ROYDEN LEPP

RUST™

DEATH OF THE ROCKET BOY

Published by
ARCHAIA™

ROYD

RU

DEATH OF TH

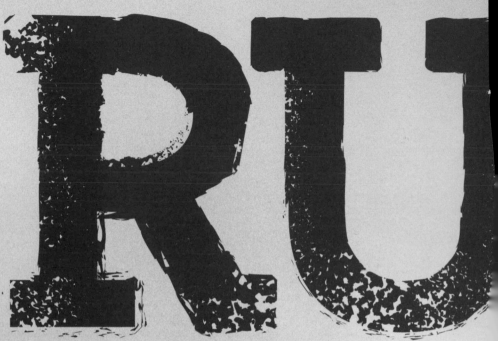

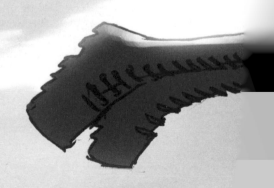

N LEPP

ST™

ROCKET BOY

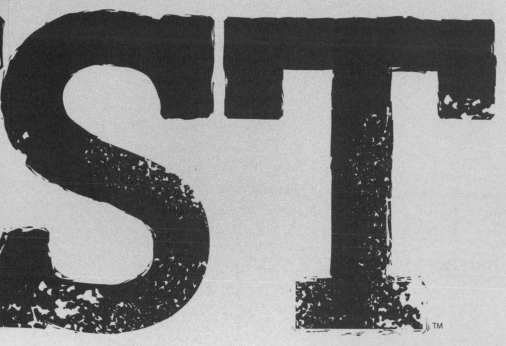

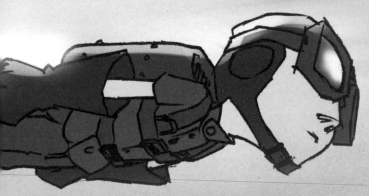

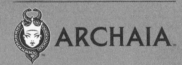

ARCHAIA™

RUST VOLUME THREE: DEATH OF THE ROCKET BOY,
September 2017. Published by Archaia, a division of
Boom Entertainment, Inc. Rust is ™ and © 2017 Royden
Lepp. All Rights Reserved. Archaia™ and the Archaia logo
are trademarks of Boom Entertainment, Inc., registered
in various countries and categories. All characters,
events, and institutions depicted herein are fictional.
Any similarity between any of the names, characters,
persons, events, and/or institutions in this publication
to actual names, characters, and persons, whether living
or dead, events, and/or institutions is unintended and
purely coincidental.

BOOM! Studios, 5670 Wilshire Boulevard, Suite 450, Los
Angeles, CA 90036-5679. Printed in China. First Printing.

ISBN: 978-1-60886-896-4, eISBN: 978-1-61398-567-0

Written & Illustrated by
Royden Lepp

Flatted by
Nechama Frier

Logo Designed by
Fawn Lau

Designer
Scott Newman

Original Series Editor
Rebecca Taylor

Collection Associate Editor
Cameron Chittock

Collection Editor
Sierra Hahn

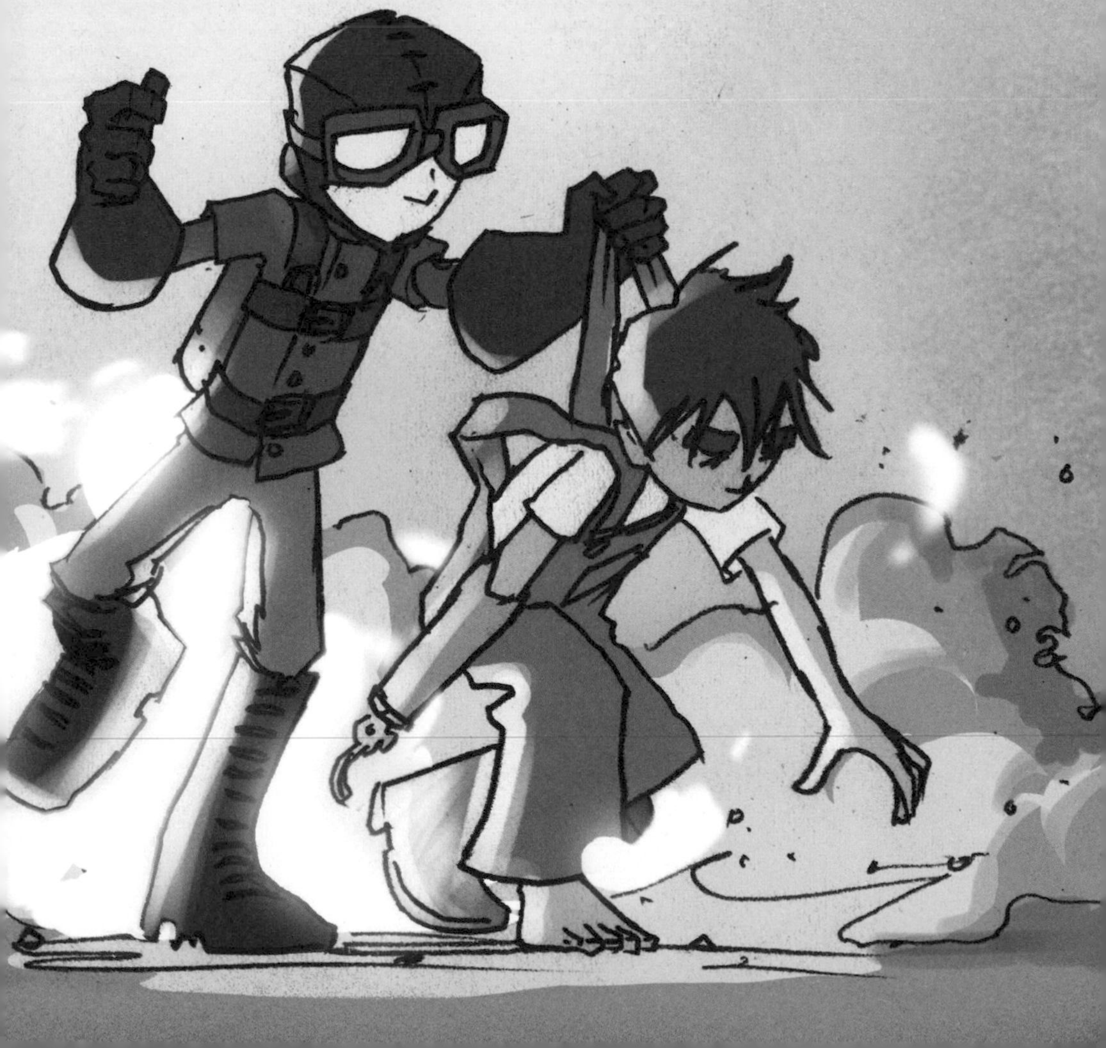

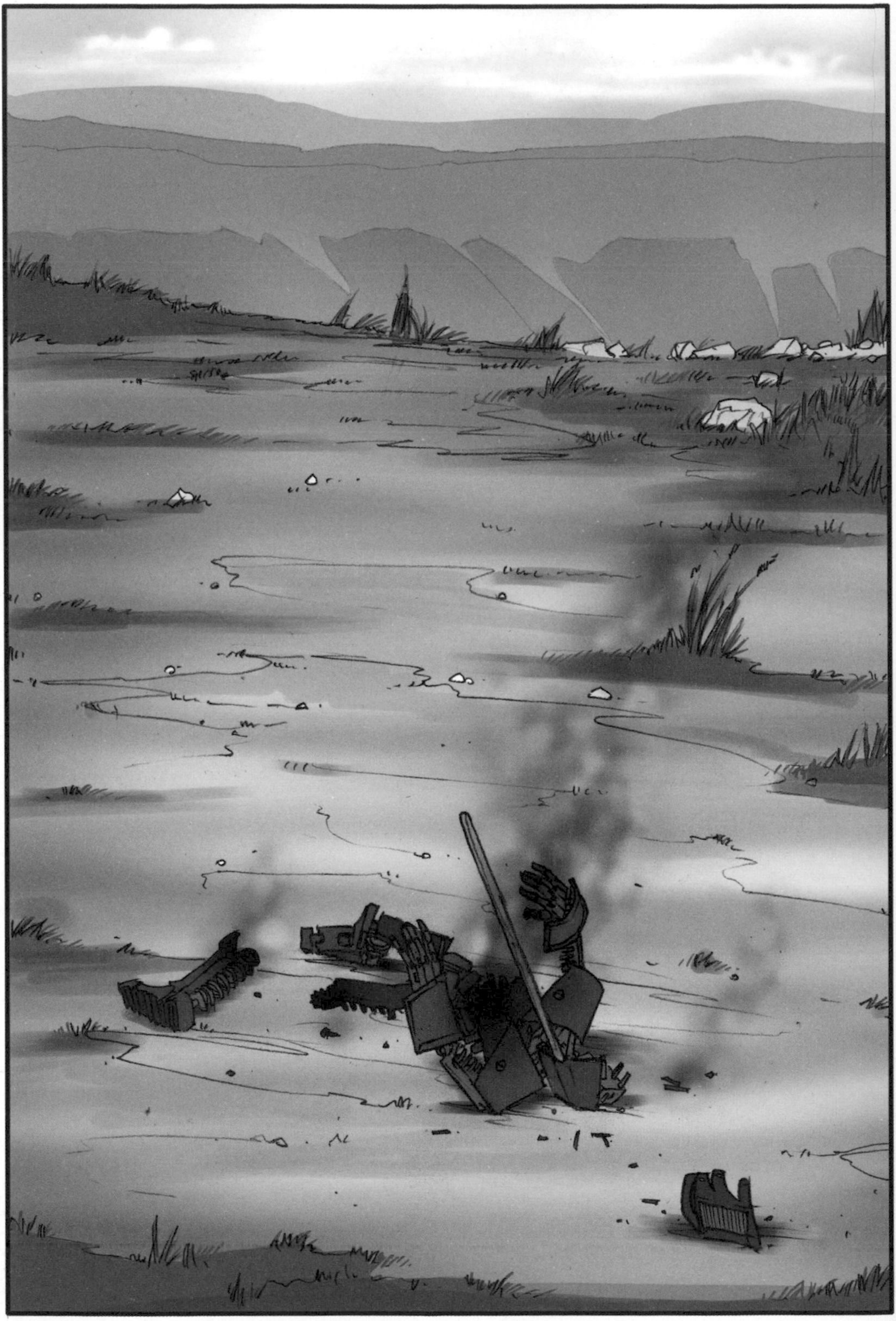

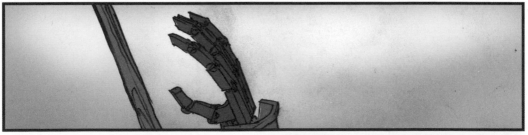

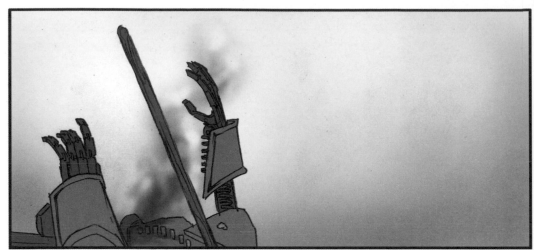

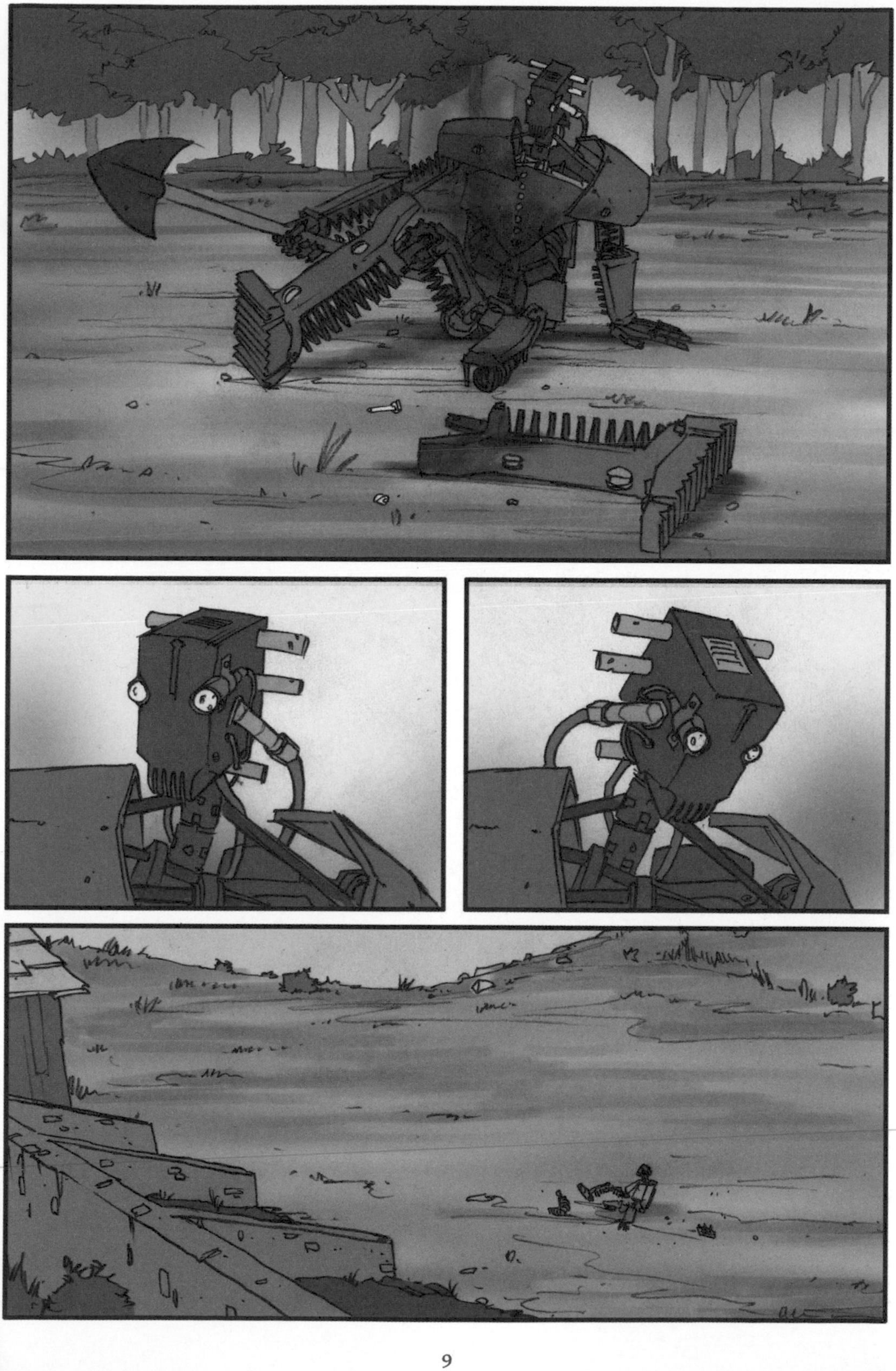

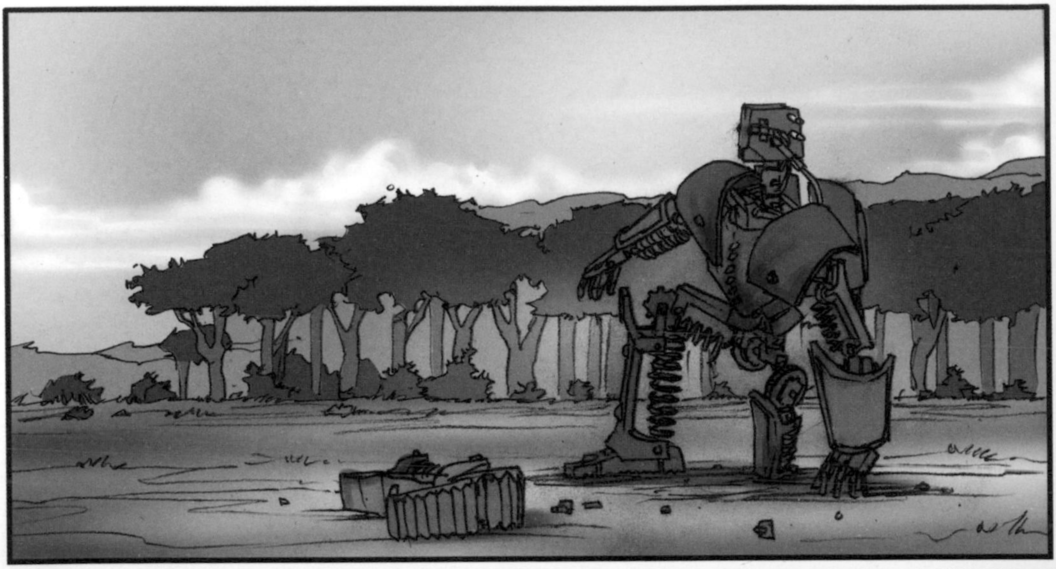

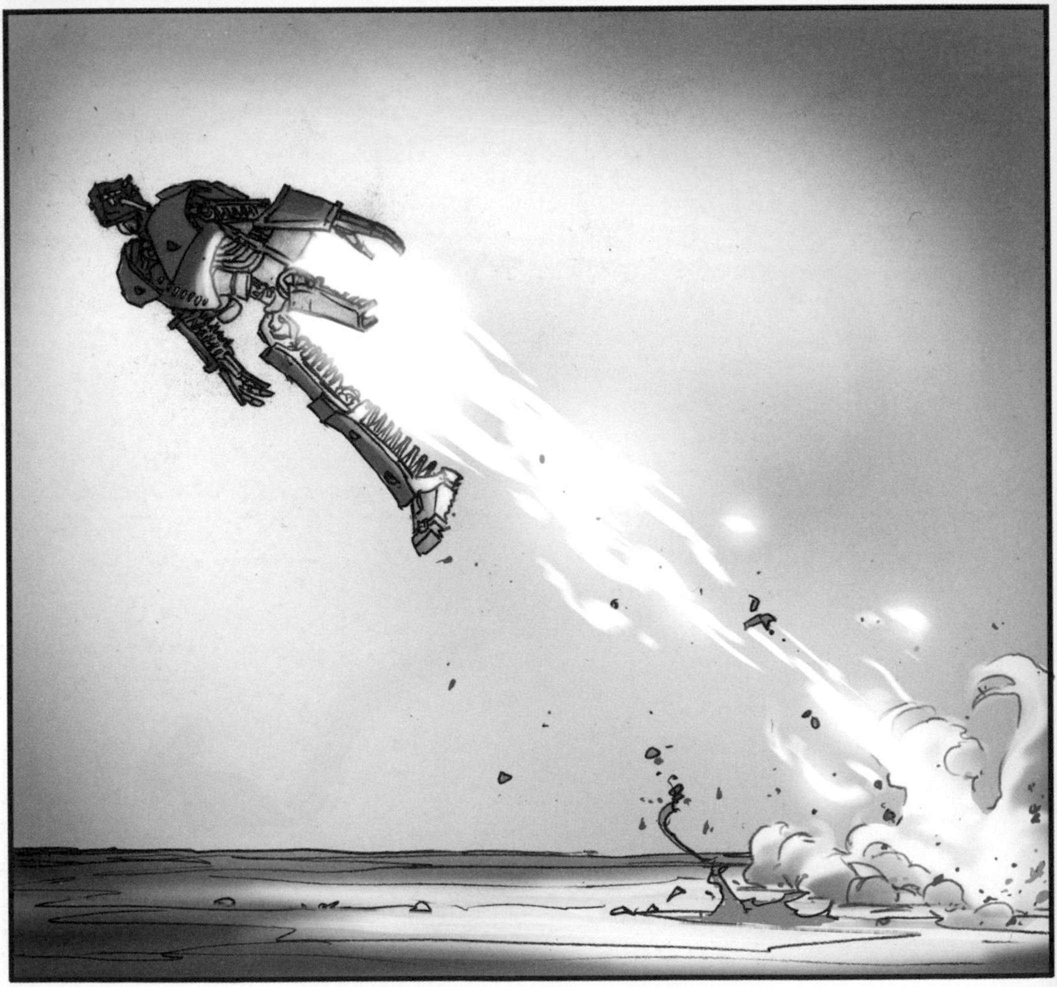

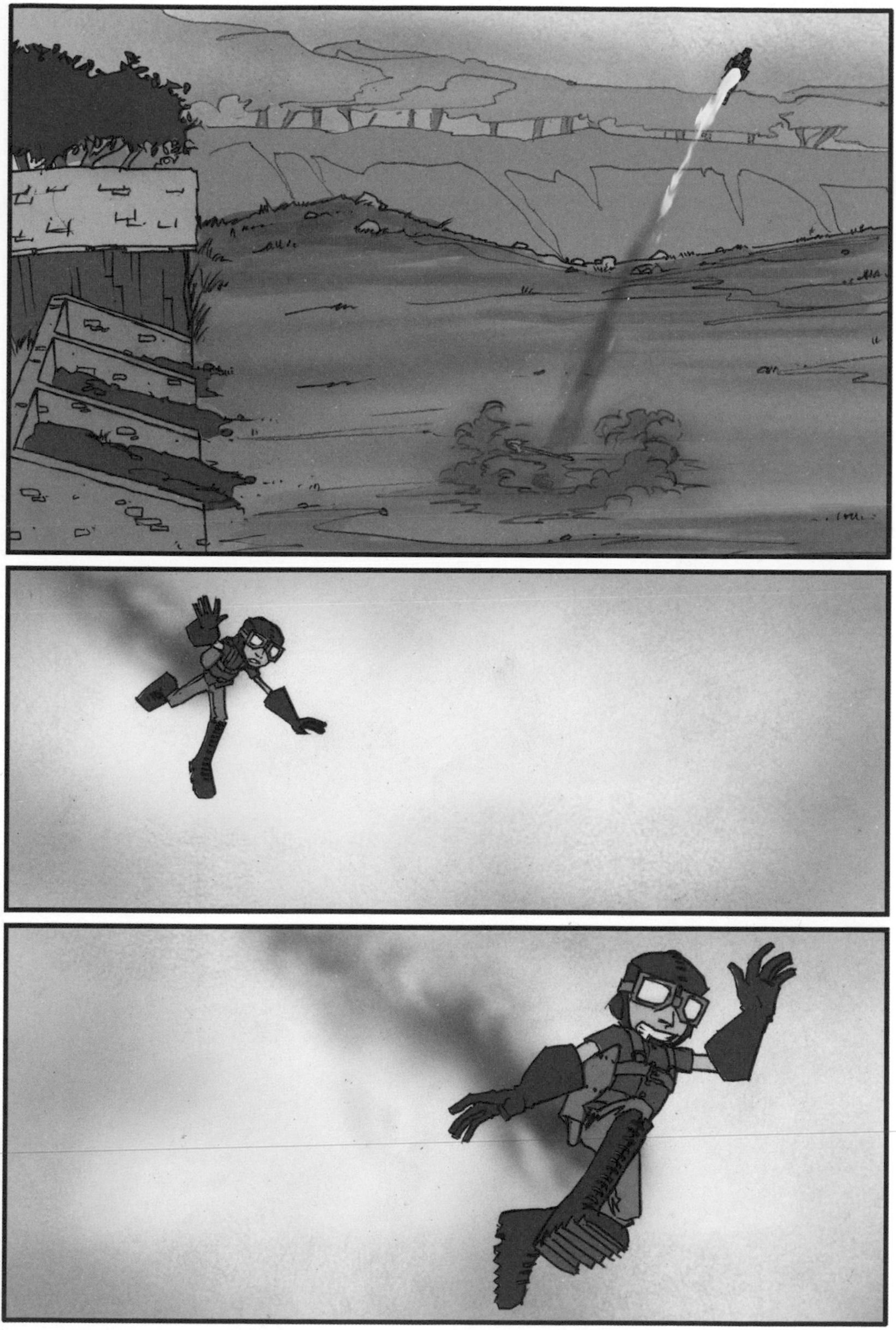

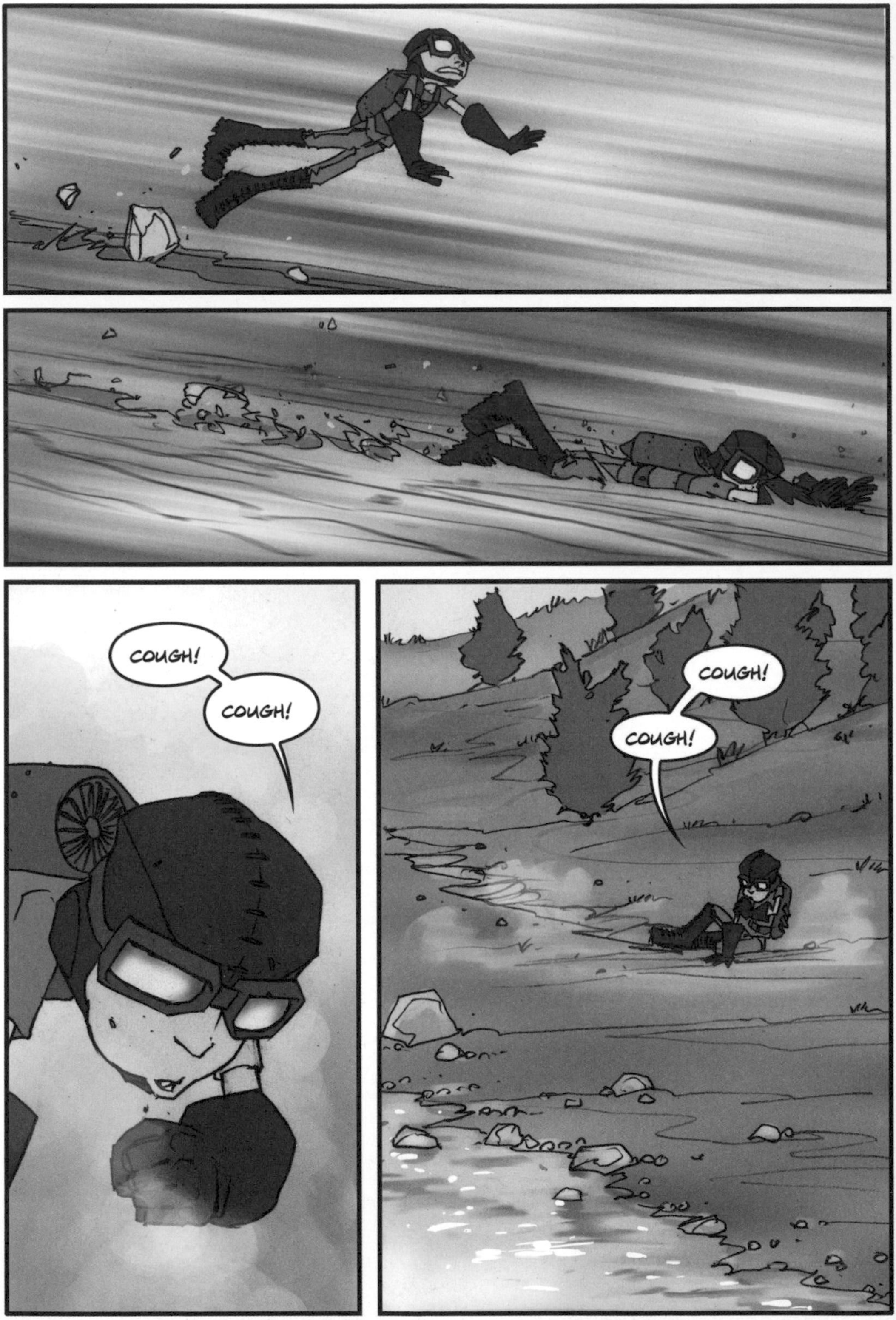
COUGH!
COUGH!
COUGH!
COUGH!

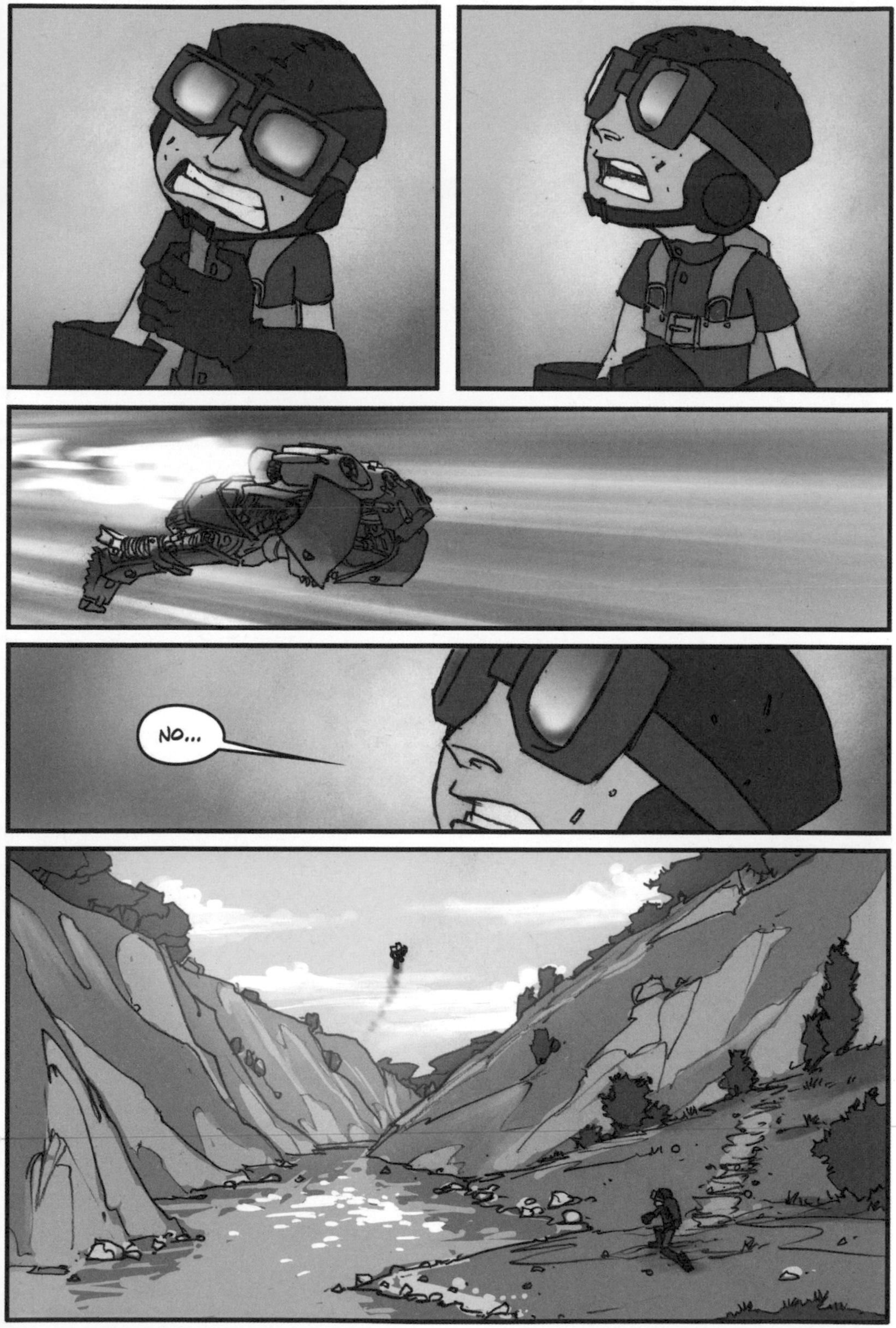
NO...

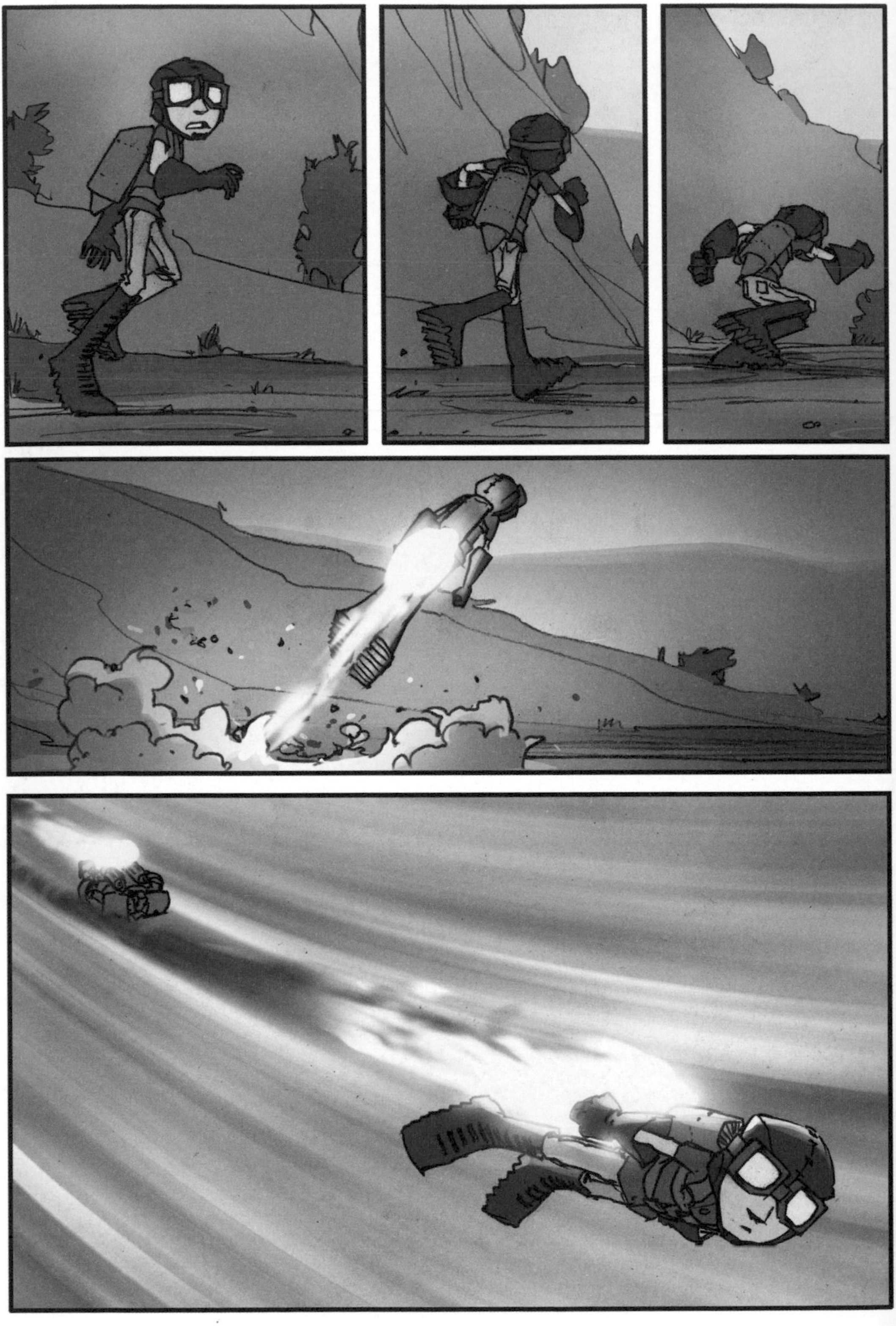

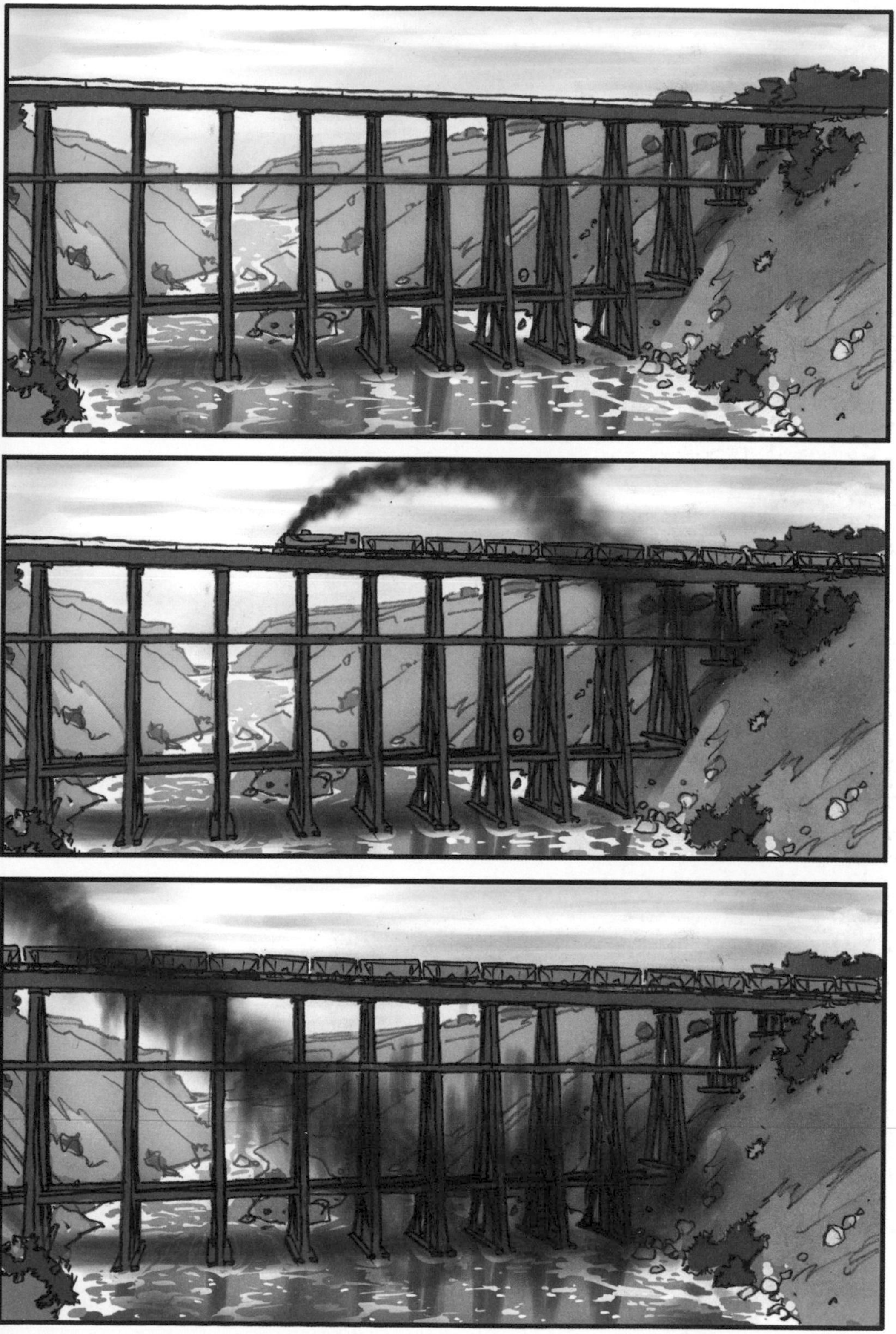

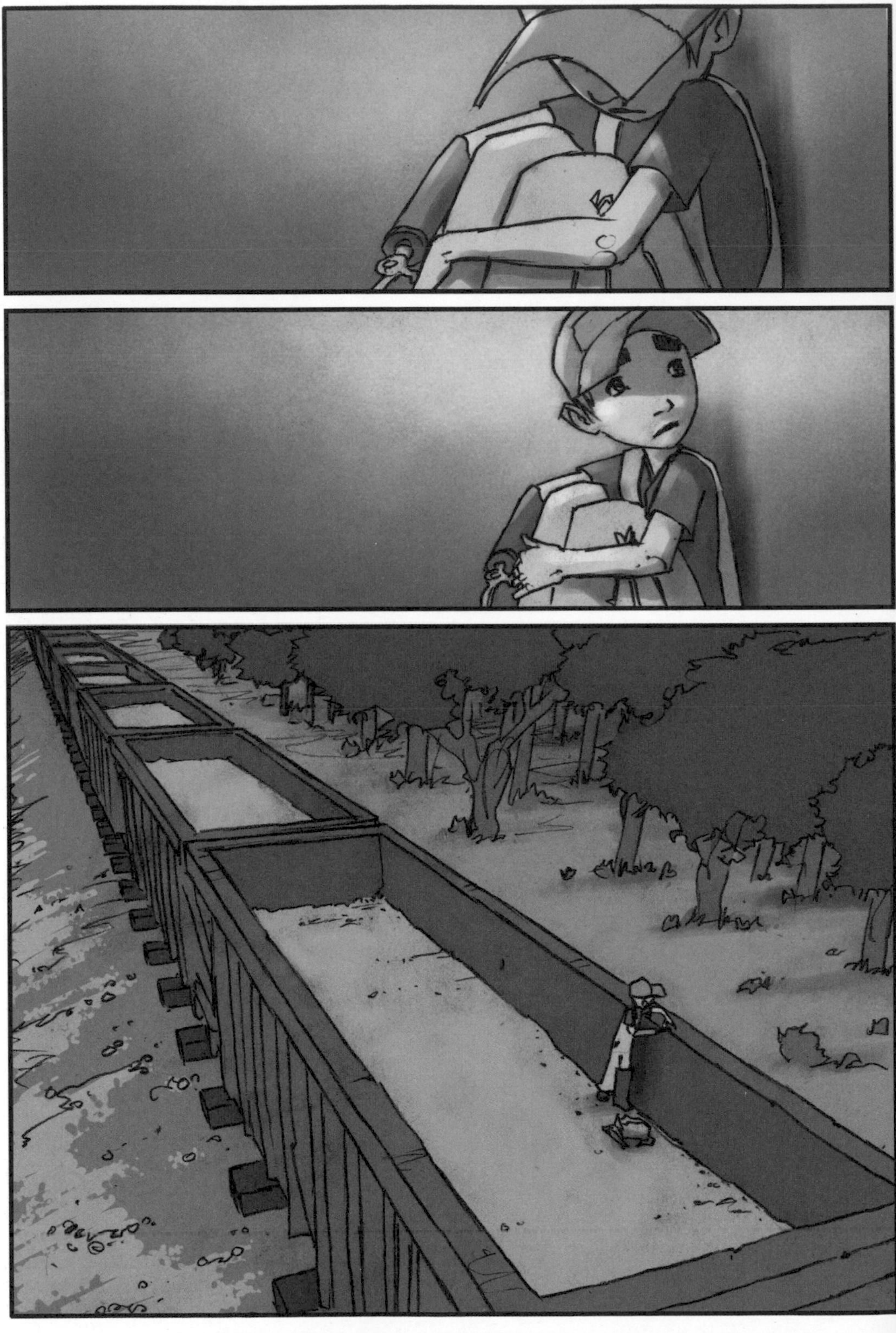

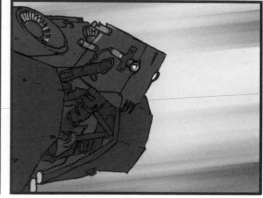

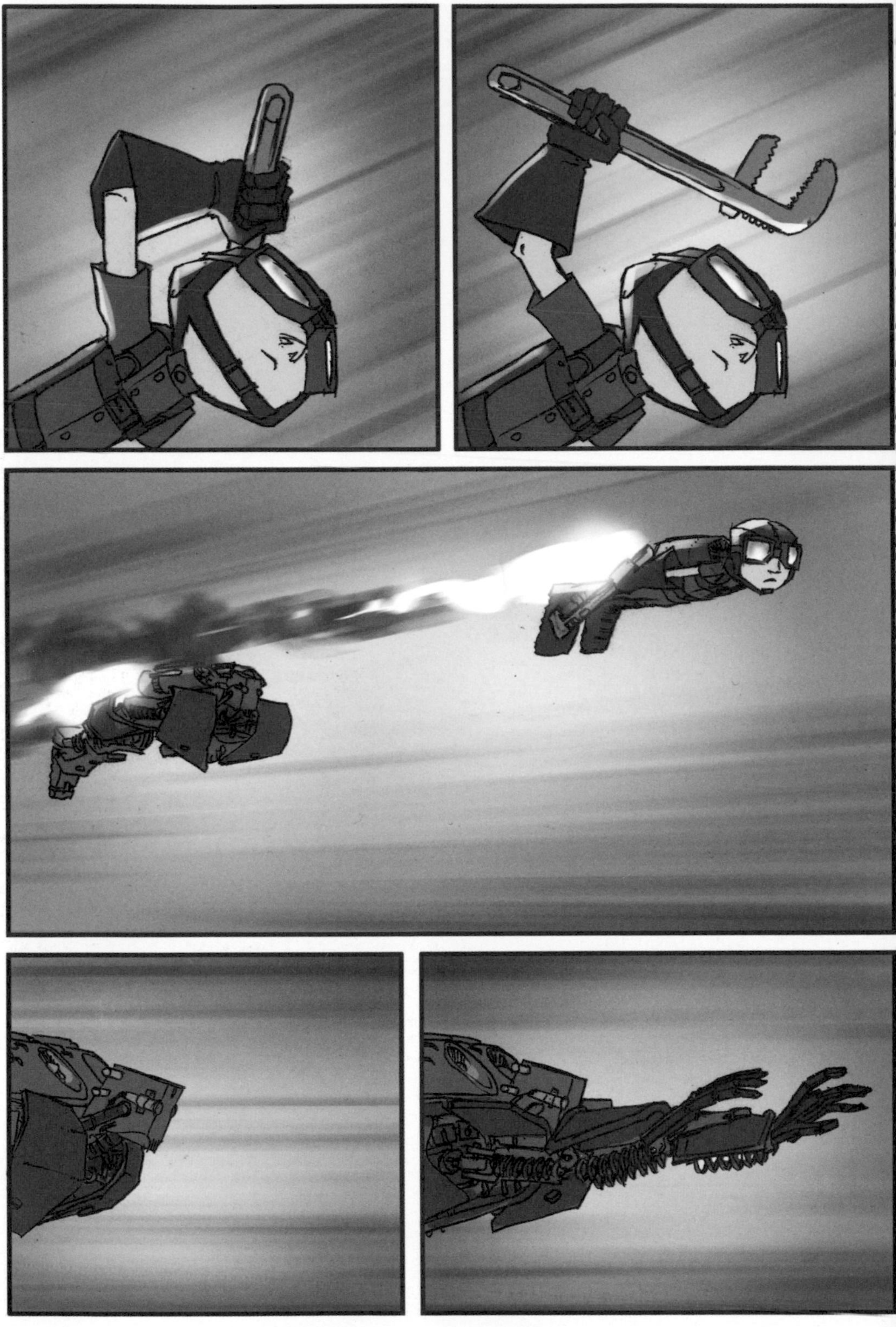

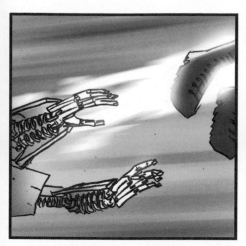

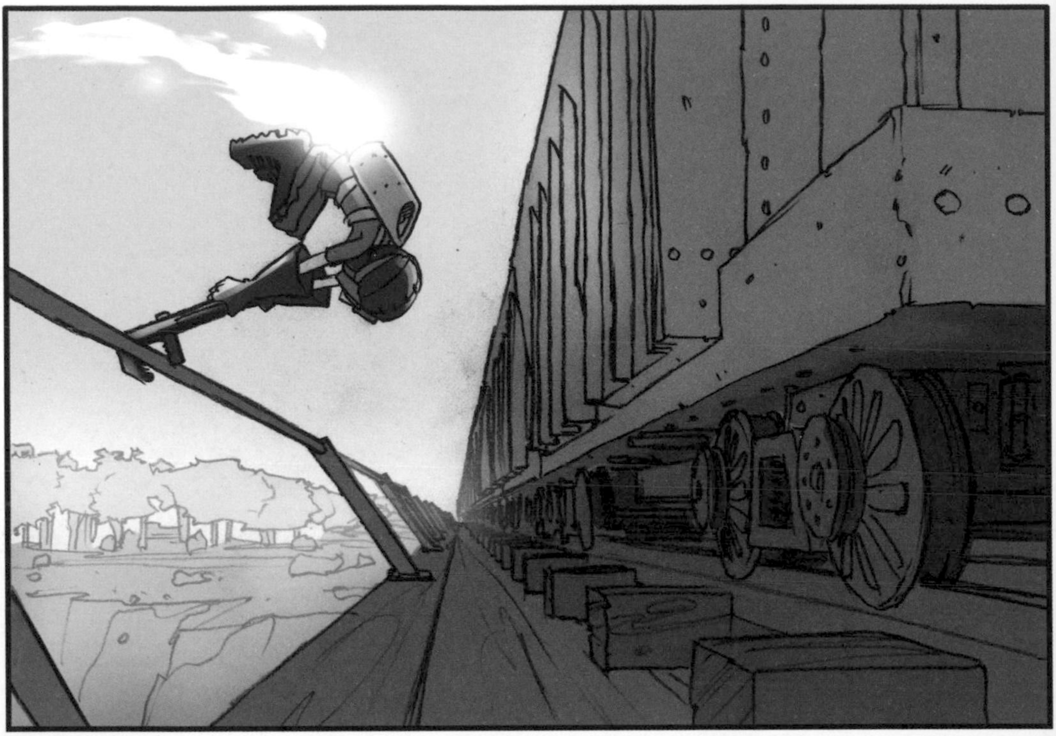

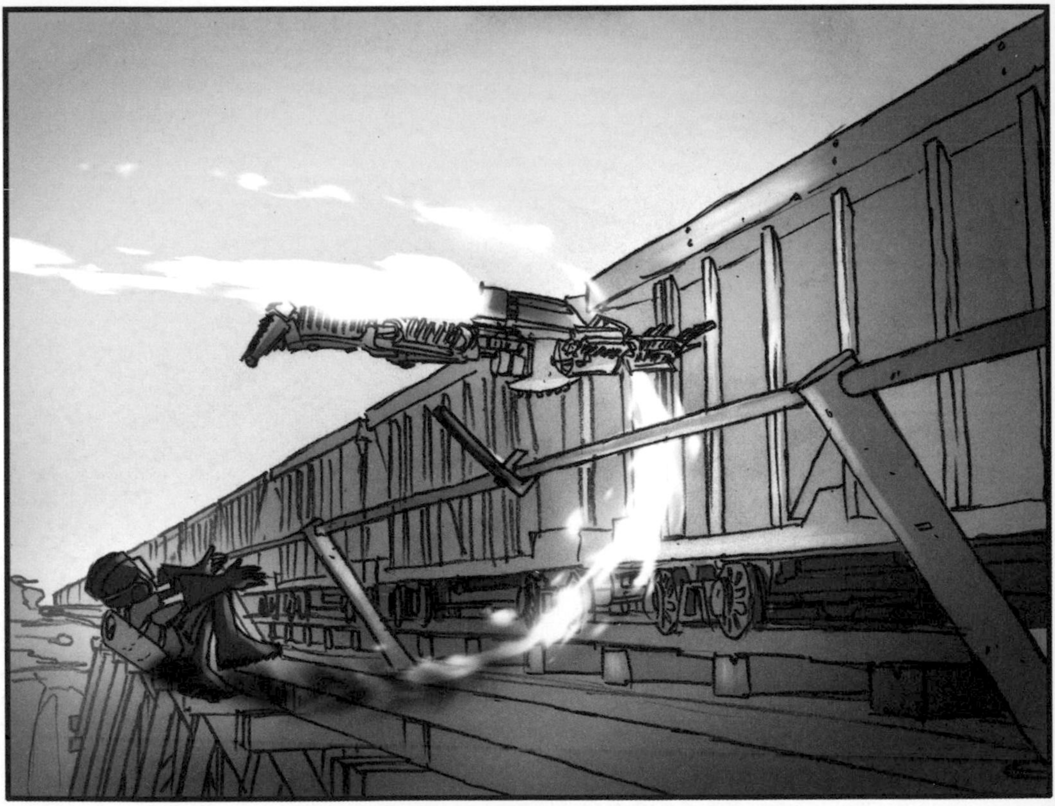

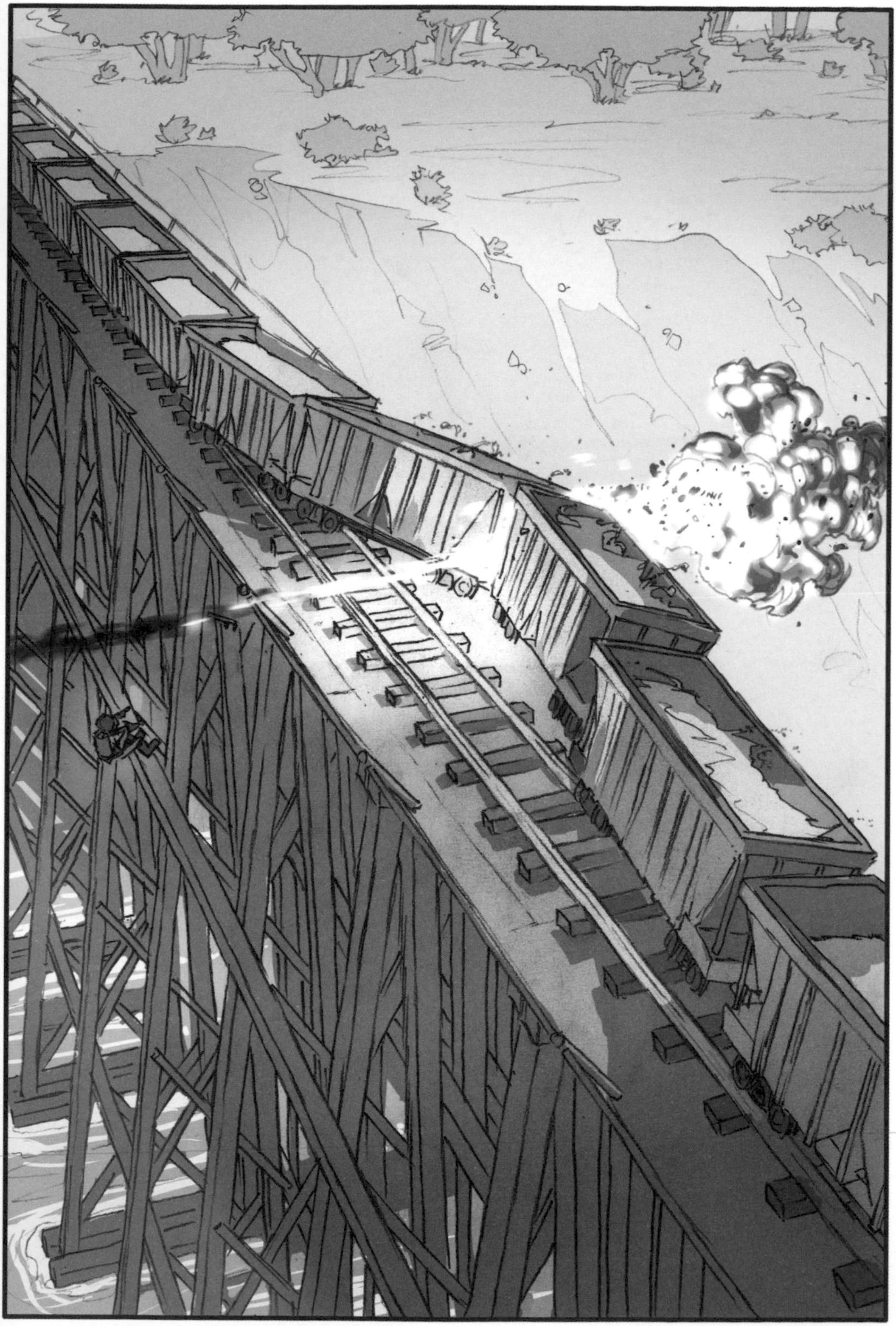

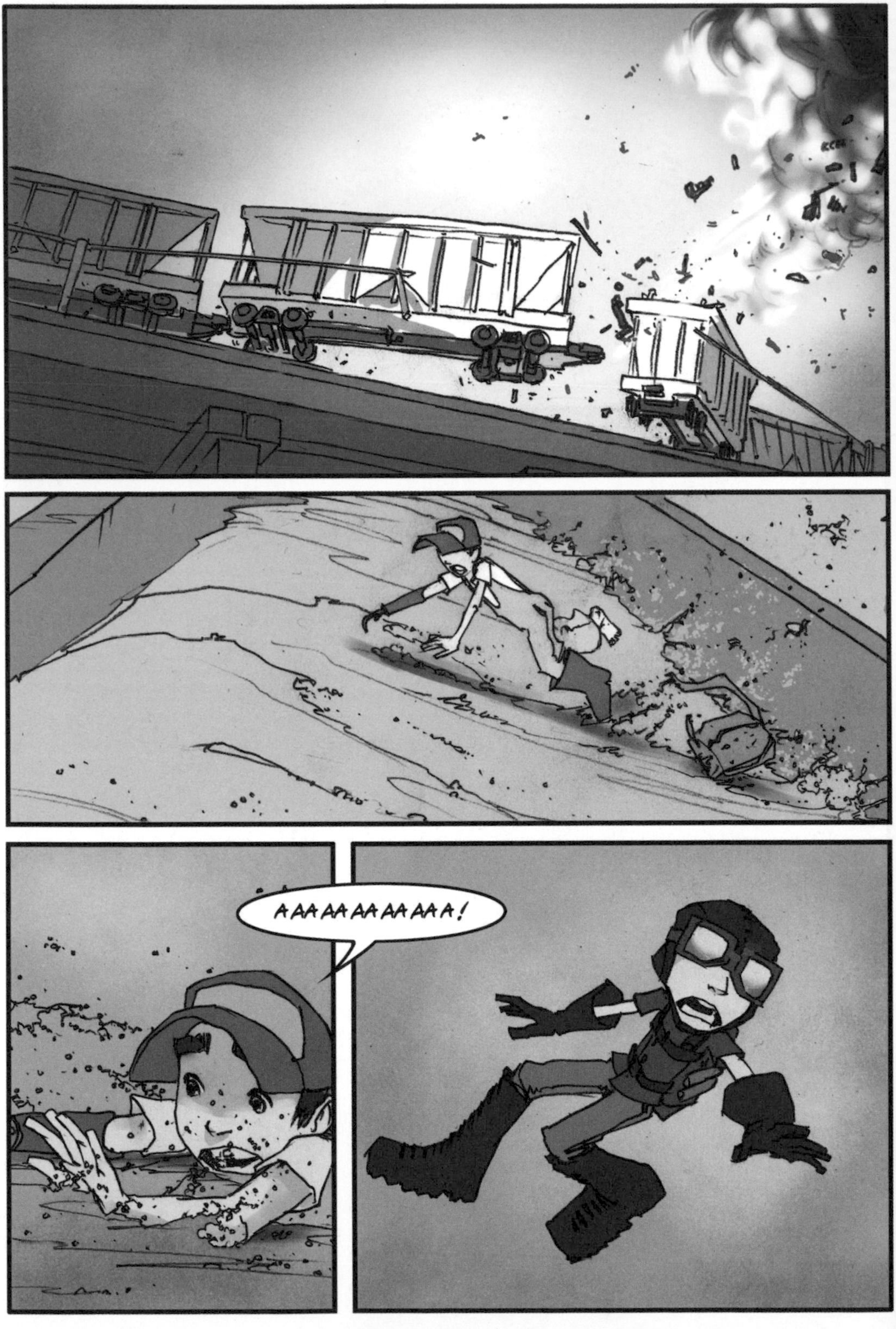
AAAAAAAAAAA!

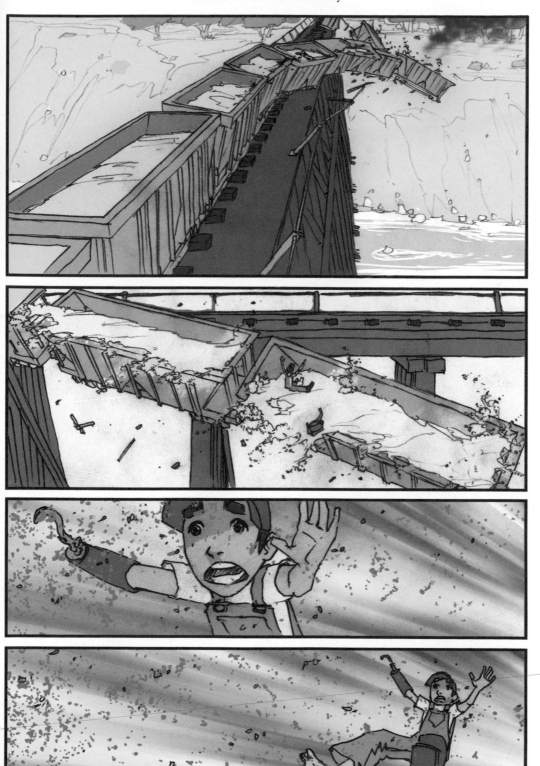

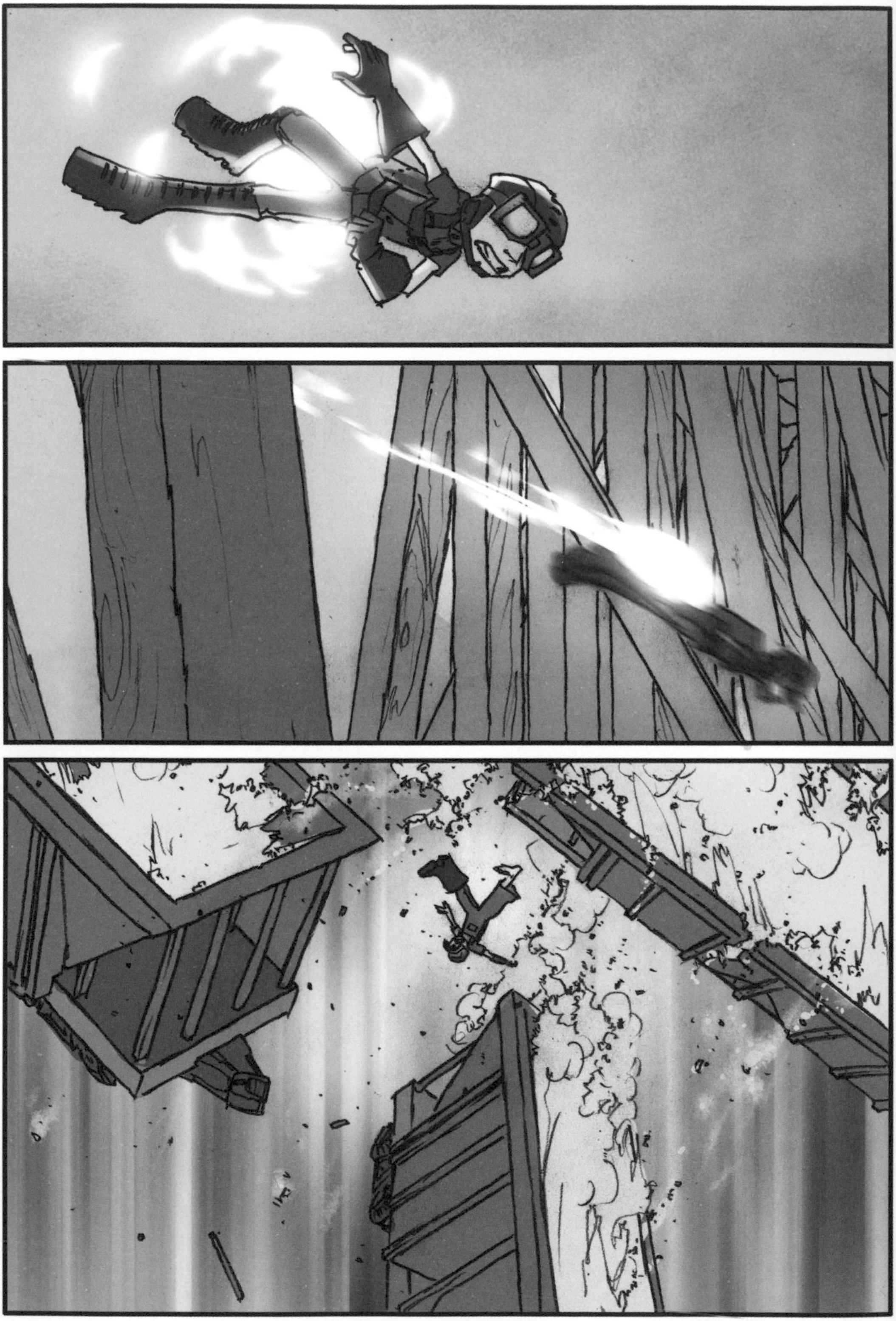

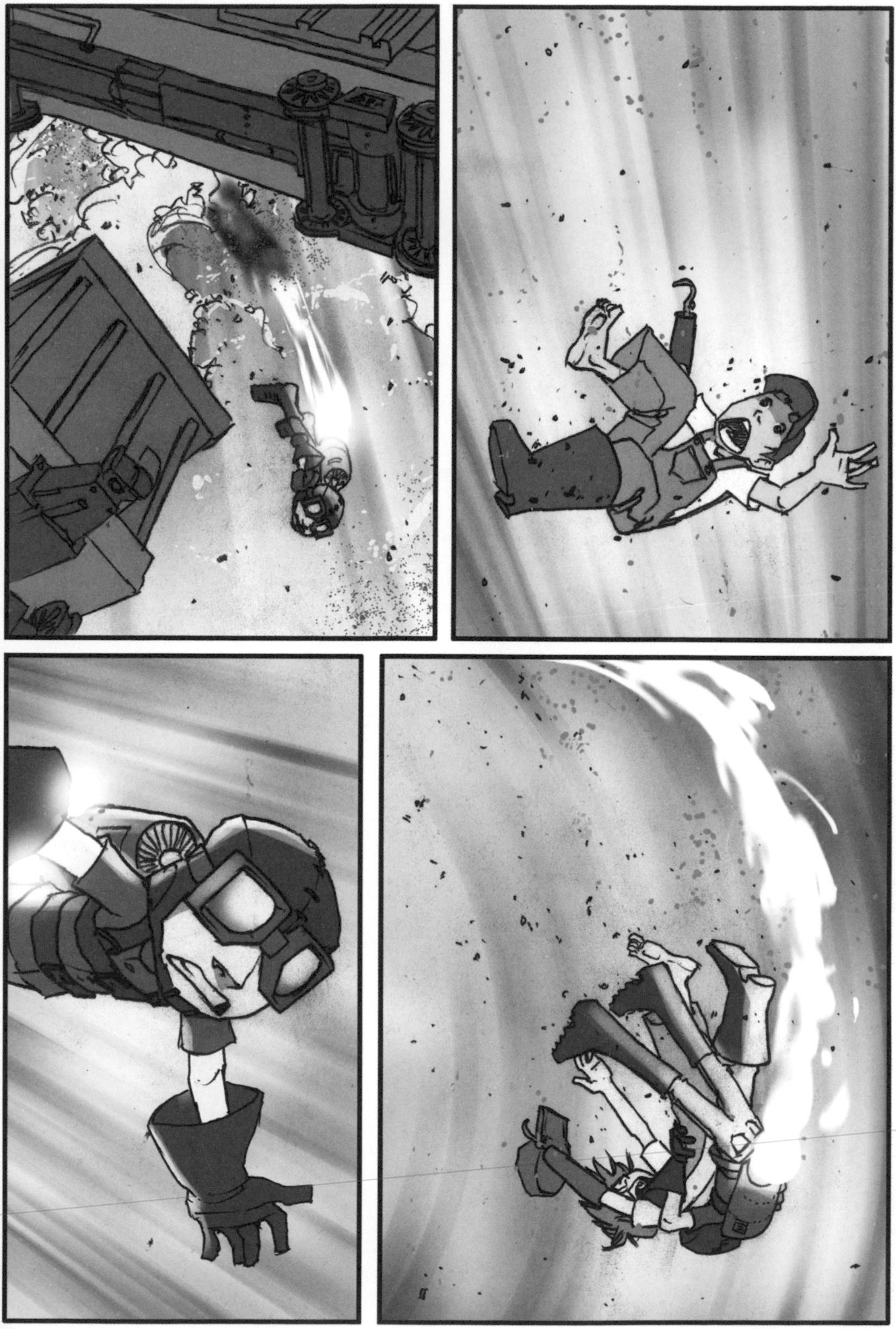

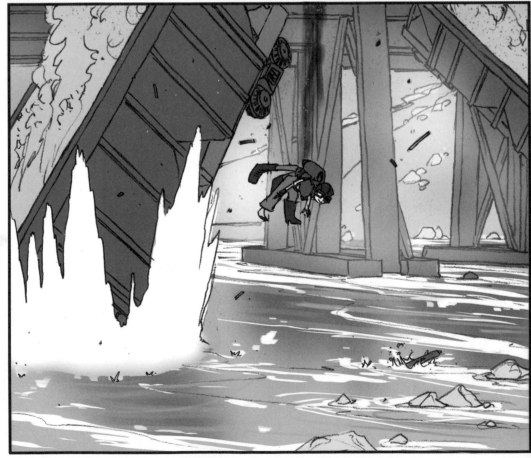

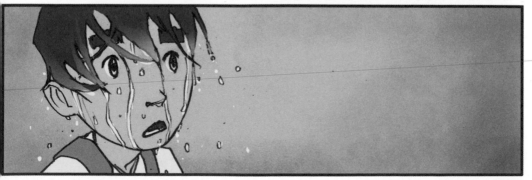

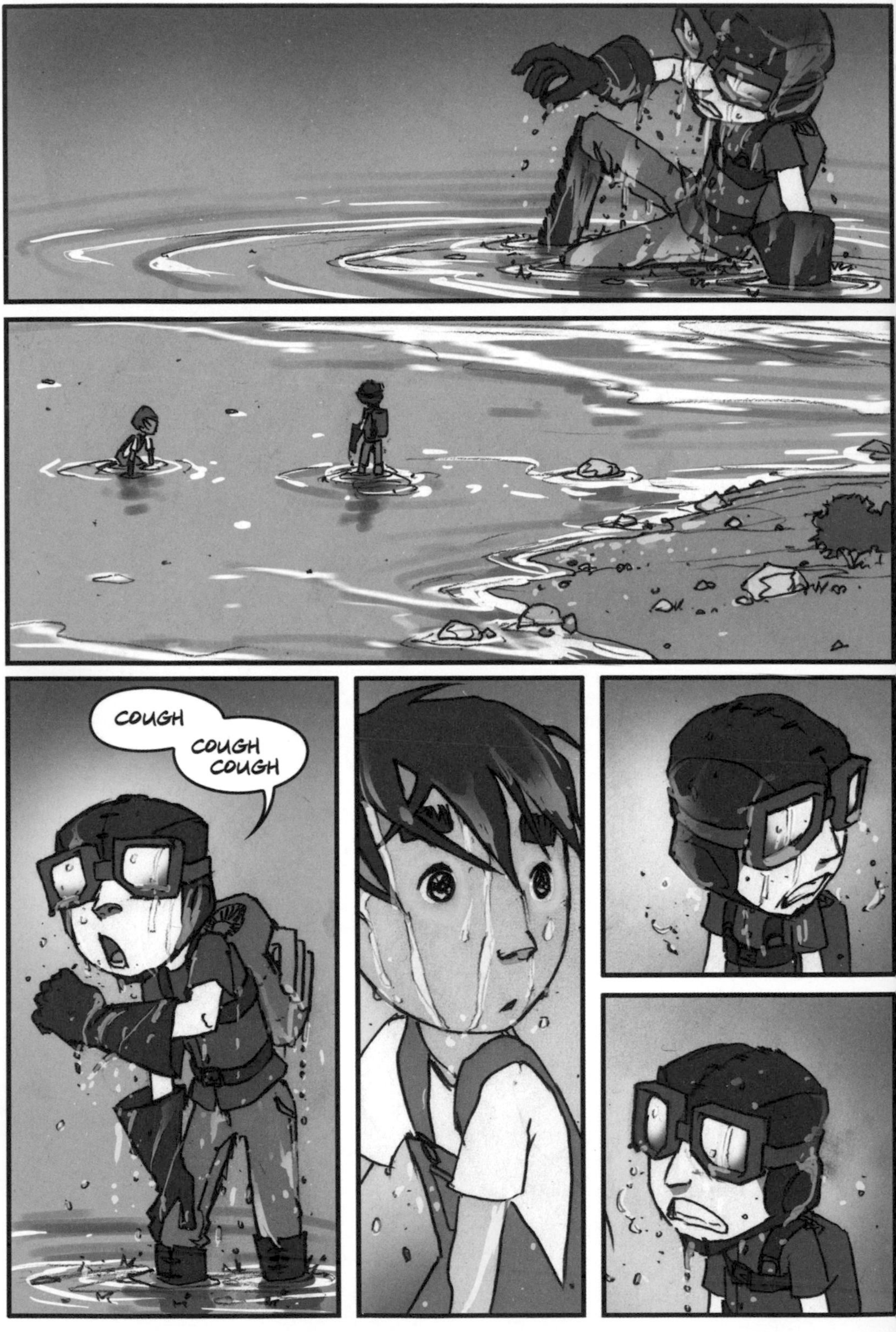
COUGH
COUGH
COUGH

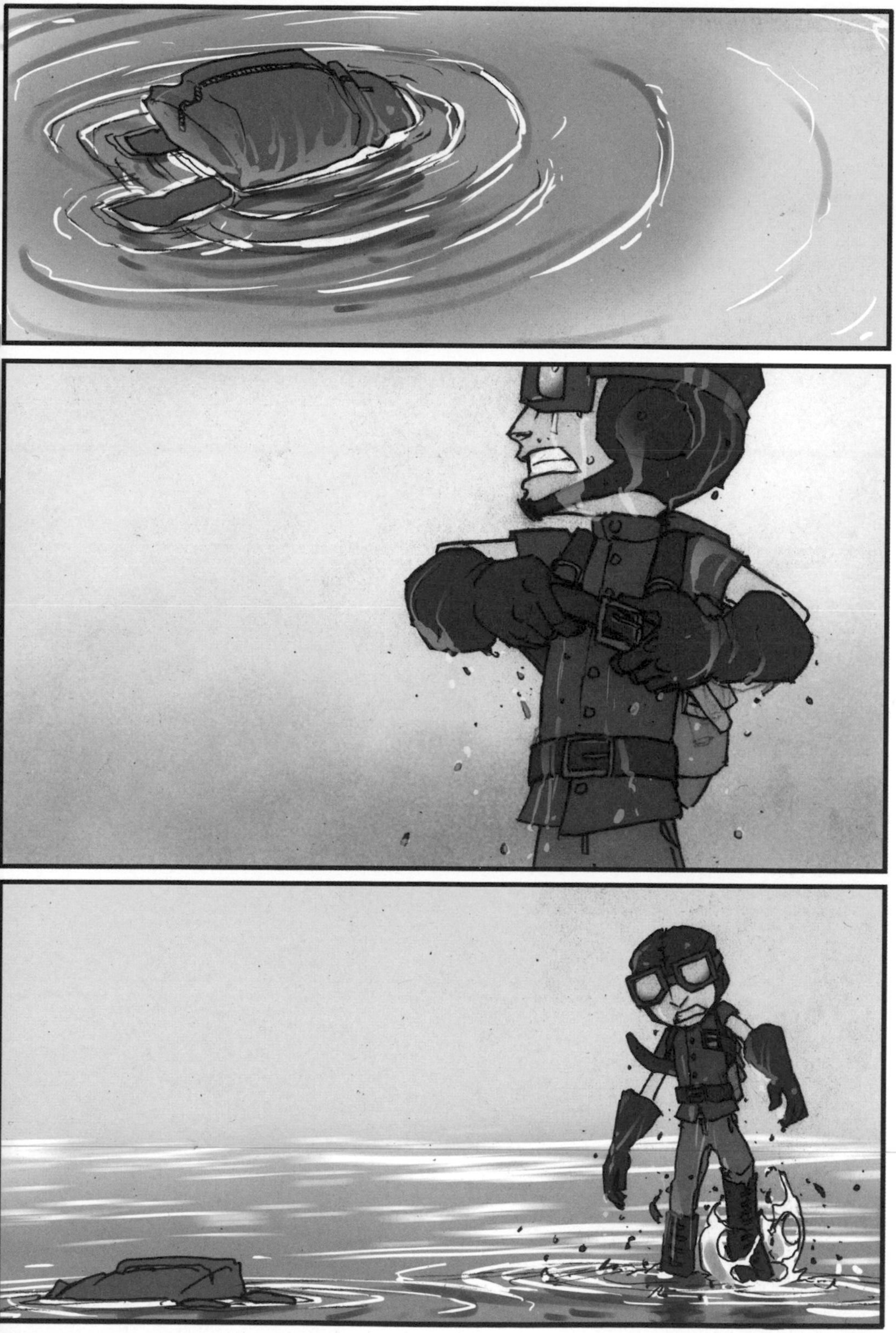

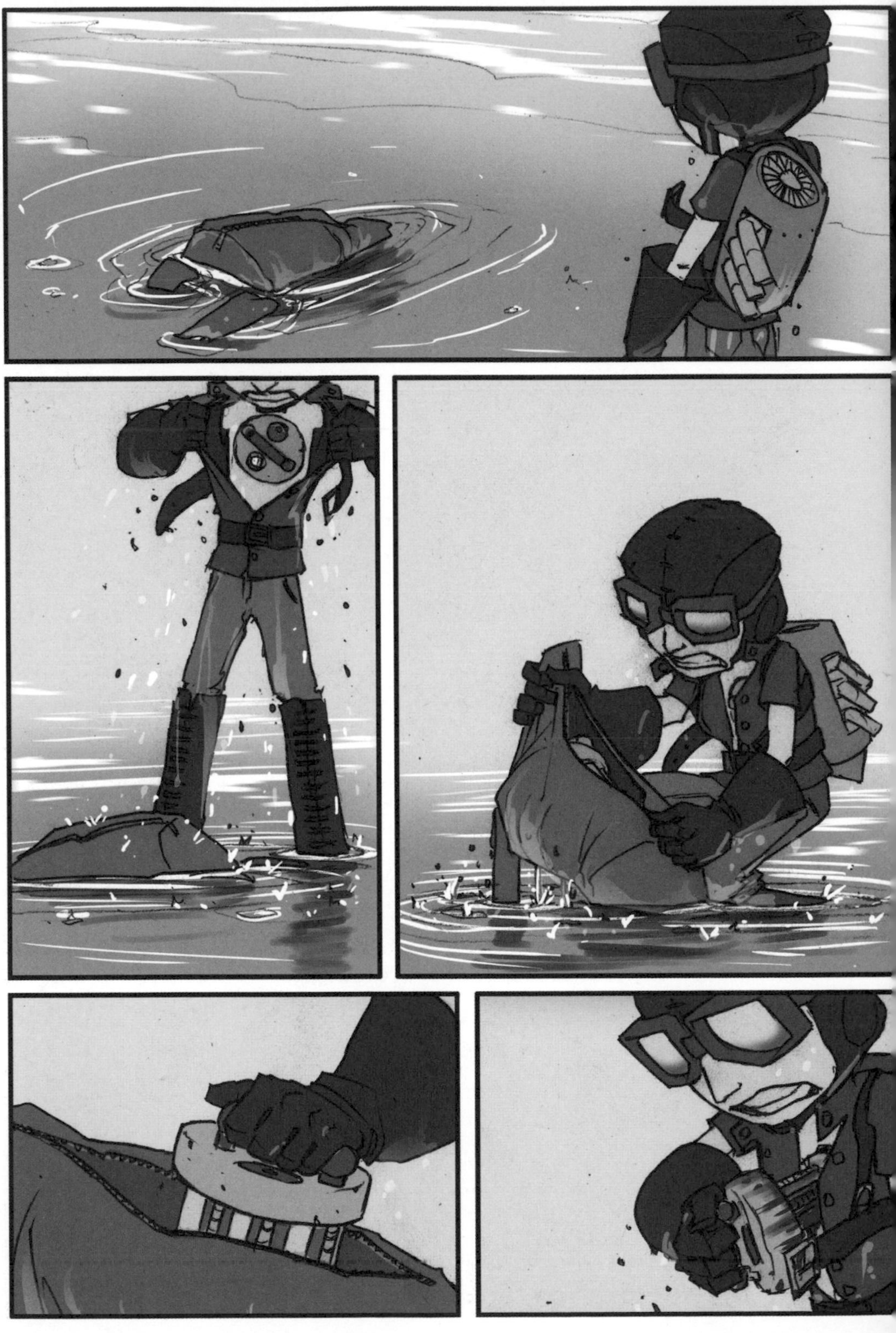

OZ!?

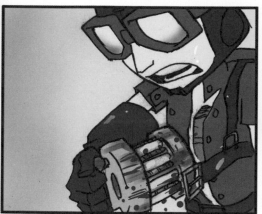

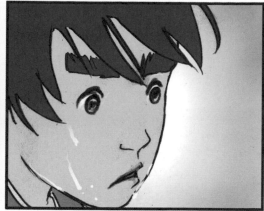

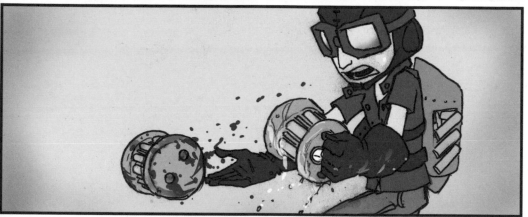

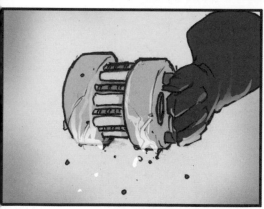

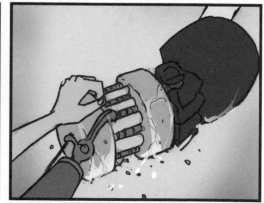

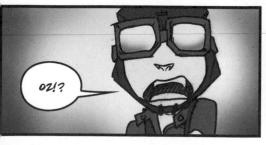

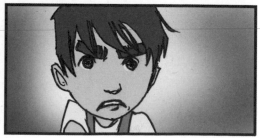

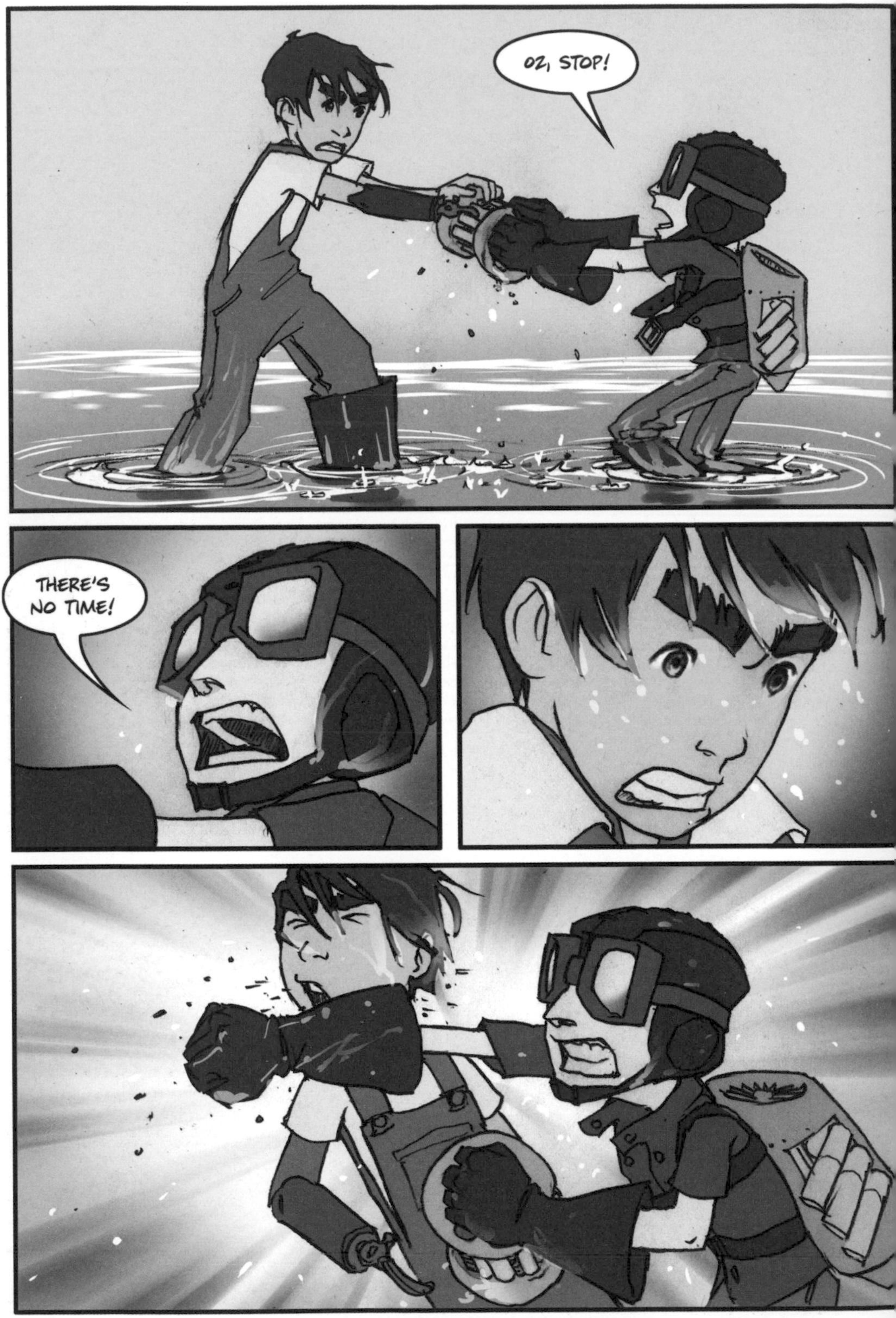
OZ, STOP!
THERE'S NO TIME!

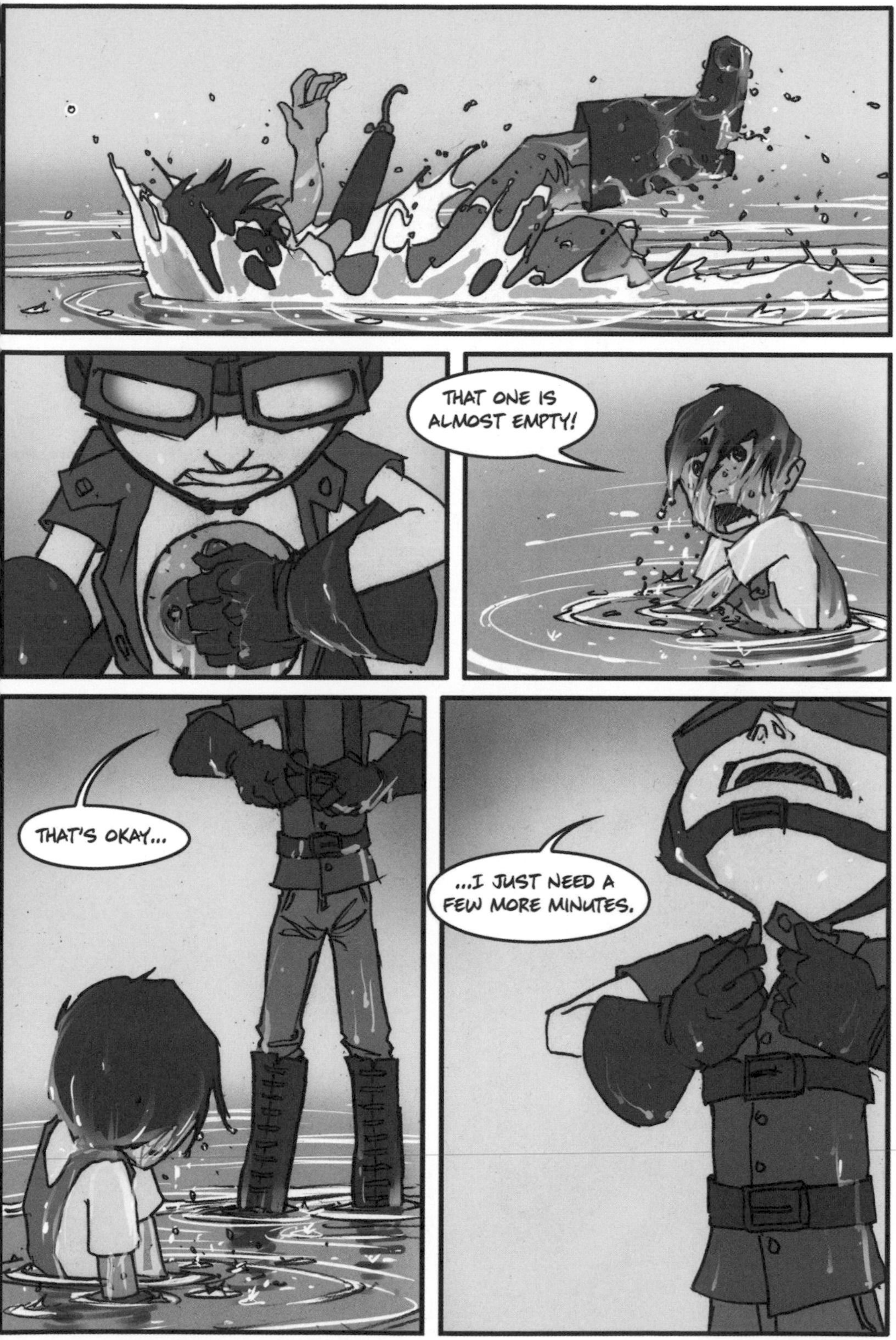
THAT ONE IS ALMOST EMPTY!
THAT'S OKAY...
...I JUST NEED A FEW MORE MINUTES.

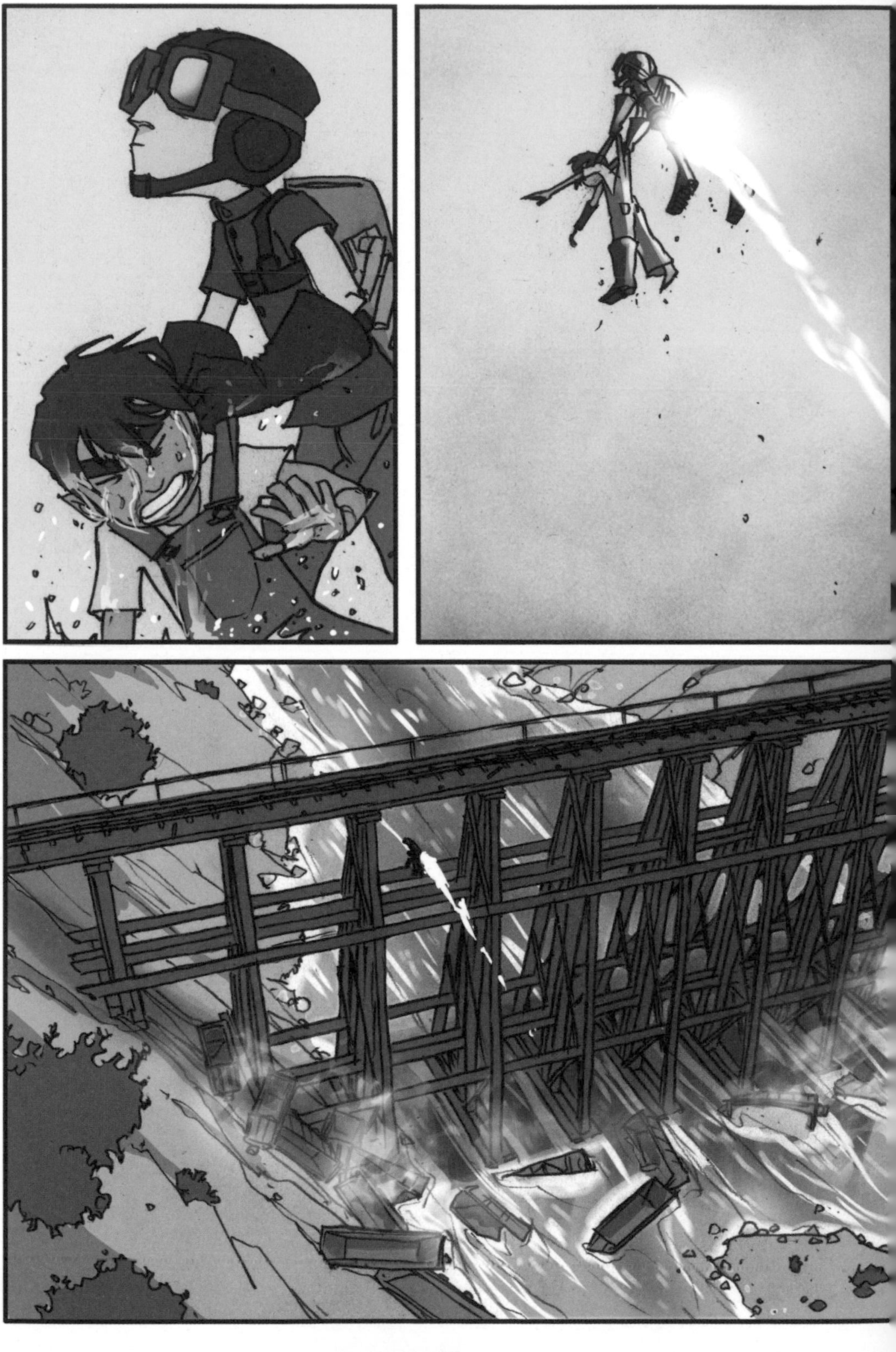

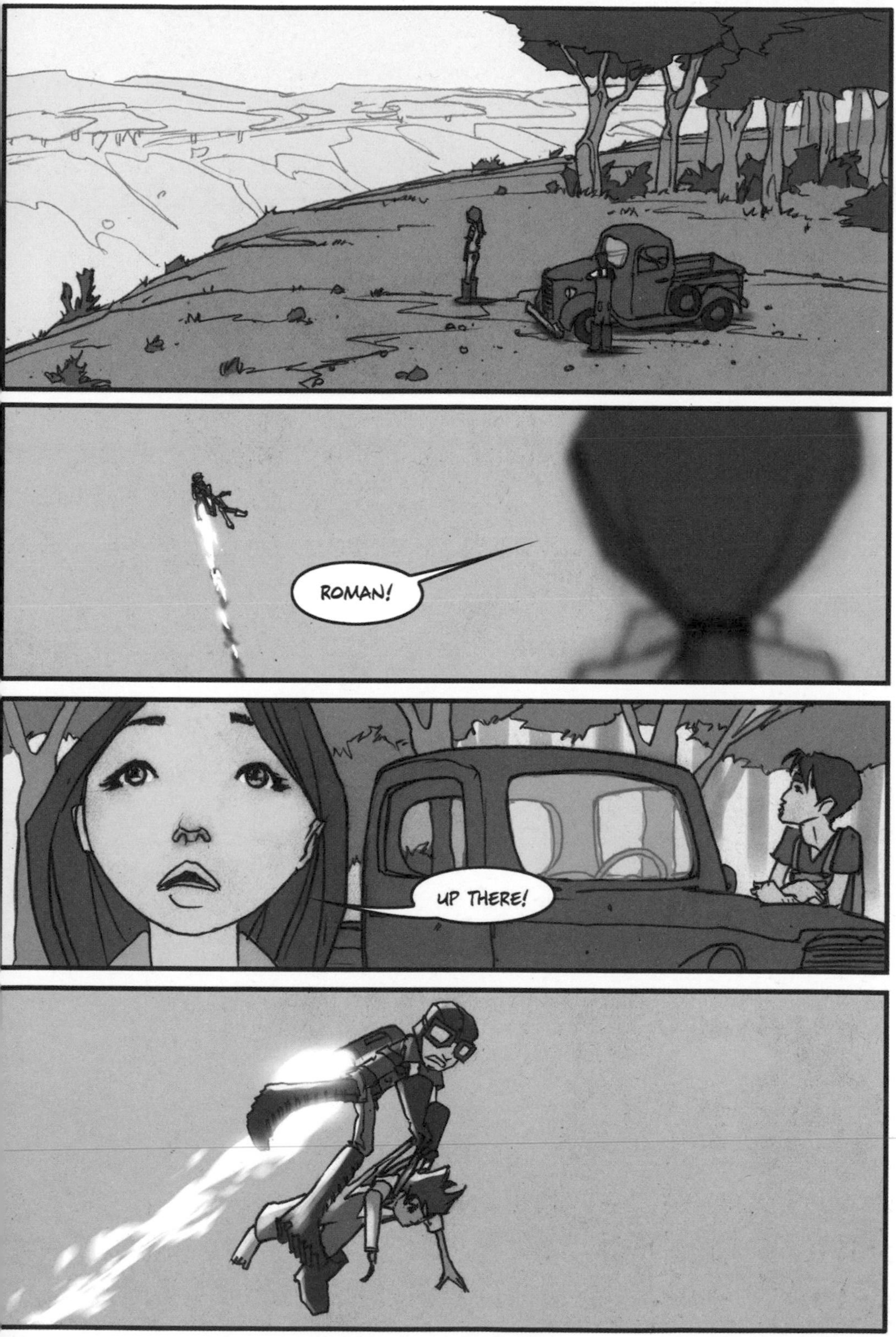
ROMAN!
UP THERE!

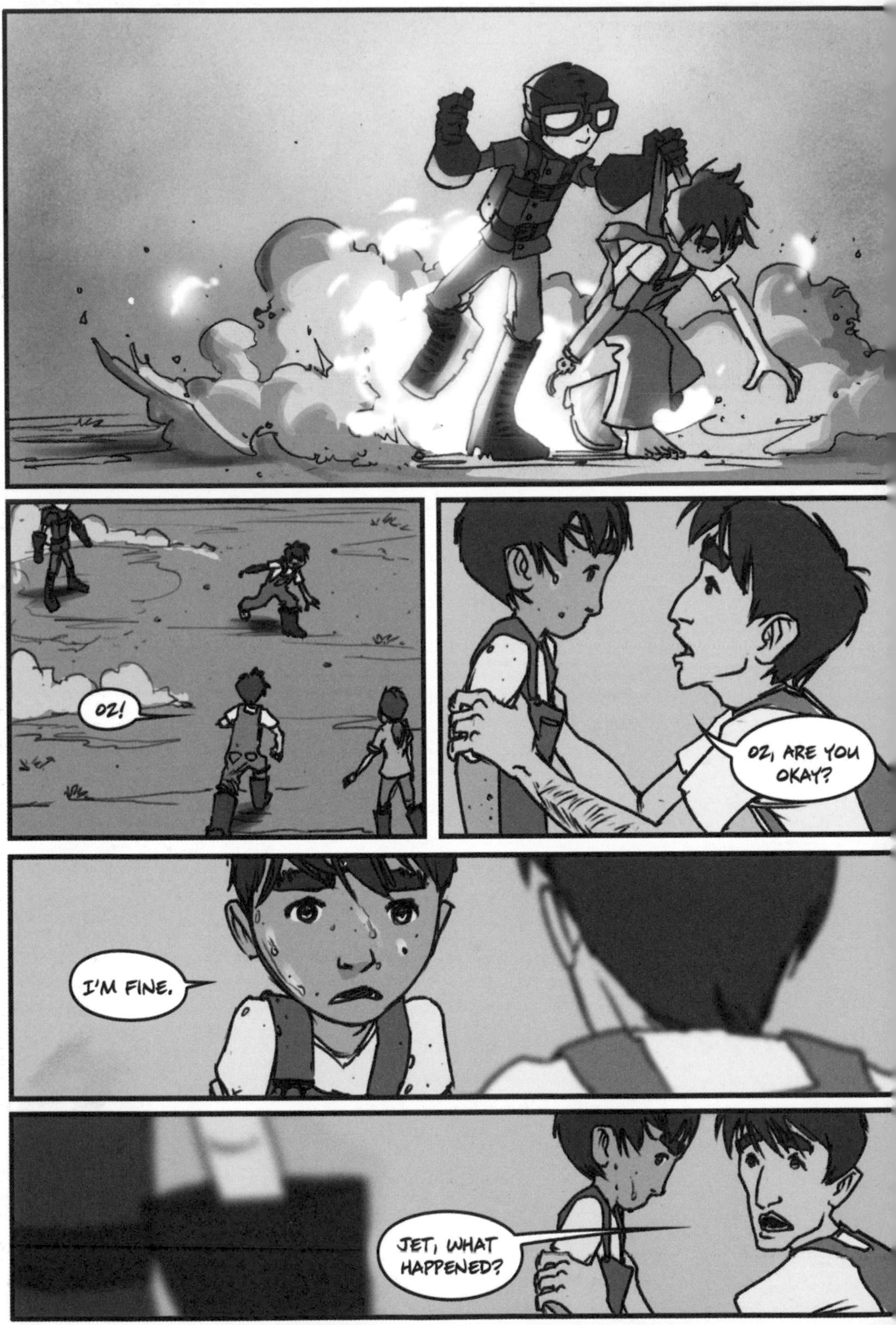
OZ!
OZ, ARE YOU OKAY?
I'M FINE.
JET, WHAT HAPPENED?

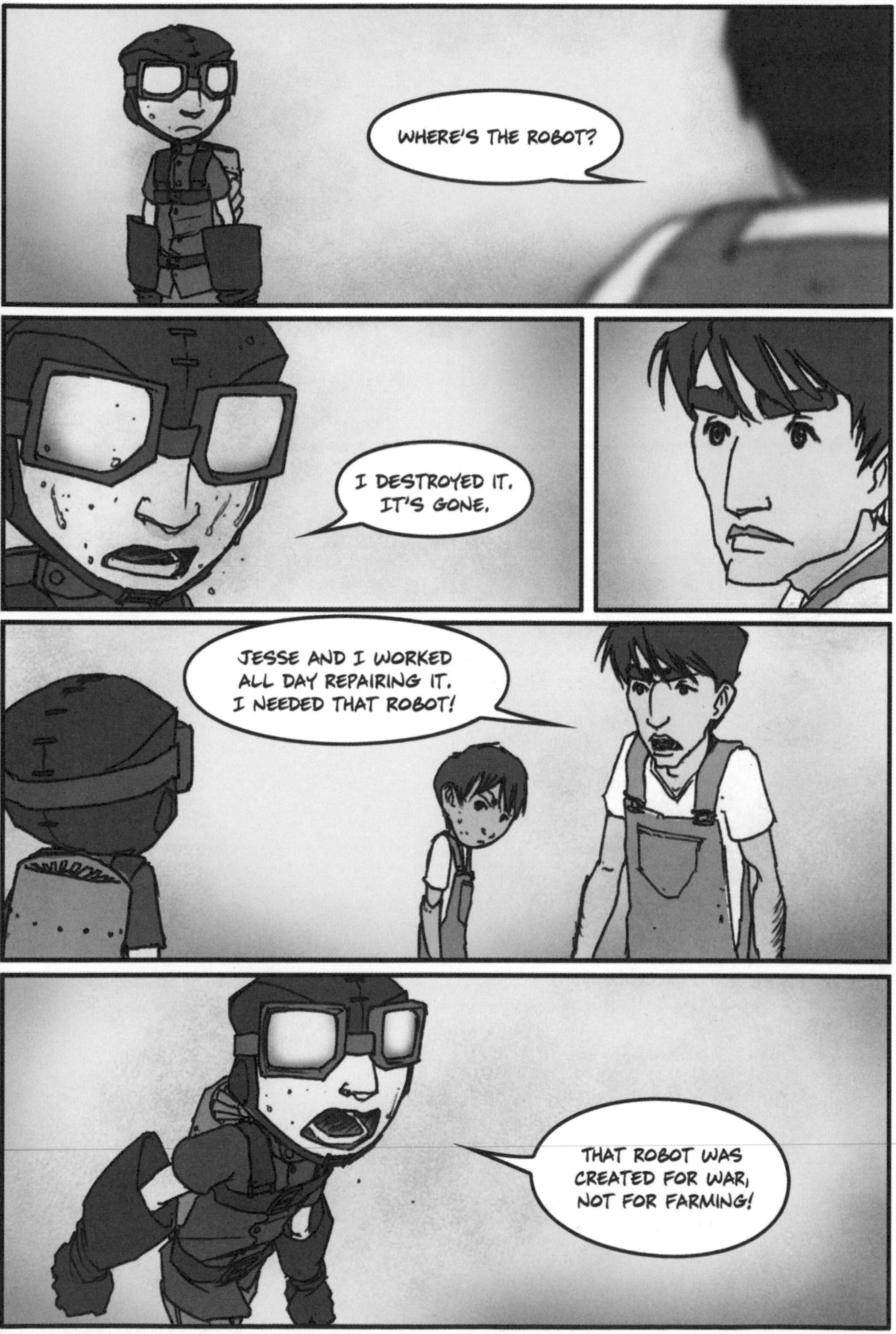
WHERE'S THE ROBOT?
I DESTROYED IT. IT'S GONE.
JESSE AND I WORKED ALL DAY REPAIRING IT. I NEEDED THAT ROBOT!
THAT ROBOT WAS CREATED FOR WAR, NOT FOR FARMING!

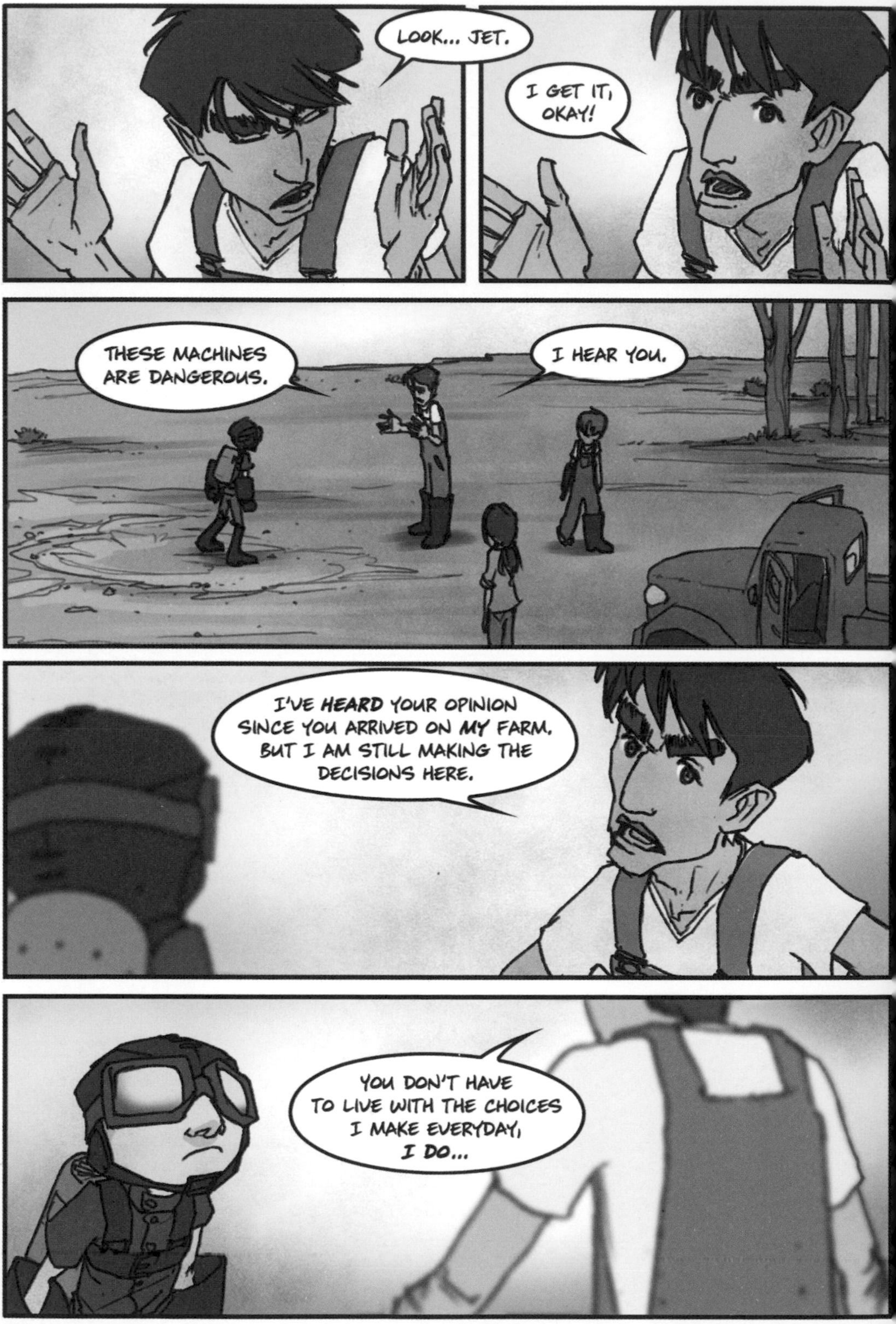
LOOK... JET.
I GET IT, OKAY!
THESE MACHINES ARE DANGEROUS.
I HEAR YOU.
I'VE HEARD YOUR OPINION SINCE YOU ARRIVED ON MY FARM. BUT I AM STILL MAKING THE DECISIONS HERE.
YOU DON'T HAVE TO LIVE WITH THE CHOICES I MAKE EVERYDAY, I DO...

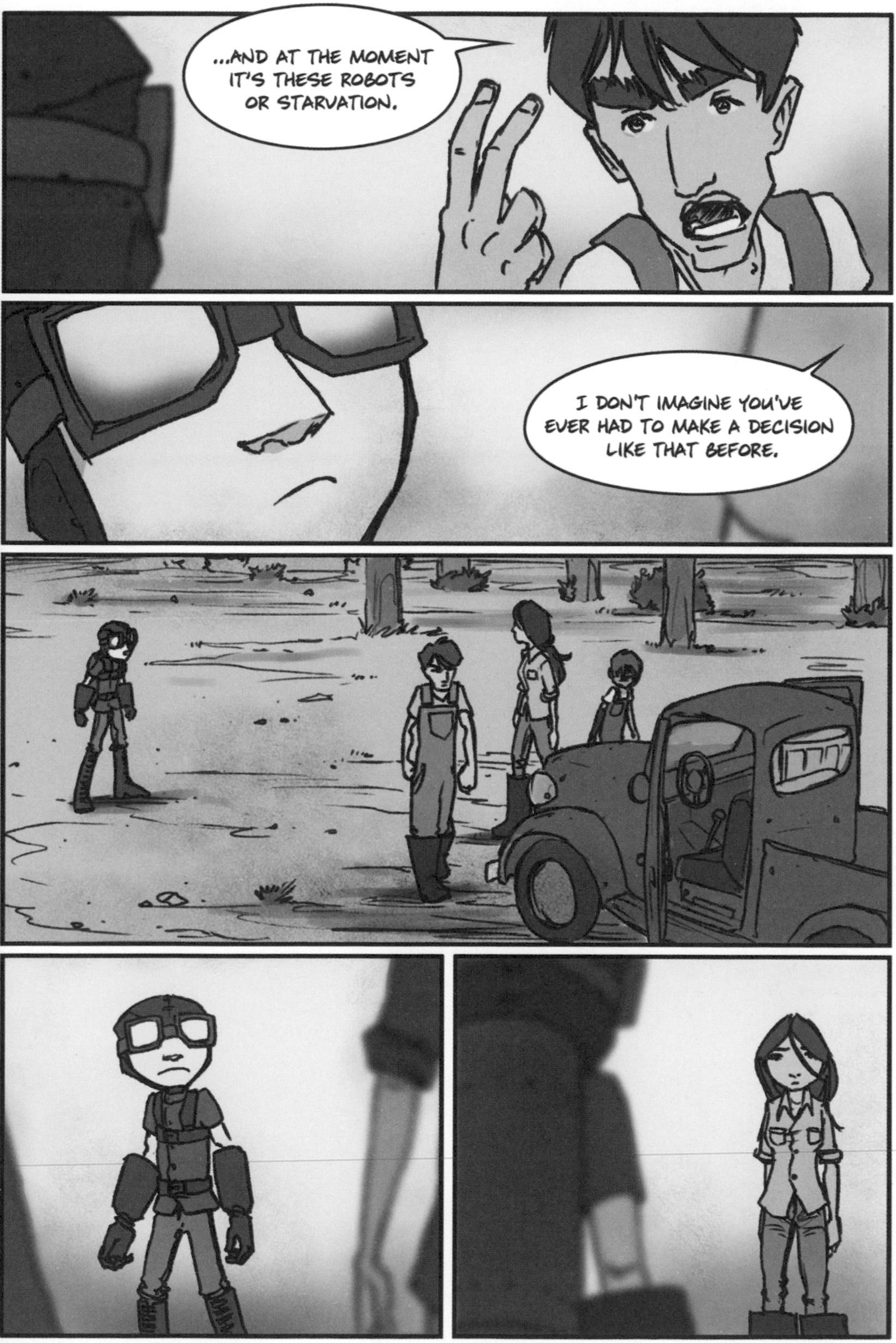
...AND AT THE MOMENT IT'S THESE ROBOTS OR STARVATION.
I DON'T IMAGINE YOU'VE EVER HAD TO MAKE A DECISION LIKE THAT BEFORE.

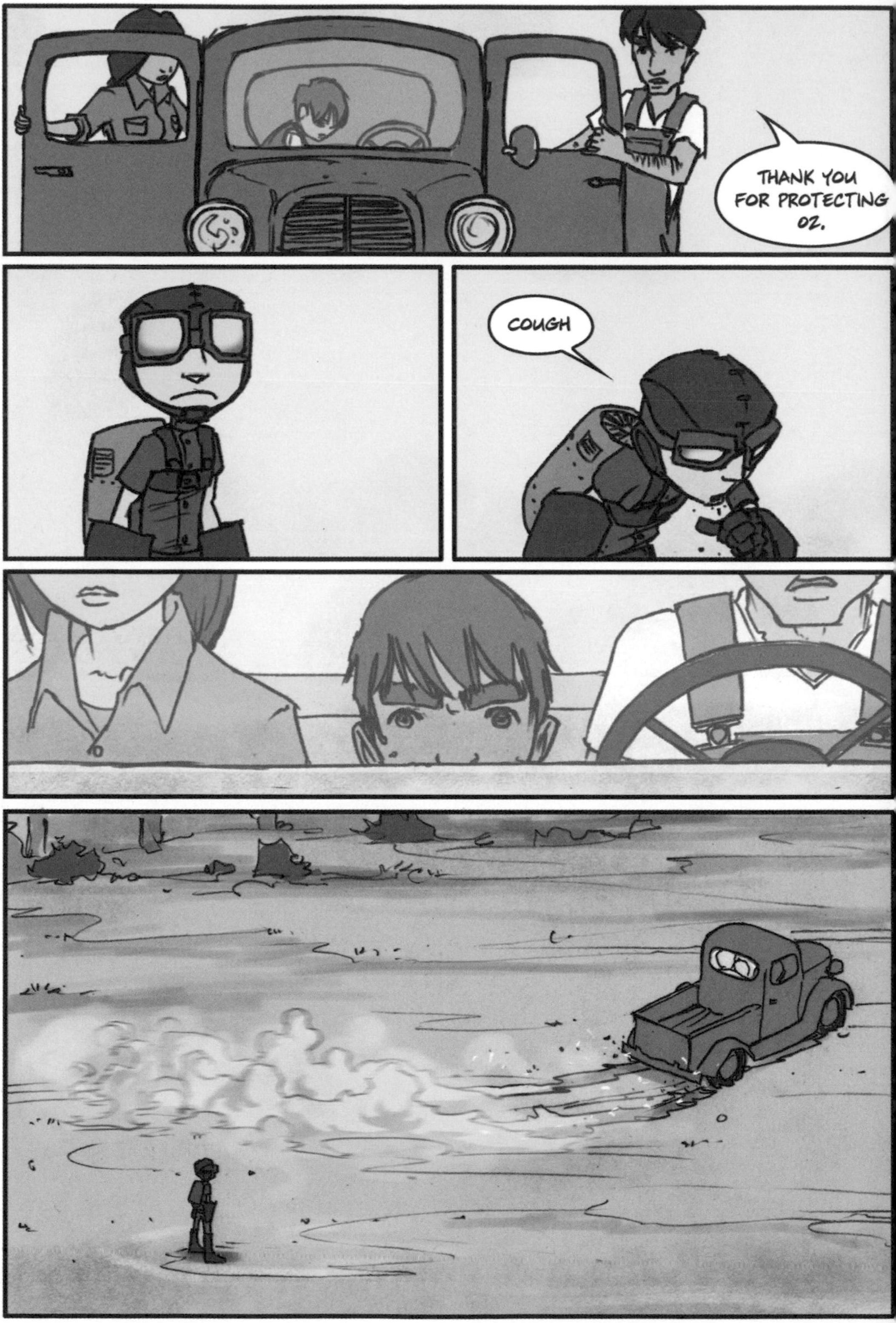
THANK YOU FOR PROTECTING OZ.
COUGH

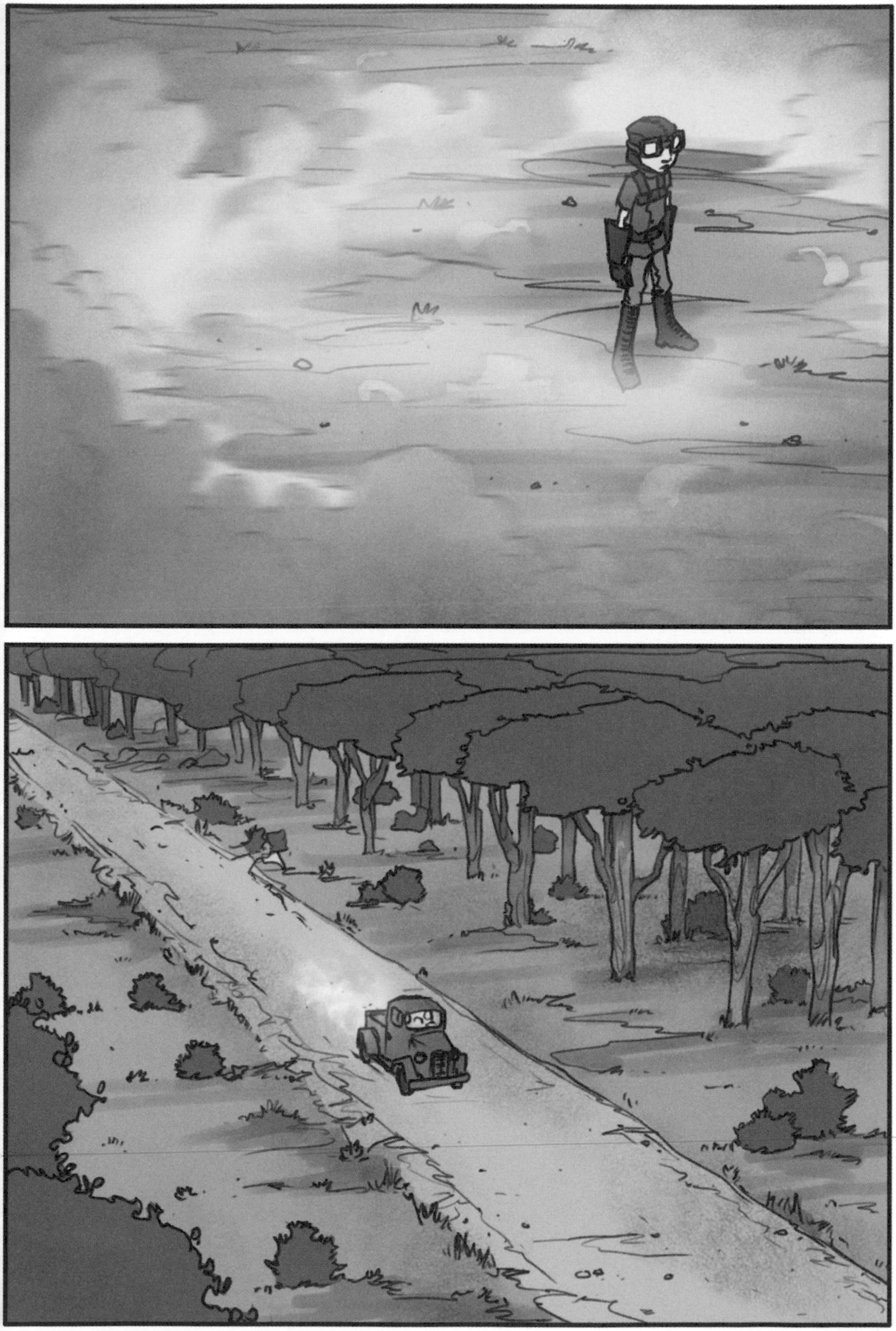

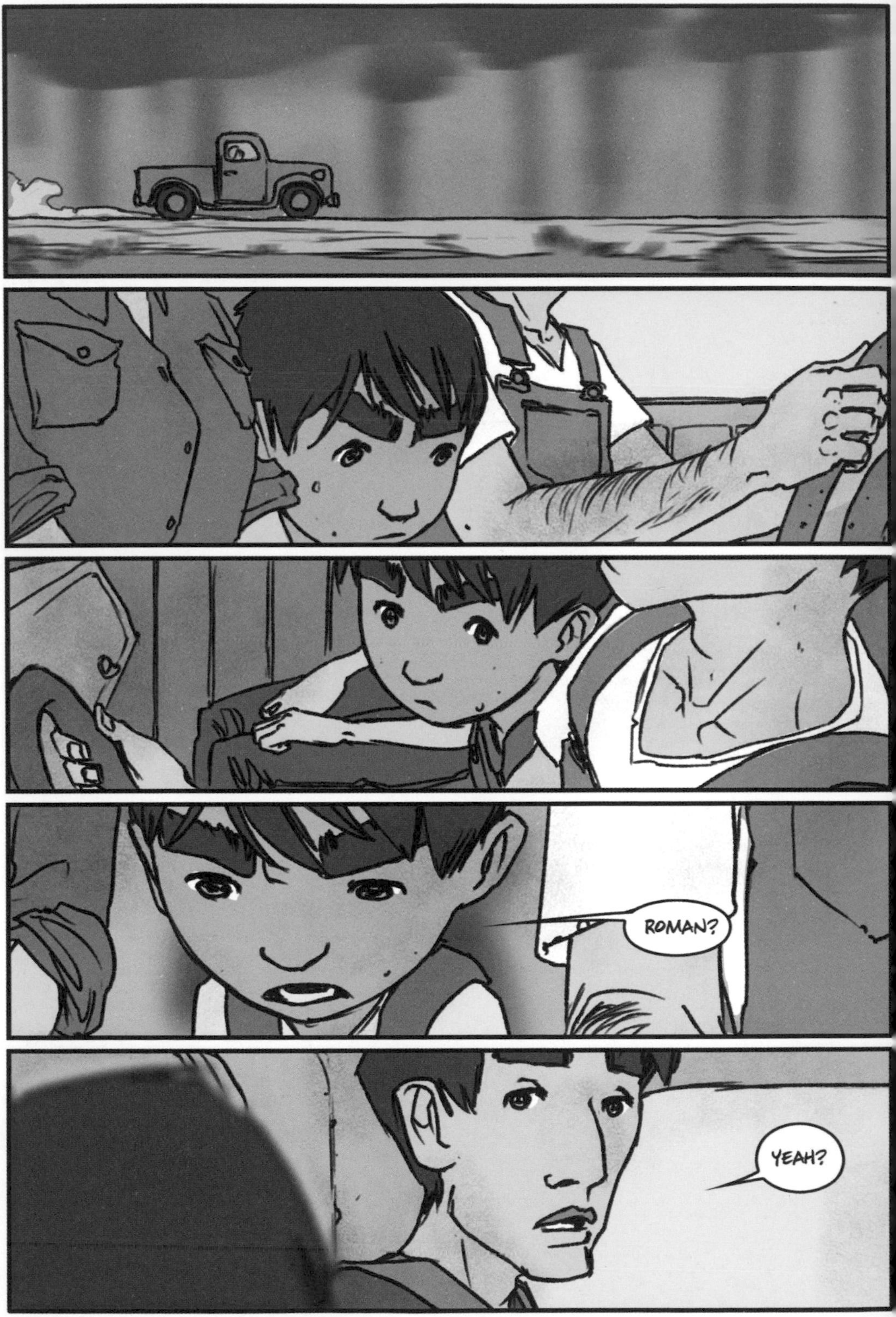
ROMAN?
YEAH?

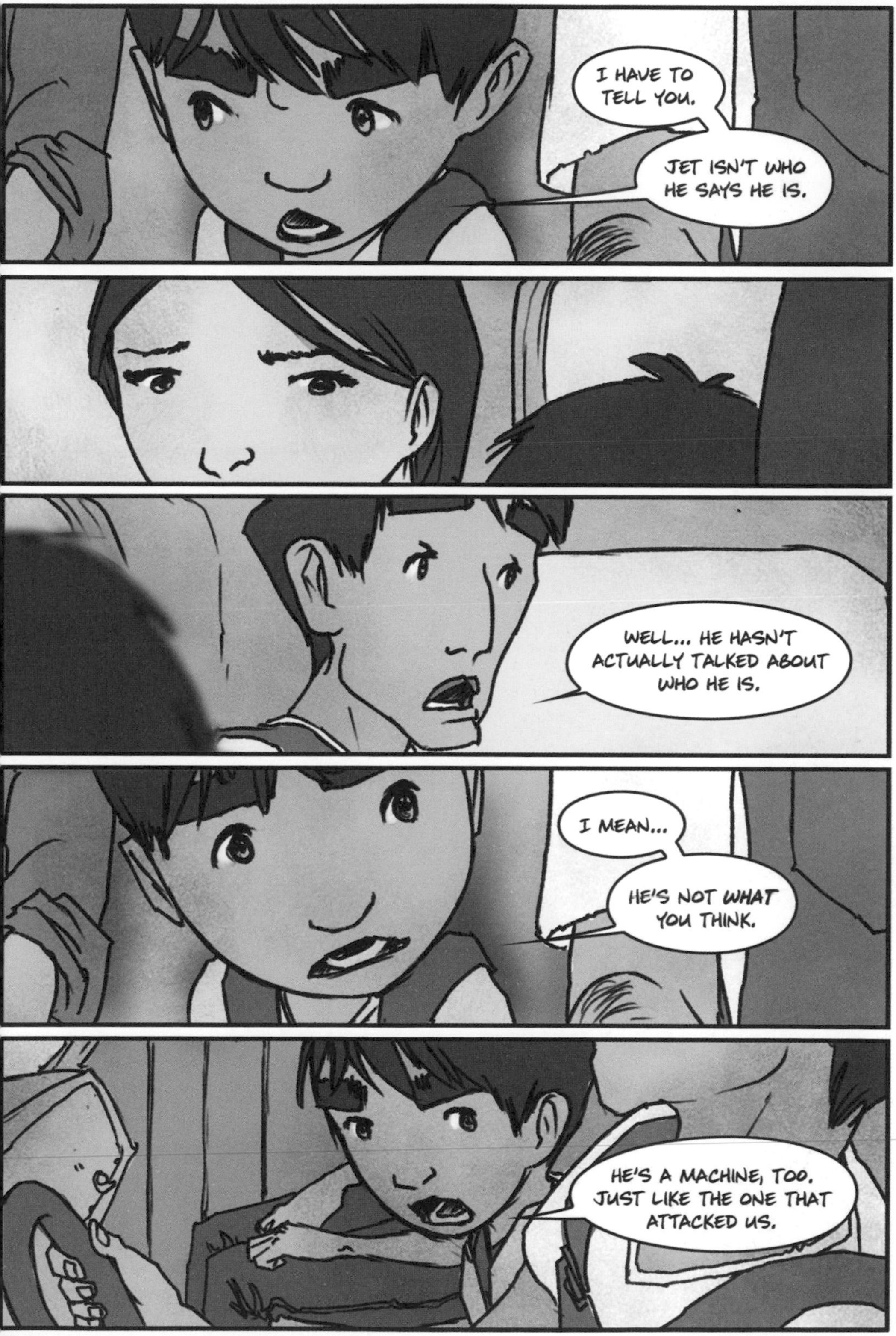
I HAVE TO TELL YOU.
JET ISN'T WHO HE SAYS HE IS.
WELL... HE HASN'T ACTUALLY TALKED ABOUT WHO HE IS.
I MEAN...
HE'S NOT WHAT YOU THINK.
HE'S A MACHINE, TOO. JUST LIKE THE ONE THAT ATTACKED US.

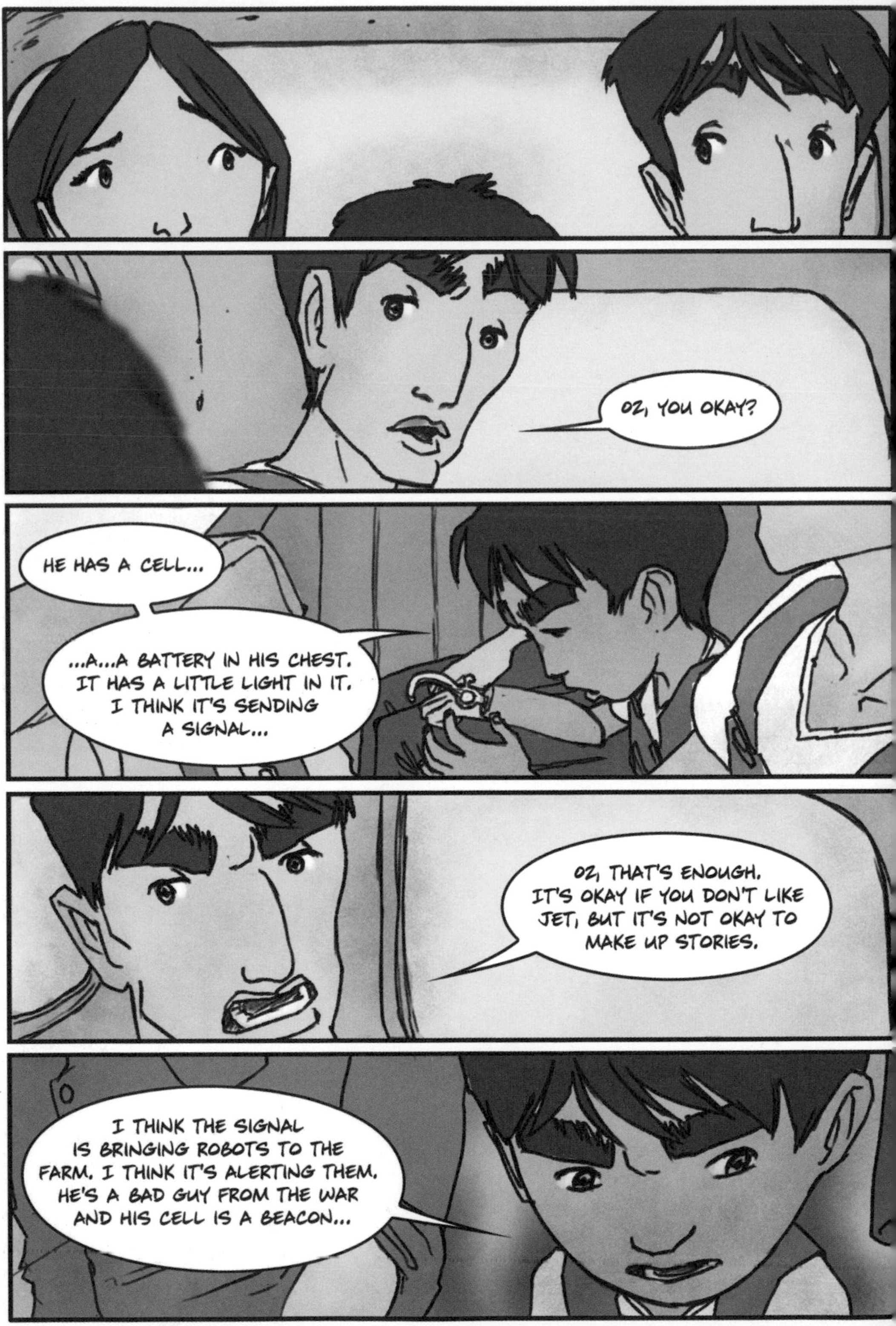
OZ, YOU OKAY?
HE HAS A CELL...
...A...A BATTERY IN HIS CHEST. IT HAS A LITTLE LIGHT IN IT. I THINK IT'S SENDING A SIGNAL...
OZ, THAT'S ENOUGH. IT'S OKAY IF YOU DON'T LIKE JET, BUT IT'S NOT OKAY TO MAKE UP STORIES.
I THINK THE SIGNAL IS BRINGING ROBOTS TO THE FARM. I THINK IT'S ALERTING THEM. HE'S A BAD GUY FROM THE WAR AND HIS CELL IS A BEACON...

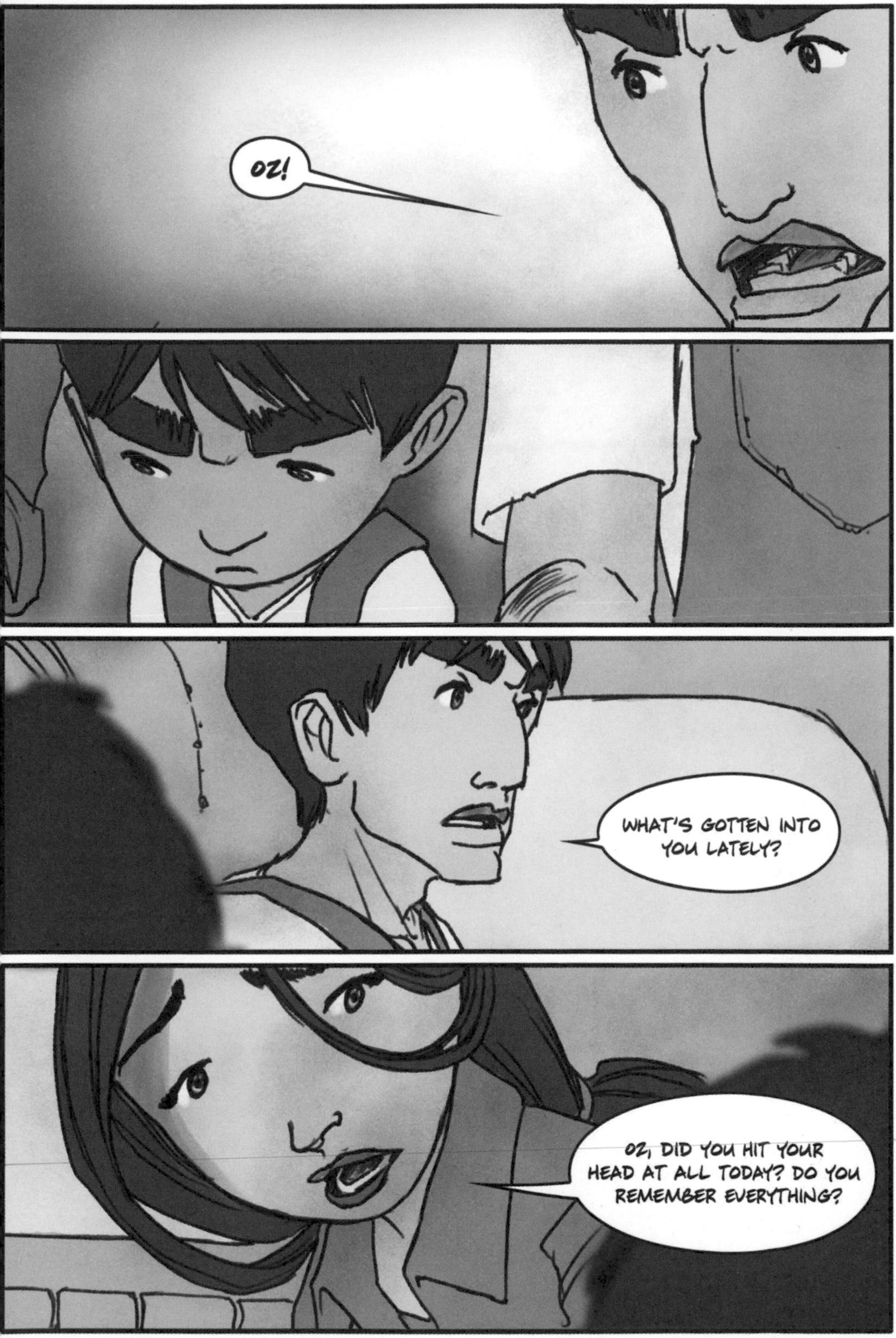
OZ!
WHAT'S GOTTEN INTO YOU LATELY?
OZ, DID YOU HIT YOUR HEAD AT ALL TODAY? DO YOU REMEMBER EVERYTHING?

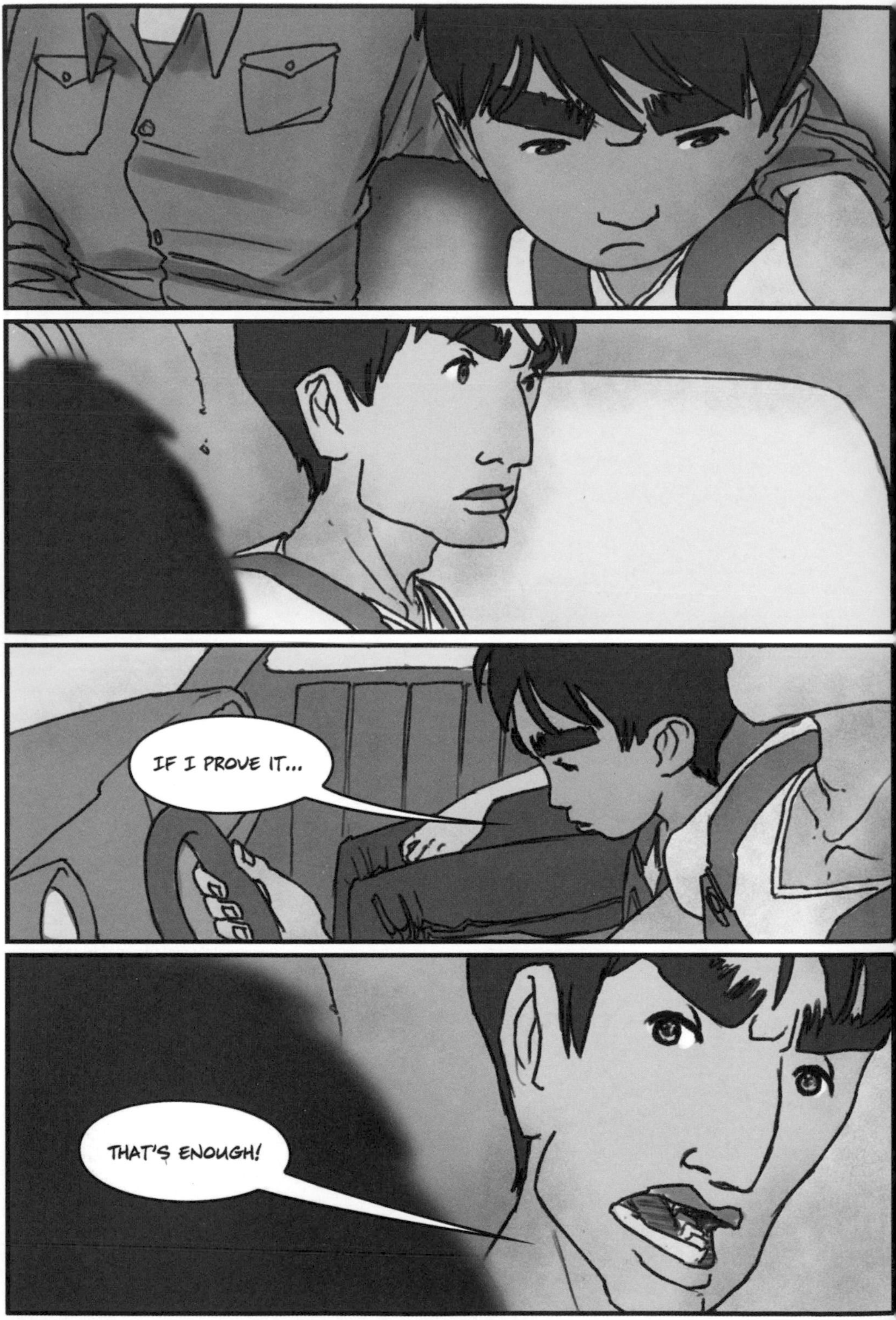
IF I PROVE IT...
THAT'S ENOUGH!

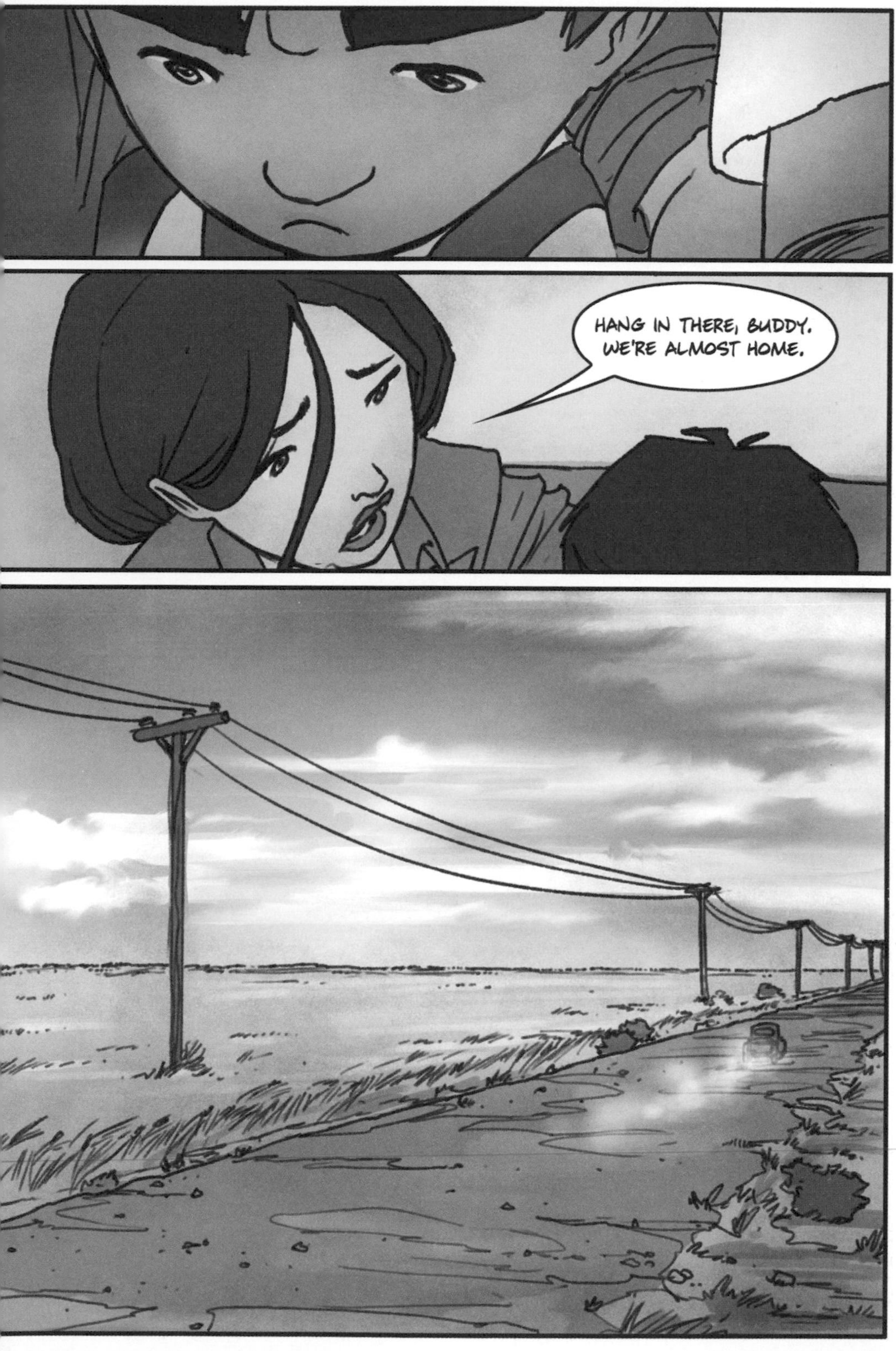
HANG IN THERE, BUDDY. WE'RE ALMOST HOME.

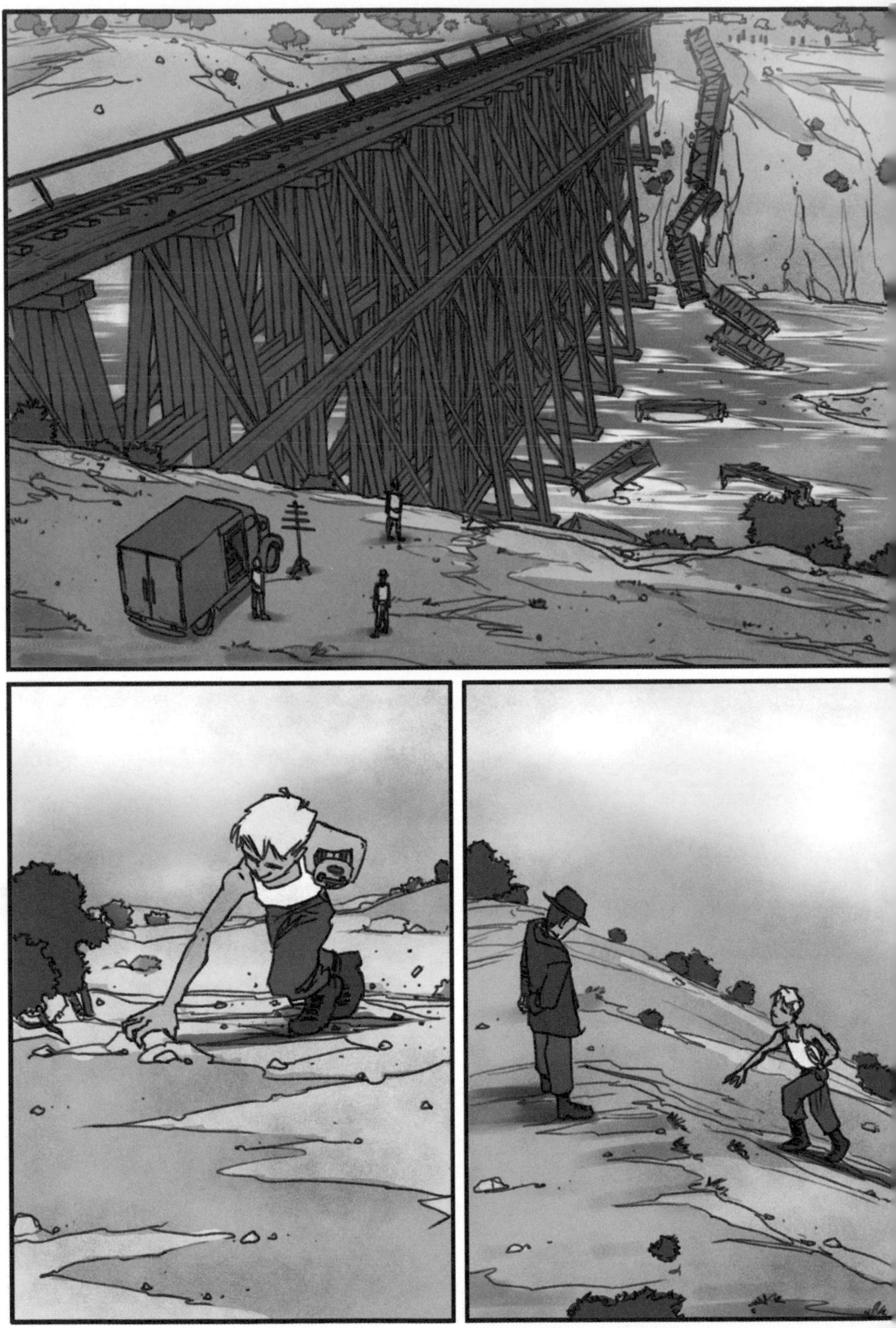

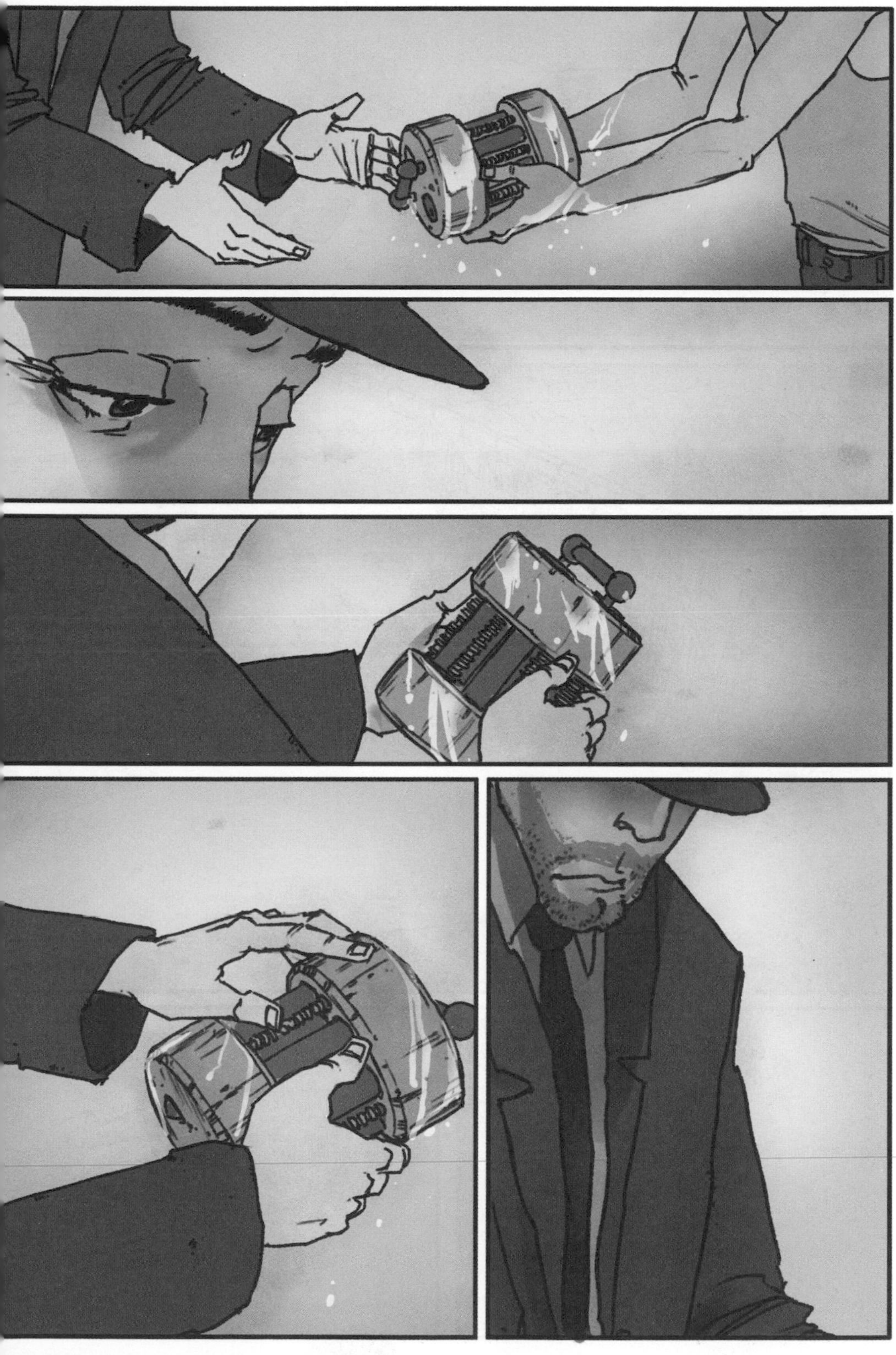

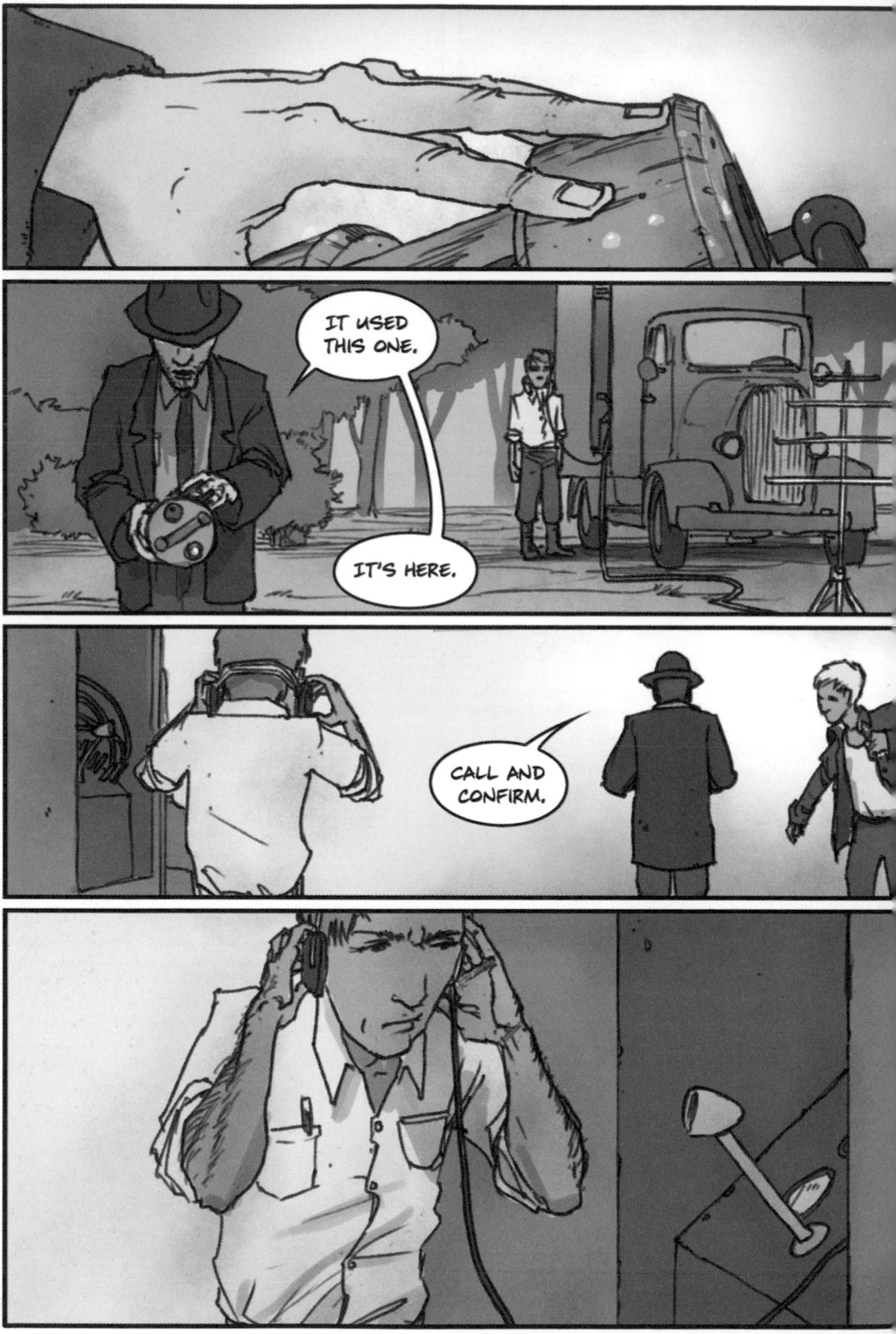
IT USED THIS ONE.
IT'S HERE.
CALL AND CONFIRM.

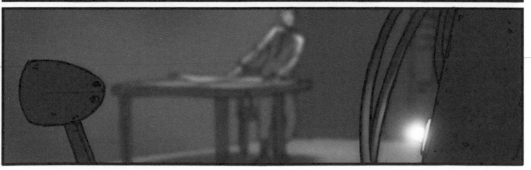

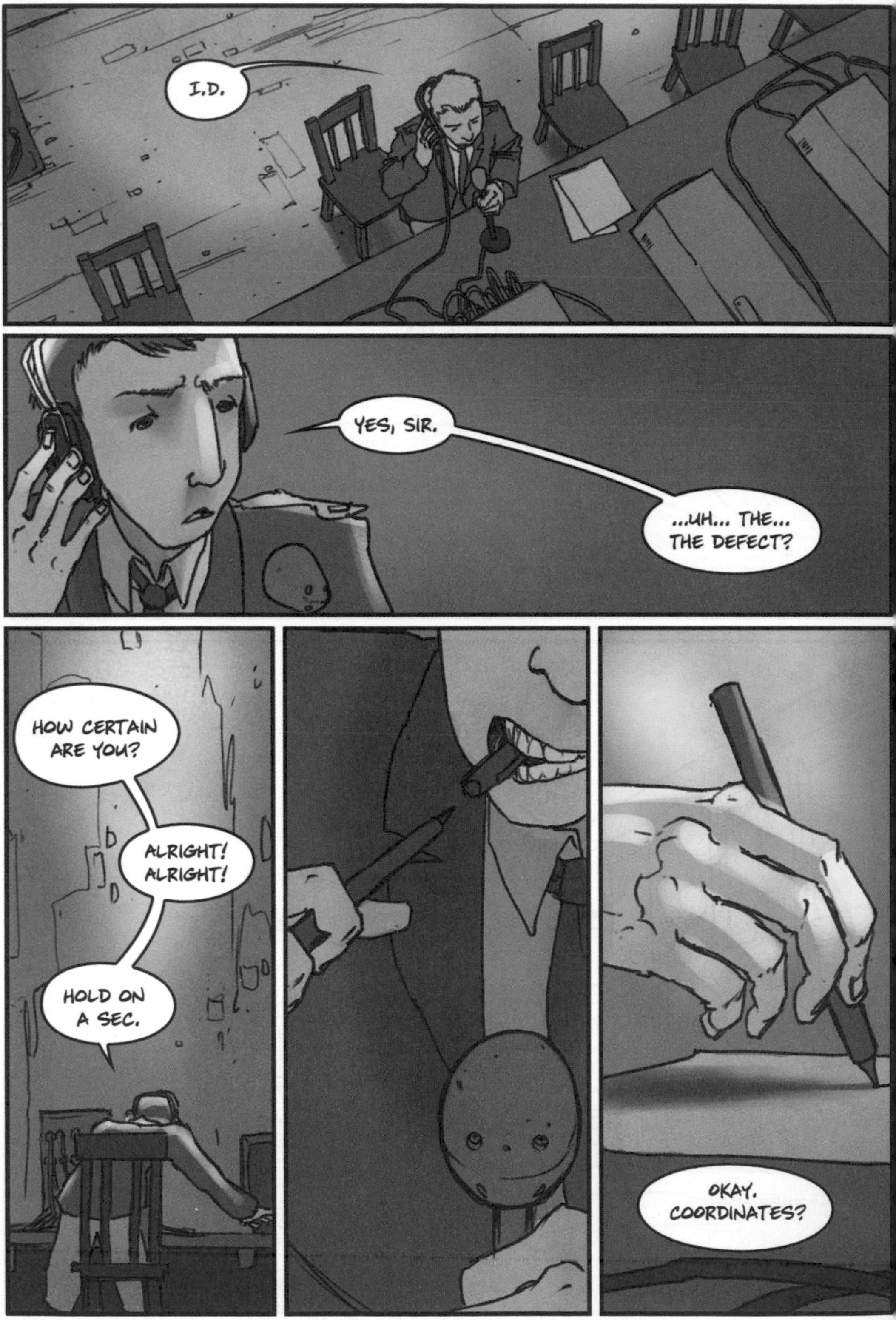
I.D.
YES, SIR.
...UH... THE...
THE DEFECT?
HOW CERTAIN
ARE YOU?
ALRIGHT!
ALRIGHT!
HOLD ON
A SEC.
OKAY.
COORDINATES?

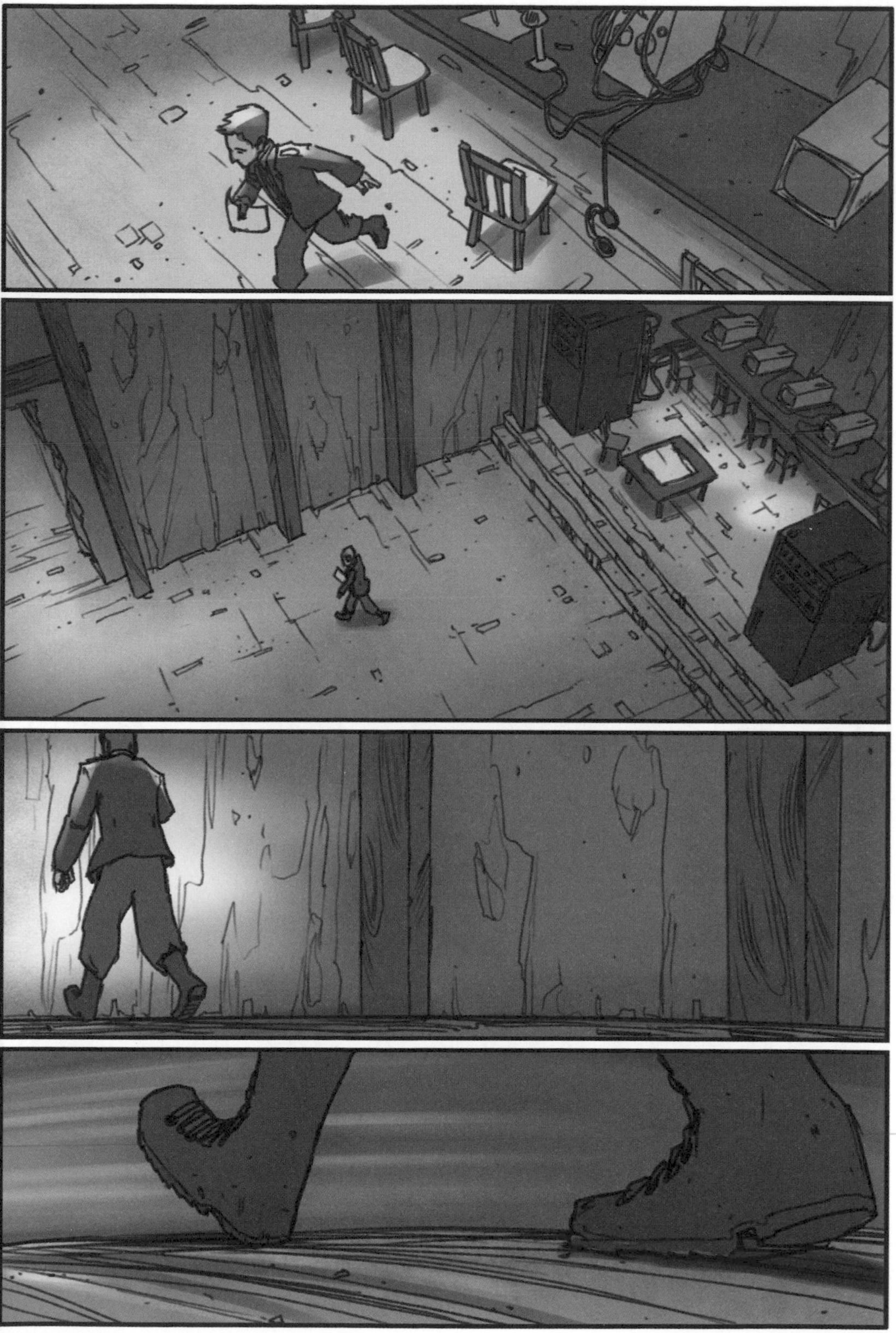

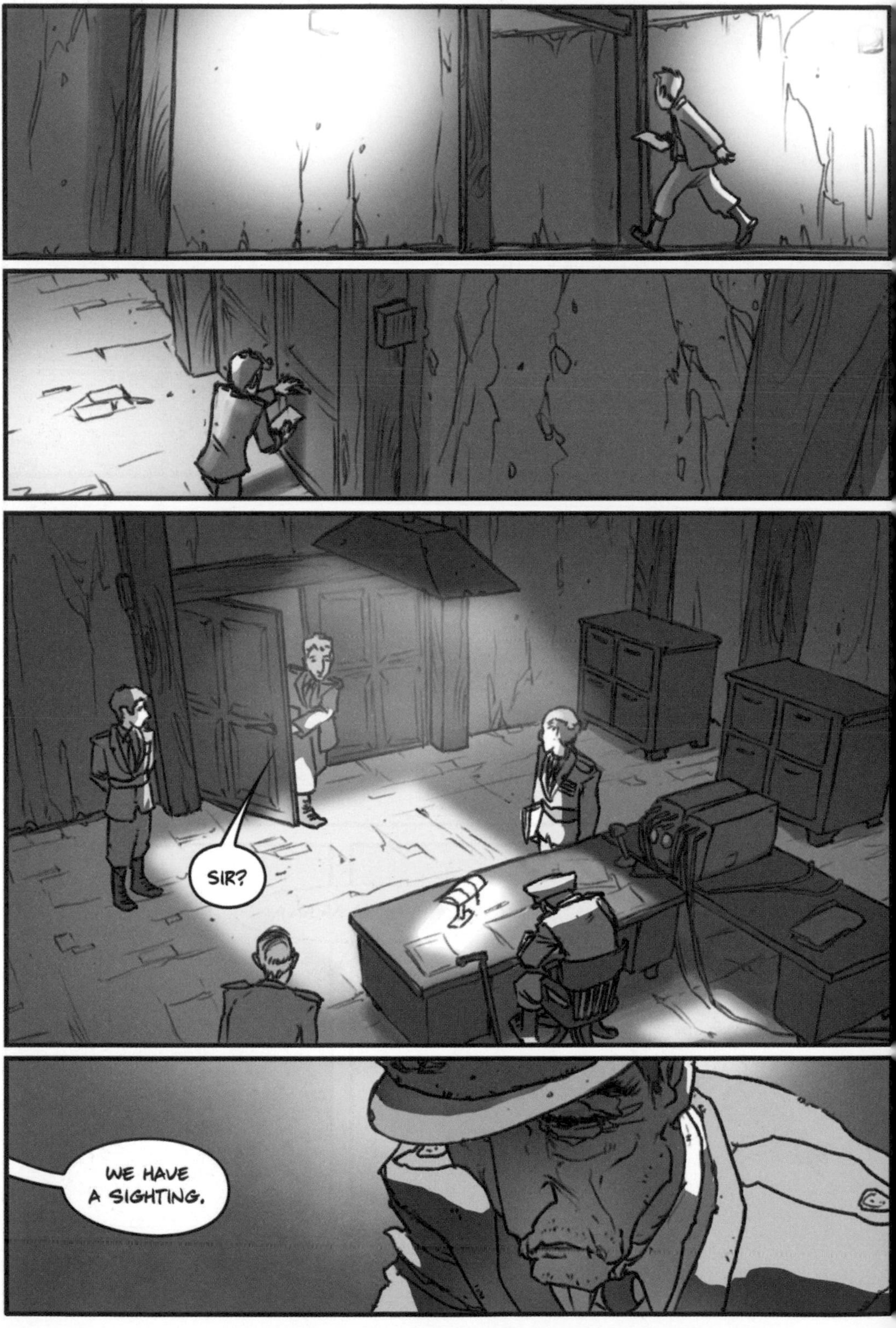
SIR?
WE HAVE A SIGHTING.

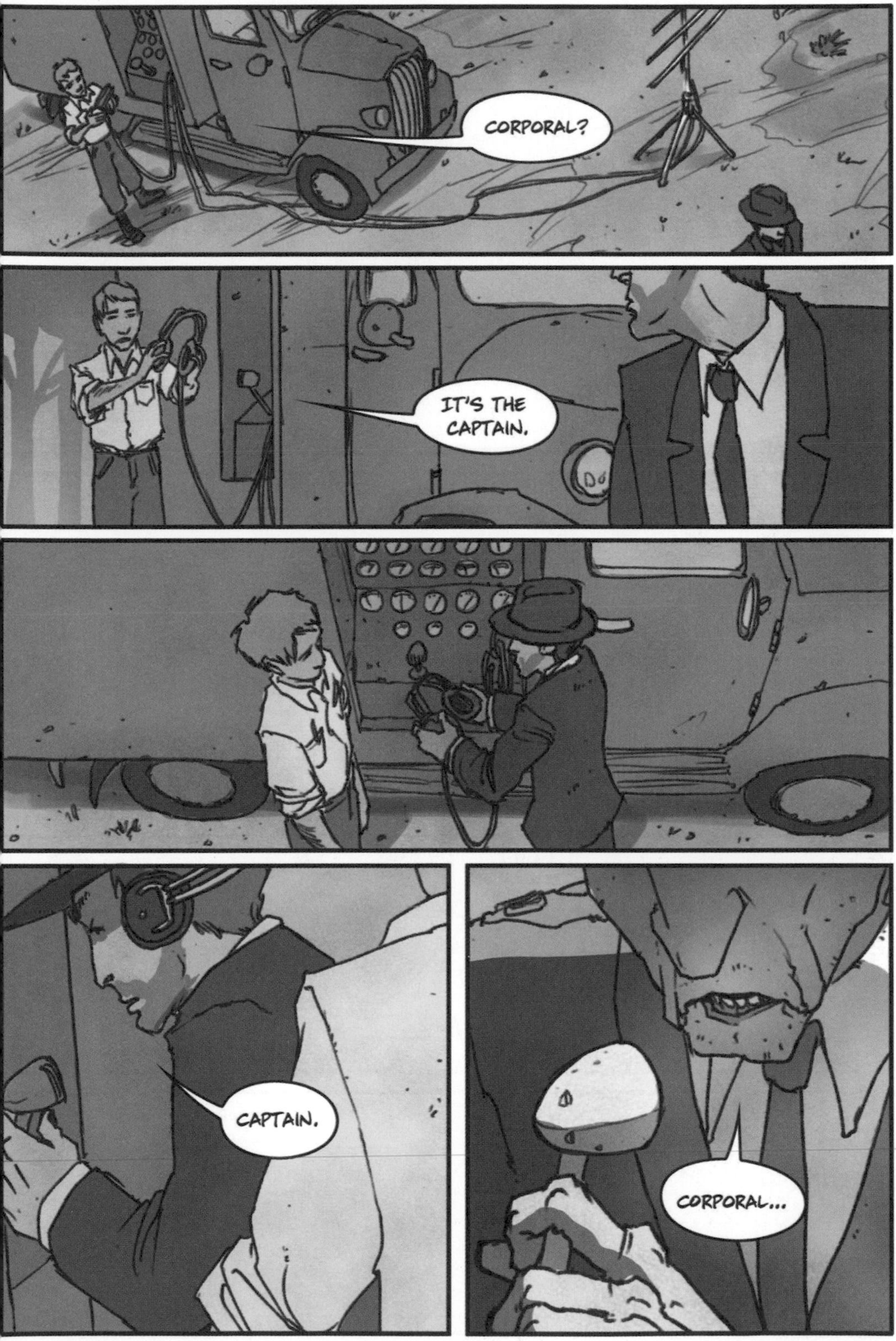
CORPORAL?
IT'S THE CAPTAIN.
CAPTAIN.
CORPORAL...

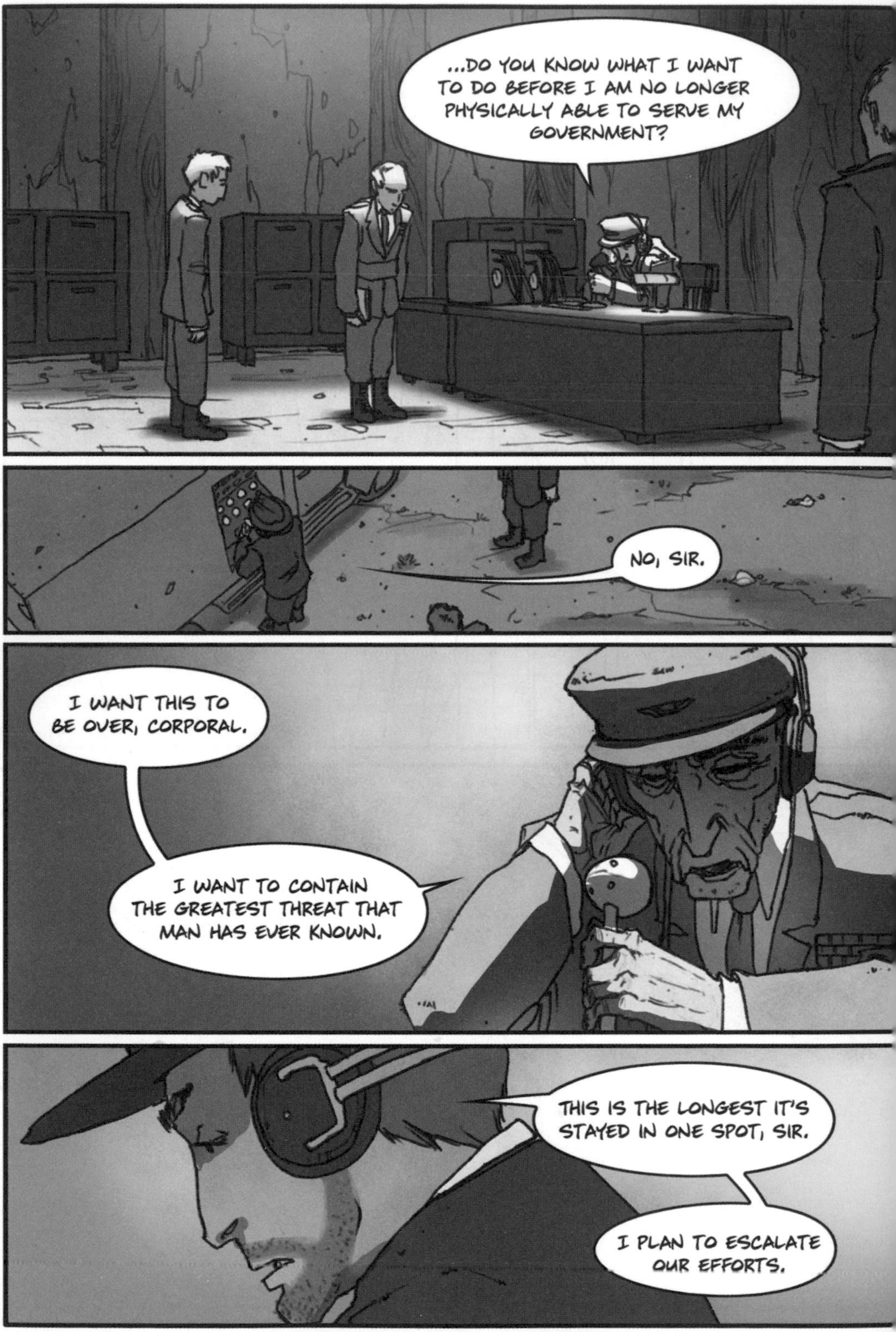
...DO YOU KNOW WHAT I WANT TO DO BEFORE I AM NO LONGER PHYSICALLY ABLE TO SERVE MY GOVERNMENT?
NO, SIR.
I WANT THIS TO BE OVER, CORPORAL.
I WANT TO CONTAIN THE GREATEST THREAT THAT MAN HAS EVER KNOWN.
THIS IS THE LONGEST IT'S STAYED IN ONE SPOT, SIR.
I PLAN TO ESCALATE OUR EFFORTS.

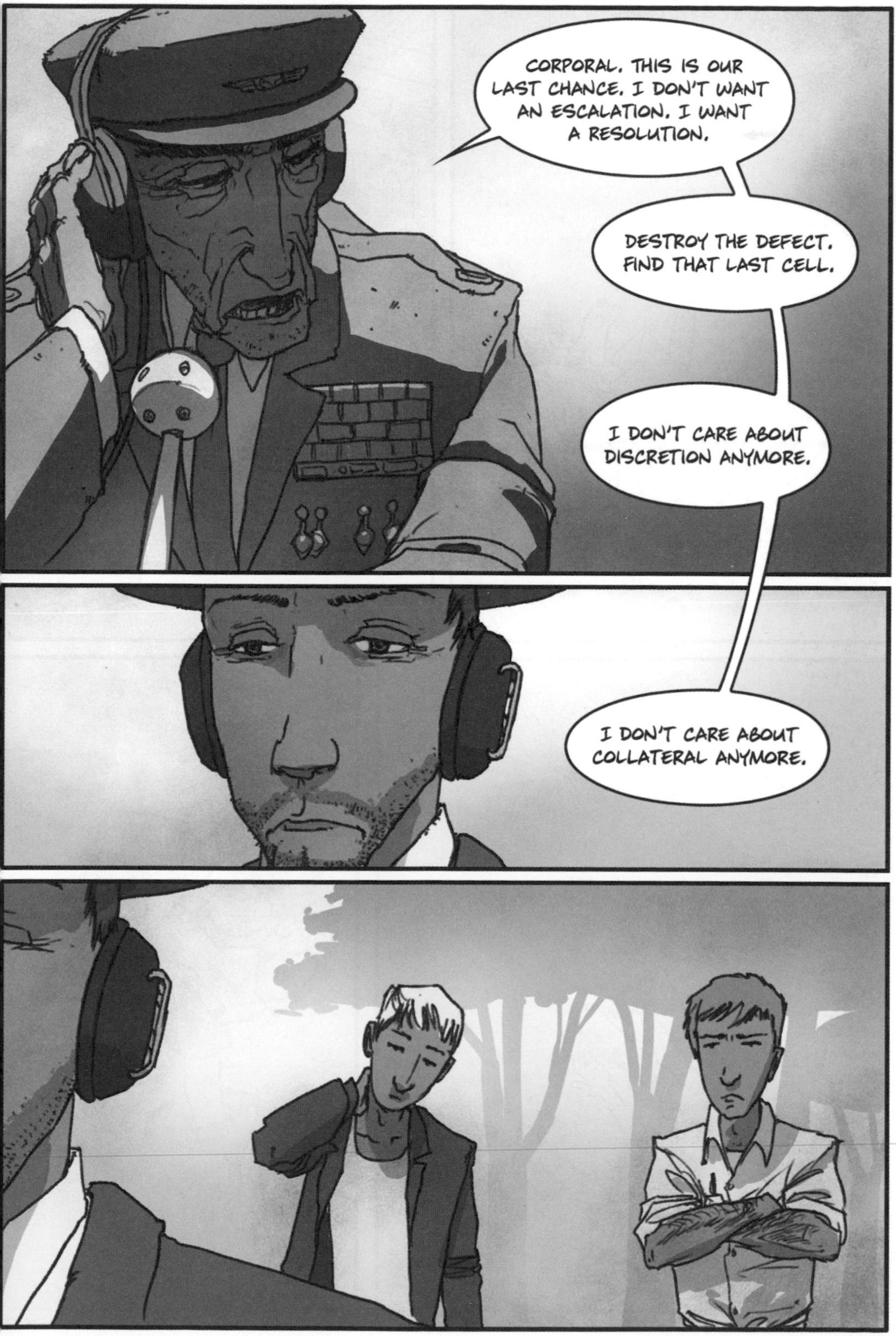
CORPORAL. THIS IS OUR LAST CHANCE. I DON'T WANT AN ESCALATION. I WANT A RESOLUTION.
DESTROY THE DEFECT. FIND THAT LAST CELL.
I DON'T CARE ABOUT DISCRETION ANYMORE.
I DON'T CARE ABOUT COLLATERAL ANYMORE.

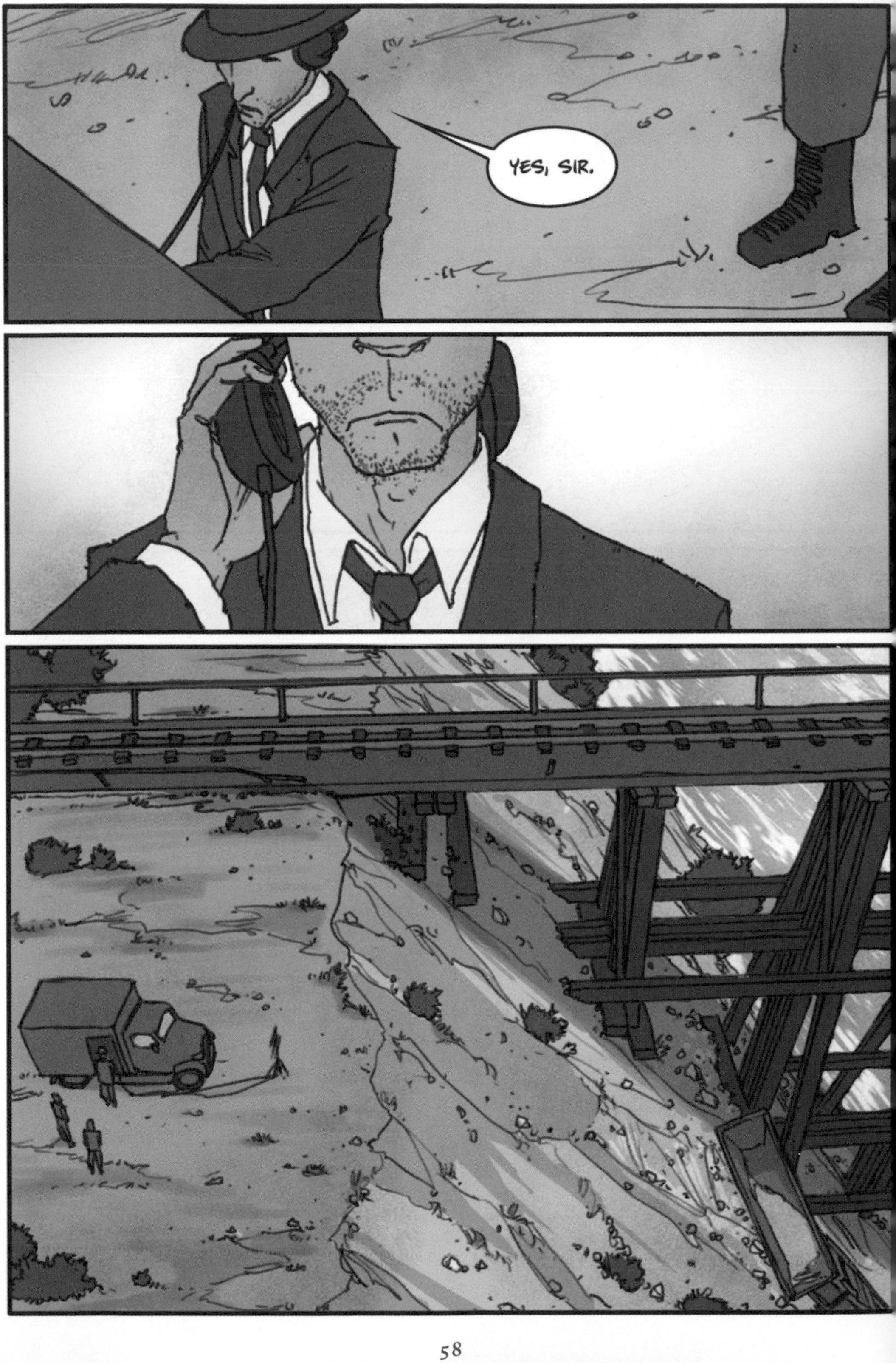
YES, SIR.

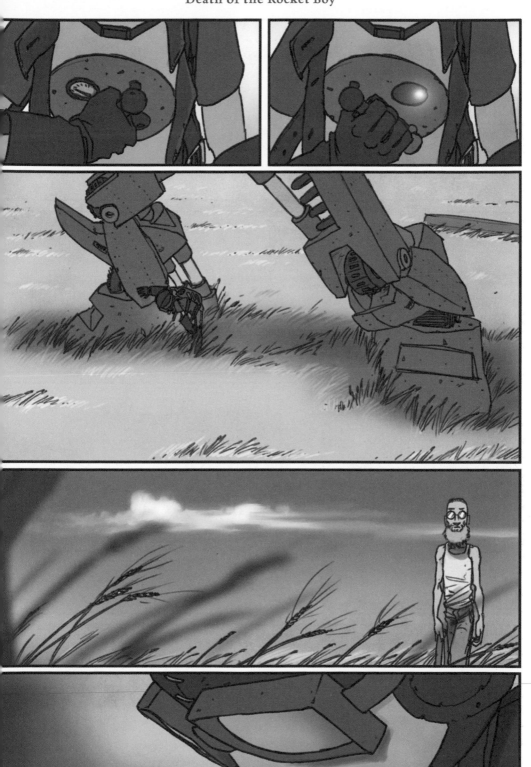

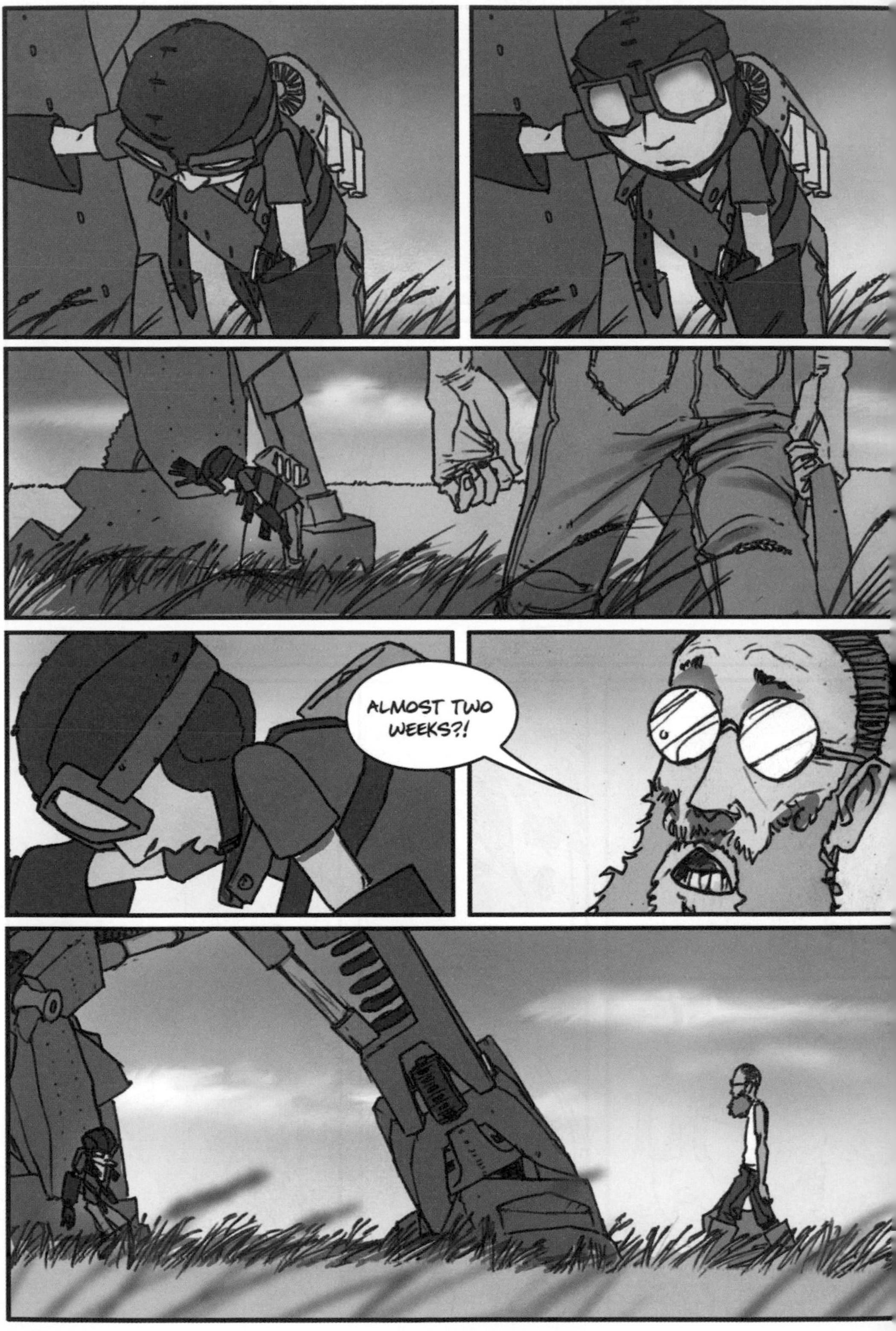
ALMOST TWO WEEKS?!

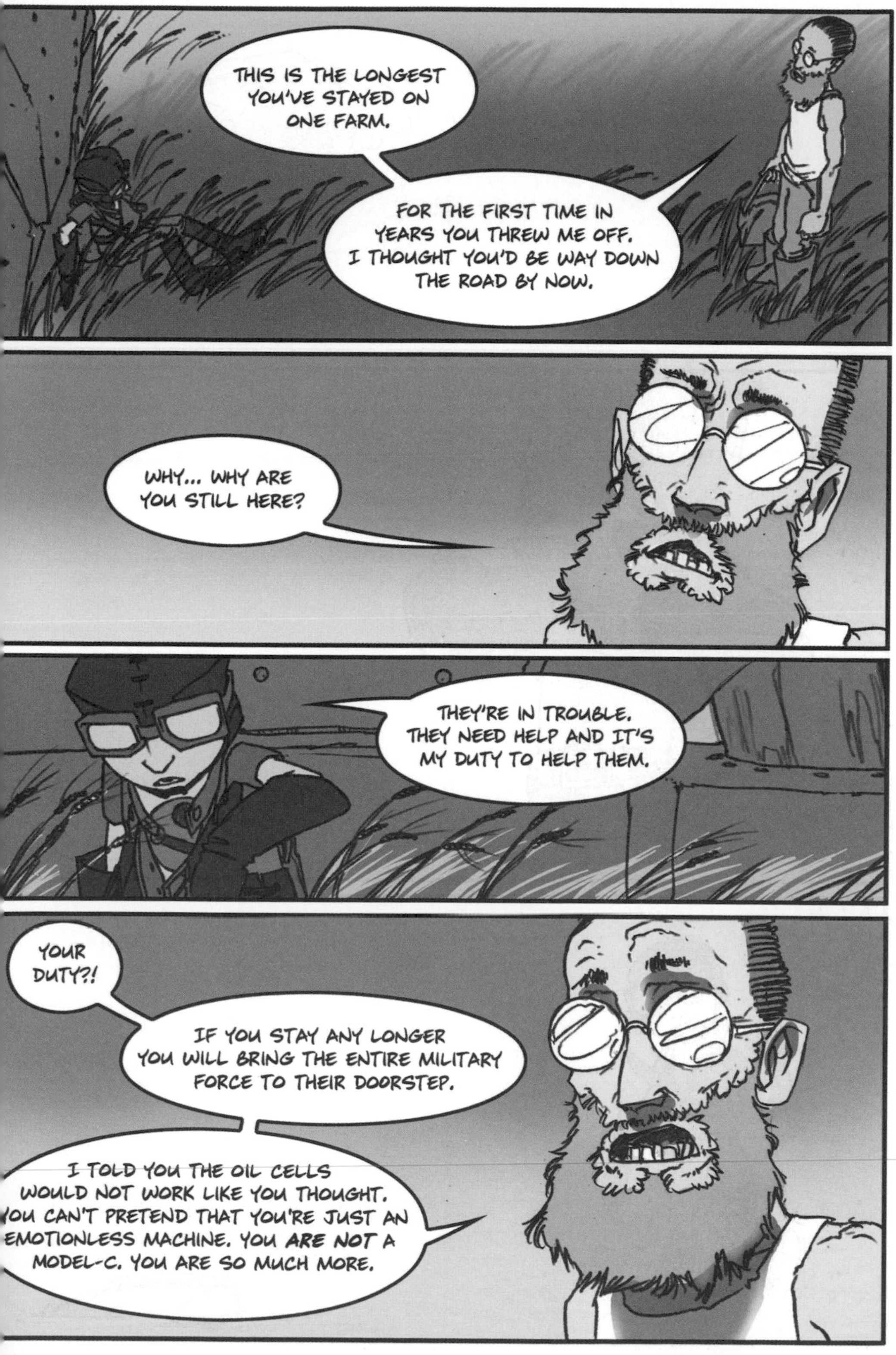
THIS IS THE LONGEST YOU'VE STAYED ON ONE FARM.
FOR THE FIRST TIME IN YEARS YOU THREW ME OFF. I THOUGHT YOU'D BE WAY DOWN THE ROAD BY NOW.
WHY... WHY ARE YOU STILL HERE?
THEY'RE IN TROUBLE. THEY NEED HELP AND IT'S MY DUTY TO HELP THEM.
YOUR DUTY?!
IF YOU STAY ANY LONGER YOU WILL BRING THE ENTIRE MILITARY FORCE TO THEIR DOORSTEP.
I TOLD YOU THE OIL CELLS WOULD NOT WORK LIKE YOU THOUGHT. YOU CAN'T PRETEND THAT YOU'RE JUST AN EMOTIONLESS MACHINE. YOU ARE NOT A MODEL-C. YOU ARE SO MUCH MORE.

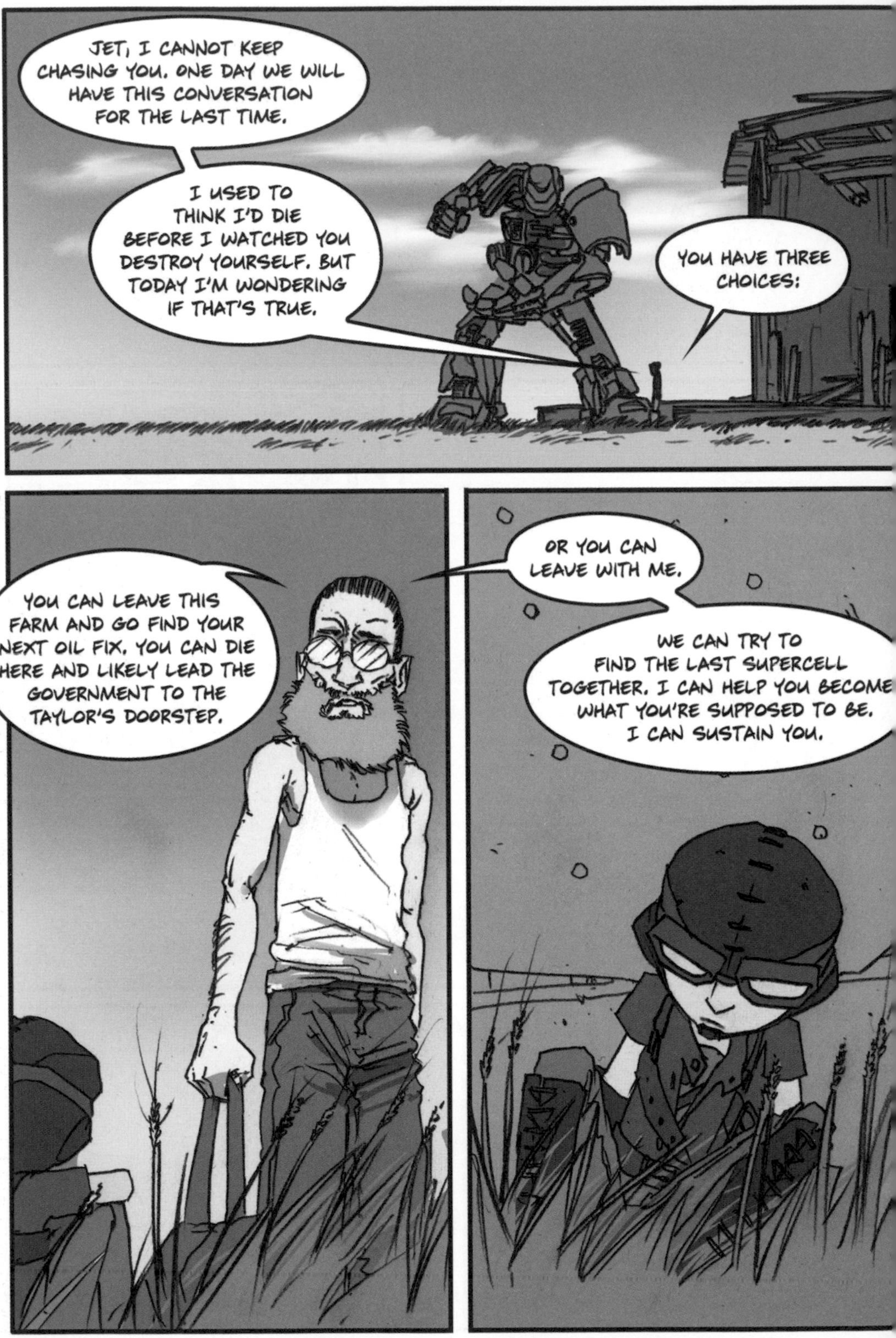
JET, I CANNOT KEEP CHASING YOU. ONE DAY WE WILL HAVE THIS CONVERSATION FOR THE LAST TIME.
I USED TO THINK I'D DIE BEFORE I WATCHED YOU DESTROY YOURSELF. BUT TODAY I'M WONDERING IF THAT'S TRUE.
YOU HAVE THREE CHOICES:
YOU CAN LEAVE THIS FARM AND GO FIND YOUR NEXT OIL FIX. YOU CAN DIE HERE AND LIKELY LEAD THE GOVERNMENT TO THE TAYLOR'S DOORSTEP.
OR YOU CAN LEAVE WITH ME.
WE CAN TRY TO FIND THE LAST SUPERCELL TOGETHER. I CAN HELP YOU BECOME WHAT YOU'RE SUPPOSED TO BE. I CAN SUSTAIN YOU.

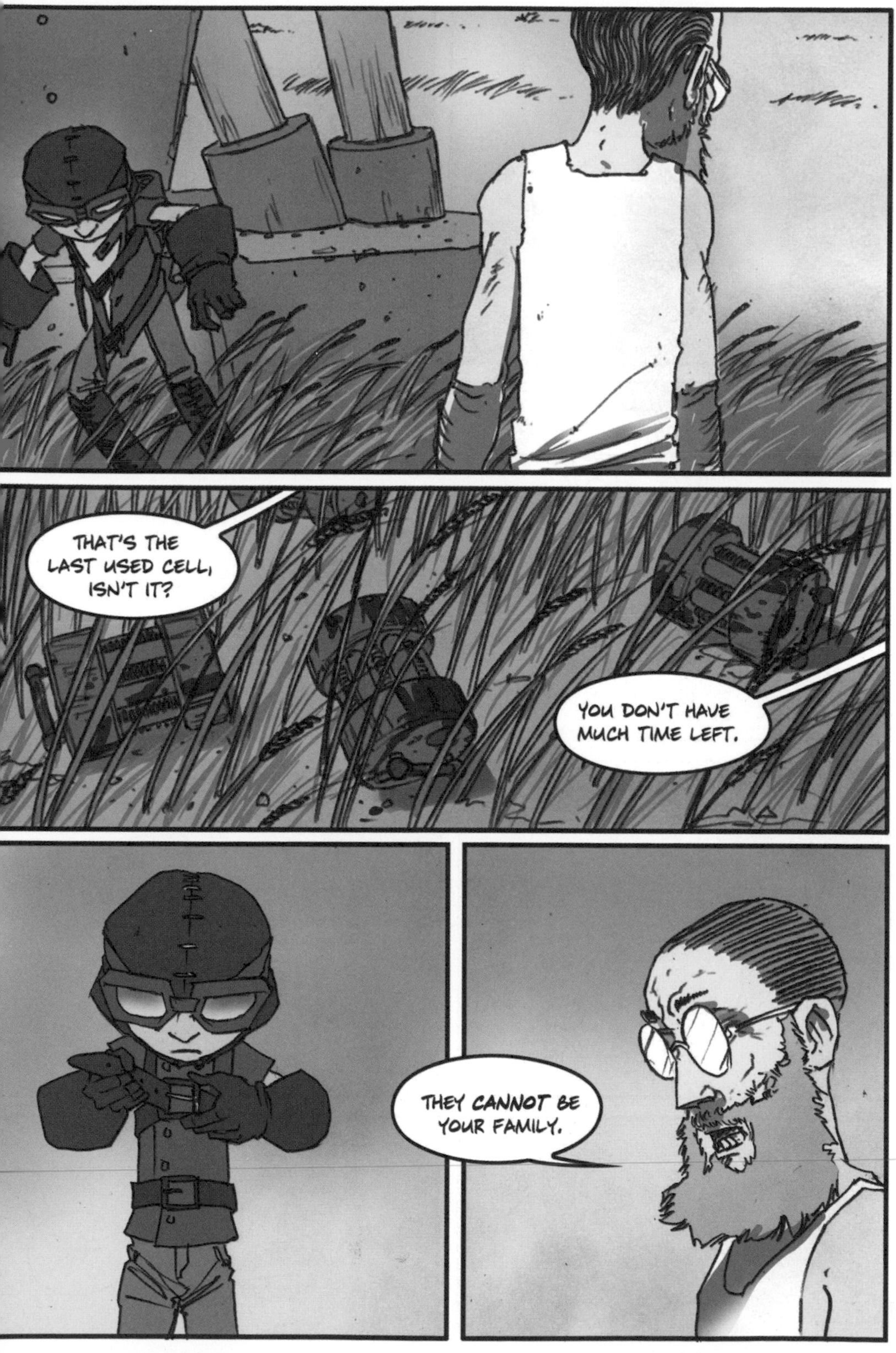
THAT'S THE LAST USED CELL, ISN'T IT?
YOU DON'T HAVE MUCH TIME LEFT.
THEY CANNOT BE YOUR FAMILY.

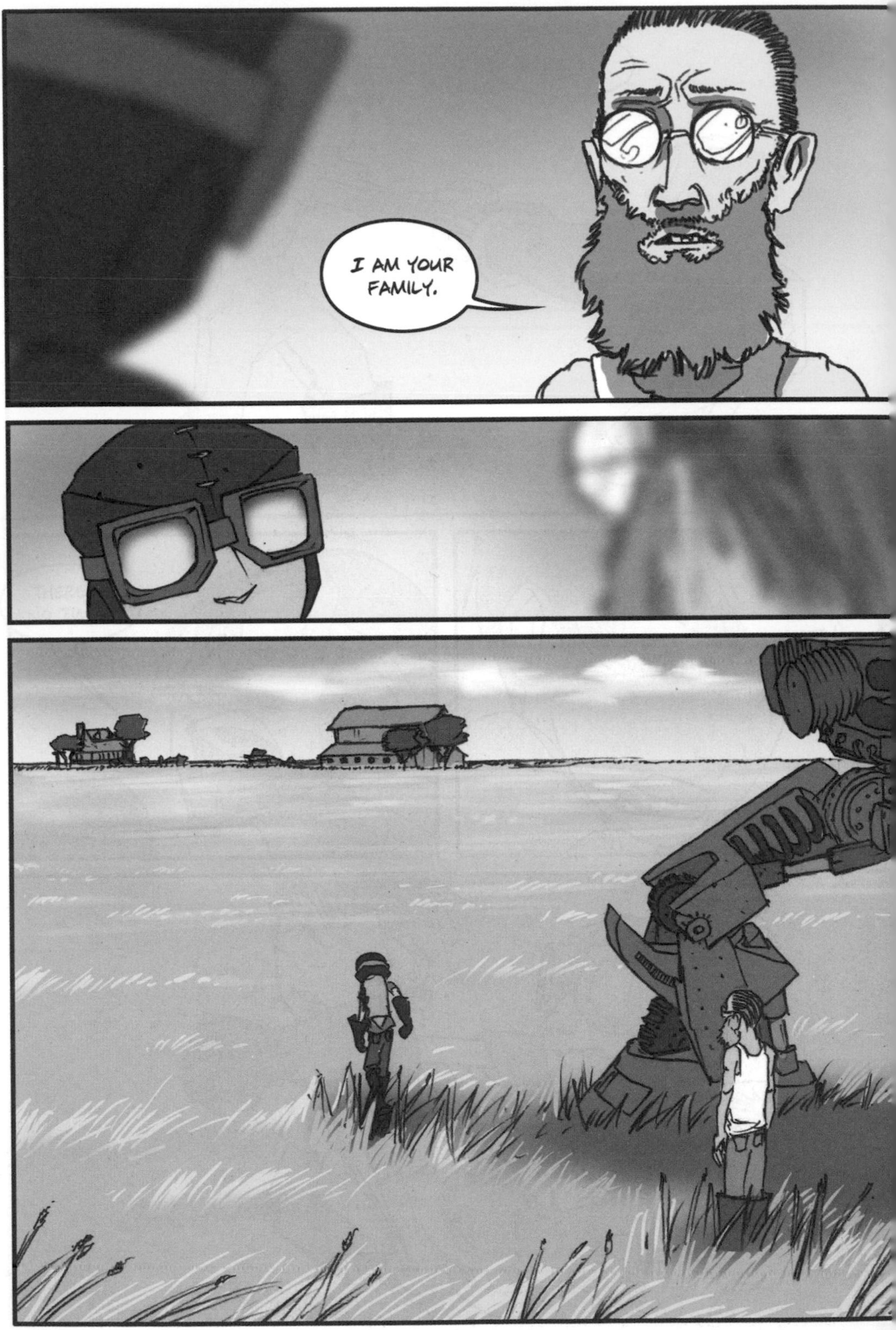
I AM YOUR FAMILY.

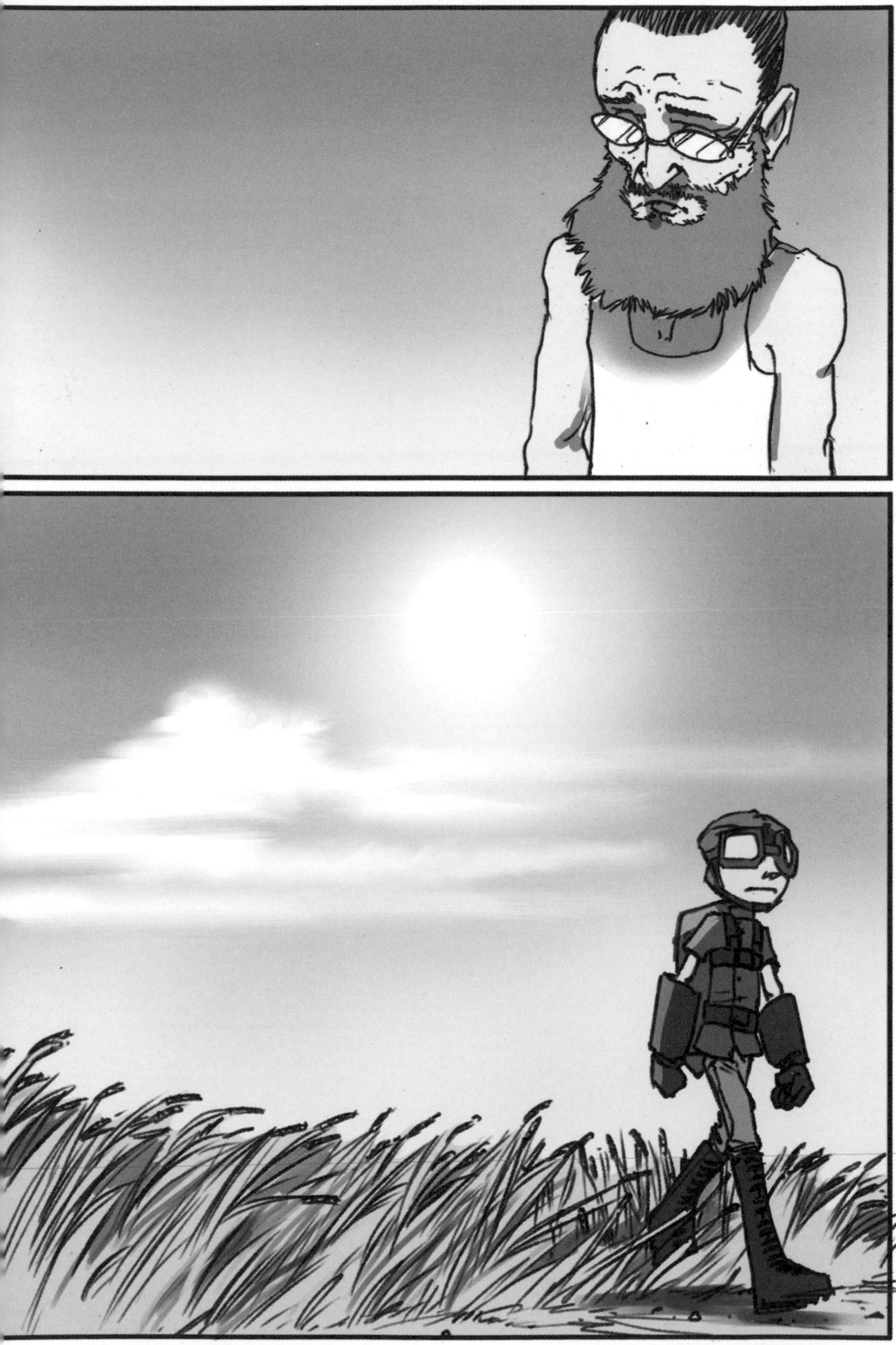

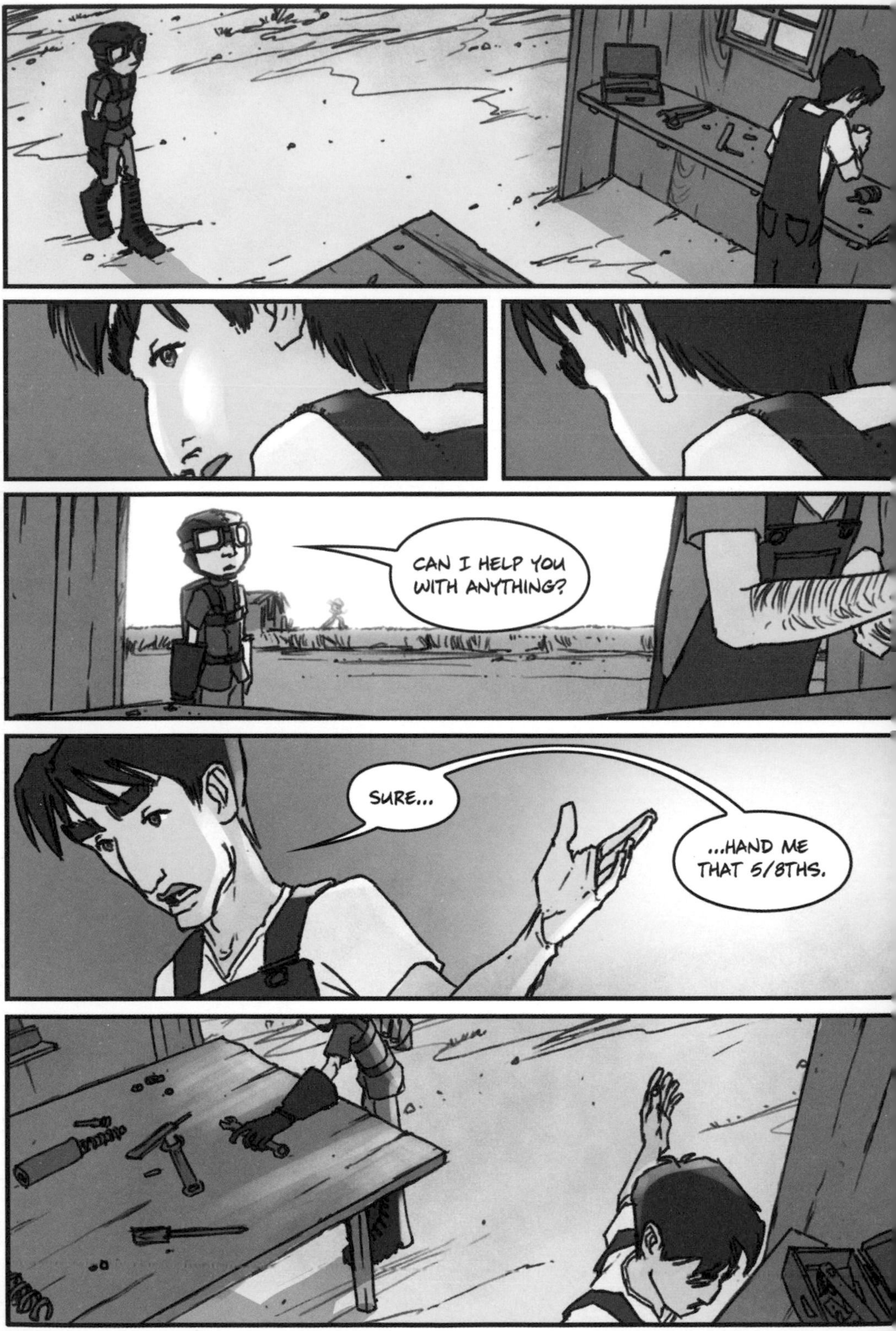
CAN I HELP YOU WITH ANYTHING?
SURE...
...HAND ME THAT 5/8THS.

I'M SORRY I YELLED AT YOU, JET. I'M SORRY WE DISAGREE.

THESE MACHINES...

...THEY START WITH A BASE CODE. YOU CAN RECODE THEM ALL YOU WANT AND THEY'LL FOLLOW THAT CODE FOR A WHILE...

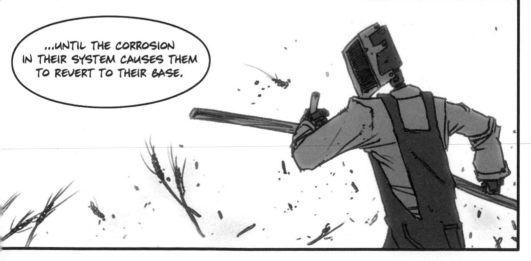

...UNTIL THE CORROSION IN THEIR SYSTEM CAUSES THEM TO REVERT TO THEIR BASE.

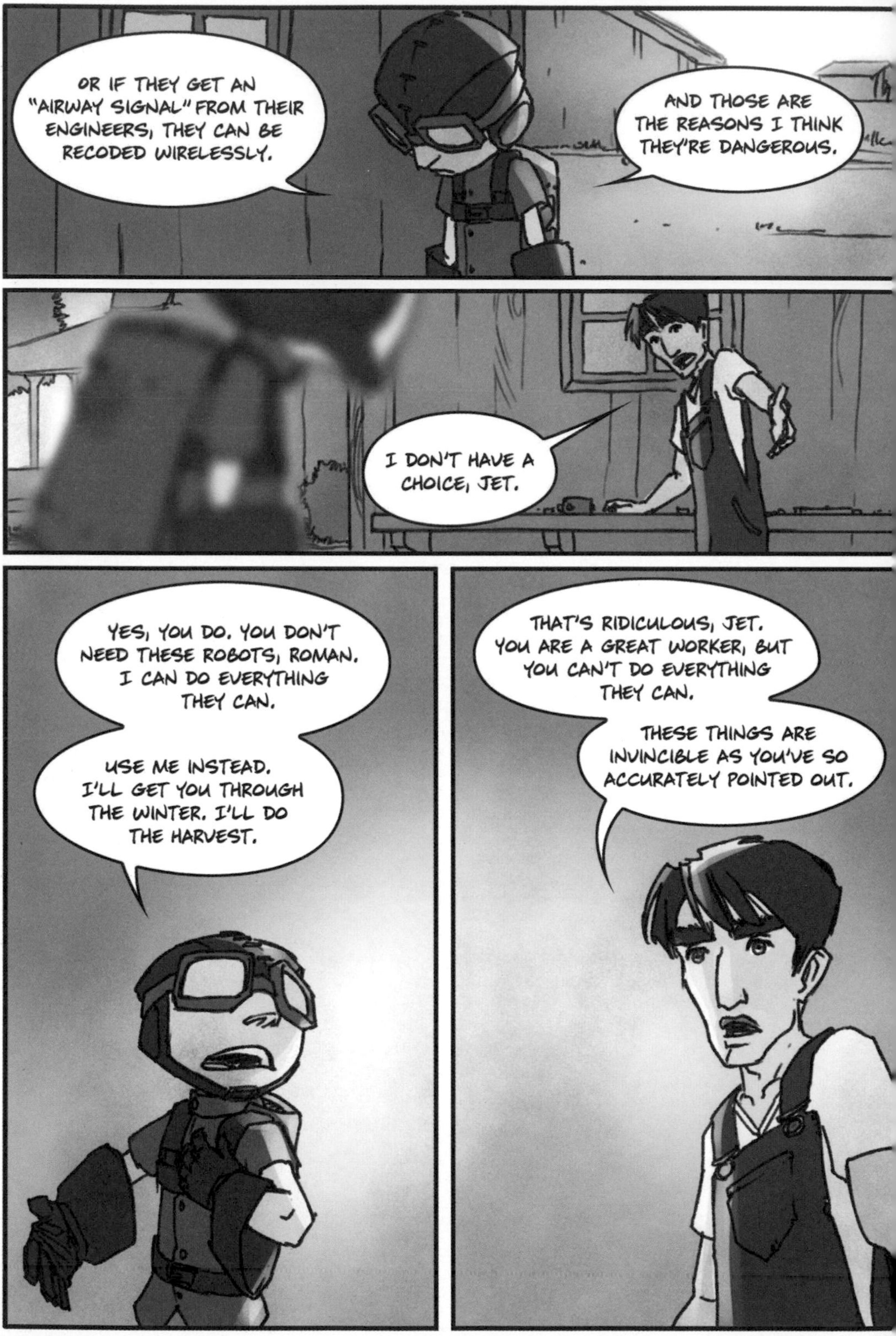
OR IF THEY GET AN "AIRWAY SIGNAL" FROM THEIR ENGINEERS, THEY CAN BE RECODED WIRELESSLY.
AND THOSE ARE THE REASONS I THINK THEY'RE DANGEROUS.
I DON'T HAVE A CHOICE, JET.
YES, YOU DO. YOU DON'T NEED THESE ROBOTS, ROMAN. I CAN DO EVERYTHING THEY CAN.
USE ME INSTEAD. I'LL GET YOU THROUGH THE WINTER. I'LL DO THE HARVEST.
THAT'S RIDICULOUS, JET. YOU ARE A GREAT WORKER, BUT YOU CAN'T DO EVERYTHING THEY CAN.
THESE THINGS ARE INVINCIBLE AS YOU'VE SO ACCURATELY POINTED OUT.

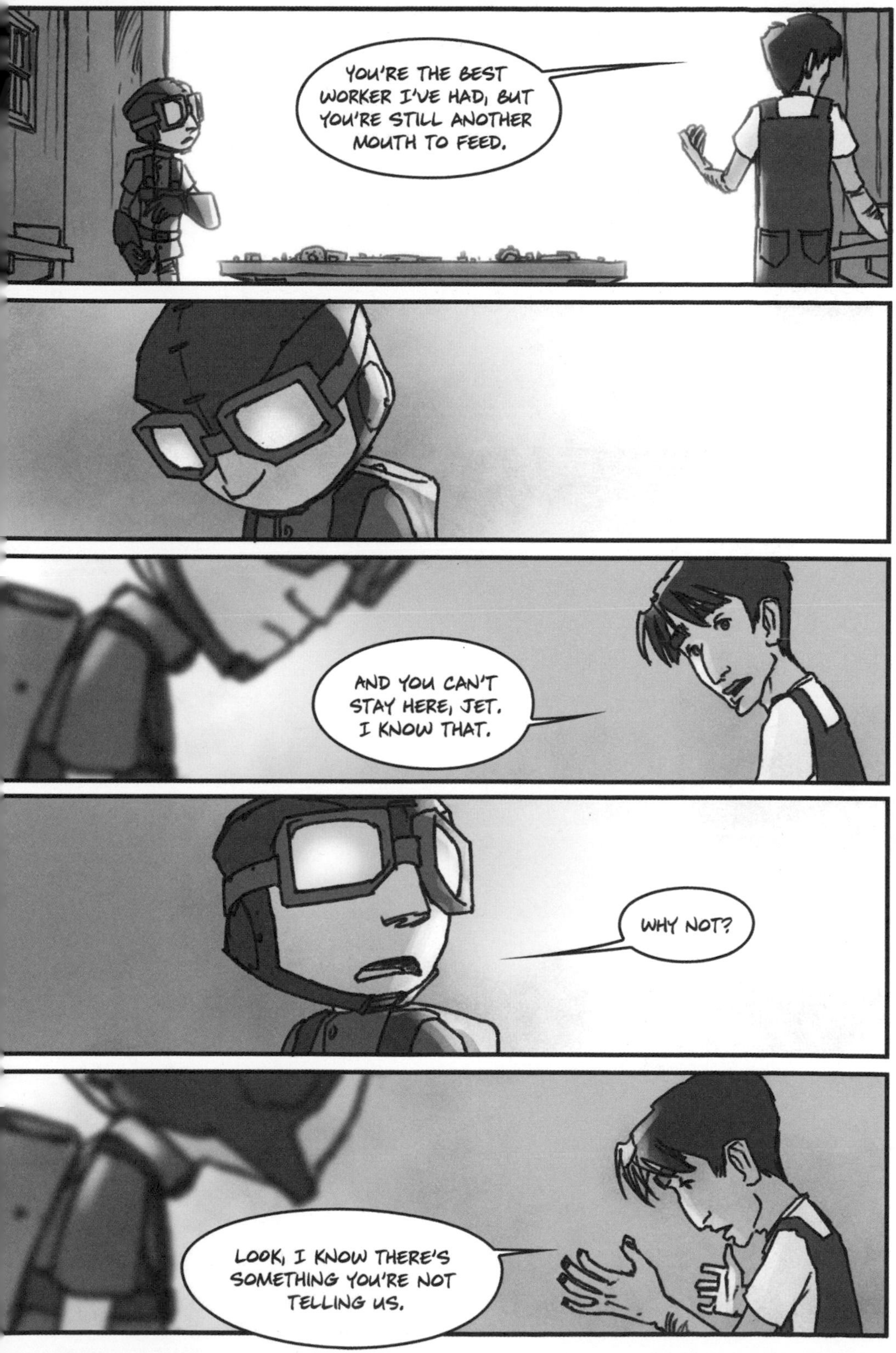
YOU'RE THE BEST WORKER I'VE HAD, BUT YOU'RE STILL ANOTHER MOUTH TO FEED.
AND YOU CAN'T STAY HERE, JET. I KNOW THAT.
WHY NOT?
LOOK, I KNOW THERE'S SOMETHING YOU'RE NOT TELLING US.

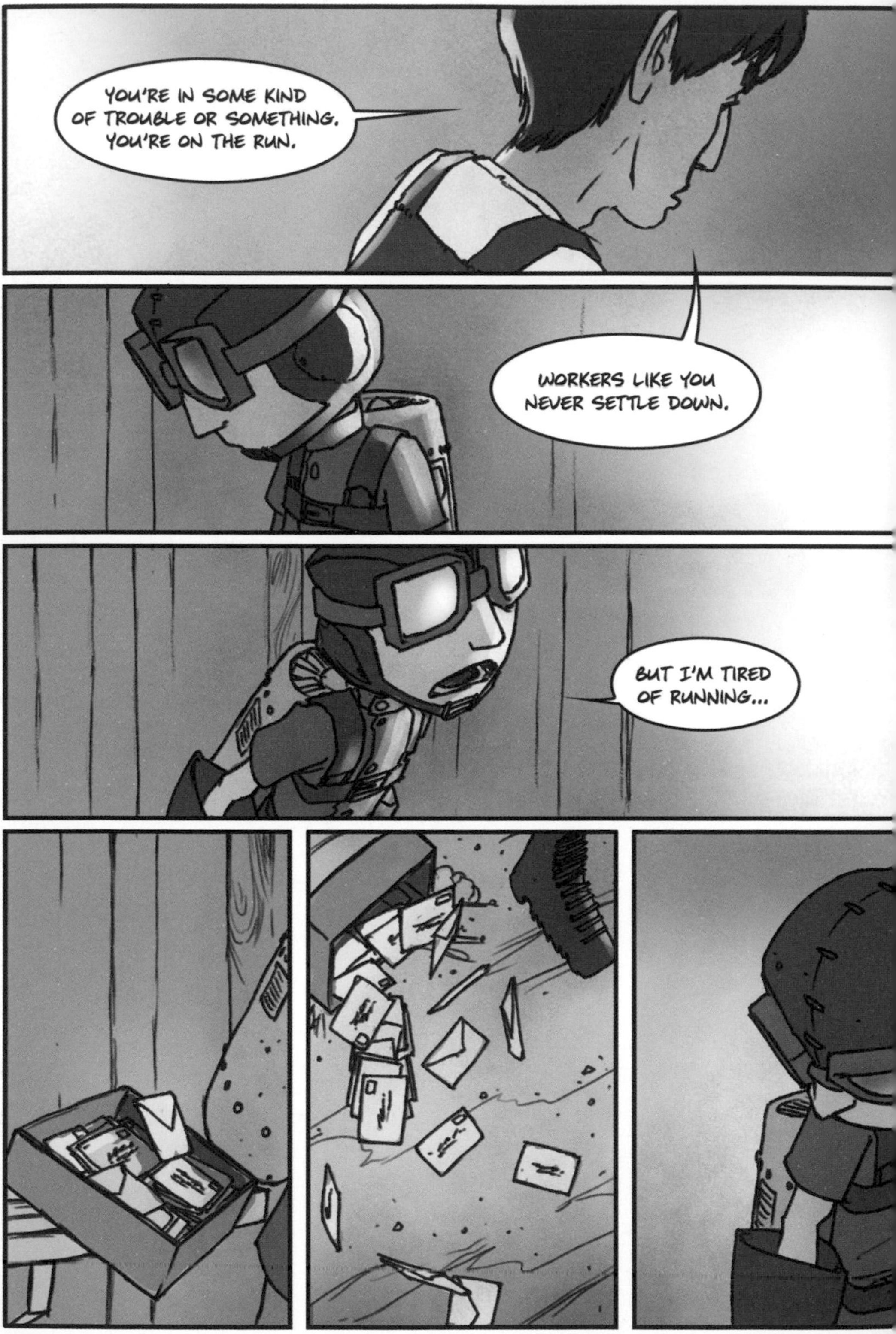
YOU'RE IN SOME KIND OF TROUBLE OR SOMETHING. YOU'RE ON THE RUN.
WORKERS LIKE YOU NEVER SETTLE DOWN.
BUT I'M TIRED OF RUNNING...

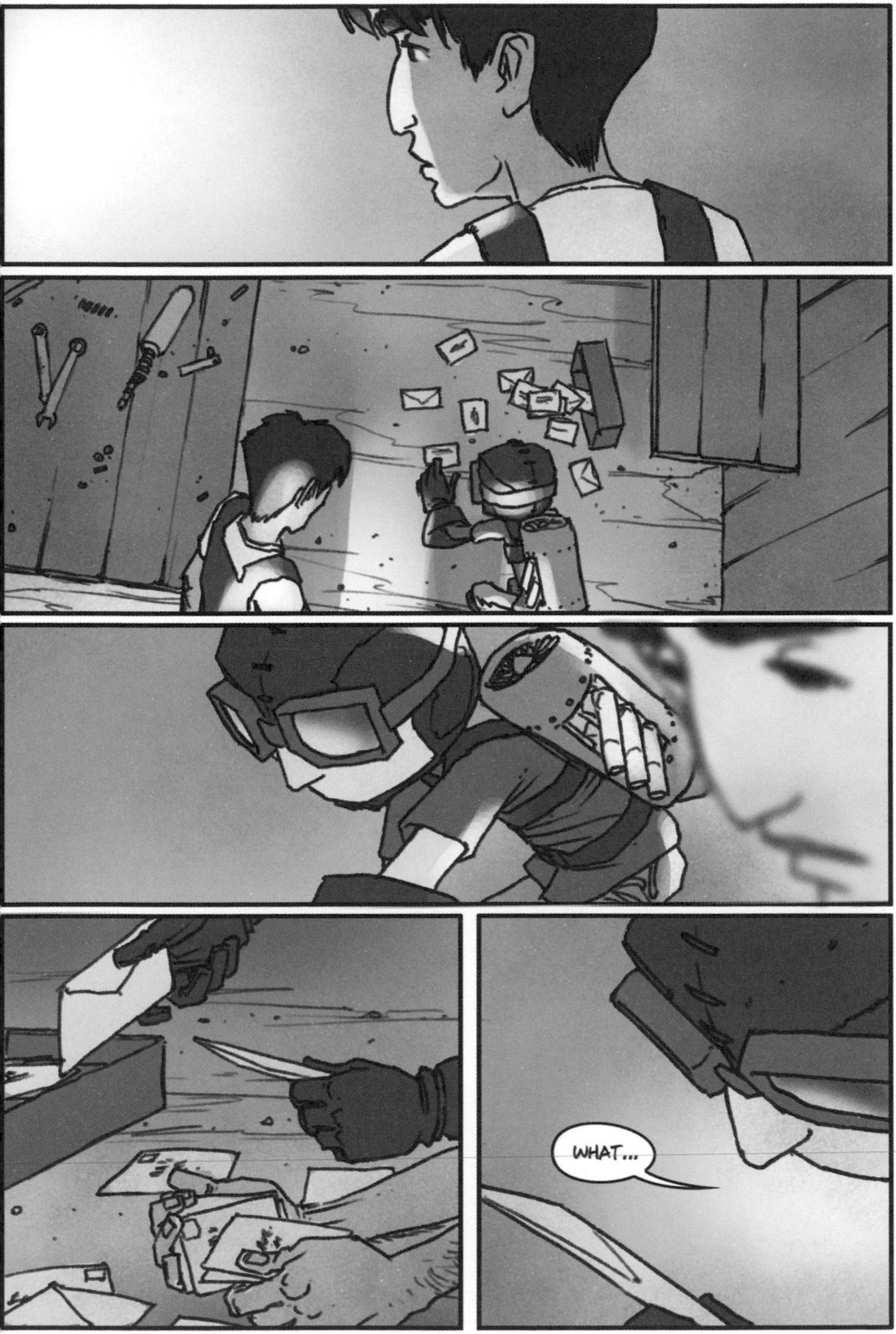
WHAT...

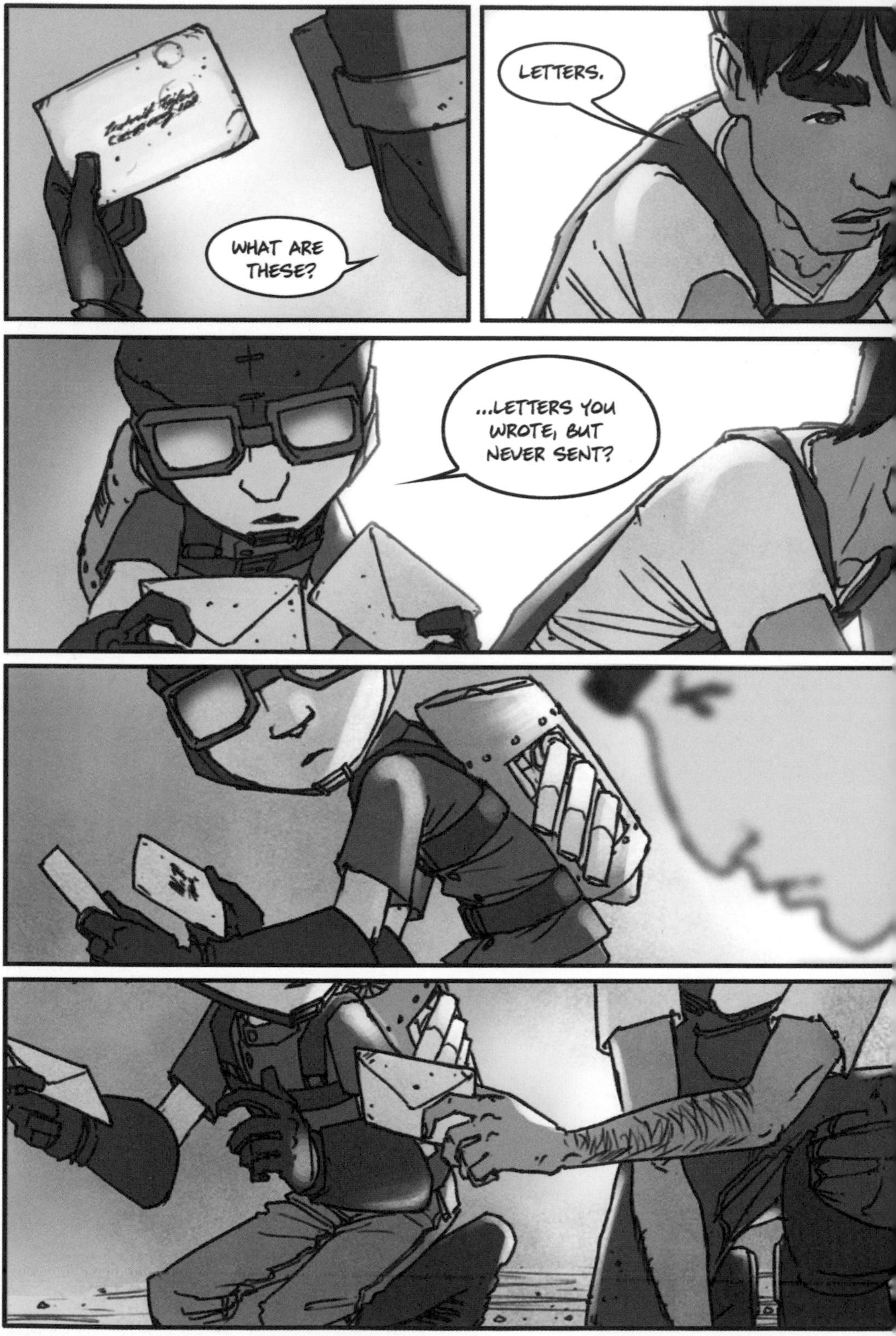
WHAT ARE THESE?
LETTERS.
...LETTERS YOU WROTE, BUT NEVER SENT?

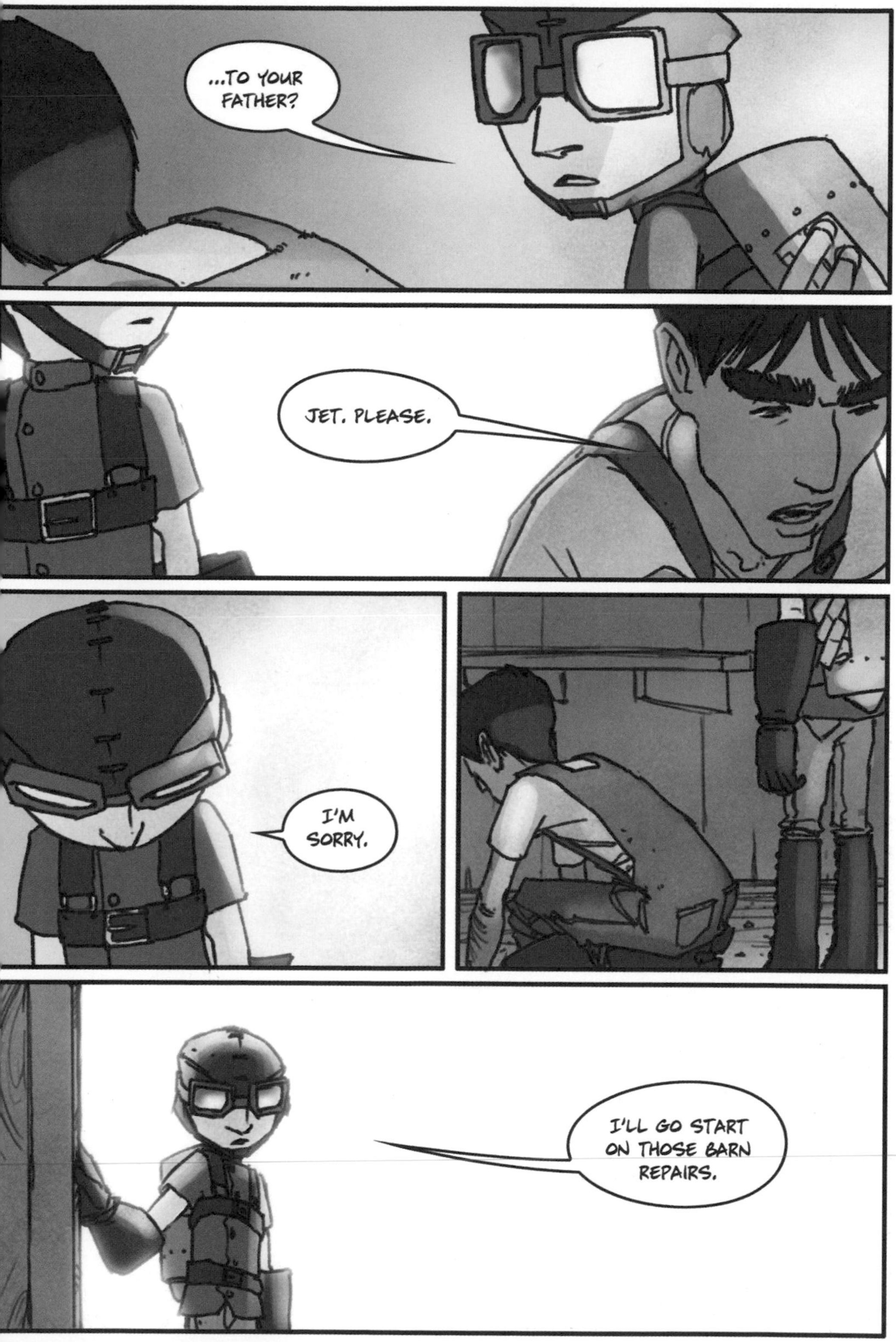
...TO YOUR FATHER?
JET. PLEASE.
I'M SORRY.
I'LL GO START ON THOSE BARN REPAIRS.

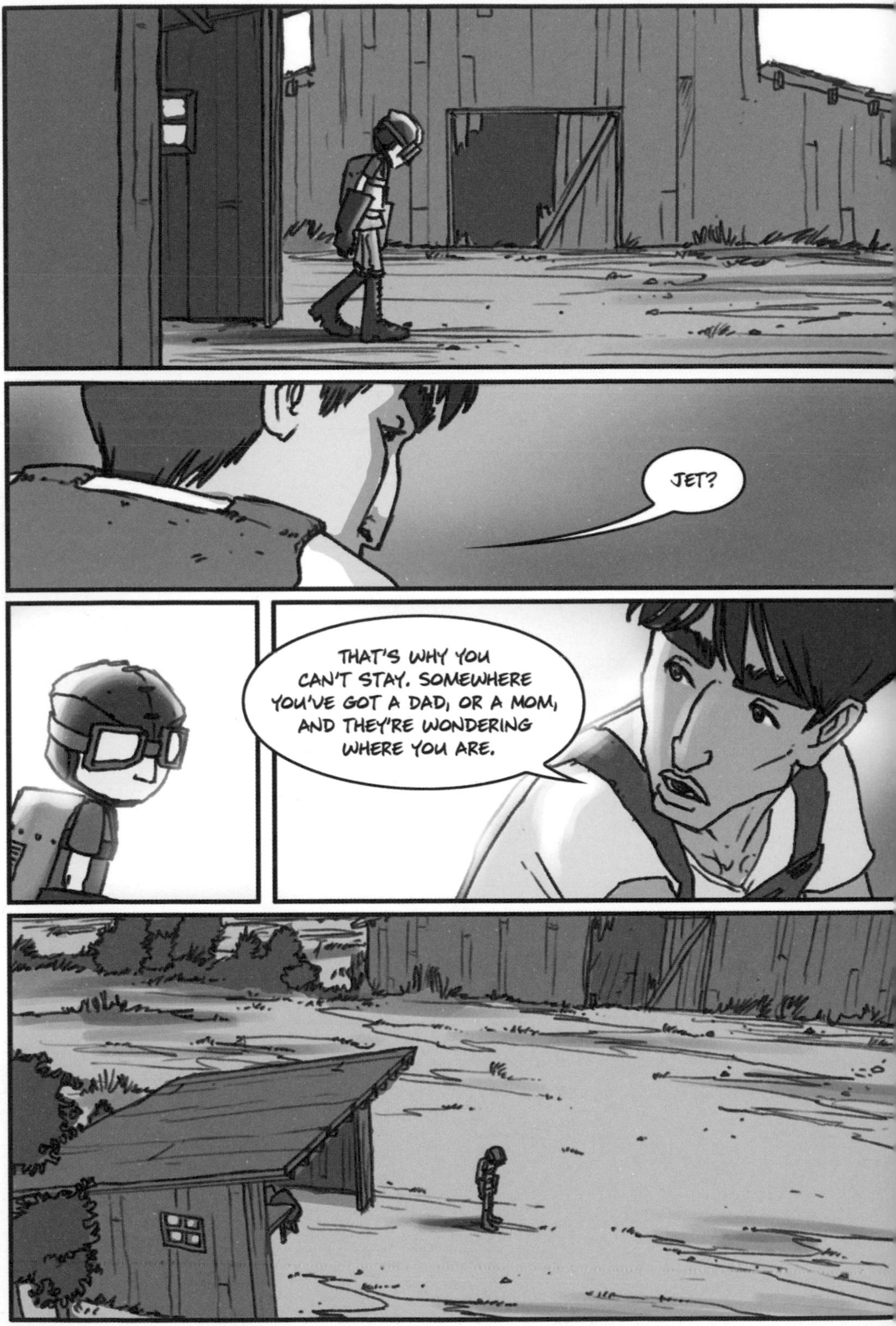
JET?
THAT'S WHY YOU CAN'T STAY. SOMEWHERE YOU'VE GOT A DAD, OR A MOM, AND THEY'RE WONDERING WHERE YOU ARE.

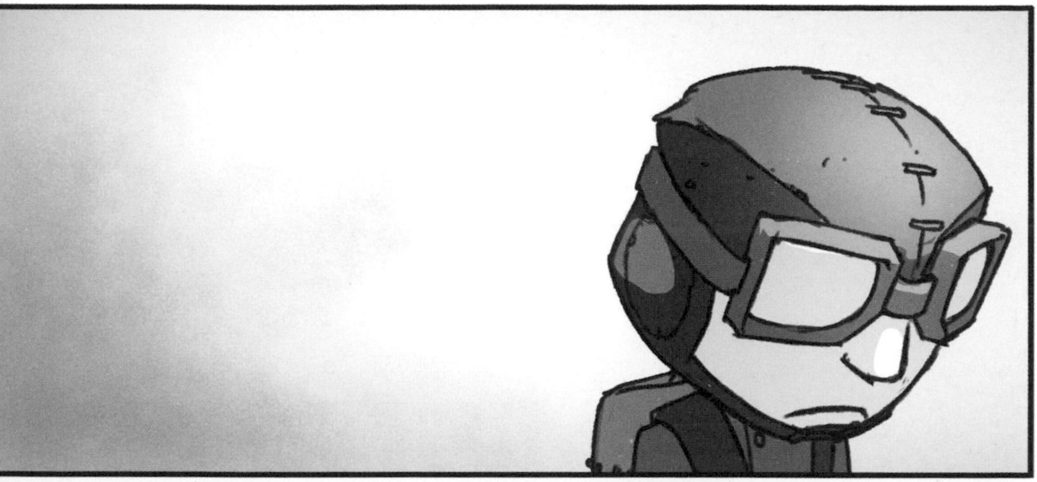

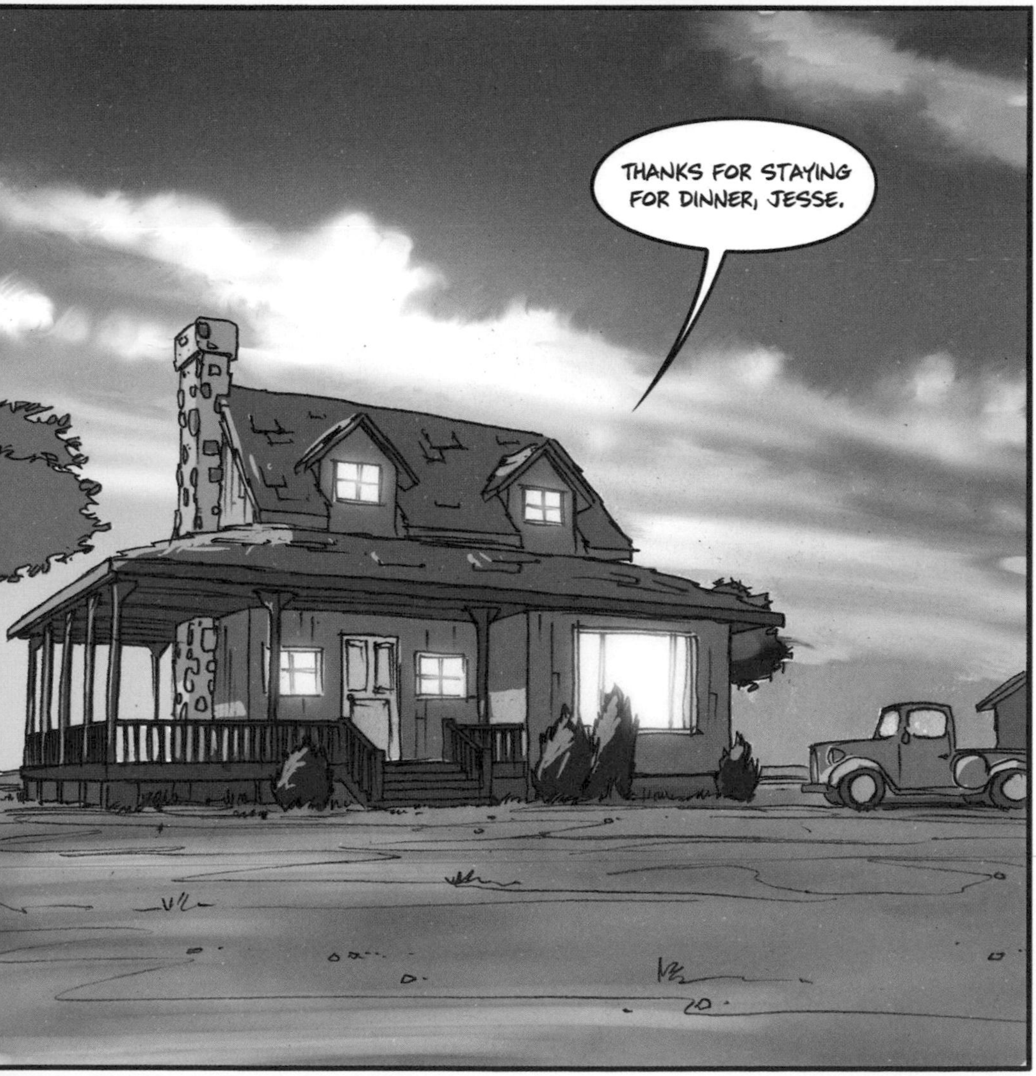
THANKS FOR STAYING FOR DINNER, JESSE.

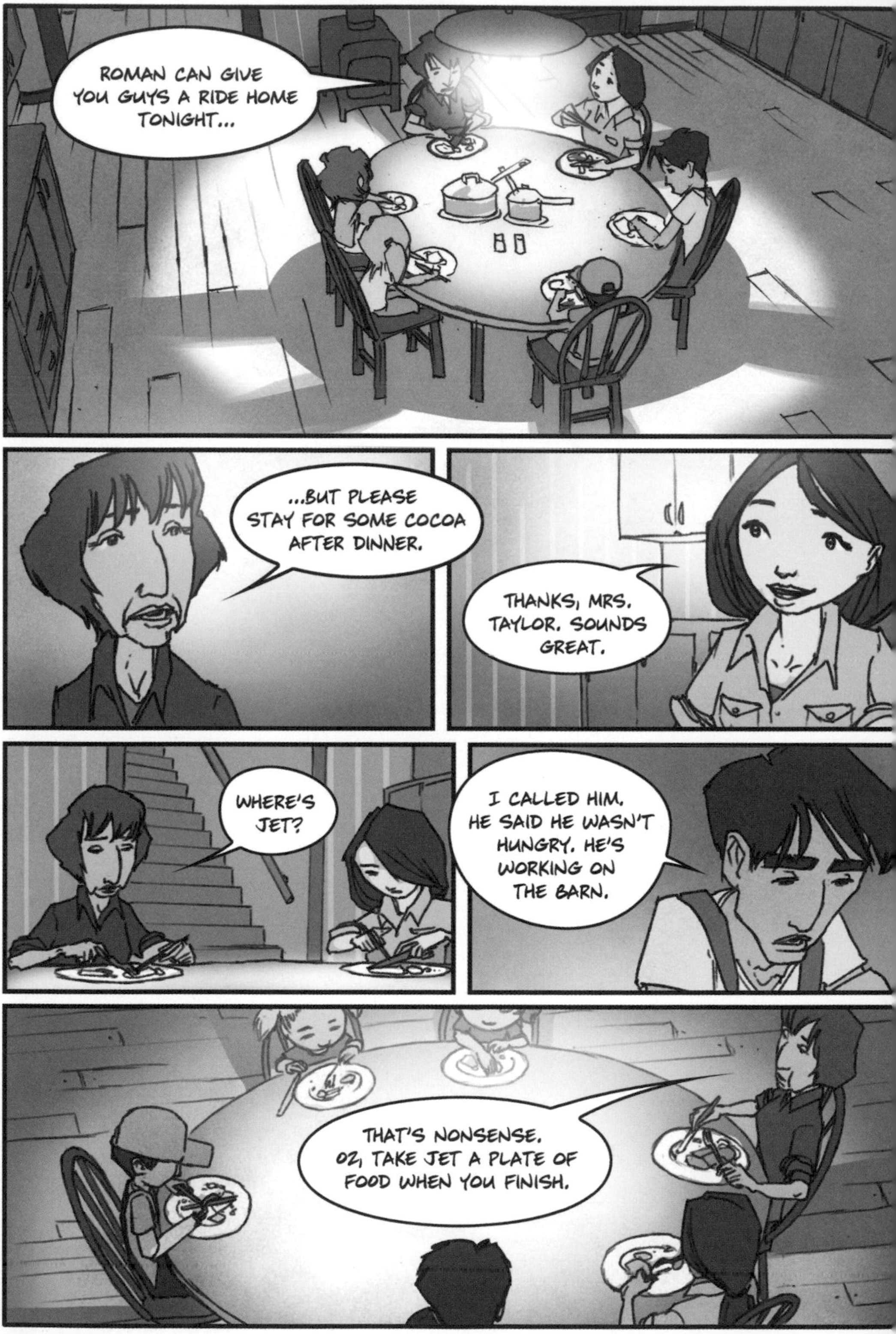
ROMAN CAN GIVE YOU GUYS A RIDE HOME TONIGHT...
...BUT PLEASE STAY FOR SOME COCOA AFTER DINNER.
THANKS, MRS. TAYLOR. SOUNDS GREAT.
WHERE'S JET?
I CALLED HIM. HE SAID HE WASN'T HUNGRY. HE'S WORKING ON THE BARN.
THAT'S NONSENSE. OZ, TAKE JET A PLATE OF FOOD WHEN YOU FINISH.

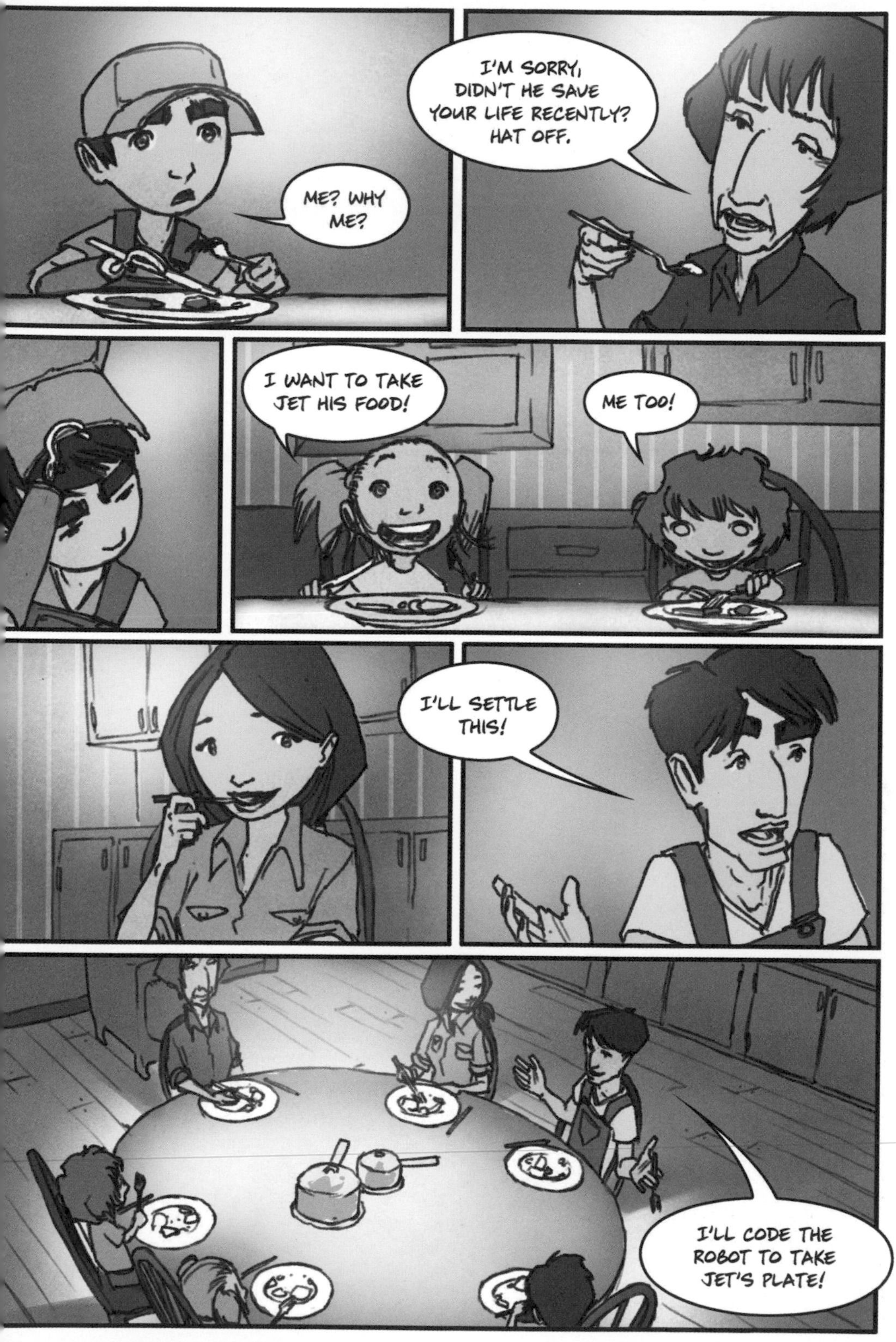
ME? WHY ME?
I'M SORRY, DIDN'T HE SAVE YOUR LIFE RECENTLY? HAT OFF.
I WANT TO TAKE JET HIS FOOD!
ME TOO!
I'LL SETTLE THIS!
I'LL CODE THE ROBOT TO TAKE JET'S PLATE!

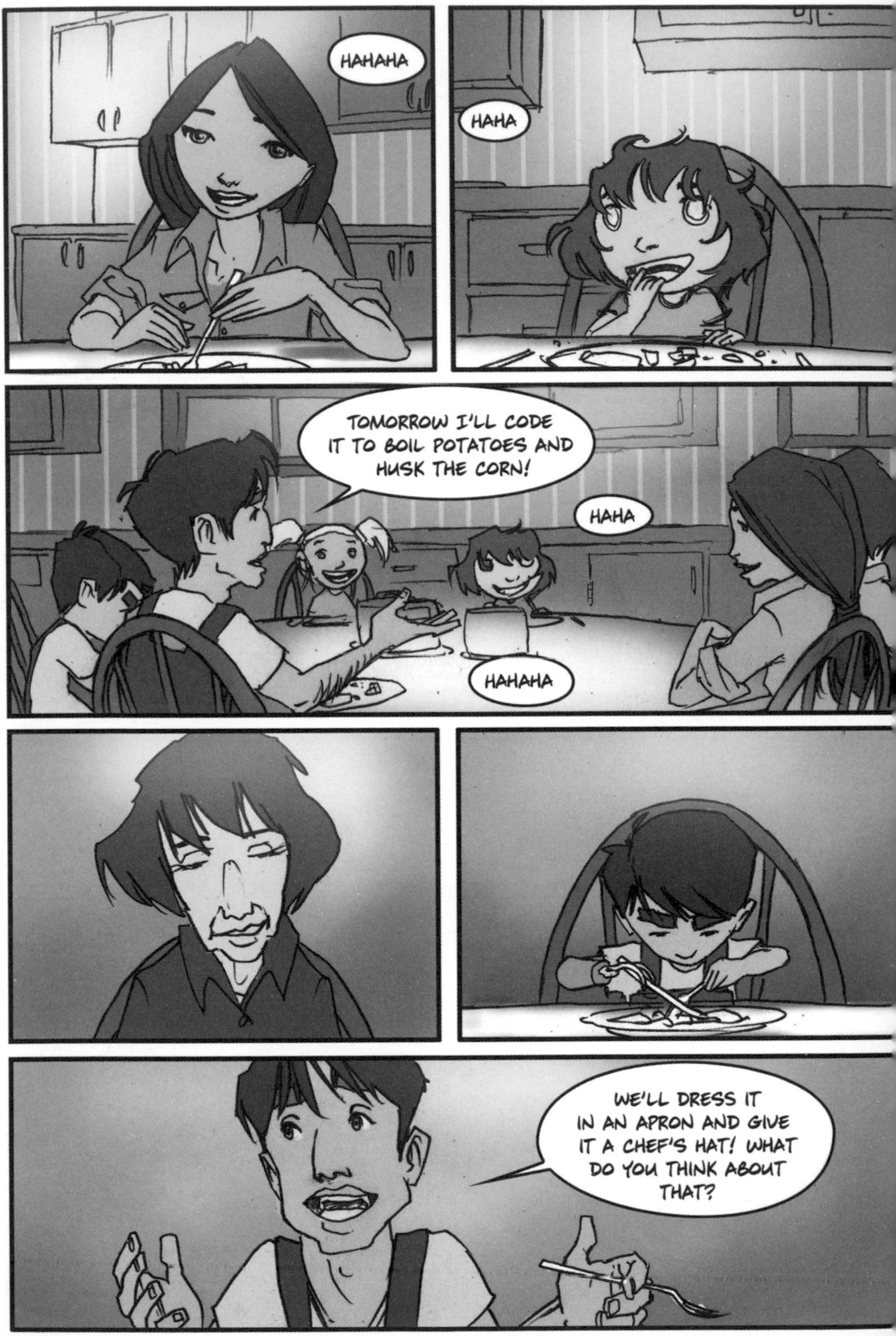
HAHAHA
HAHA
TOMORROW I'LL CODE IT TO BOIL POTATOES AND HUSK THE CORN!
HAHA
HAHAHA
WE'LL DRESS IT IN AN APRON AND GIVE IT A CHEF'S HAT! WHAT DO YOU THINK ABOUT THAT?

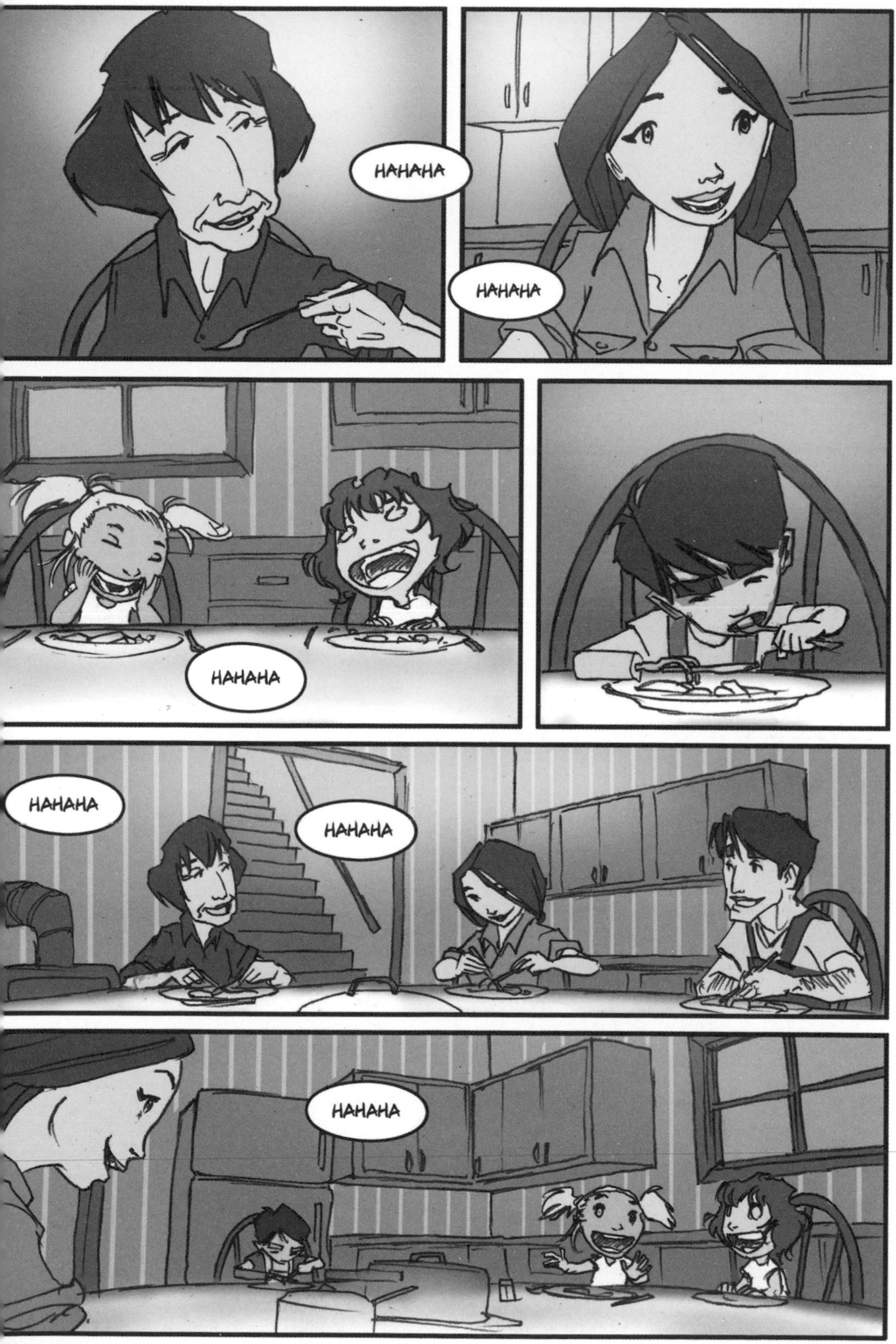
HAHAHA
HAHAHA
HAHAHA
HAHAHA
HAHAHA
HAHAHA

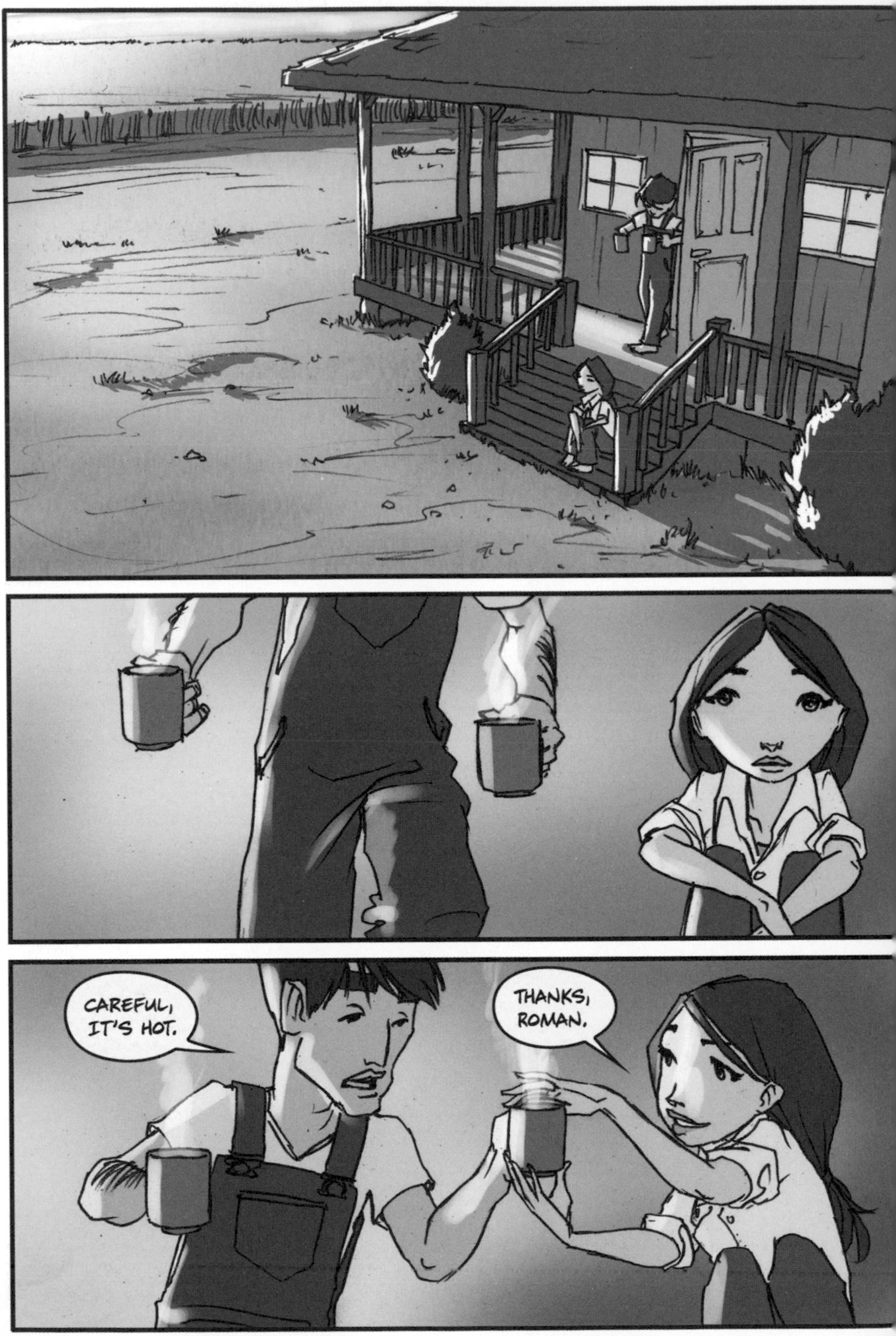
CAREFUL, IT'S HOT.
THANKS, ROMAN.

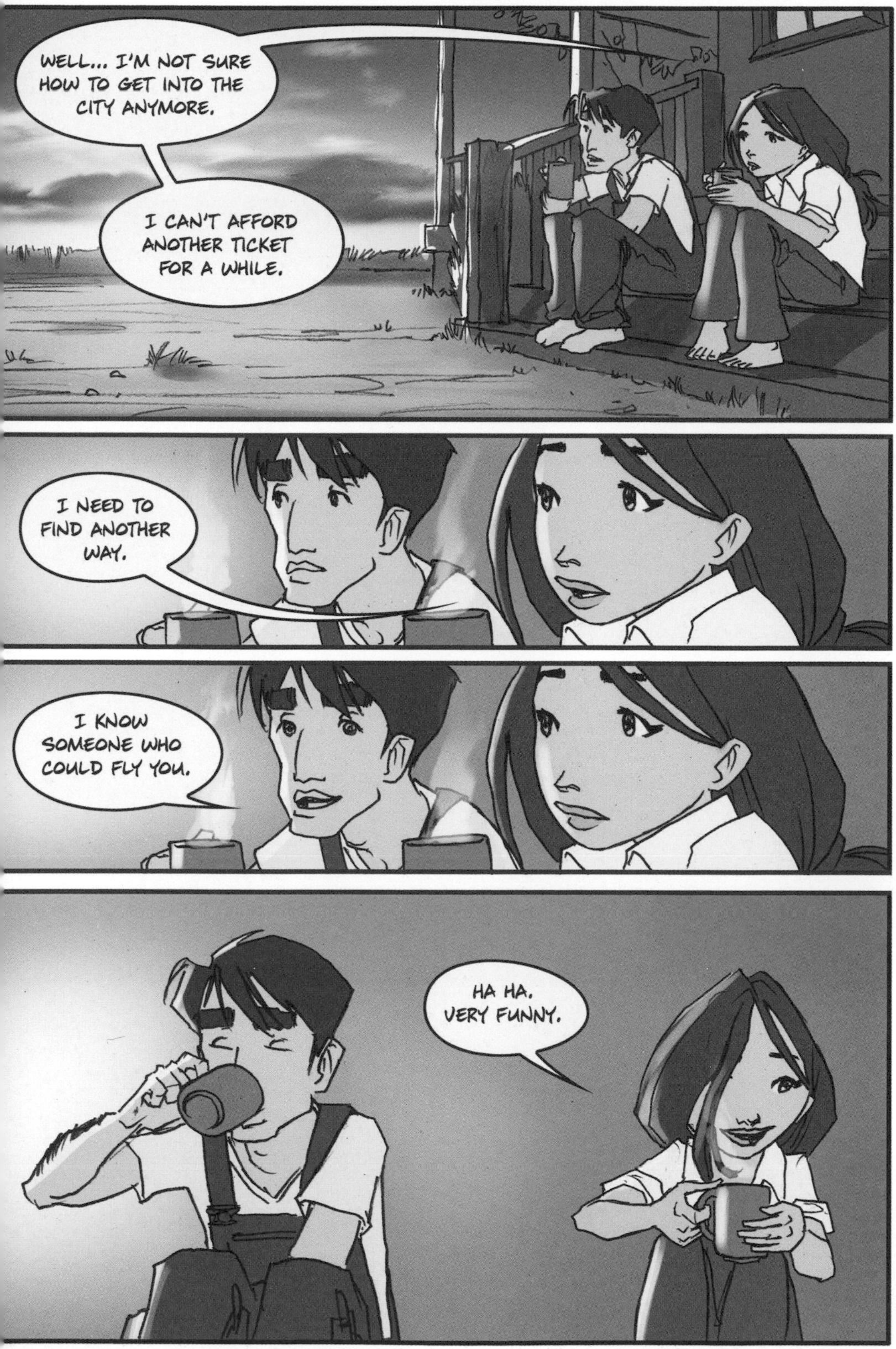
WELL... I'M NOT SURE HOW TO GET INTO THE CITY ANYMORE.
I CAN'T AFFORD ANOTHER TICKET FOR A WHILE.
I NEED TO FIND ANOTHER WAY.
I KNOW SOMEONE WHO COULD FLY YOU.
HA HA. VERY FUNNY.

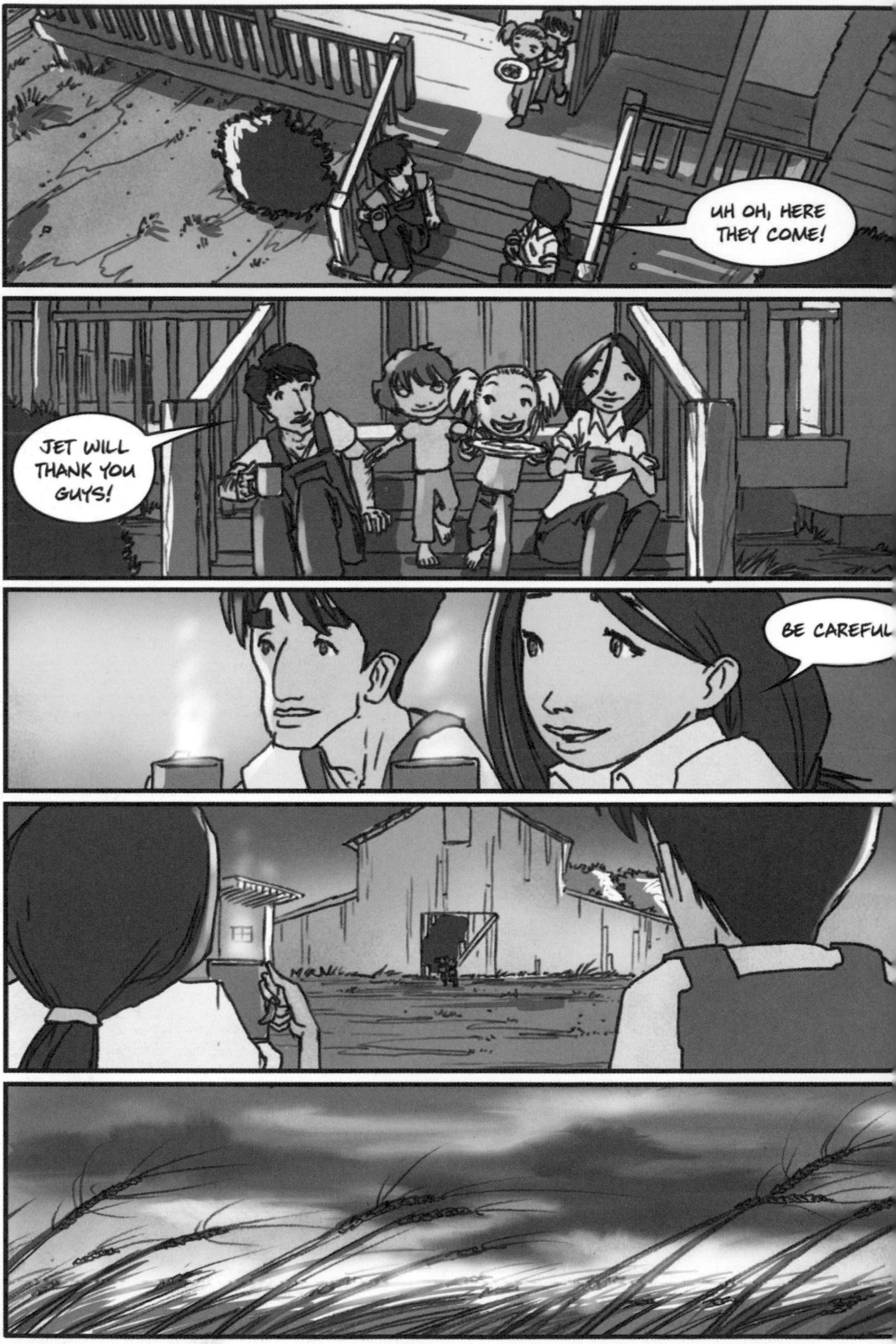
UH OH, HERE THEY COME!
JET WILL THANK YOU GUYS!
BE CAREFUL

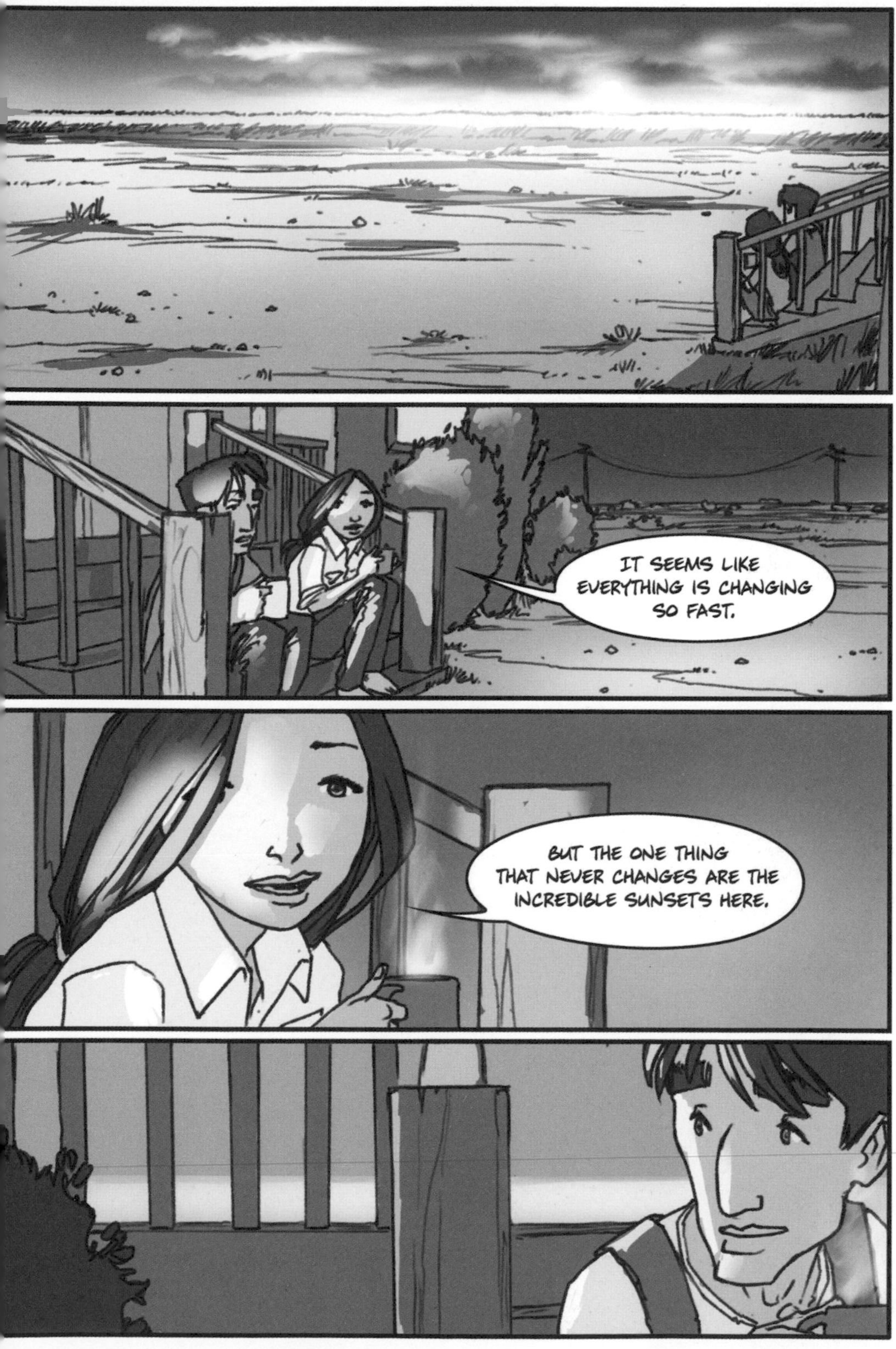
IT SEEMS LIKE EVERYTHING IS CHANGING SO FAST.
BUT THE ONE THING THAT NEVER CHANGES ARE THE INCREDIBLE SUNSETS HERE.

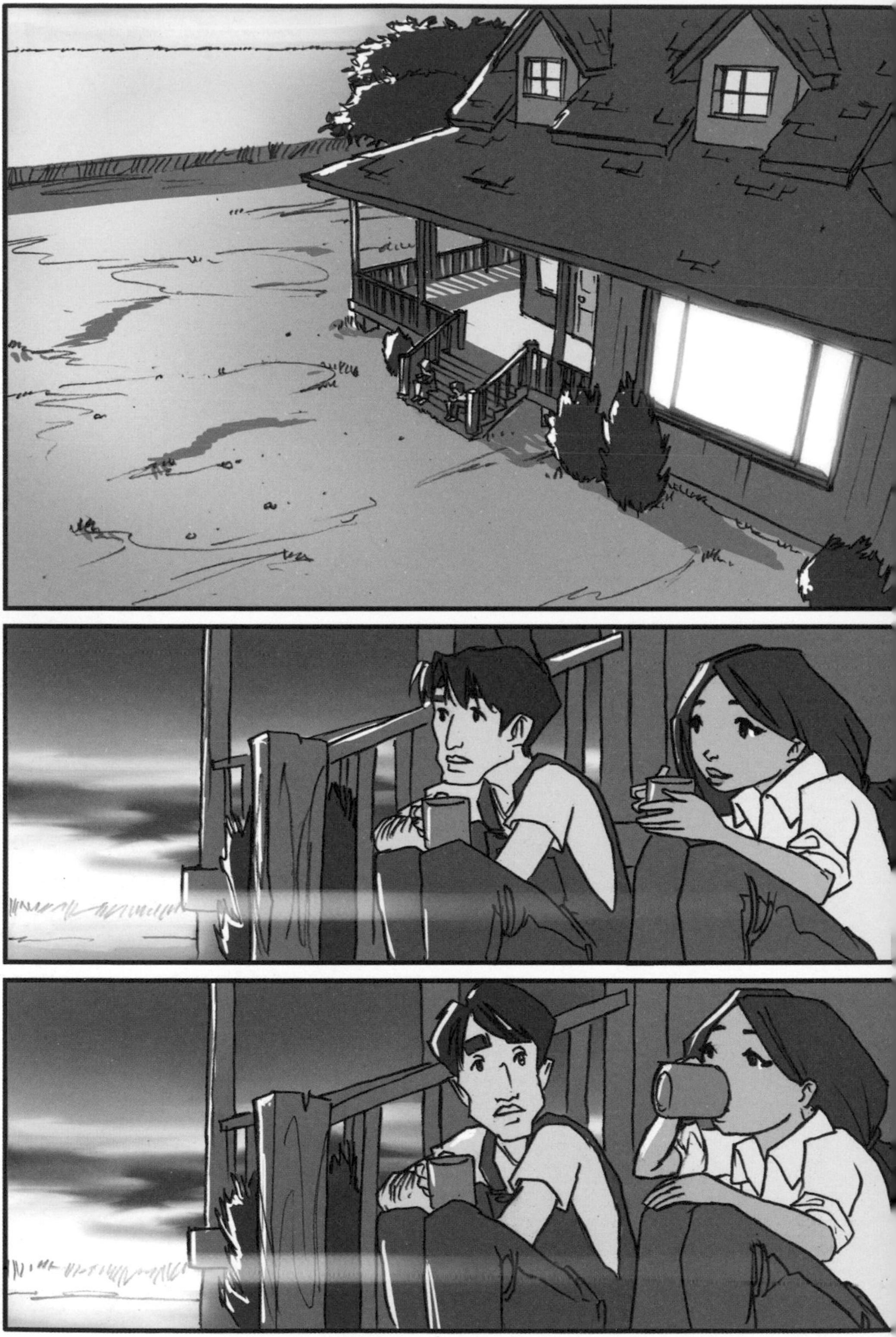

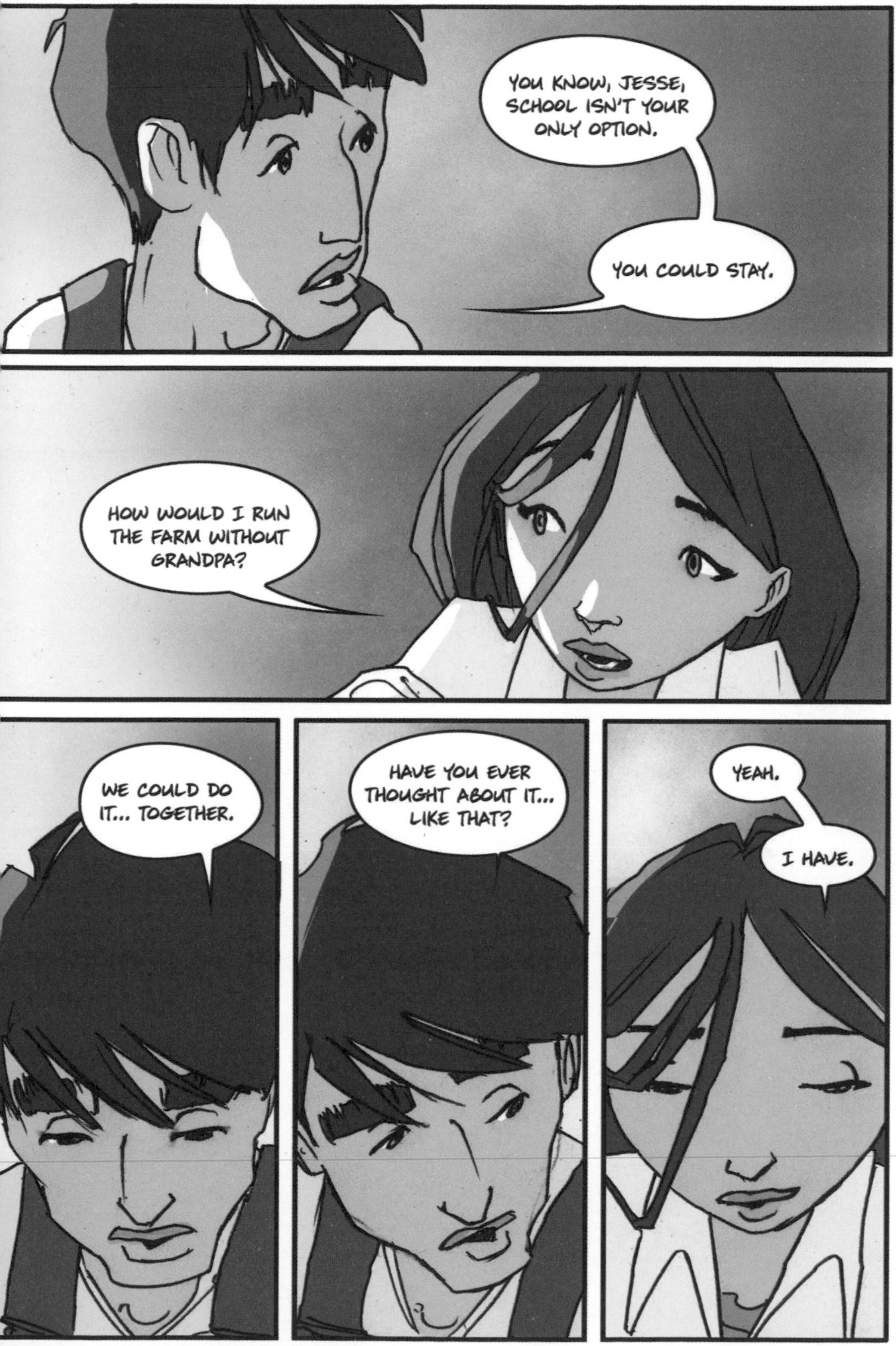
YOU KNOW, JESSE, SCHOOL ISN'T YOUR ONLY OPTION.
YOU COULD STAY.
HOW WOULD I RUN THE FARM WITHOUT GRANDPA?
WE COULD DO IT... TOGETHER.
HAVE YOU EVER THOUGHT ABOUT IT... LIKE THAT?
YEAH.
I HAVE.

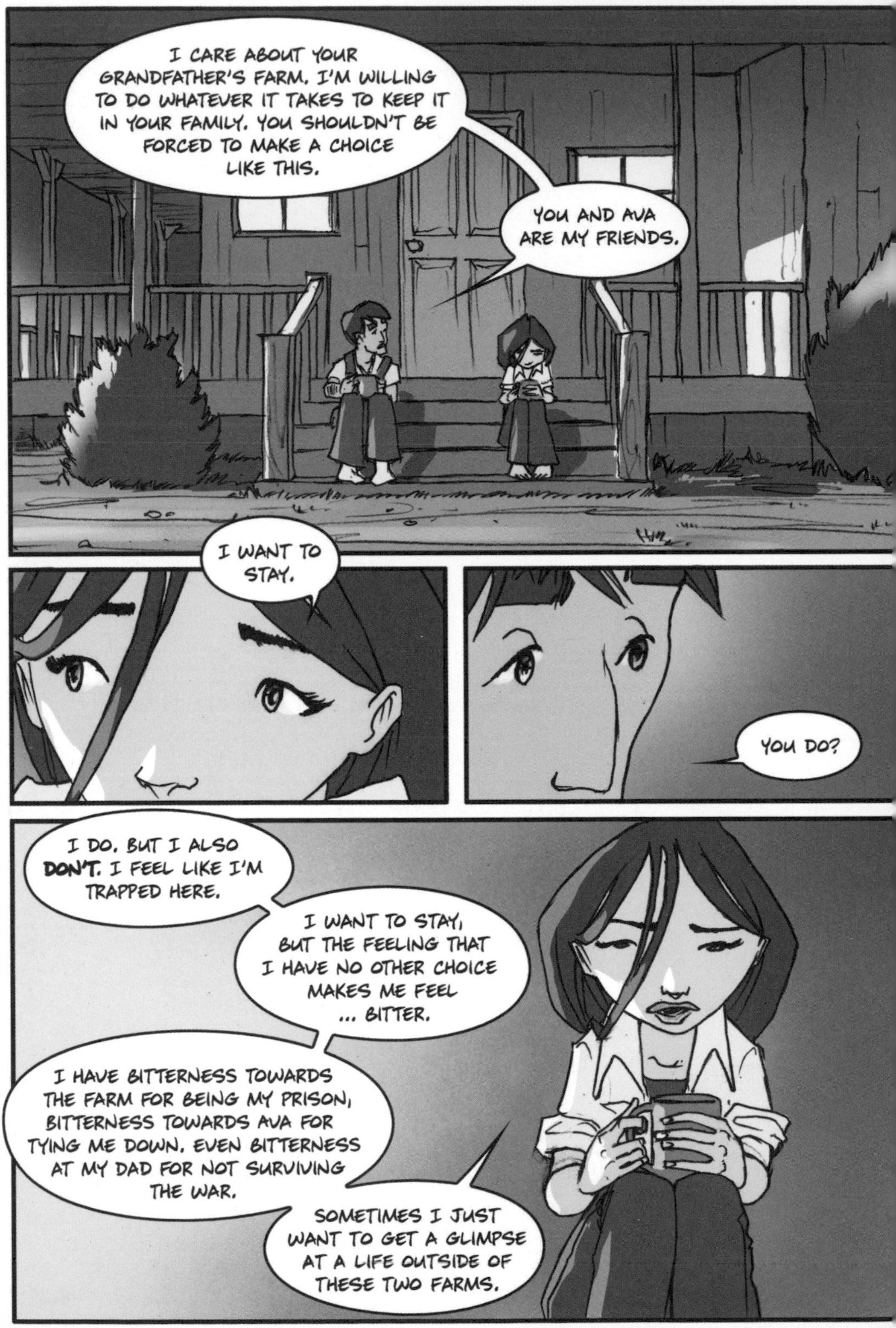
I CARE ABOUT YOUR GRANDFATHER'S FARM. I'M WILLING TO DO WHATEVER IT TAKES TO KEEP IT IN YOUR FAMILY. YOU SHOULDN'T BE FORCED TO MAKE A CHOICE LIKE THIS.
YOU AND AVA ARE MY FRIENDS.
I WANT TO STAY.
YOU DO?
I DO. BUT I ALSO **DON'T**. I FEEL LIKE I'M TRAPPED HERE.
I WANT TO STAY, BUT THE FEELING THAT I HAVE NO OTHER CHOICE MAKES ME FEEL ... BITTER.
I HAVE BITTERNESS TOWARDS THE FARM FOR BEING MY PRISON, BITTERNESS TOWARDS AVA FOR TYING ME DOWN. EVEN BITTERNESS AT MY DAD FOR NOT SURVIVING THE WAR.
SOMETIMES I JUST WANT TO GET A GLIMPSE AT A LIFE OUTSIDE OF THESE TWO FARMS.

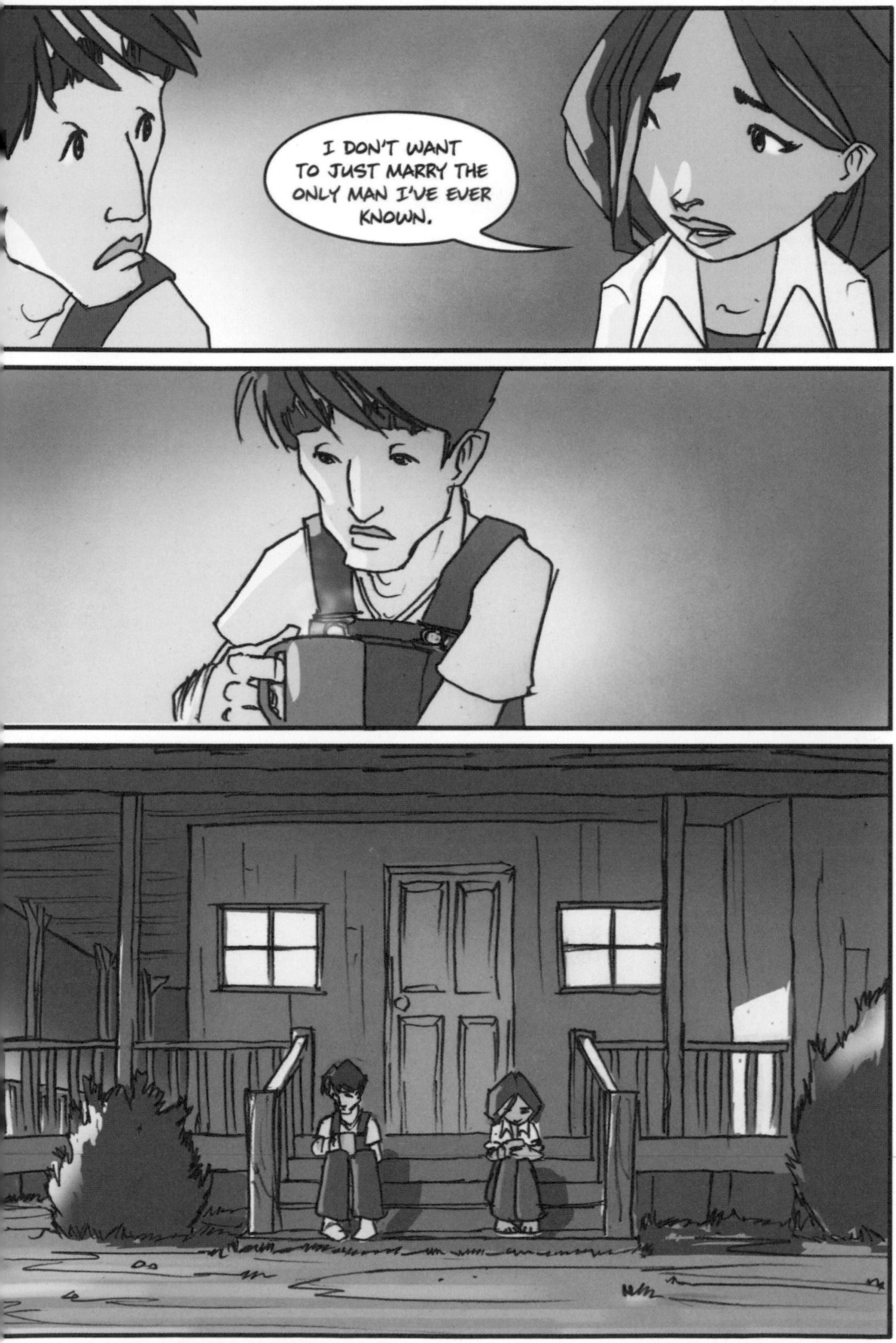
I DON'T WANT TO JUST MARRY THE ONLY MAN I'VE EVER KNOWN.

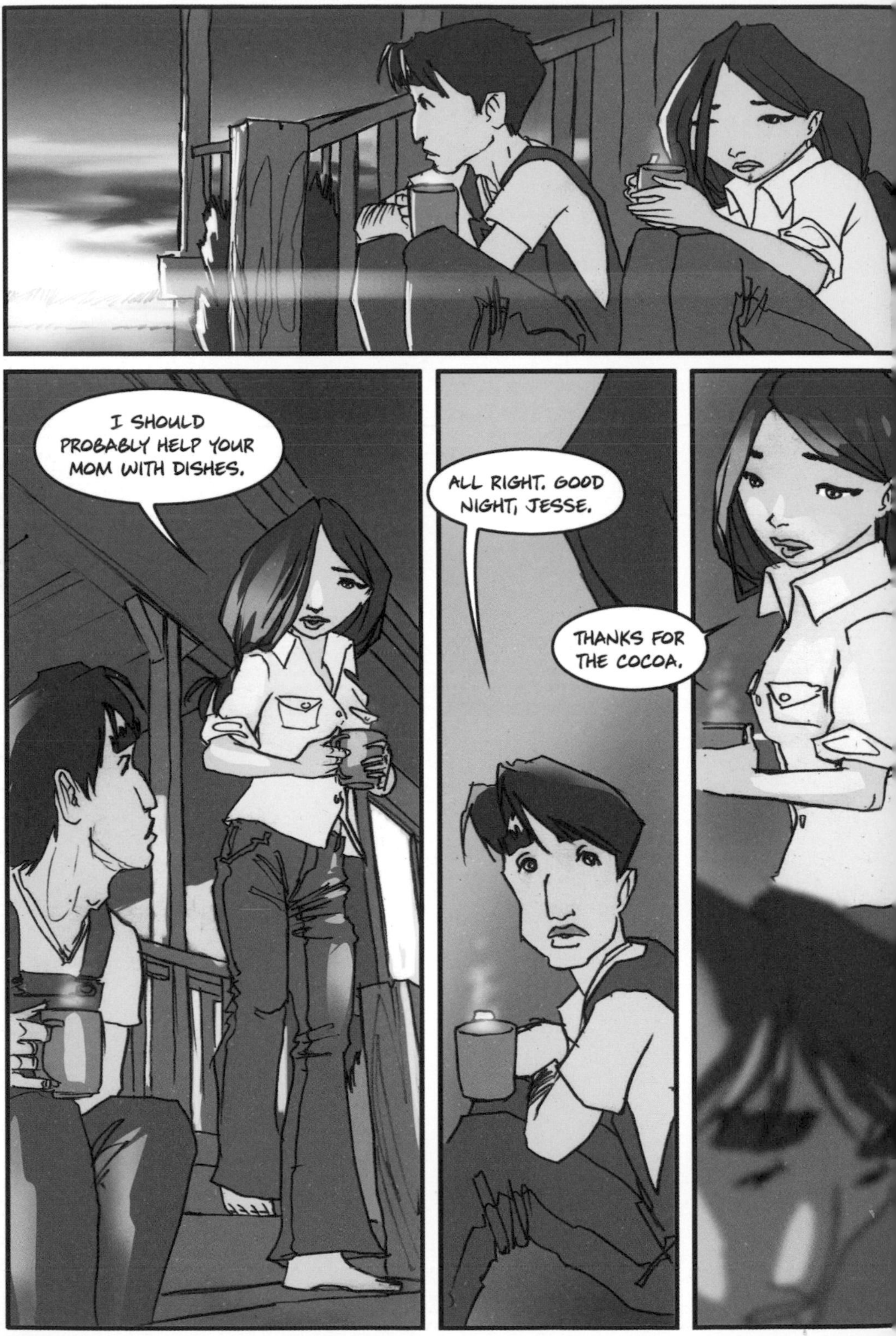
I SHOULD PROBABLY HELP YOUR MOM WITH DISHES.
ALL RIGHT. GOOD NIGHT, JESSE.
THANKS FOR THE COCOA.

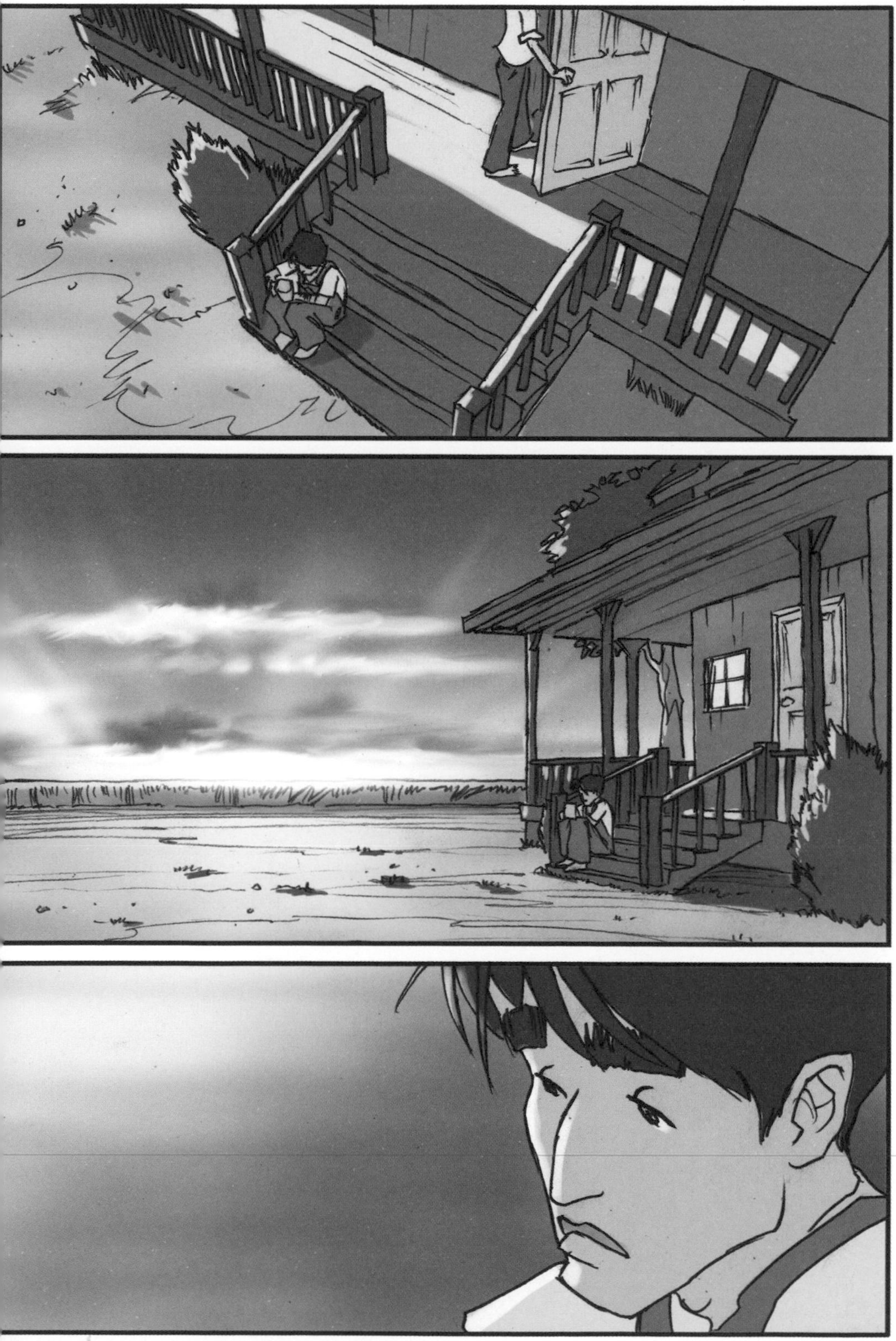

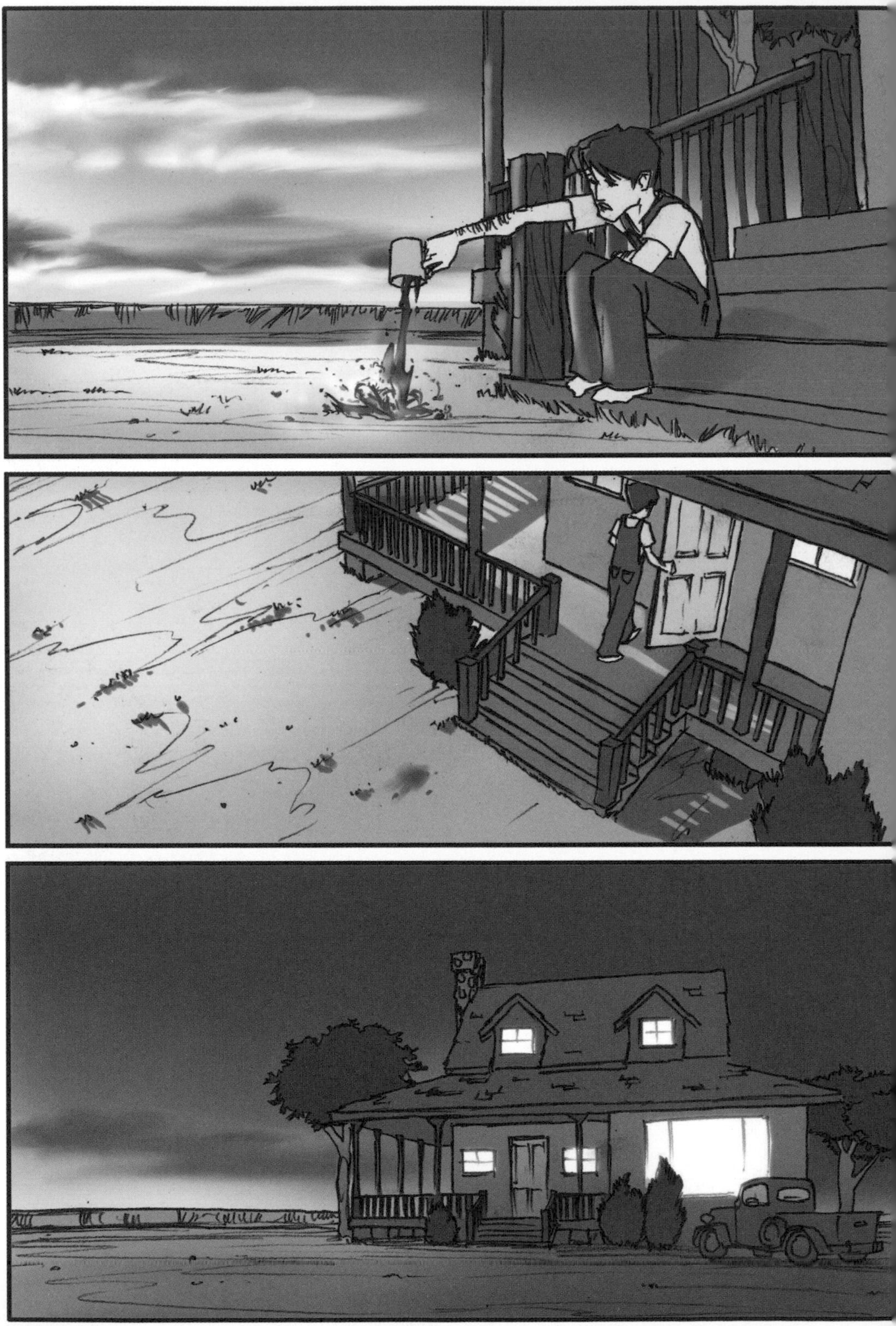

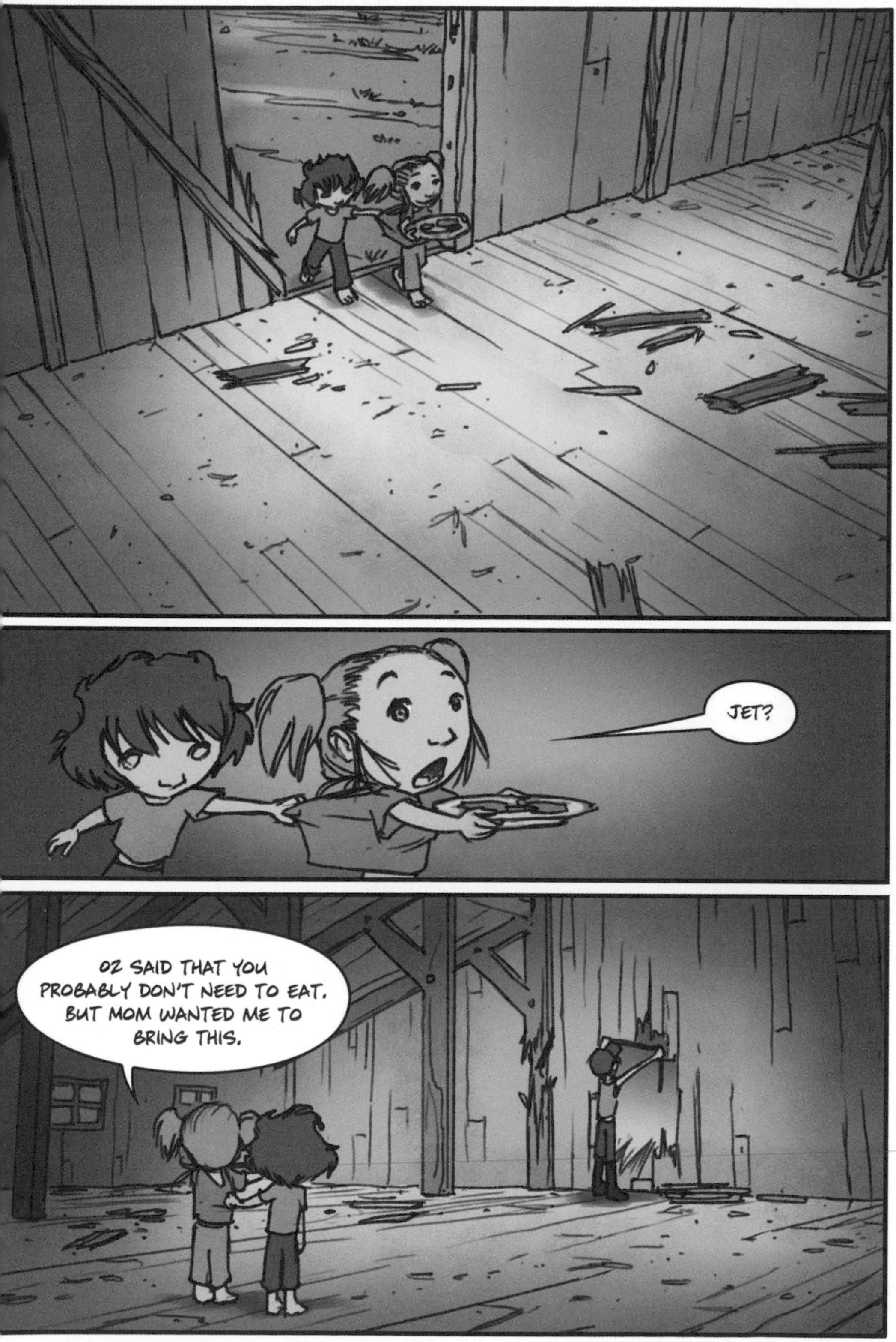
JET?
OZ SAID THAT YOU PROBABLY DON'T NEED TO EAT. BUT MOM WANTED ME TO BRING THIS.

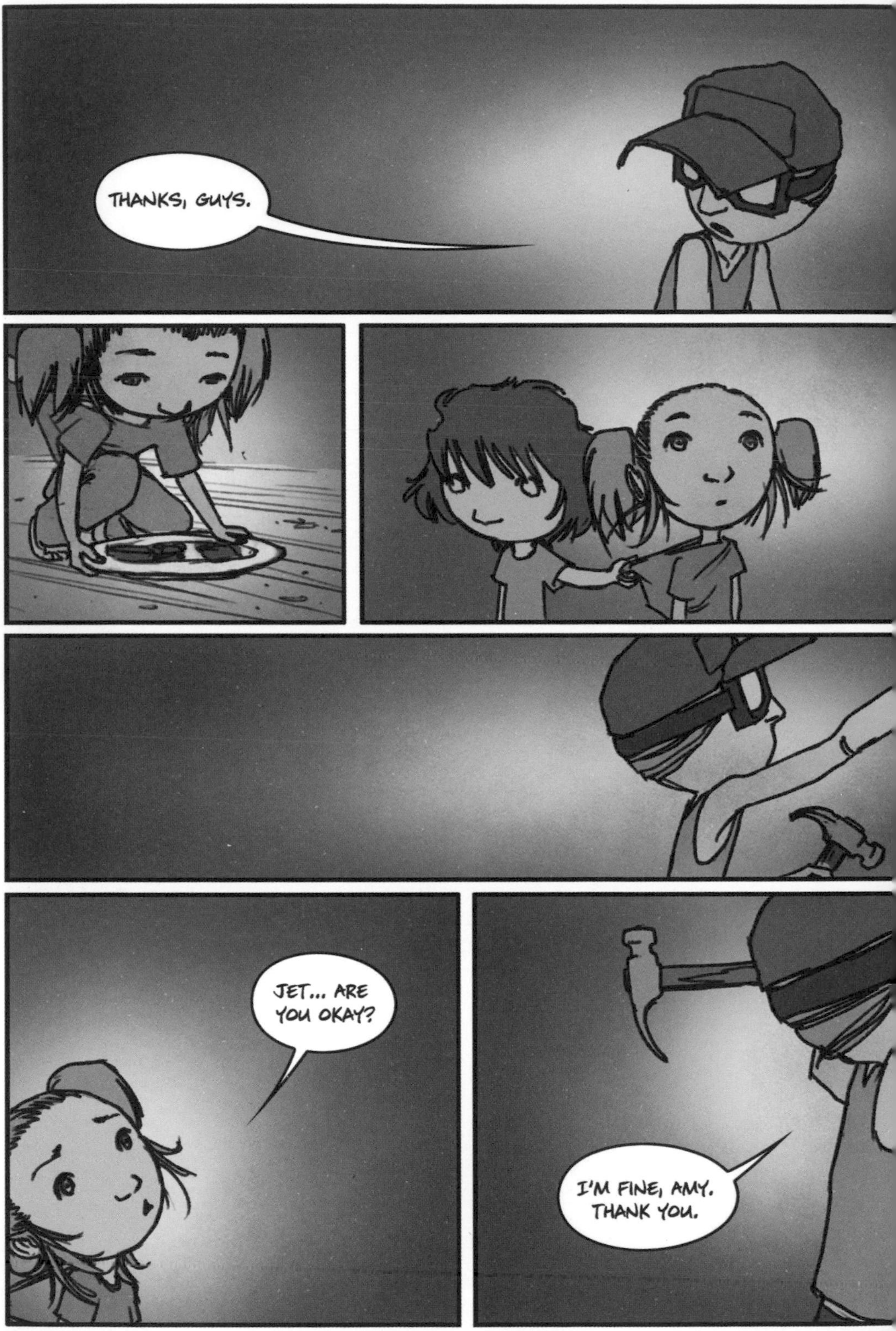
THANKS, GUYS.
JET... ARE YOU OKAY?
I'M FINE, AMY. THANK YOU.

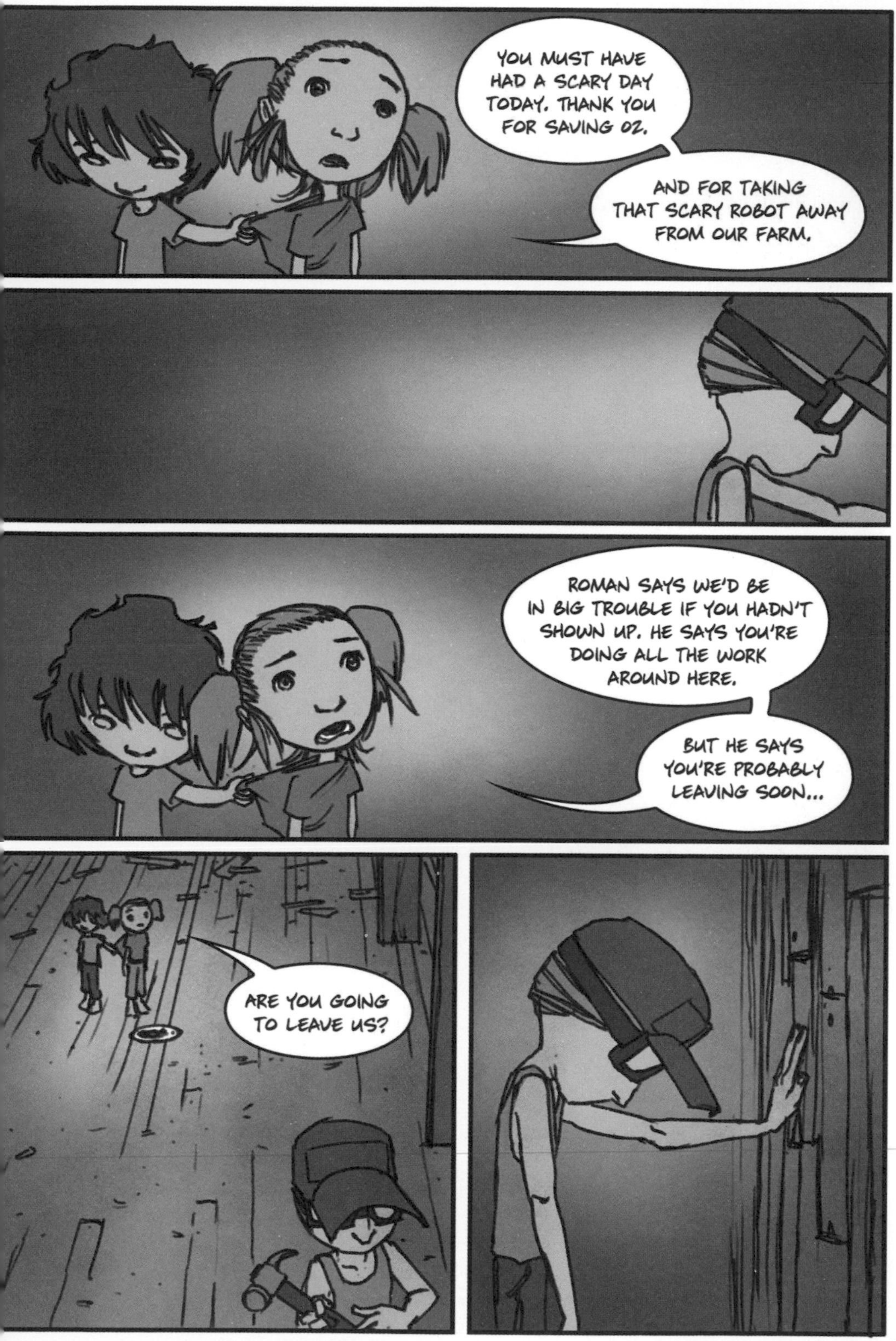
YOU MUST HAVE HAD A SCARY DAY TODAY. THANK YOU FOR SAVING OZ.
AND FOR TAKING THAT SCARY ROBOT AWAY FROM OUR FARM.
ROMAN SAYS WE'D BE IN BIG TROUBLE IF YOU HADN'T SHOWN UP. HE SAYS YOU'RE DOING ALL THE WORK AROUND HERE.
BUT HE SAYS YOU'RE PROBABLY LEAVING SOON...
ARE YOU GOING TO LEAVE US?

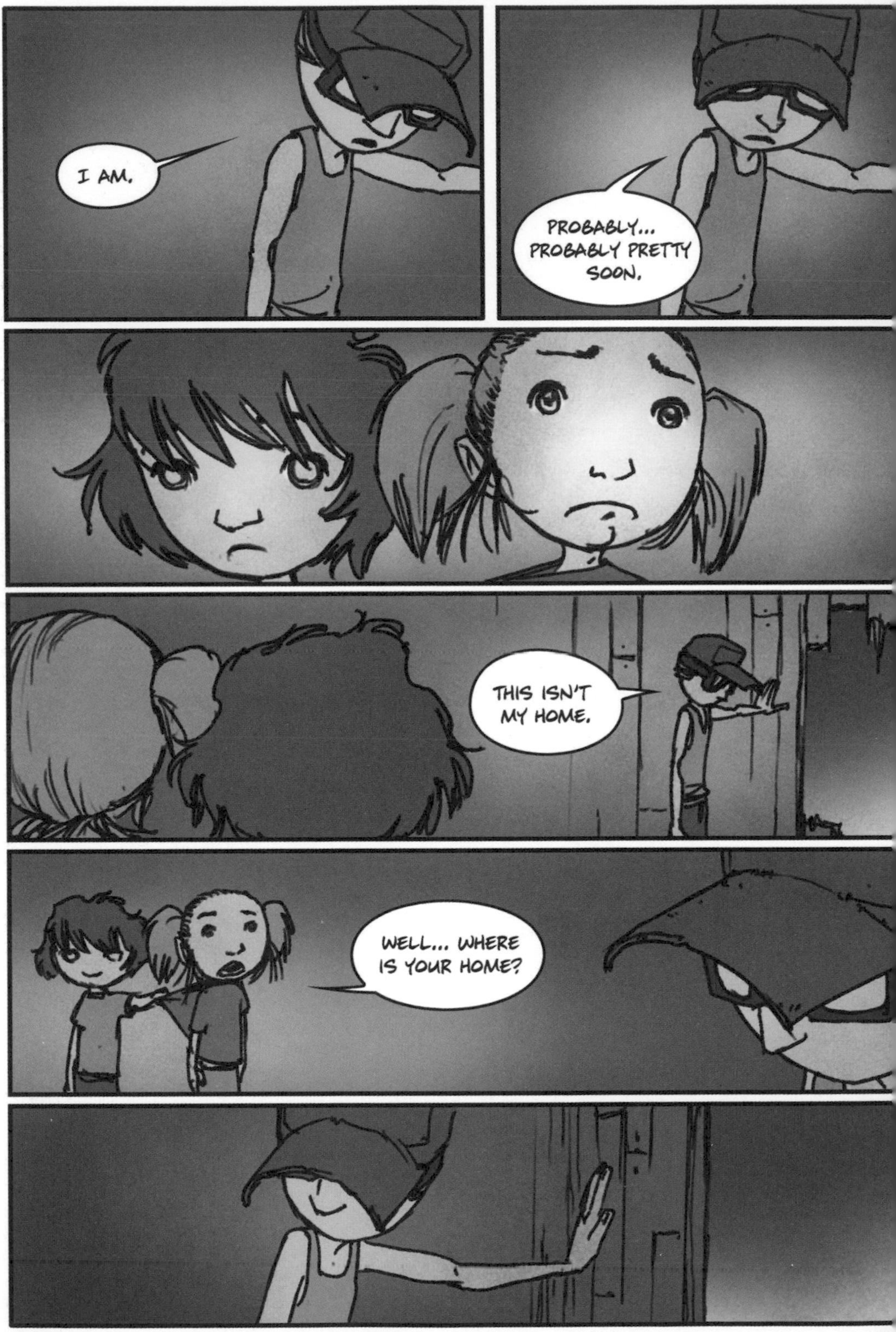
I AM.
PROBABLY... PROBABLY PRETTY SOON.
THIS ISN'T MY HOME.
WELL... WHERE IS YOUR HOME?

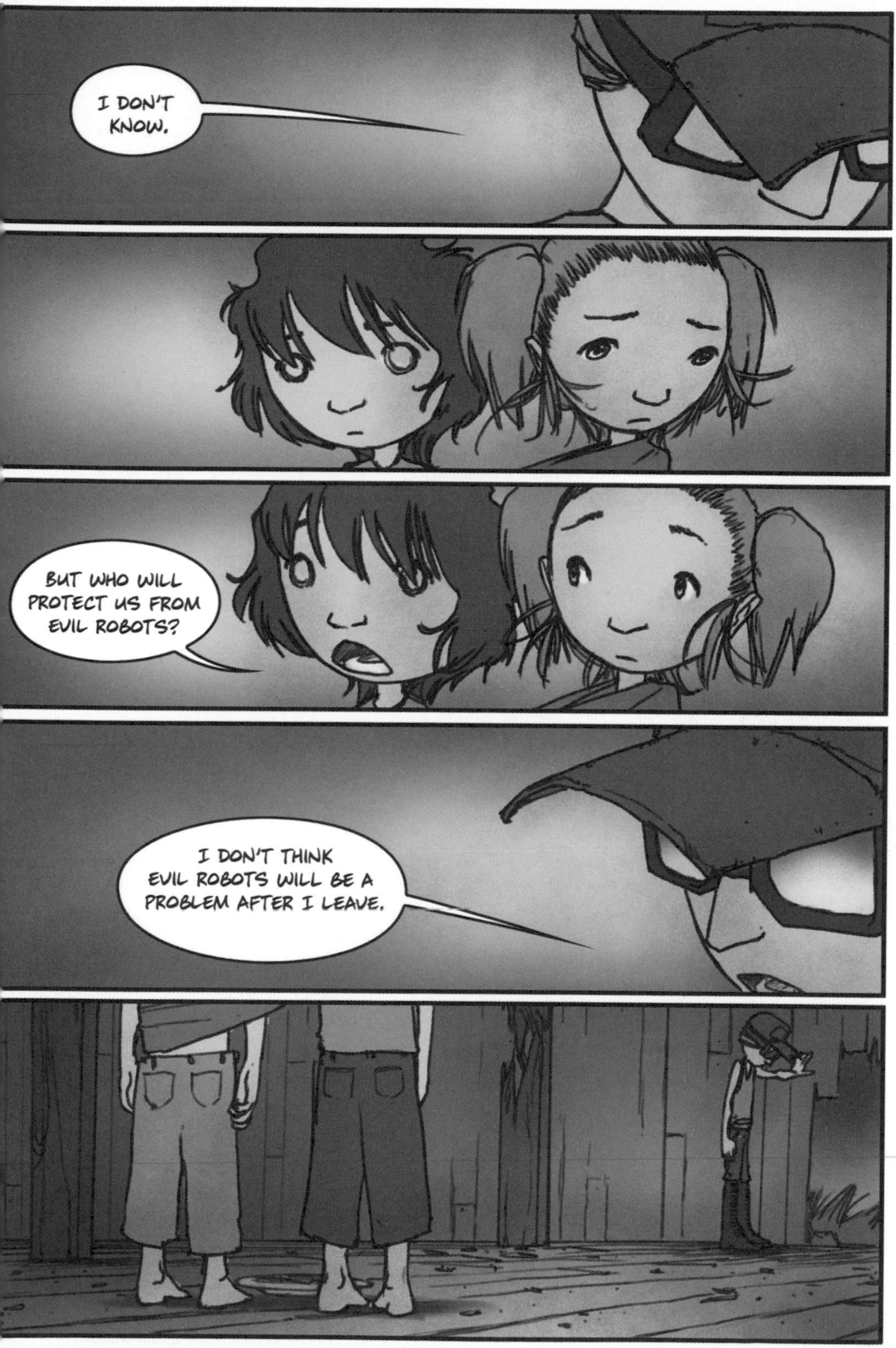
I DON'T KNOW.
BUT WHO WILL PROTECT US FROM EVIL ROBOTS?
I DON'T THINK EVIL ROBOTS WILL BE A PROBLEM AFTER I LEAVE.

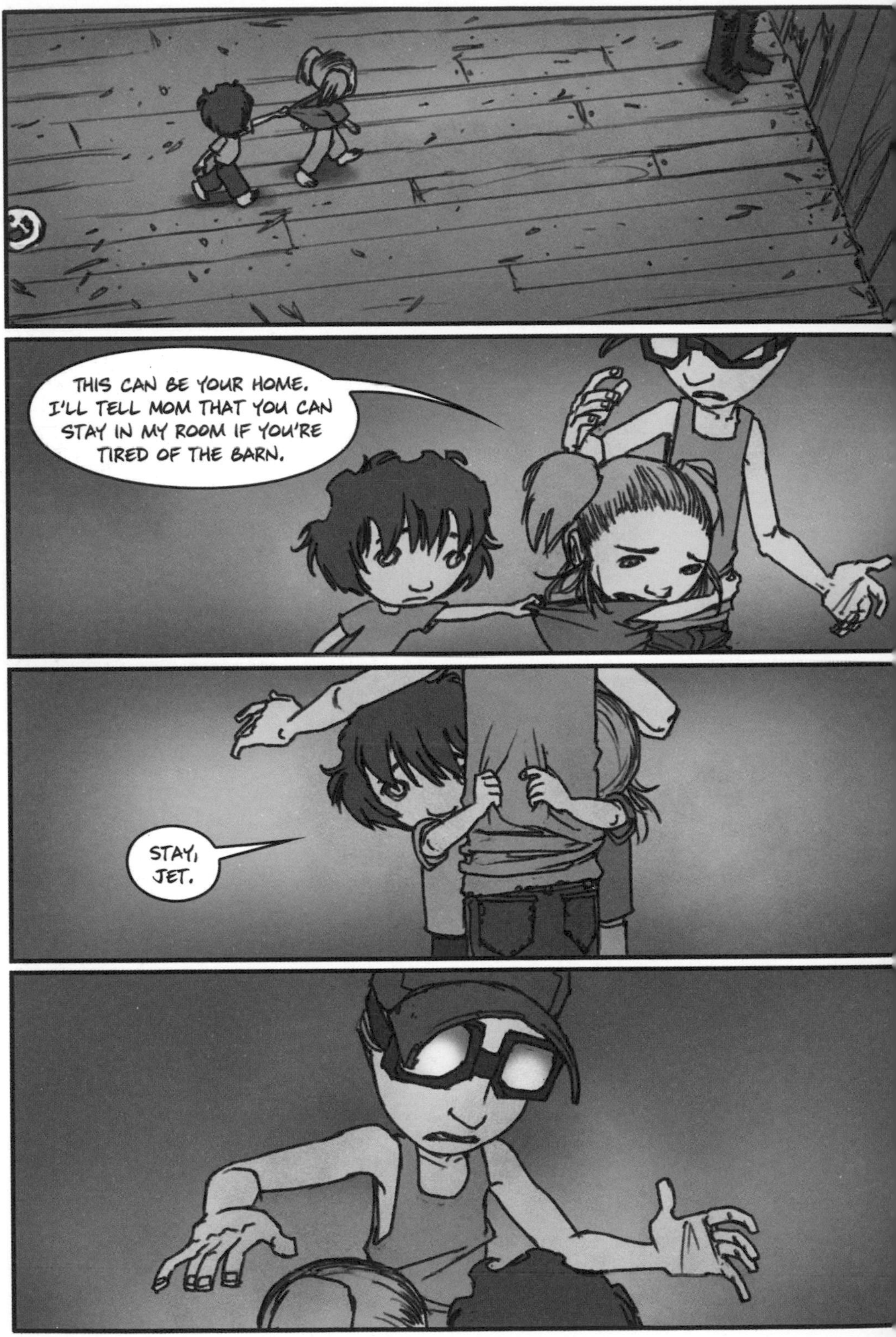
THIS CAN BE YOUR HOME. I'LL TELL MOM THAT YOU CAN STAY IN MY ROOM IF YOU'RE TIRED OF THE BARN.
STAY, JET.

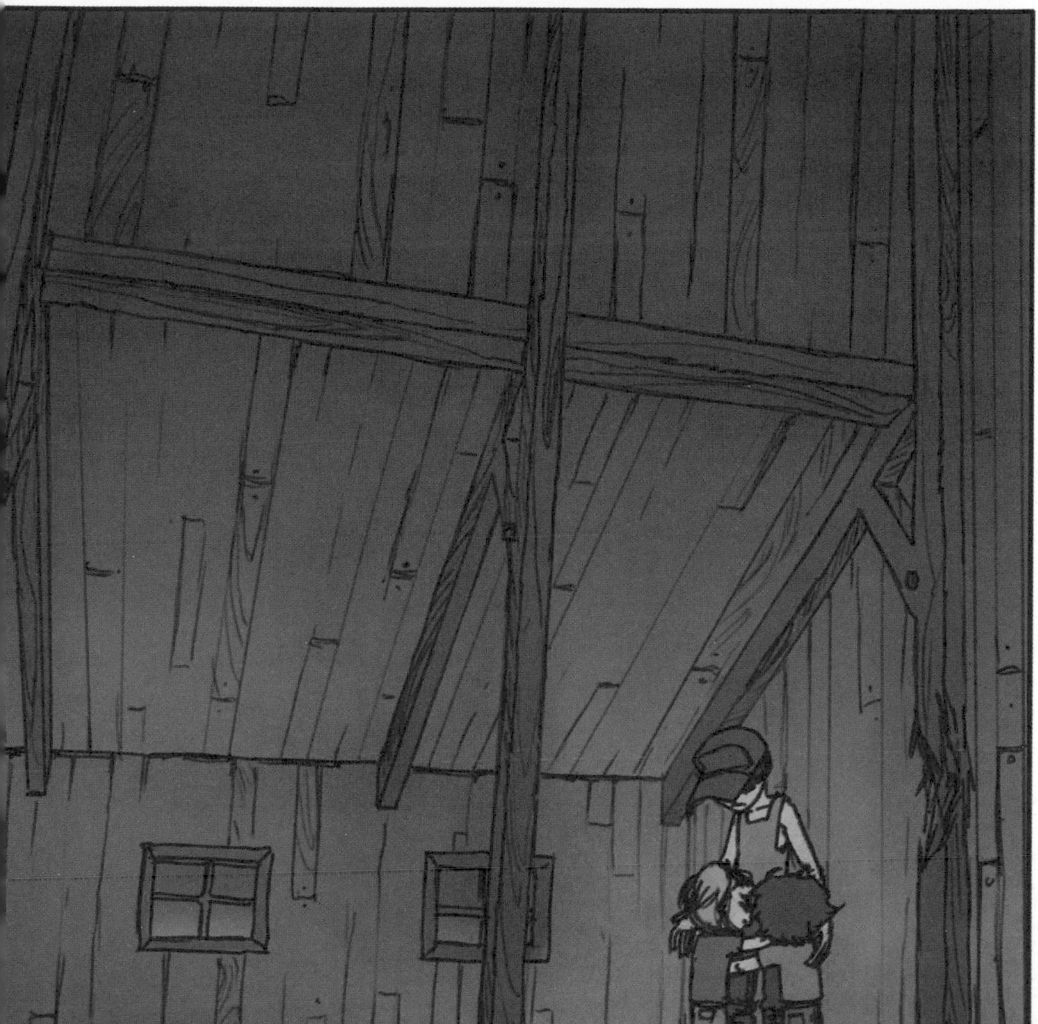

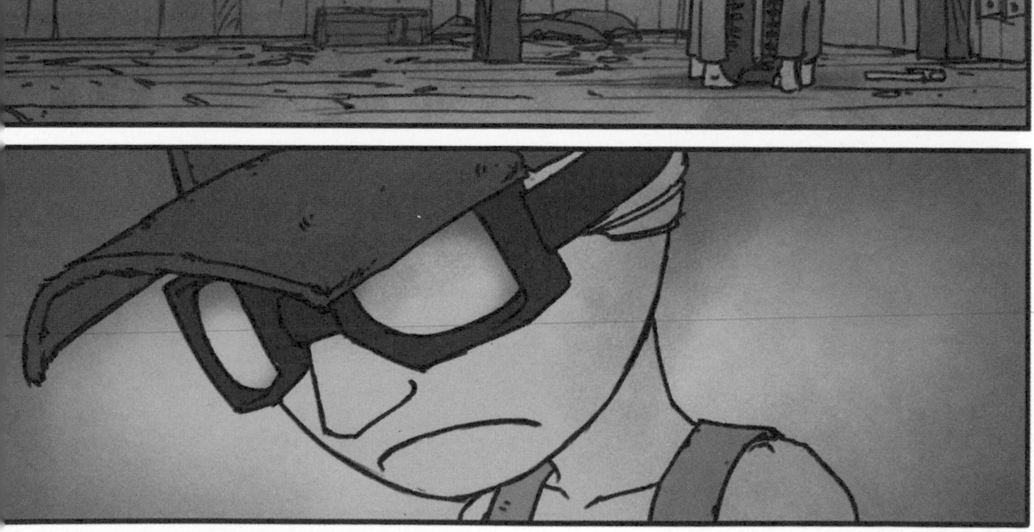

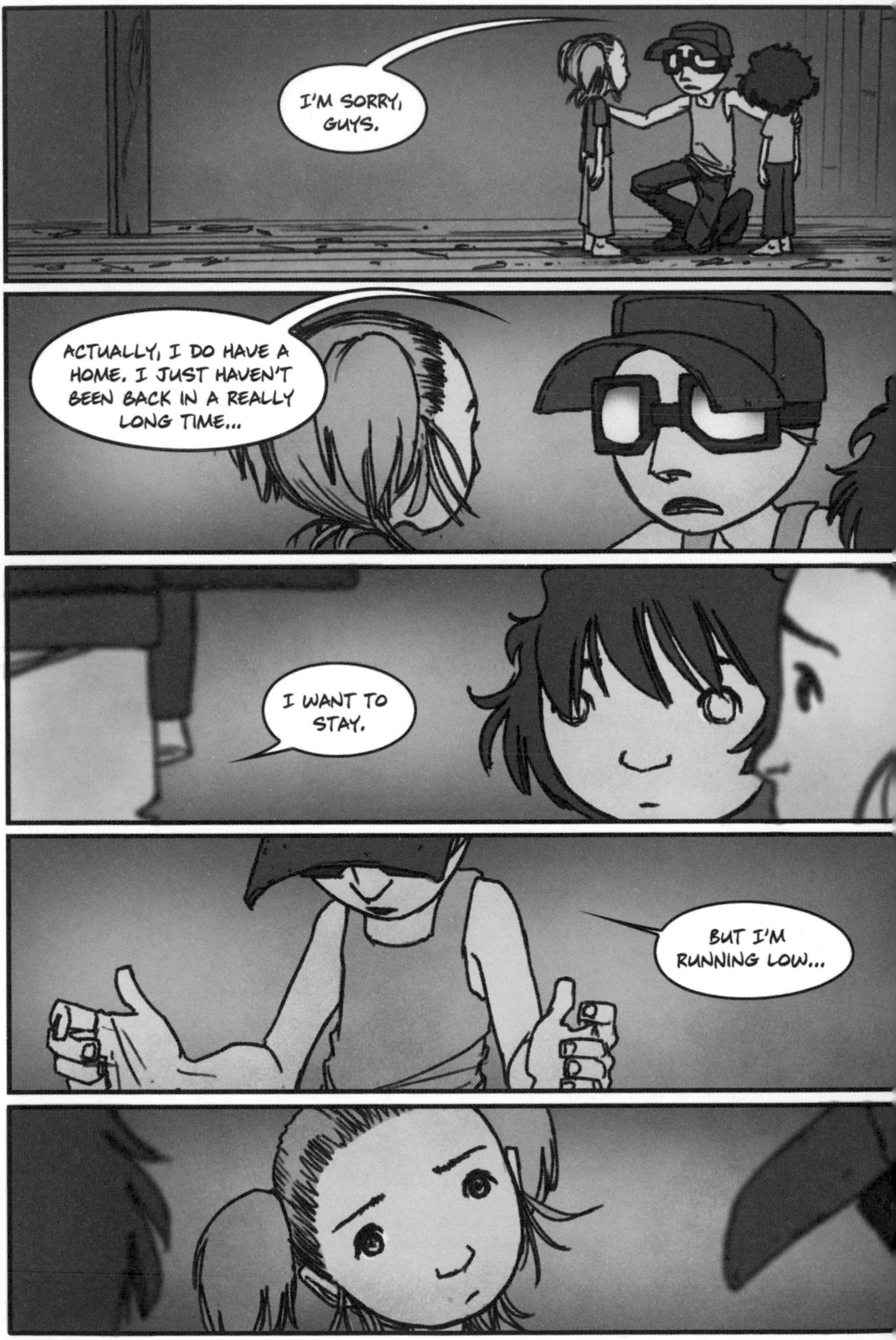
I'M SORRY, GUYS.
ACTUALLY, I DO HAVE A HOME. I JUST HAVEN'T BEEN BACK IN A REALLY LONG TIME...
I WANT TO STAY.
BUT I'M RUNNING LOW...

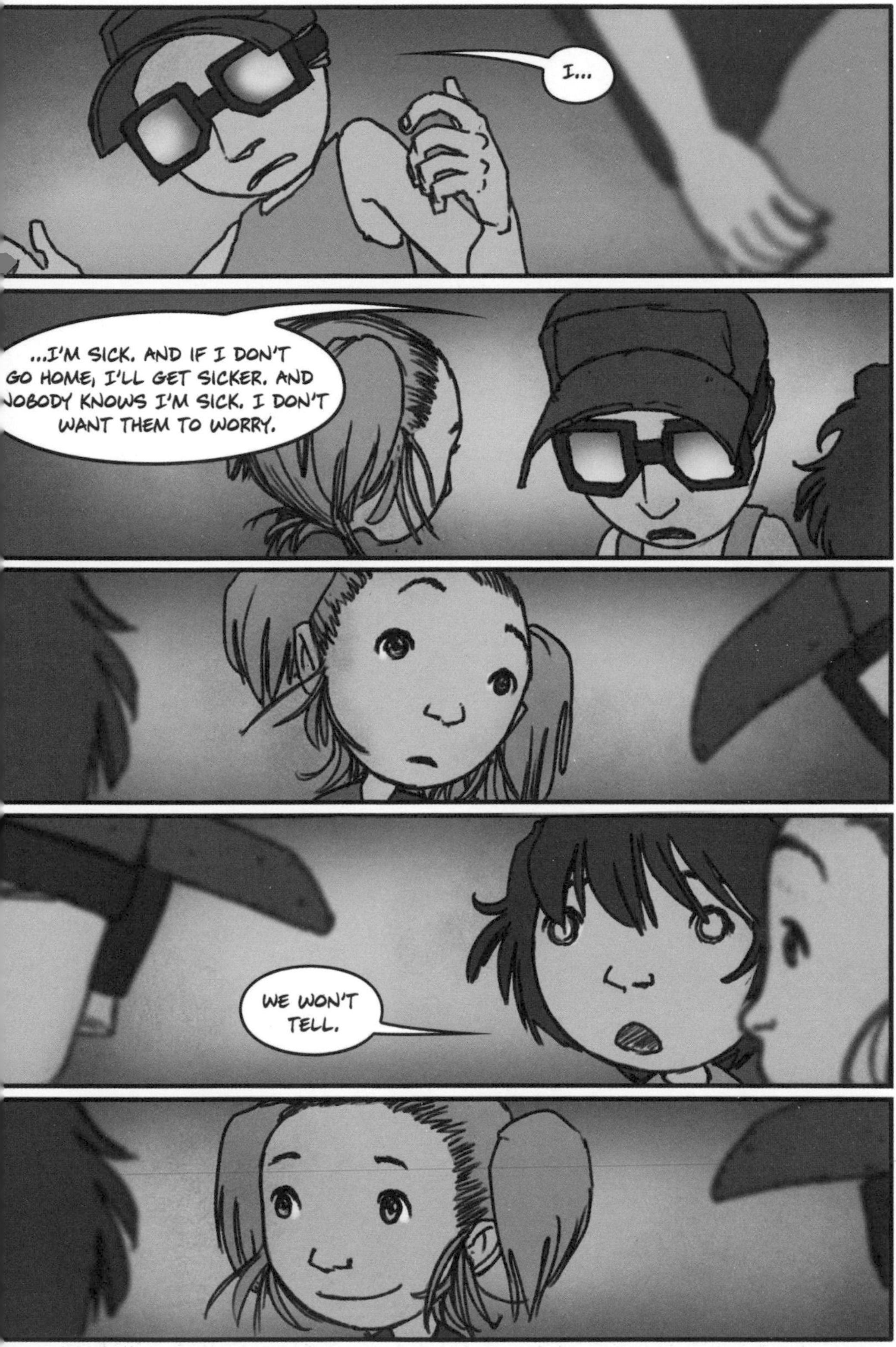
I...
...I'M SICK. AND IF I DON'T GO HOME, I'LL GET SICKER. AND NOBODY KNOWS I'M SICK. I DON'T WANT THEM TO WORRY.
WE WON'T TELL.

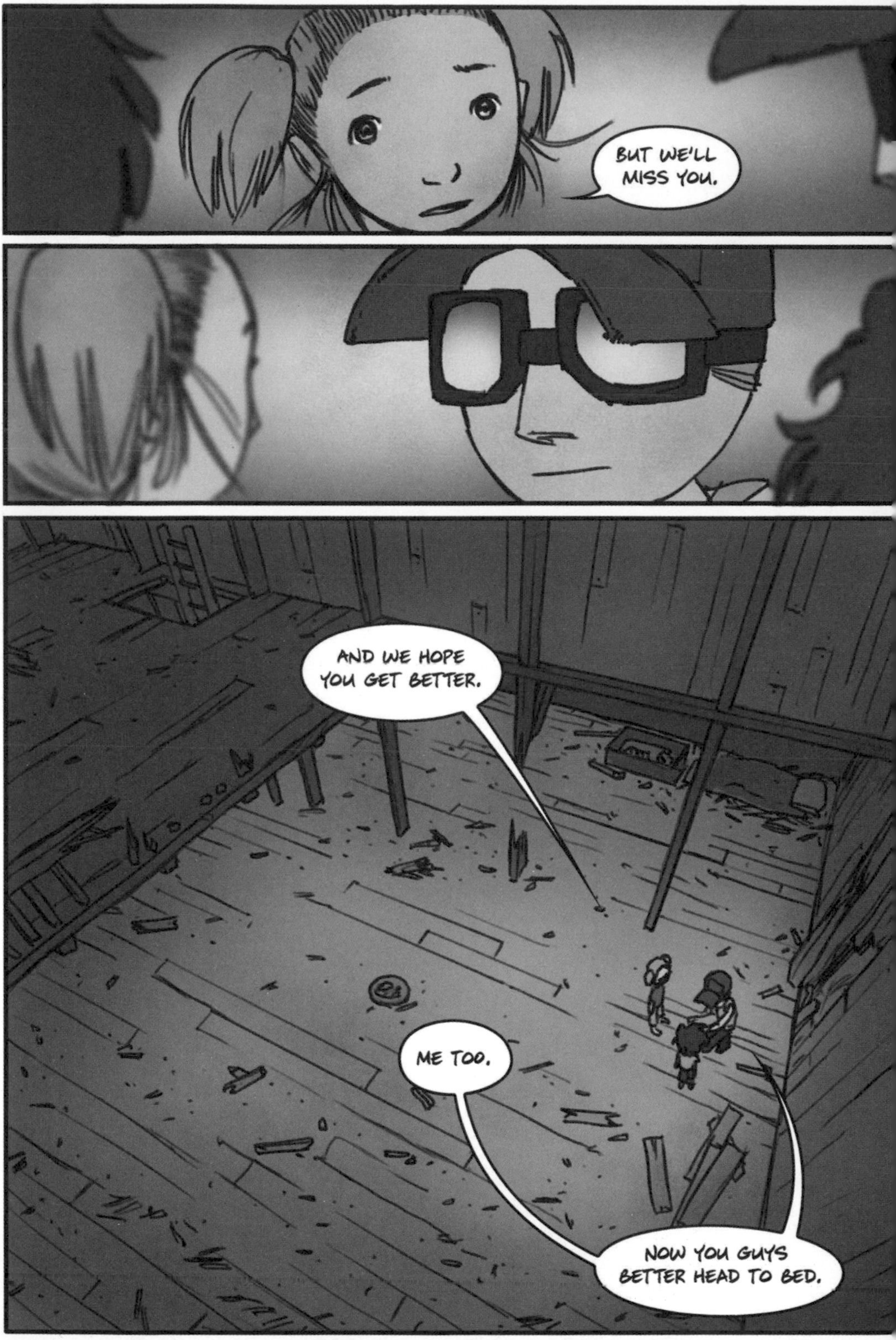
BUT WE'LL MISS YOU.
AND WE HOPE YOU GET BETTER.
ME TOO.
NOW YOU GUYS BETTER HEAD TO BED.

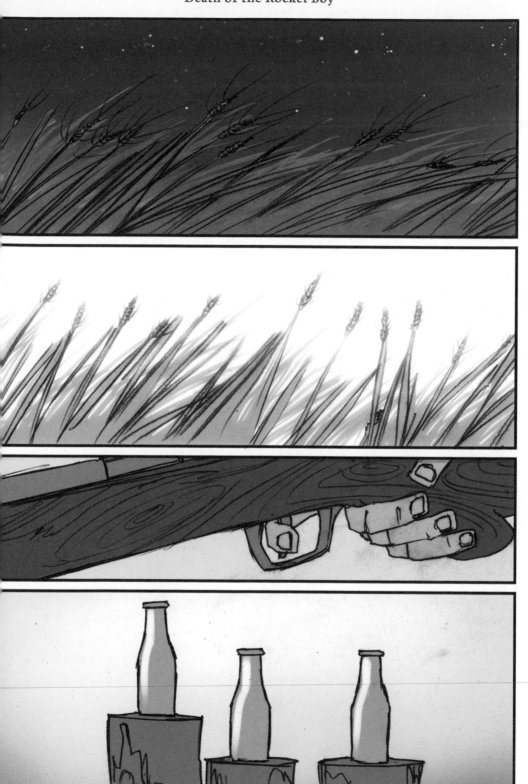

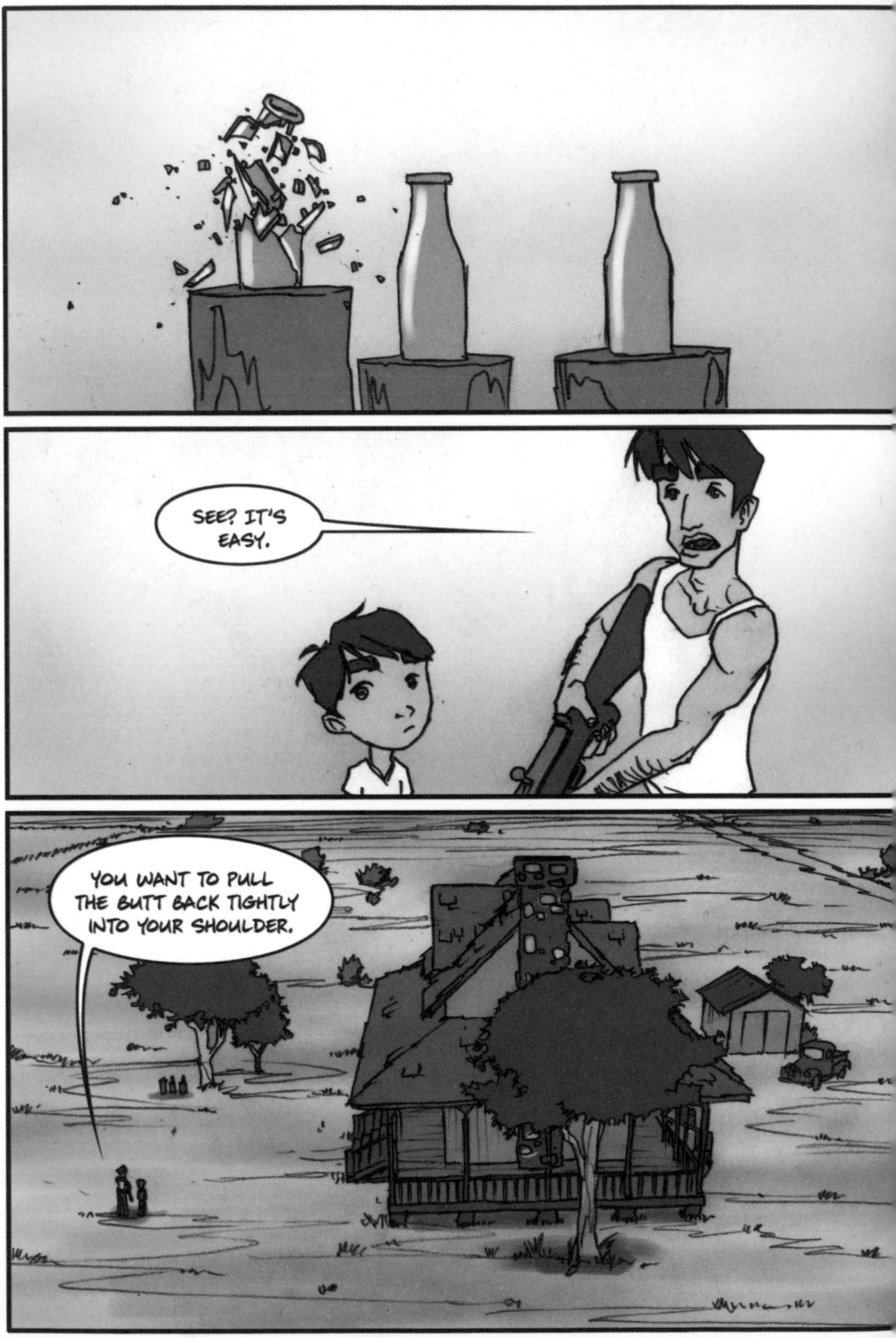
SEE? IT'S EASY.
YOU WANT TO PULL THE BUTT BACK TIGHTLY INTO YOUR SHOULDER.

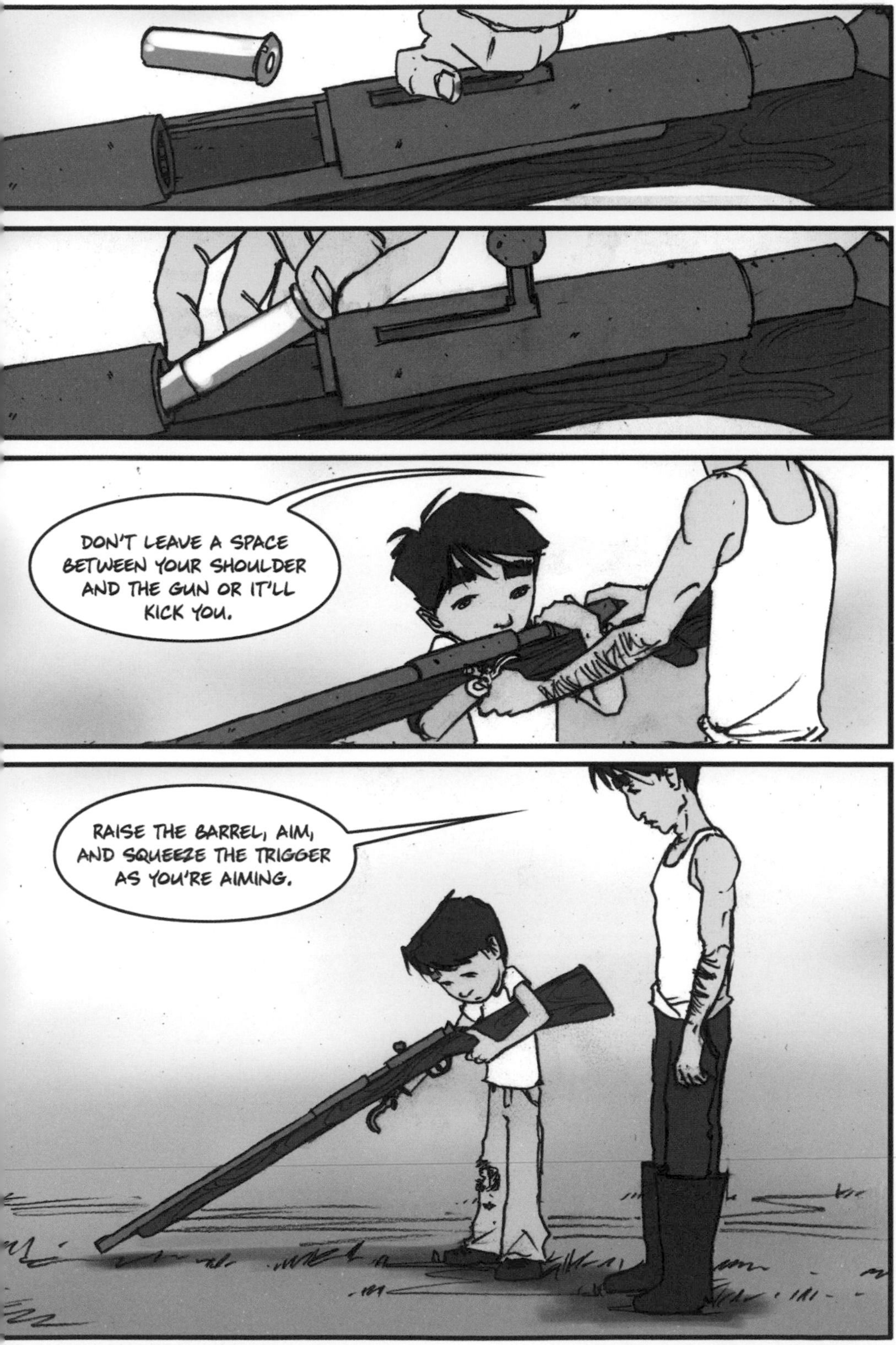
DON'T LEAVE A SPACE BETWEEN YOUR SHOULDER AND THE GUN OR IT'LL KICK YOU.
RAISE THE BARREL, AIM, AND SQUEEZE THE TRIGGER AS YOU'RE AIMING.

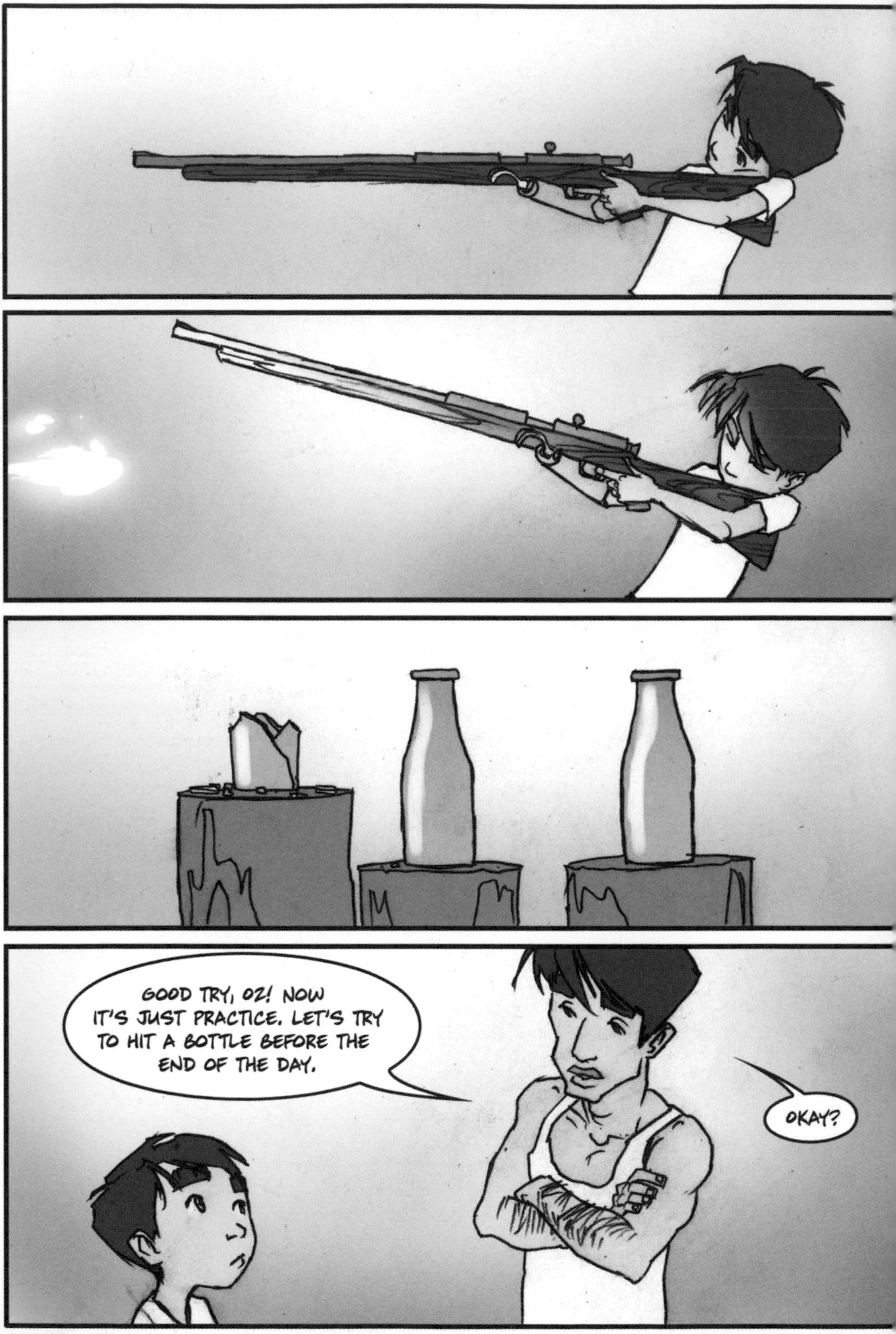
GOOD TRY, OZ! NOW IT'S JUST PRACTICE. LET'S TRY TO HIT A BOTTLE BEFORE THE END OF THE DAY.
OKAY?

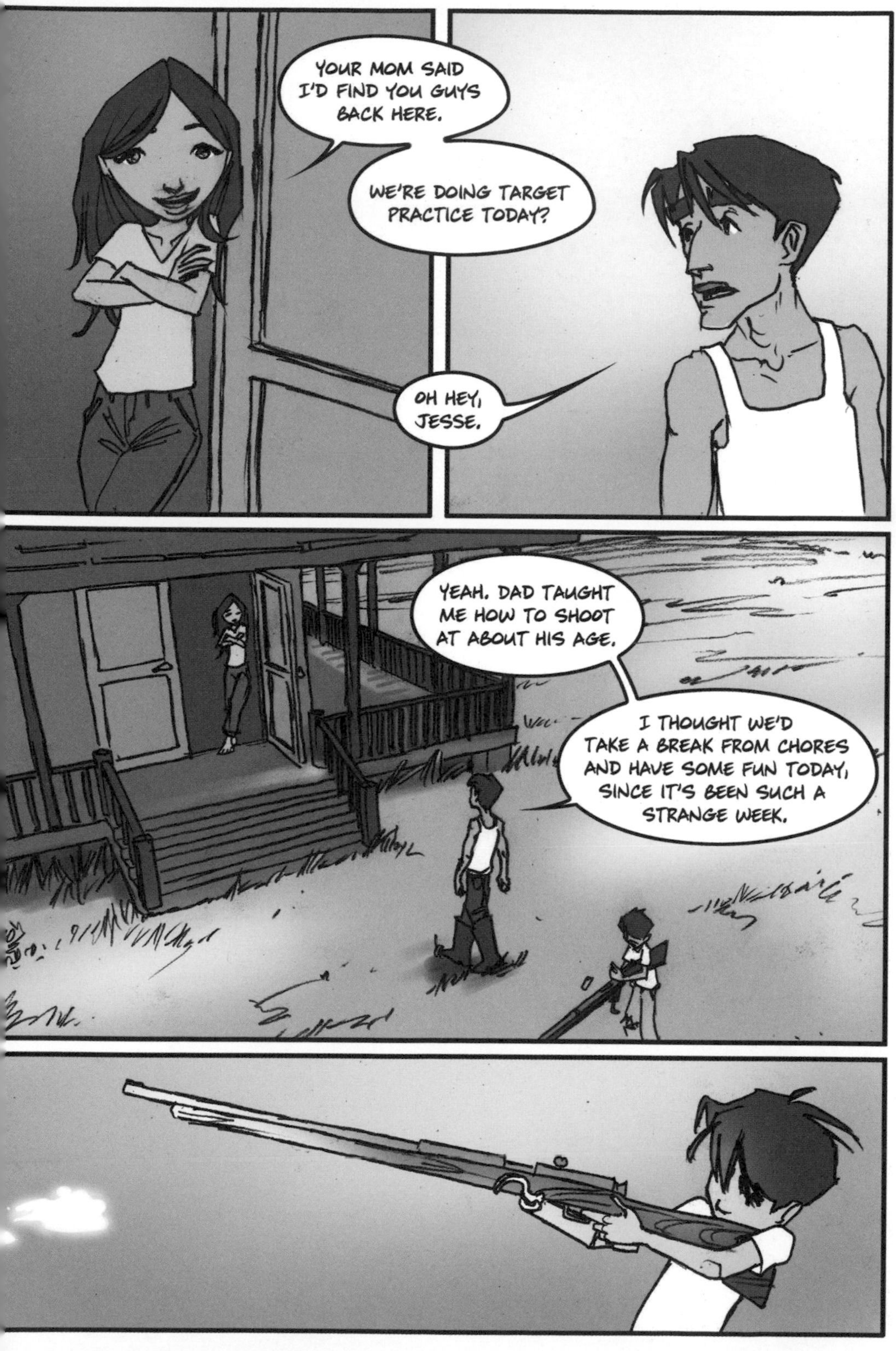
YOUR MOM SAID I'D FIND YOU GUYS BACK HERE.
WE'RE DOING TARGET PRACTICE TODAY?
OH HEY, JESSE.
YEAH. DAD TAUGHT ME HOW TO SHOOT AT ABOUT HIS AGE.
I THOUGHT WE'D TAKE A BREAK FROM CHORES AND HAVE SOME FUN TODAY, SINCE IT'S BEEN SUCH A STRANGE WEEK.

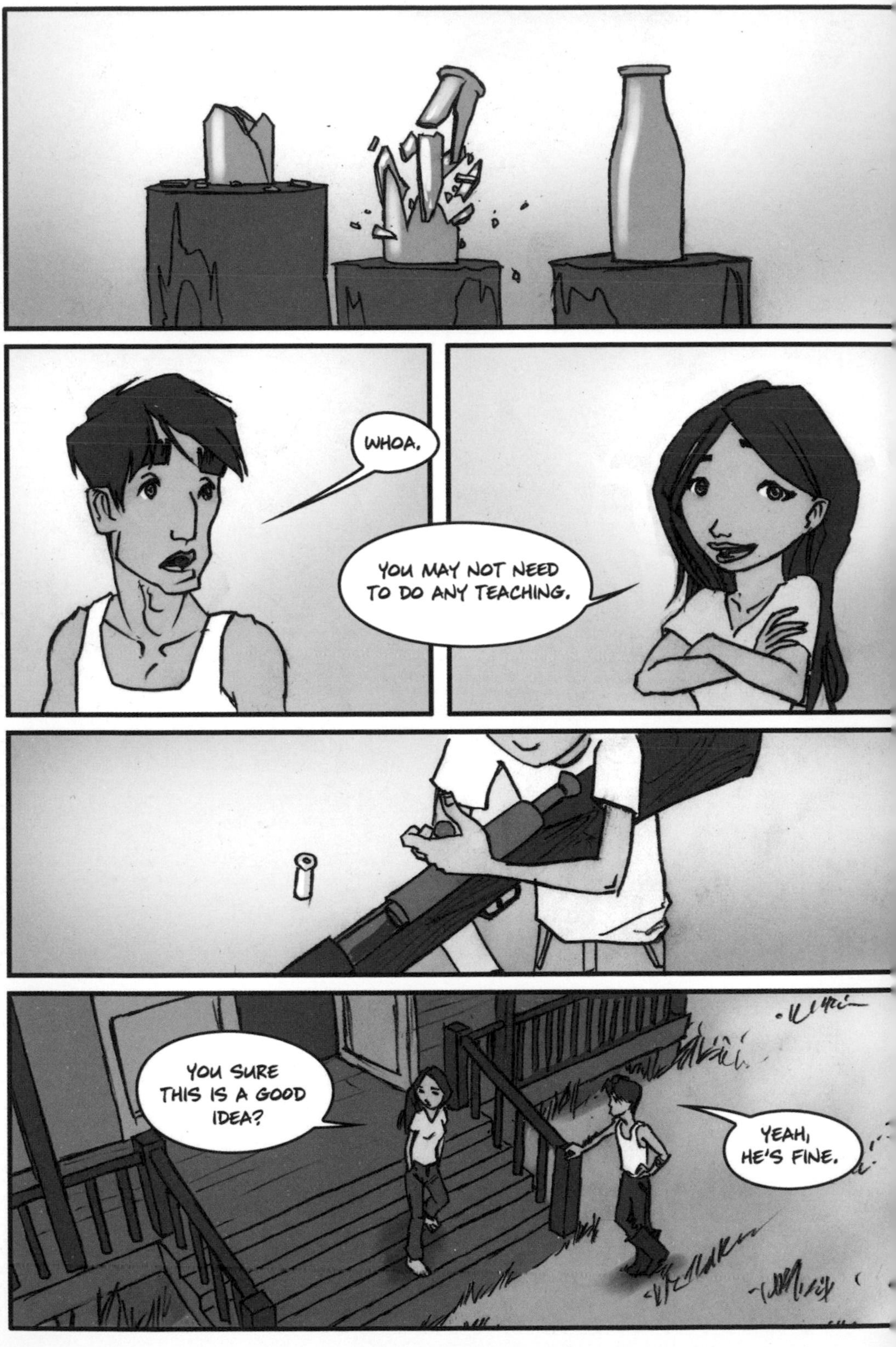
WHOA.
YOU MAY NOT NEED TO DO ANY TEACHING.
YOU SURE THIS IS A GOOD IDEA?
YEAH, HE'S FINE.

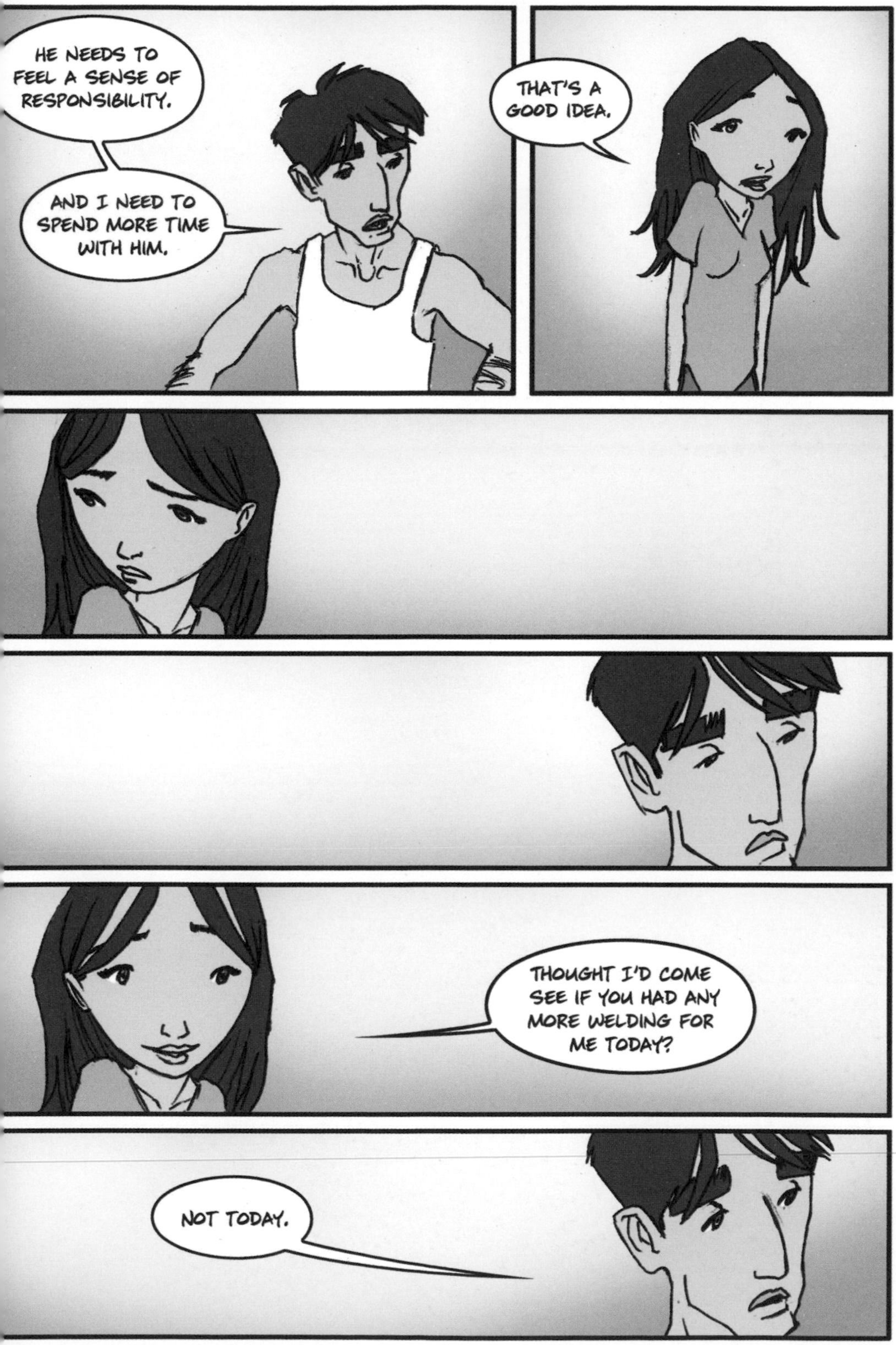
HE NEEDS TO FEEL A SENSE OF RESPONSIBILITY.
AND I NEED TO SPEND MORE TIME WITH HIM.
THAT'S A GOOD IDEA.
THOUGHT I'D COME SEE IF YOU HAD ANY MORE WELDING FOR ME TODAY?
NOT TODAY.

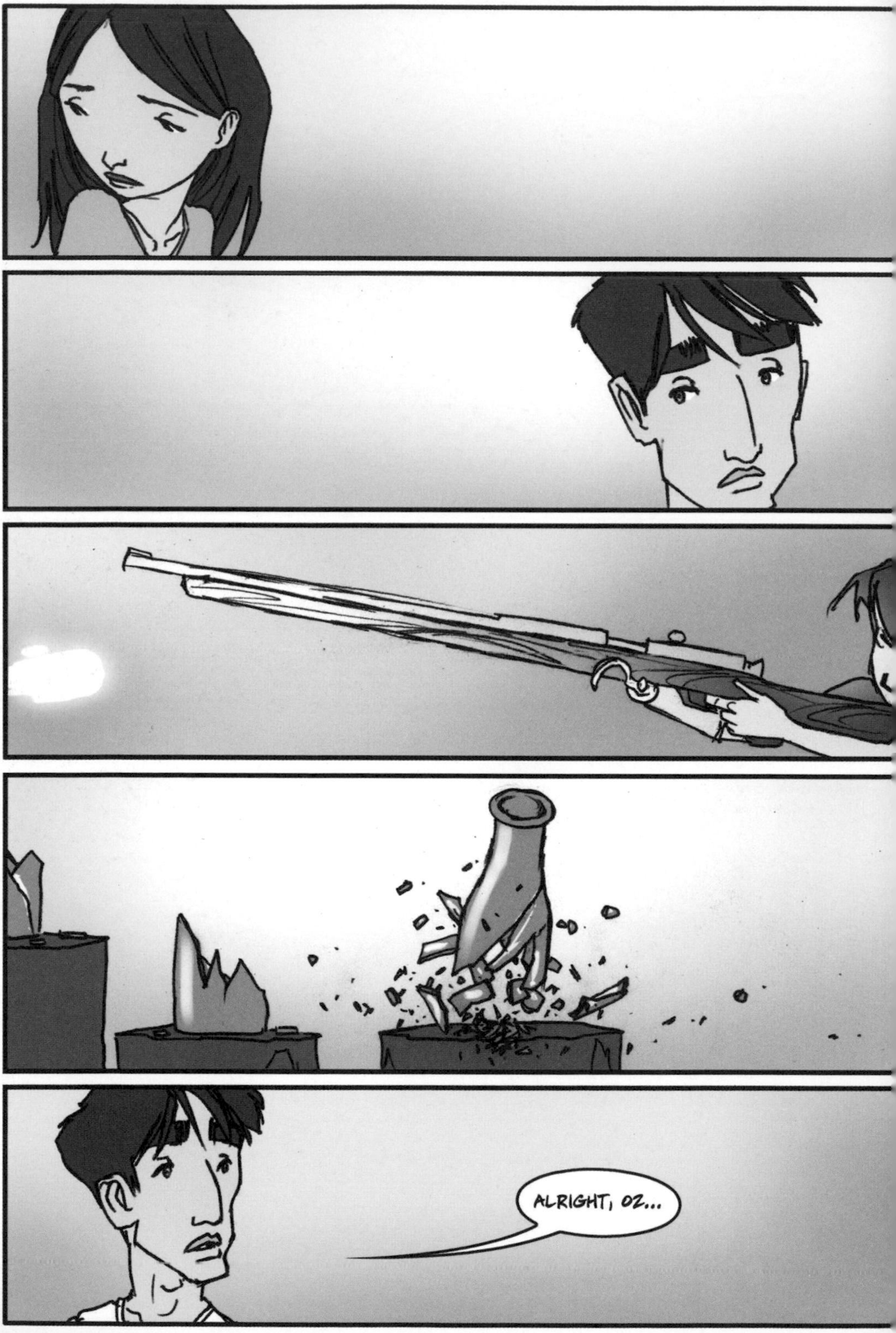
ALRIGHT, OZ...

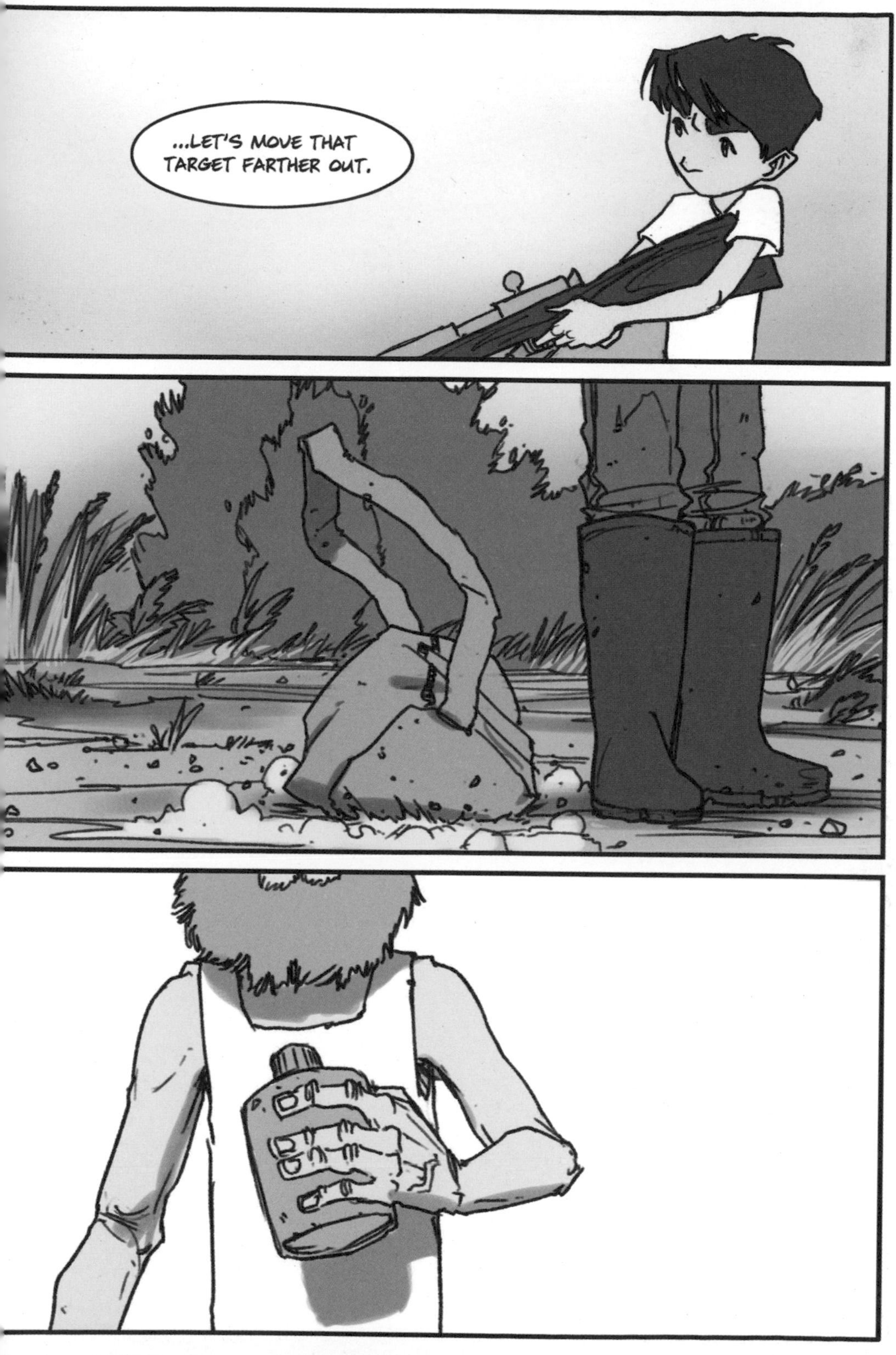
...LET'S MOVE THAT TARGET FARTHER OUT.

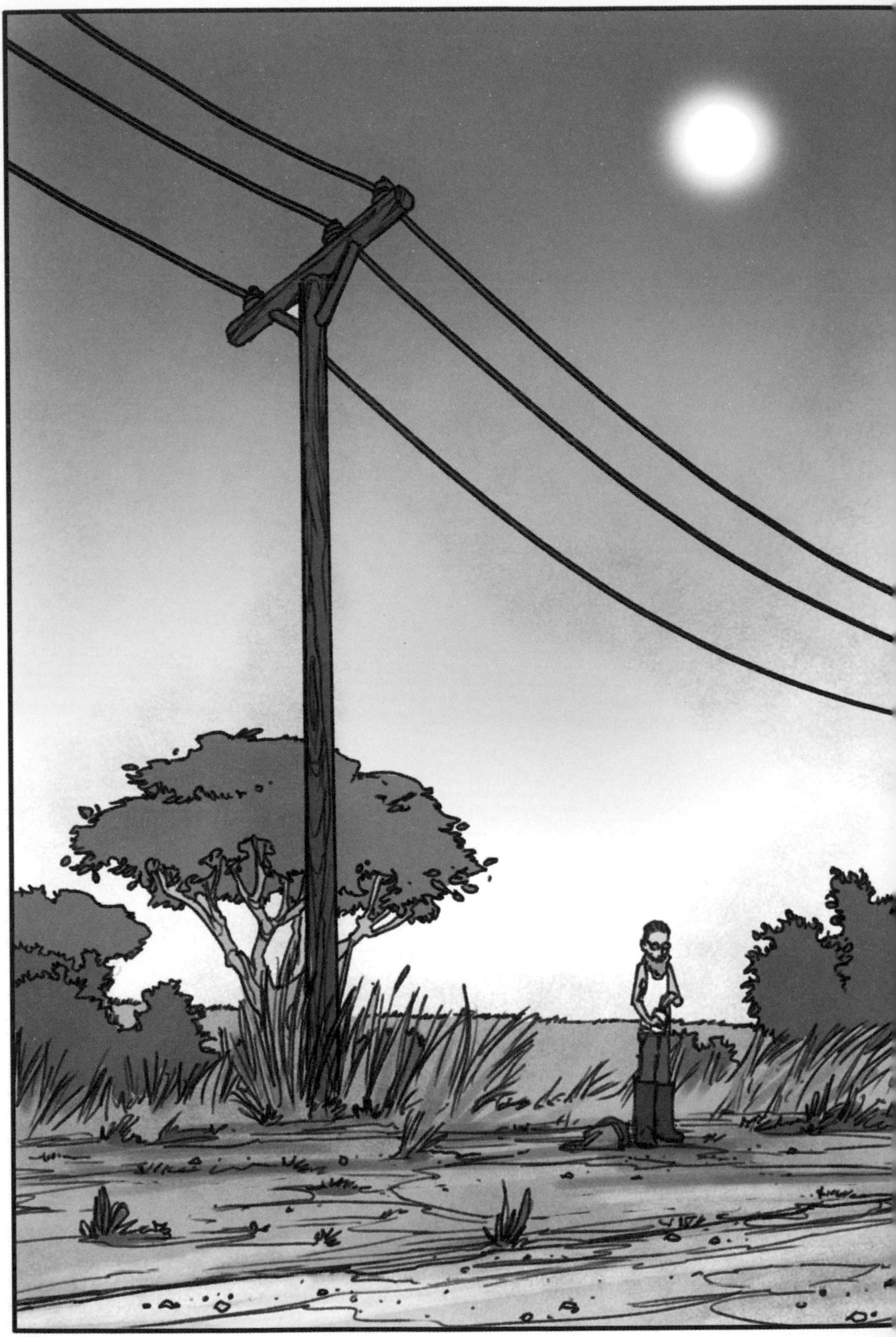

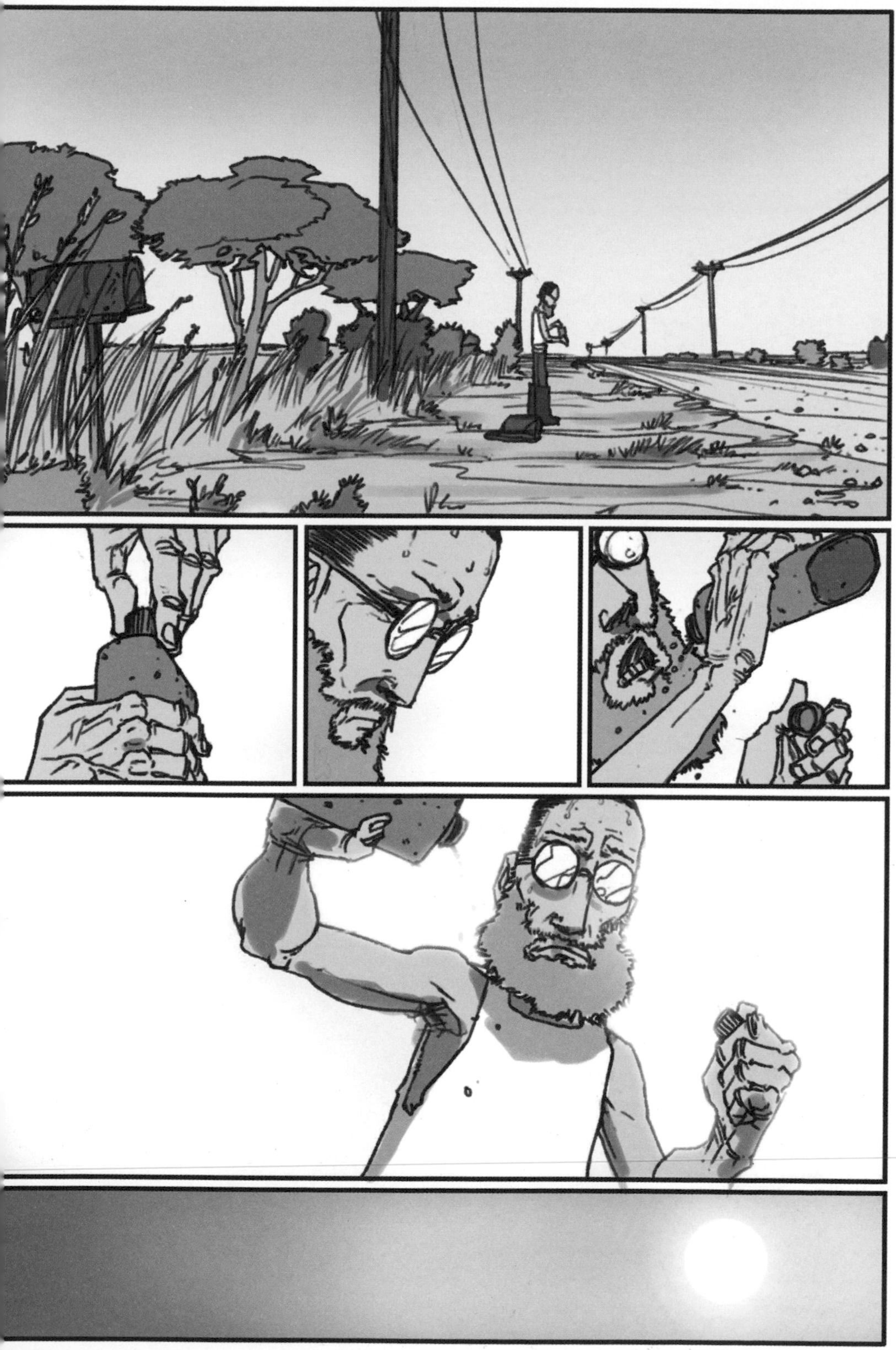

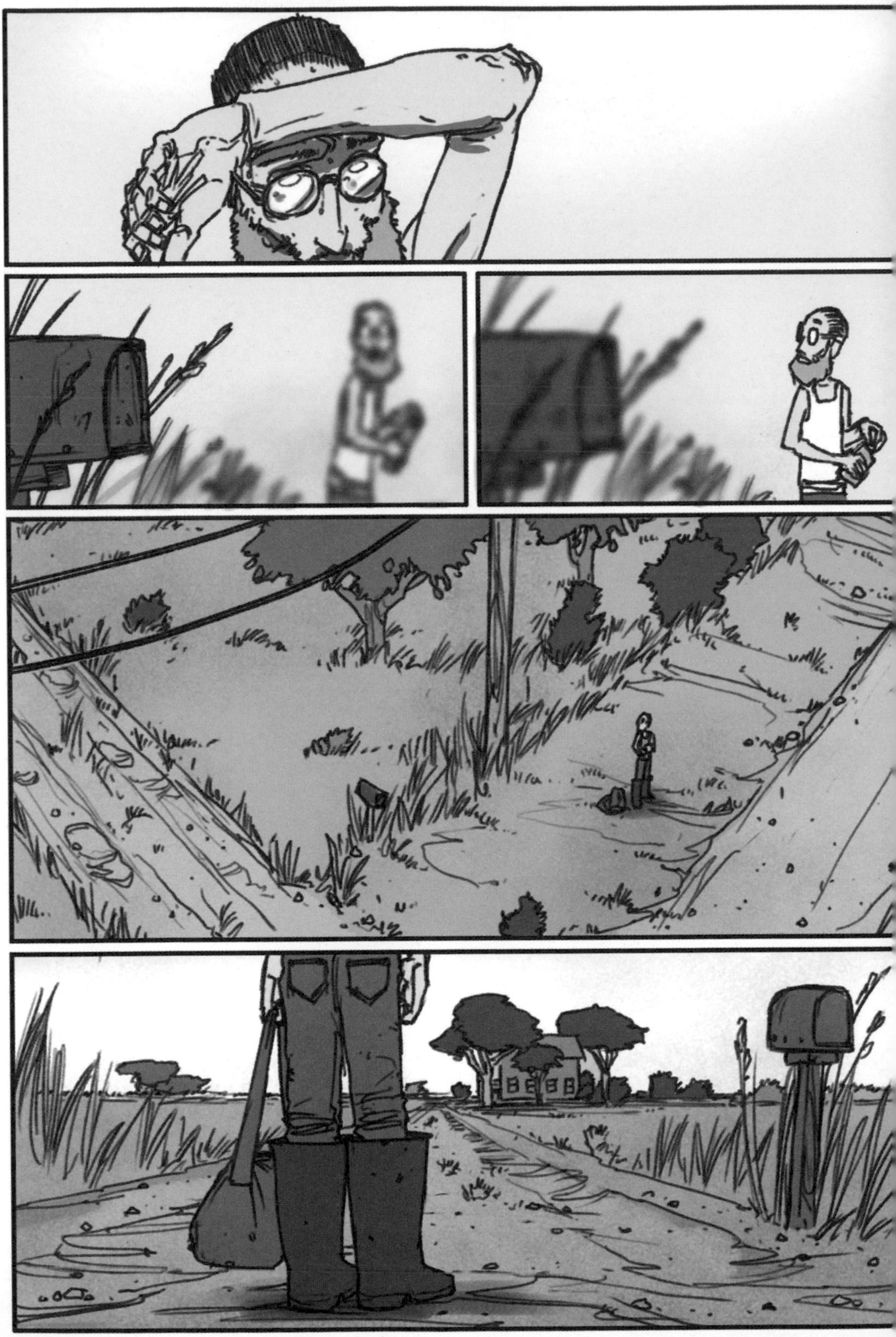

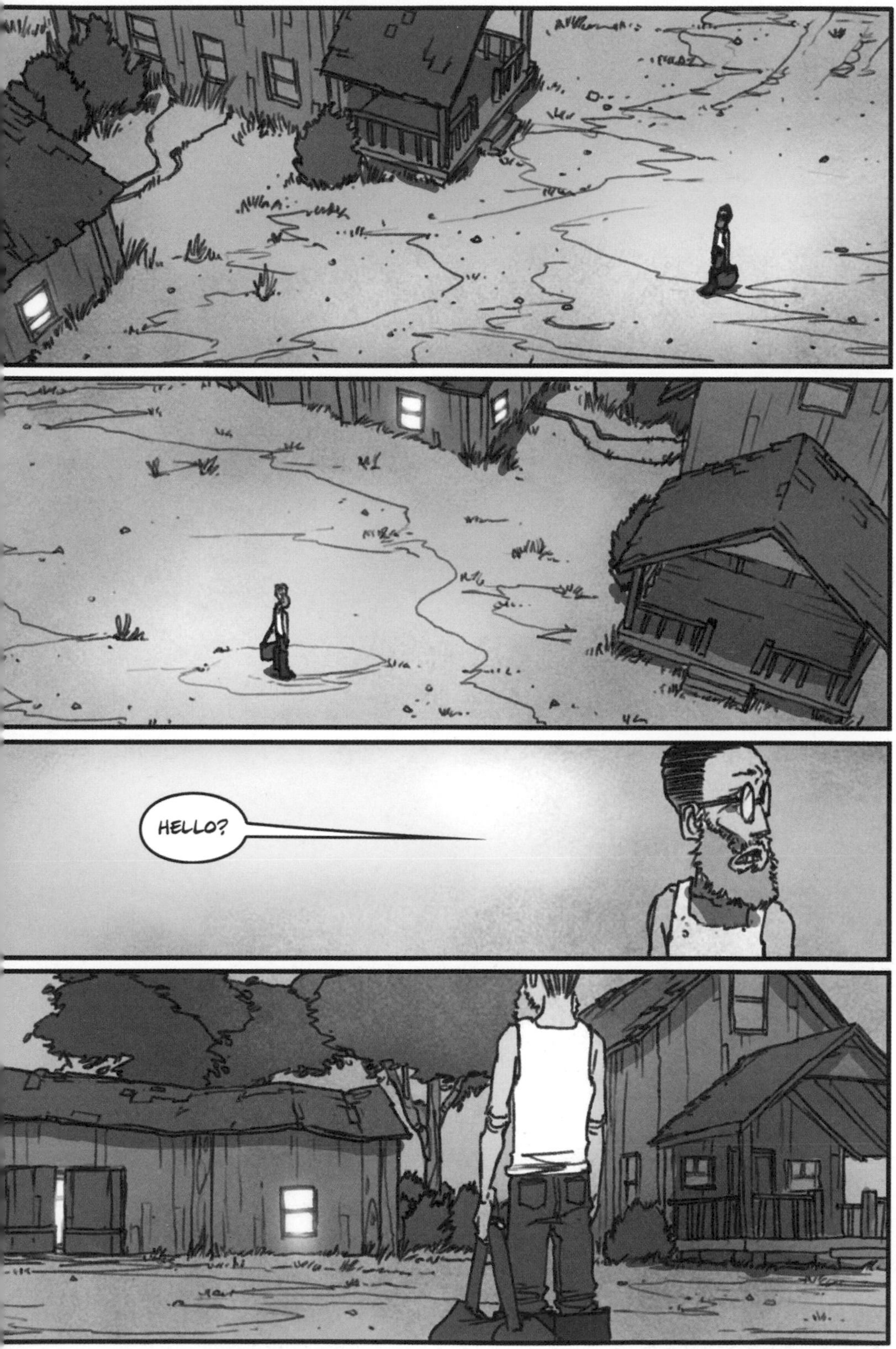
HELLO?

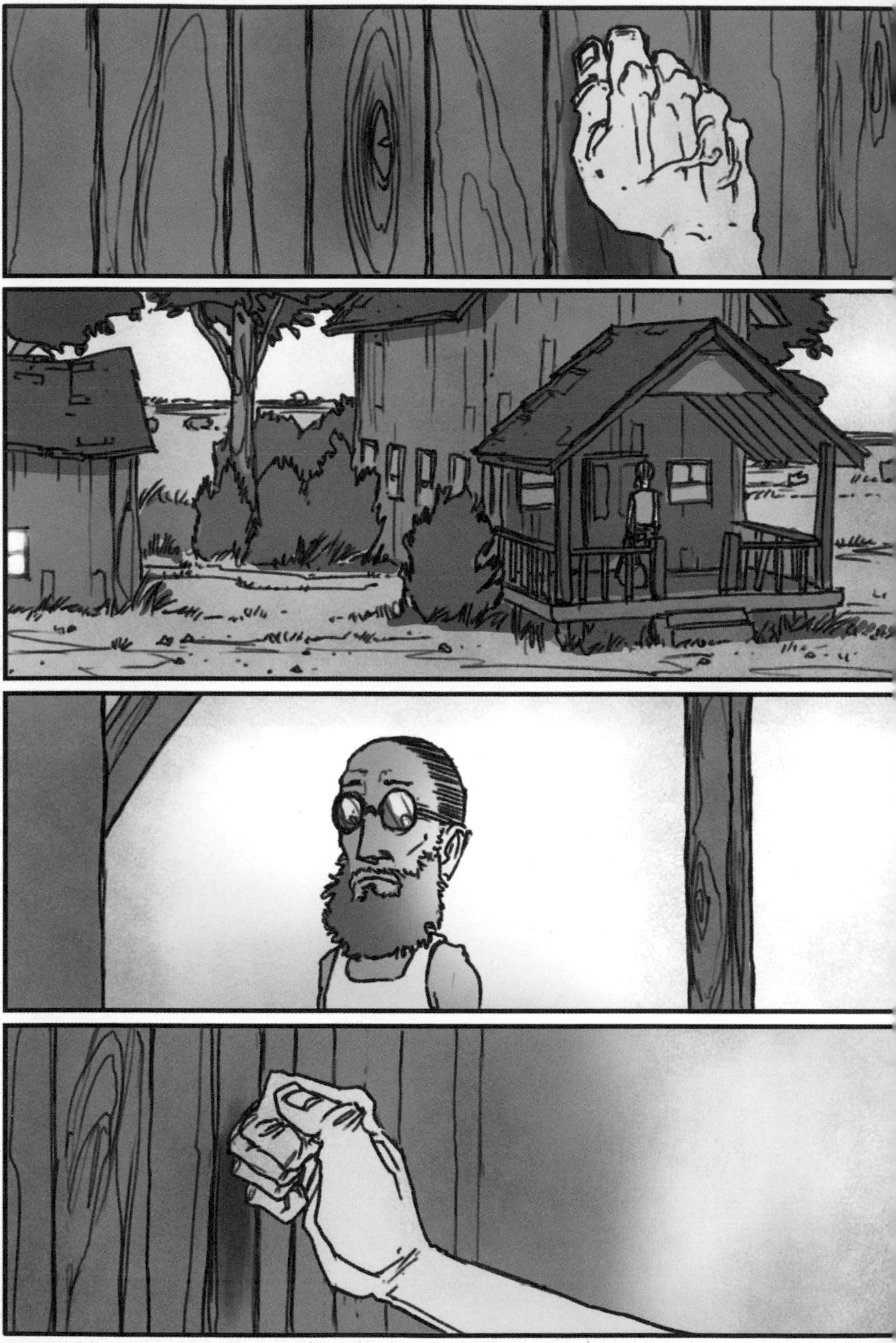

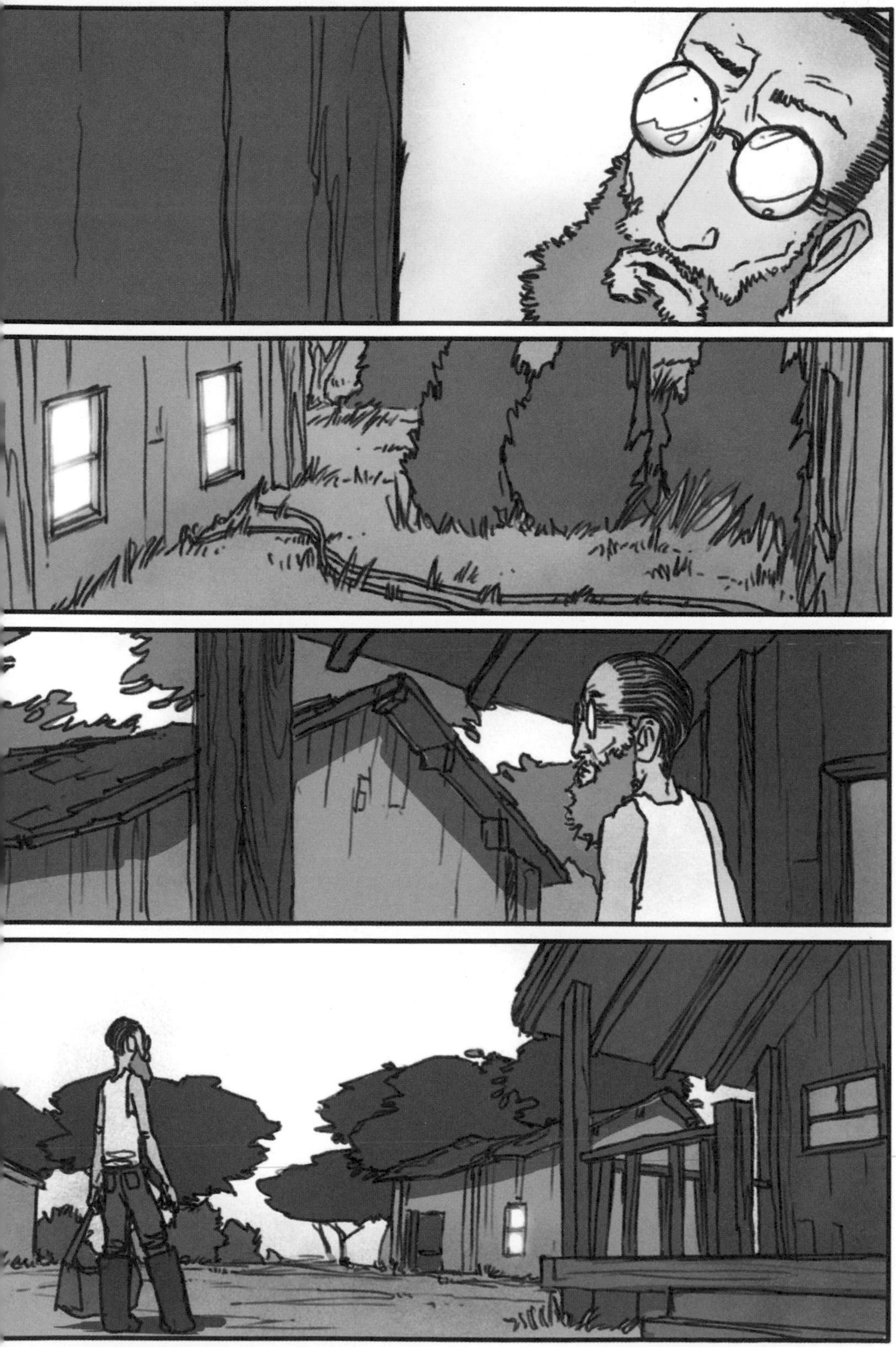

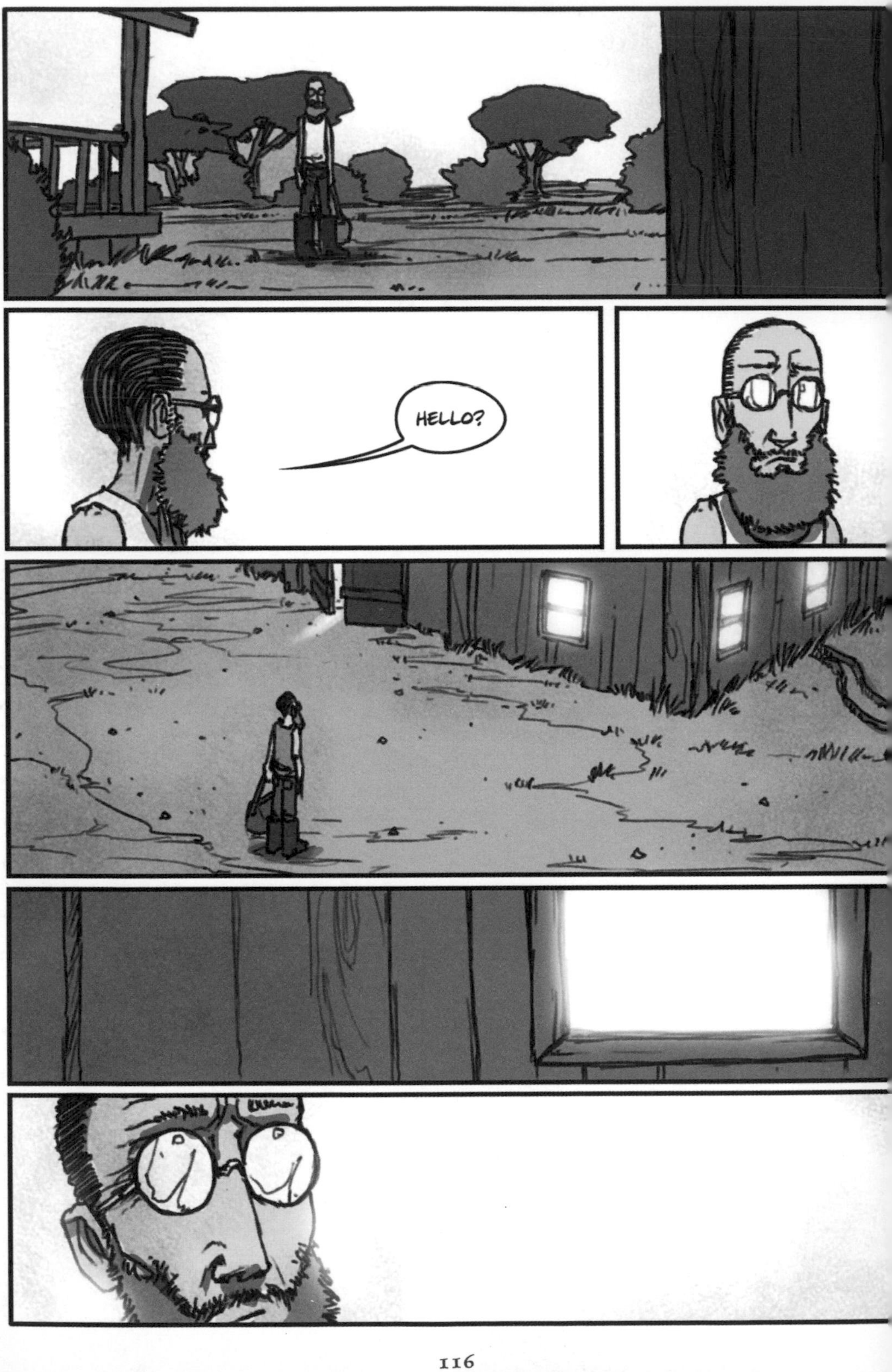
HELLO?

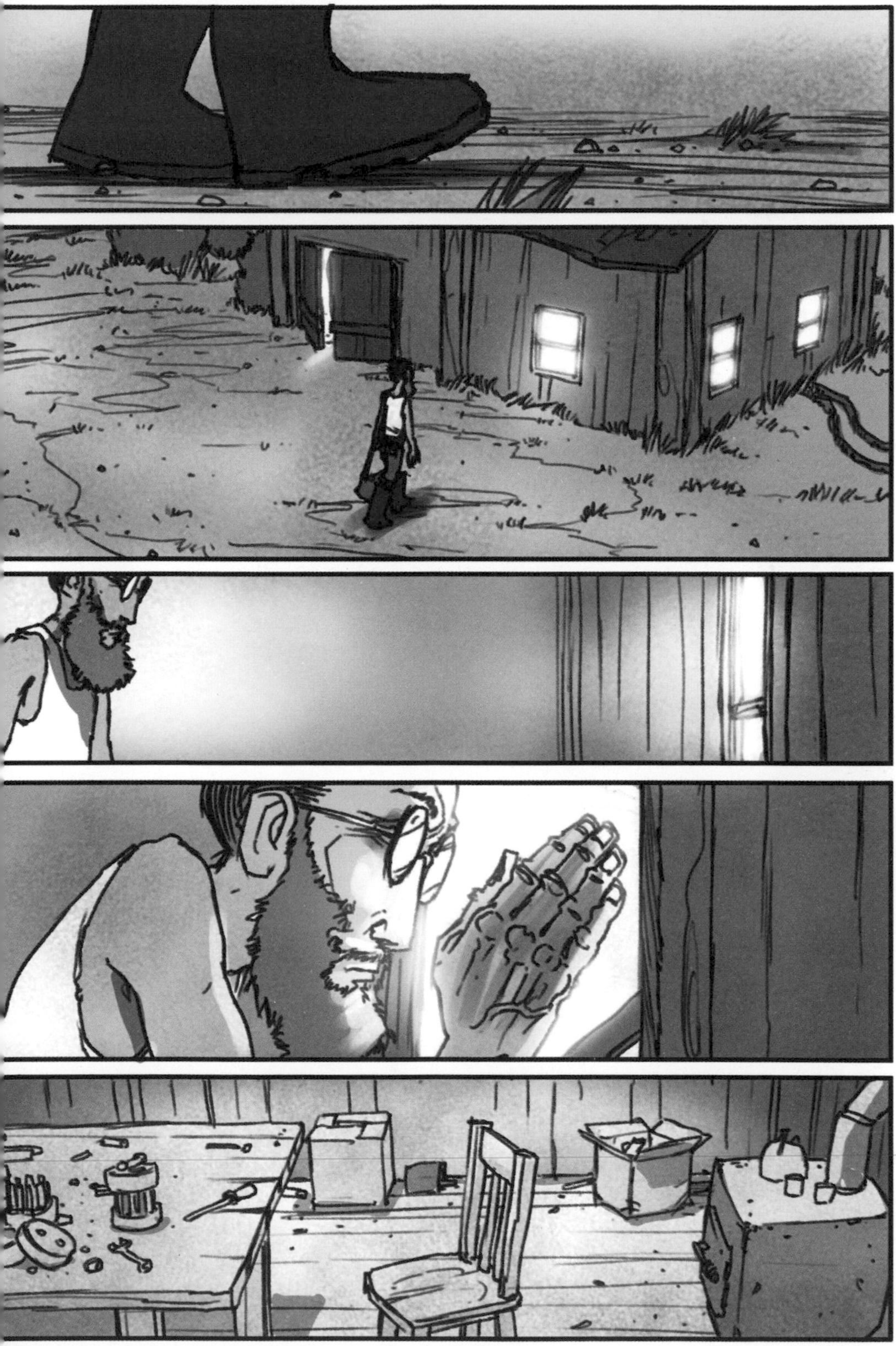

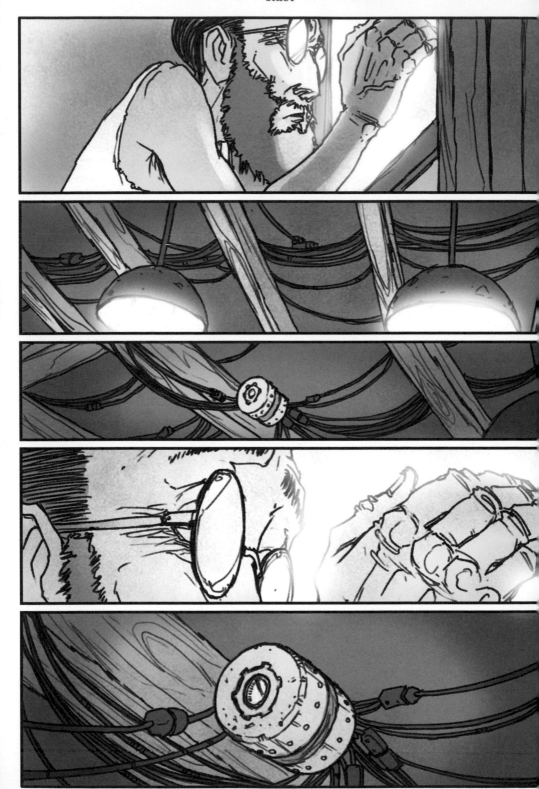

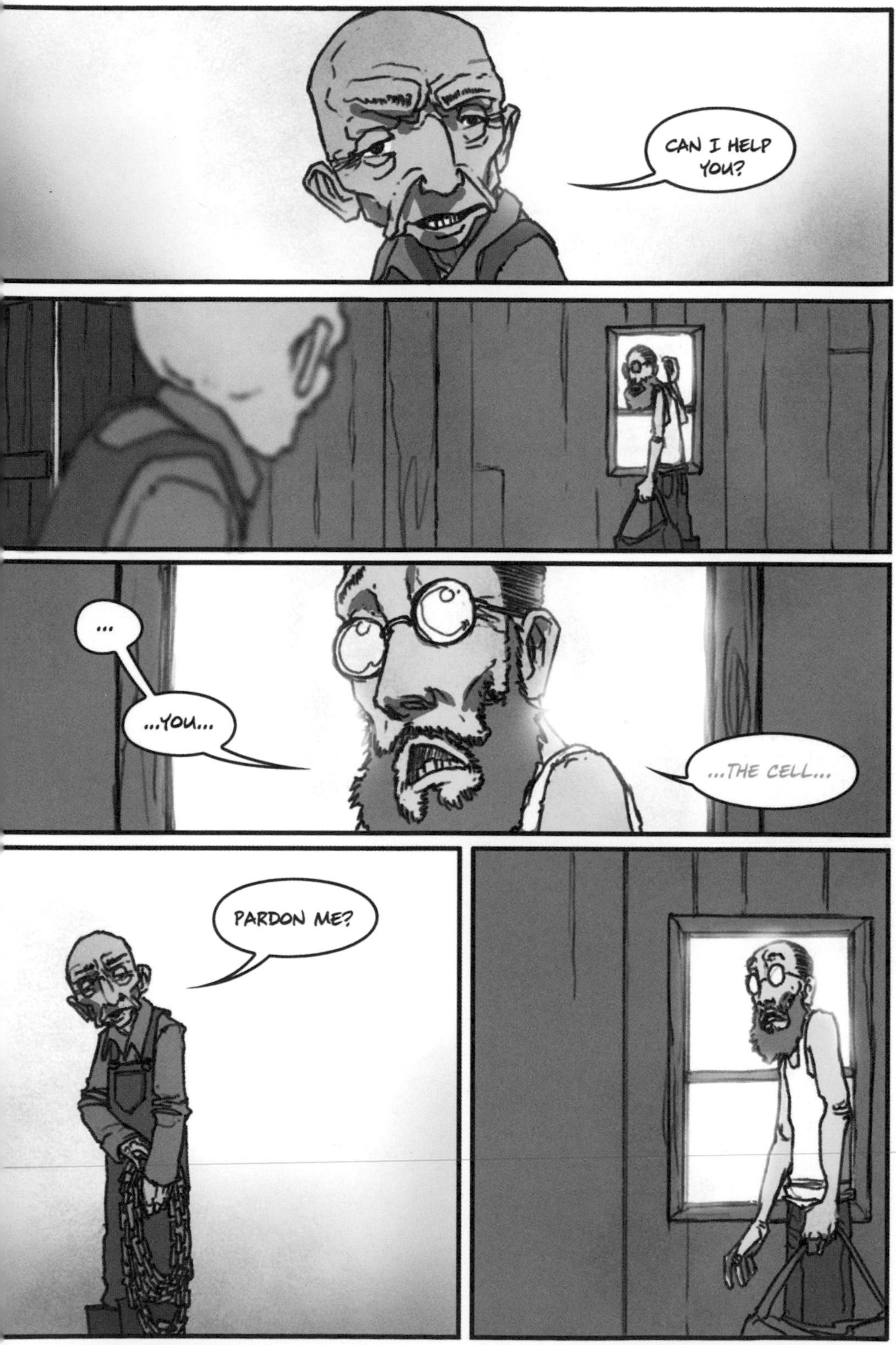
CAN I HELP YOU?
...
...YOU...
...THE CELL...
PARDON ME?

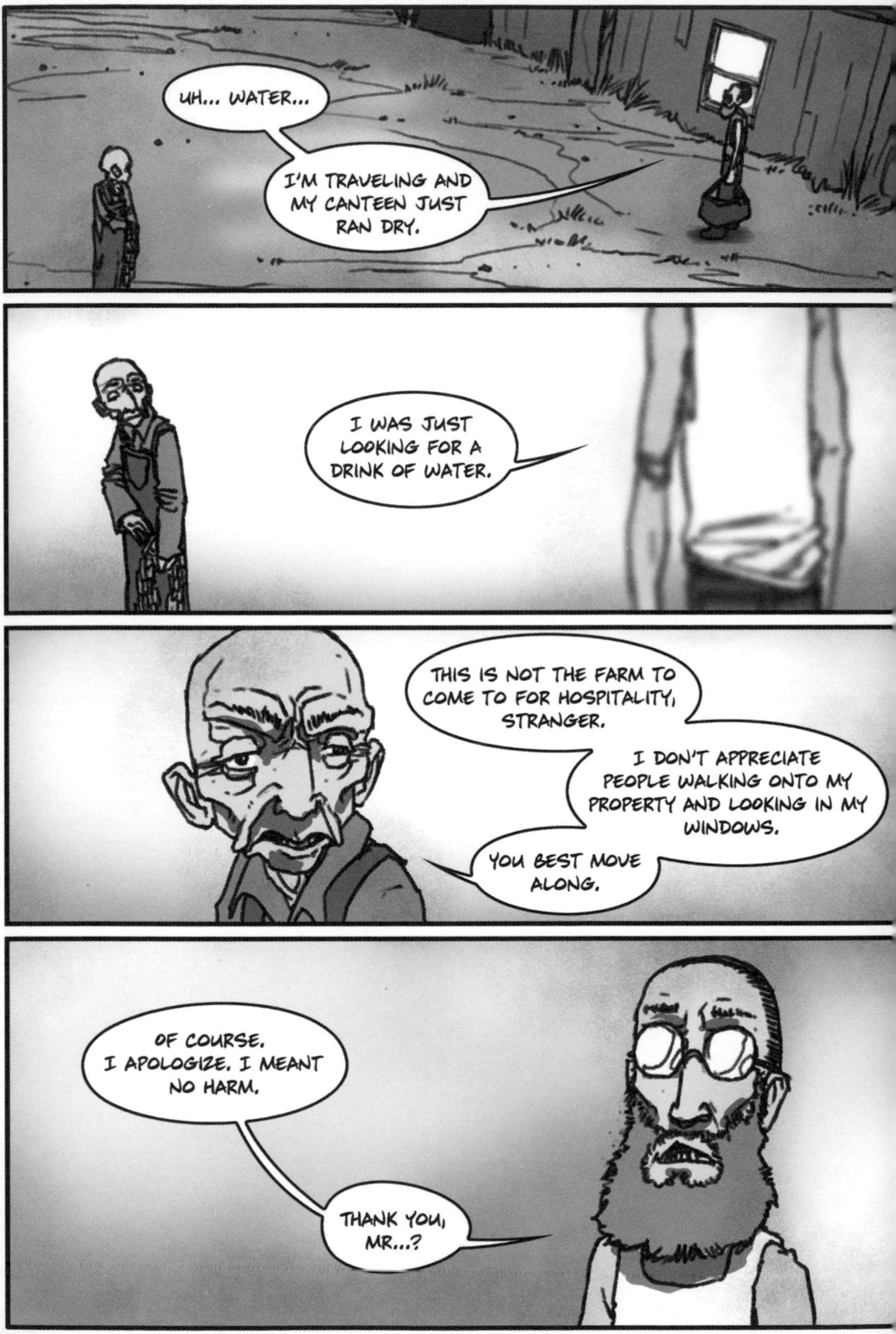
UH... WATER...
I'M TRAVELING AND MY CANTEEN JUST RAN DRY.
I WAS JUST LOOKING FOR A DRINK OF WATER.
THIS IS NOT THE FARM TO COME TO FOR HOSPITALITY, STRANGER.
I DON'T APPRECIATE PEOPLE WALKING ONTO MY PROPERTY AND LOOKING IN MY WINDOWS.
YOU BEST MOVE ALONG.
OF COURSE. I APOLOGIZE. I MEANT NO HARM.
THANK YOU, MR...?

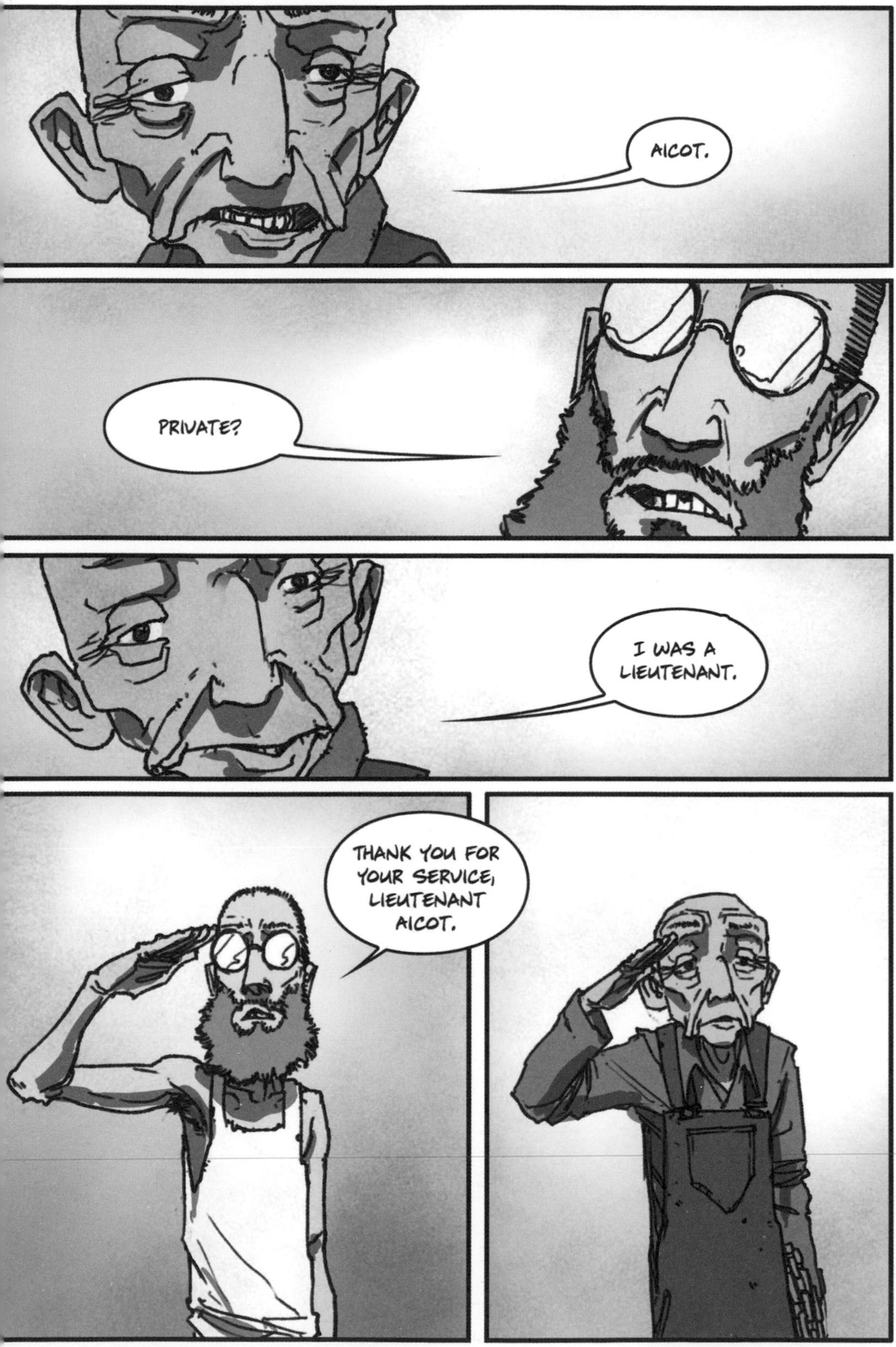
AICOT.
PRIVATE?
I WAS A LIEUTENANT.
THANK YOU FOR YOUR SERVICE, LIEUTENANT AICOT.

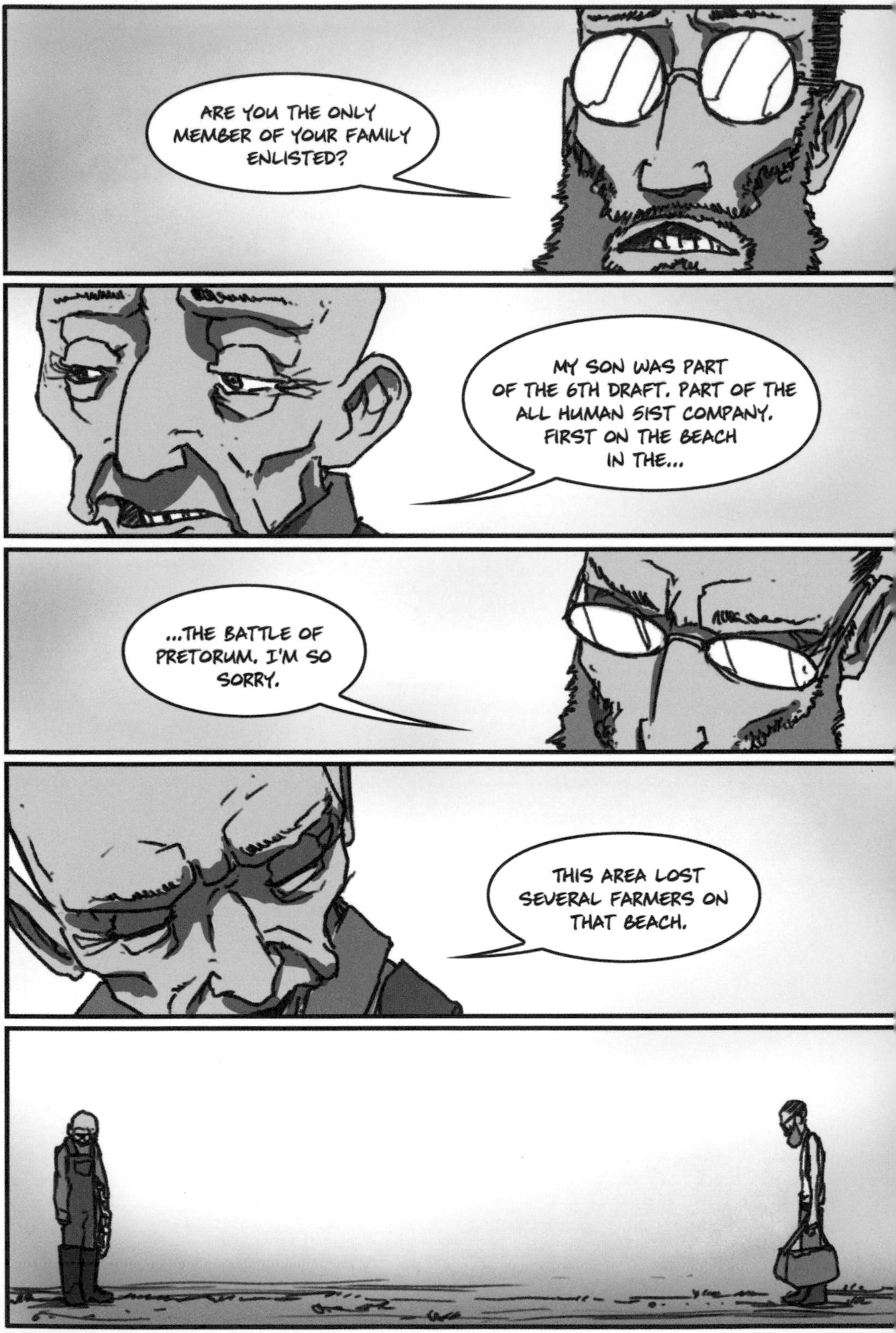
ARE YOU THE ONLY MEMBER OF YOUR FAMILY ENLISTED?
MY SON WAS PART OF THE 6TH DRAFT. PART OF THE ALL HUMAN 51ST COMPANY. FIRST ON THE BEACH IN THE...
...THE BATTLE OF PRETORUM. I'M SO SORRY.
THIS AREA LOST SEVERAL FARMERS ON THAT BEACH.

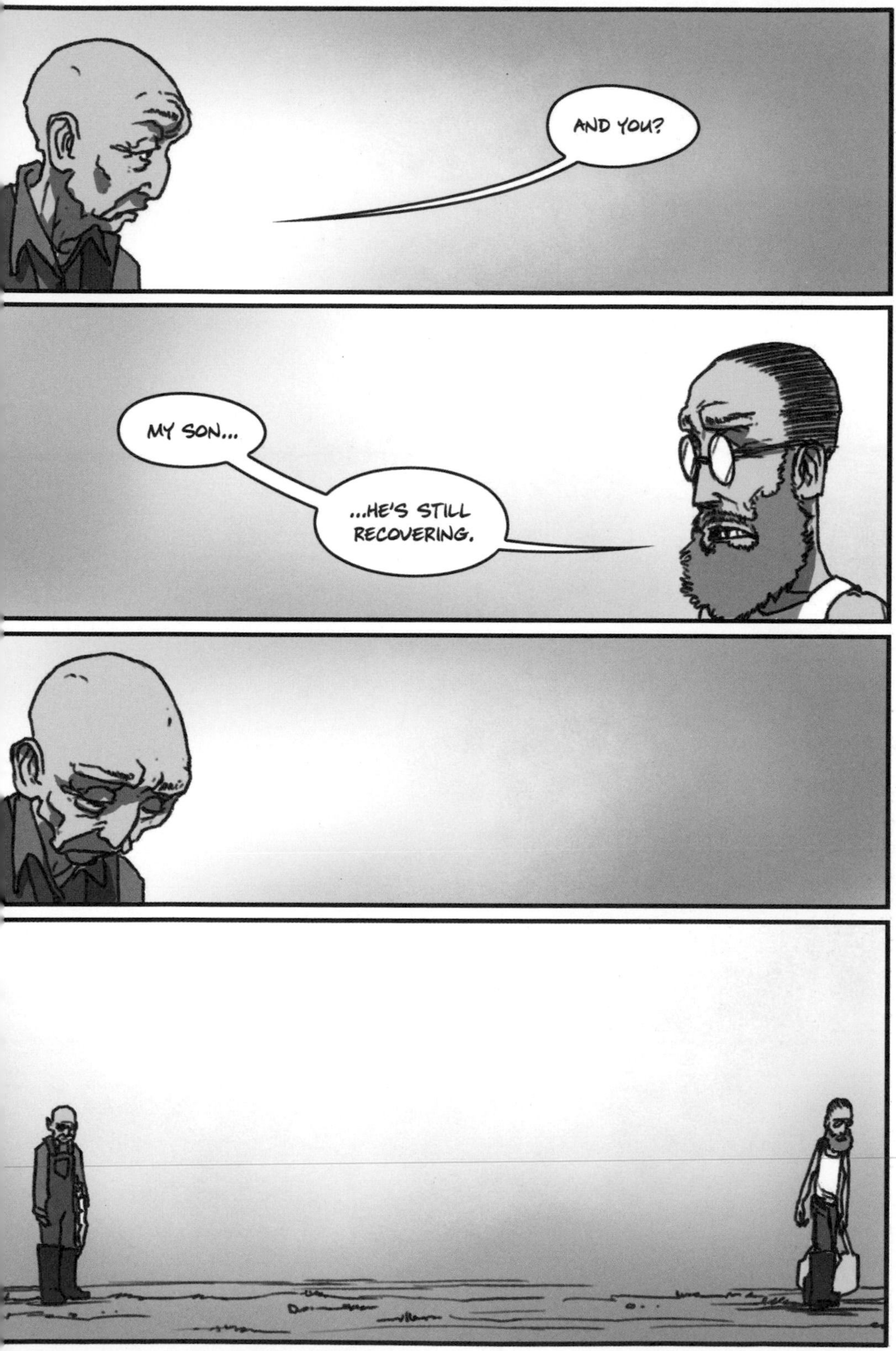
AND YOU?
MY SON...
...HE'S STILL RECOVERING.

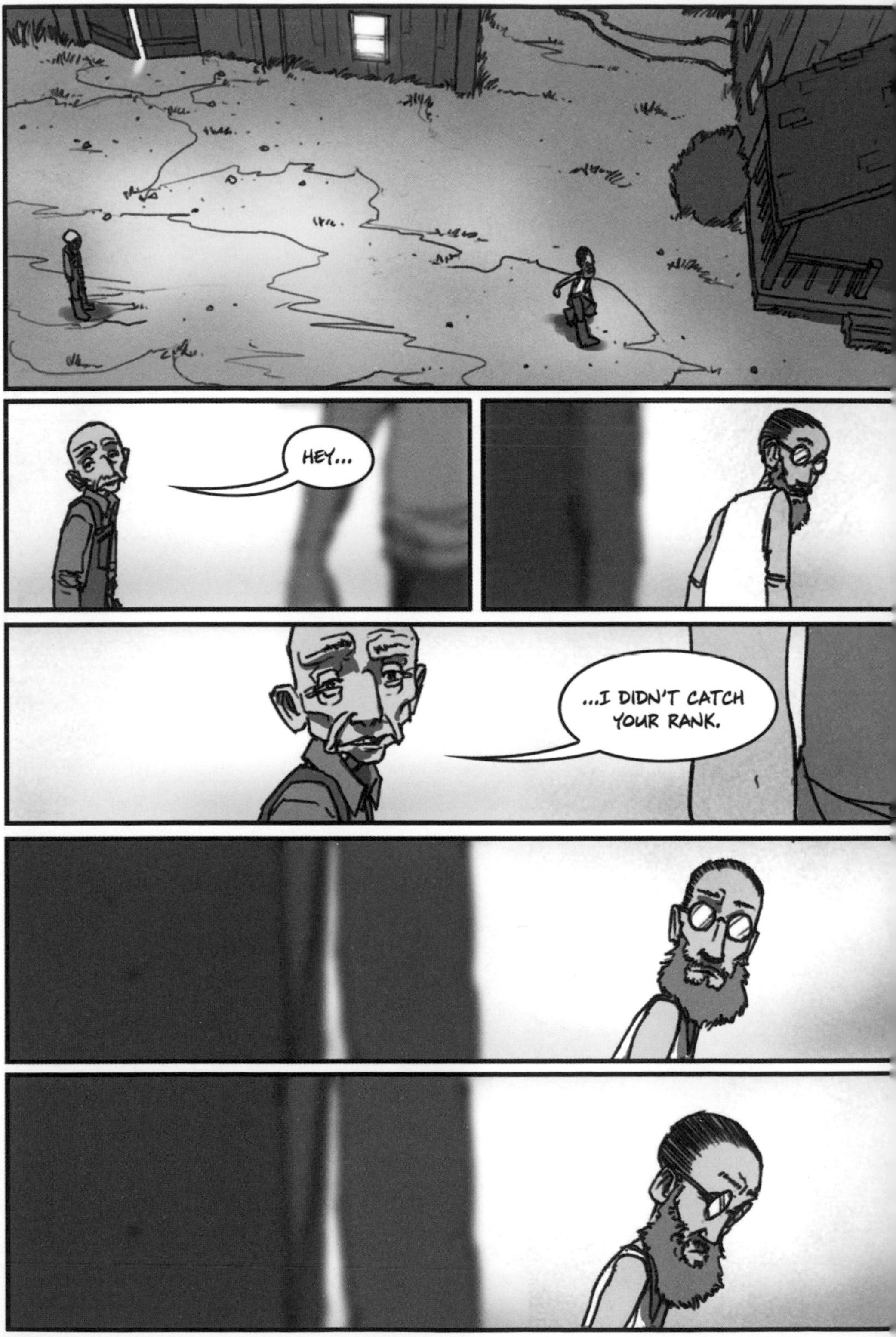
HEY...
...I DIDN'T CATCH YOUR RANK.

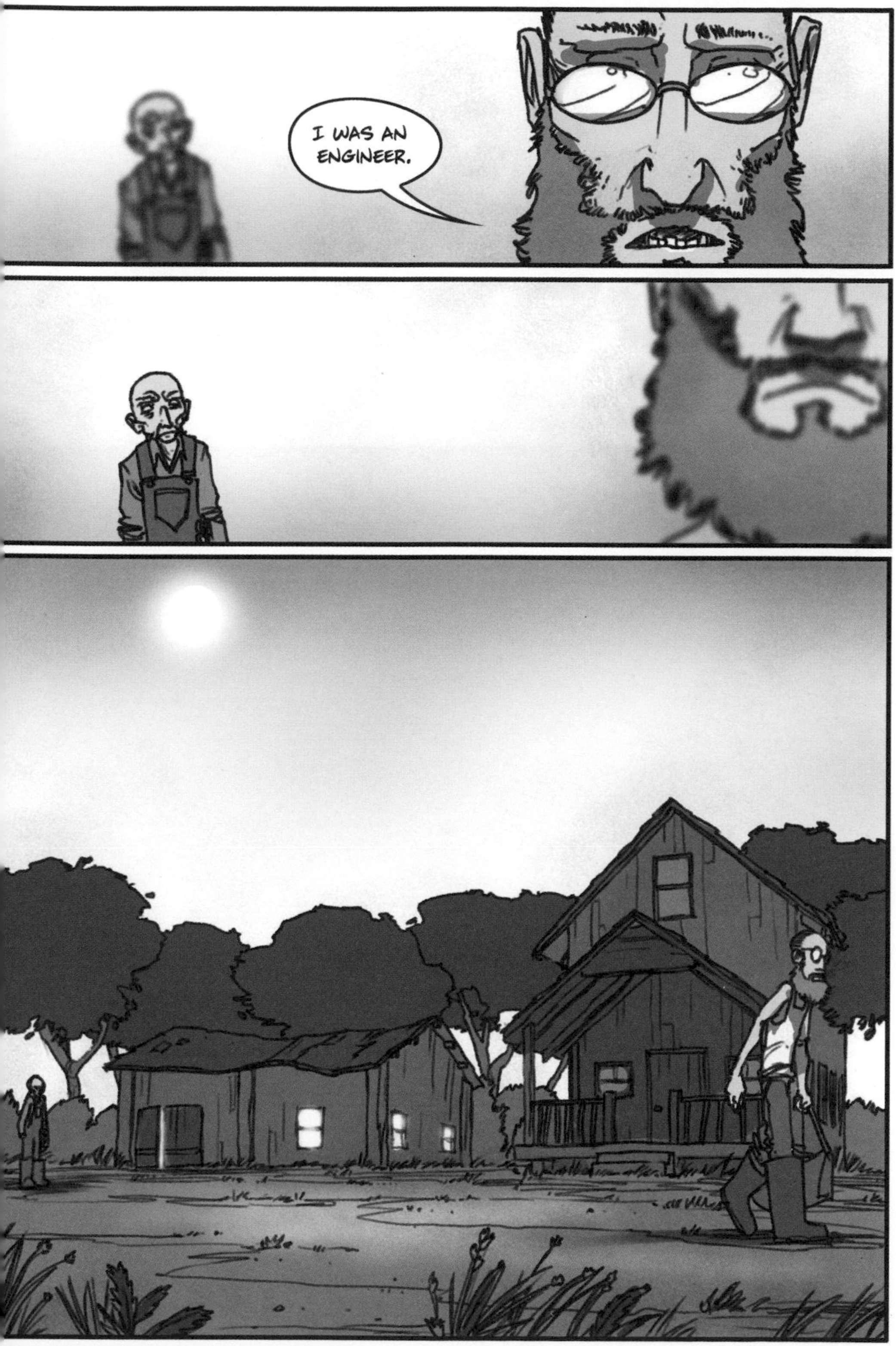
I WAS AN ENGINEER.

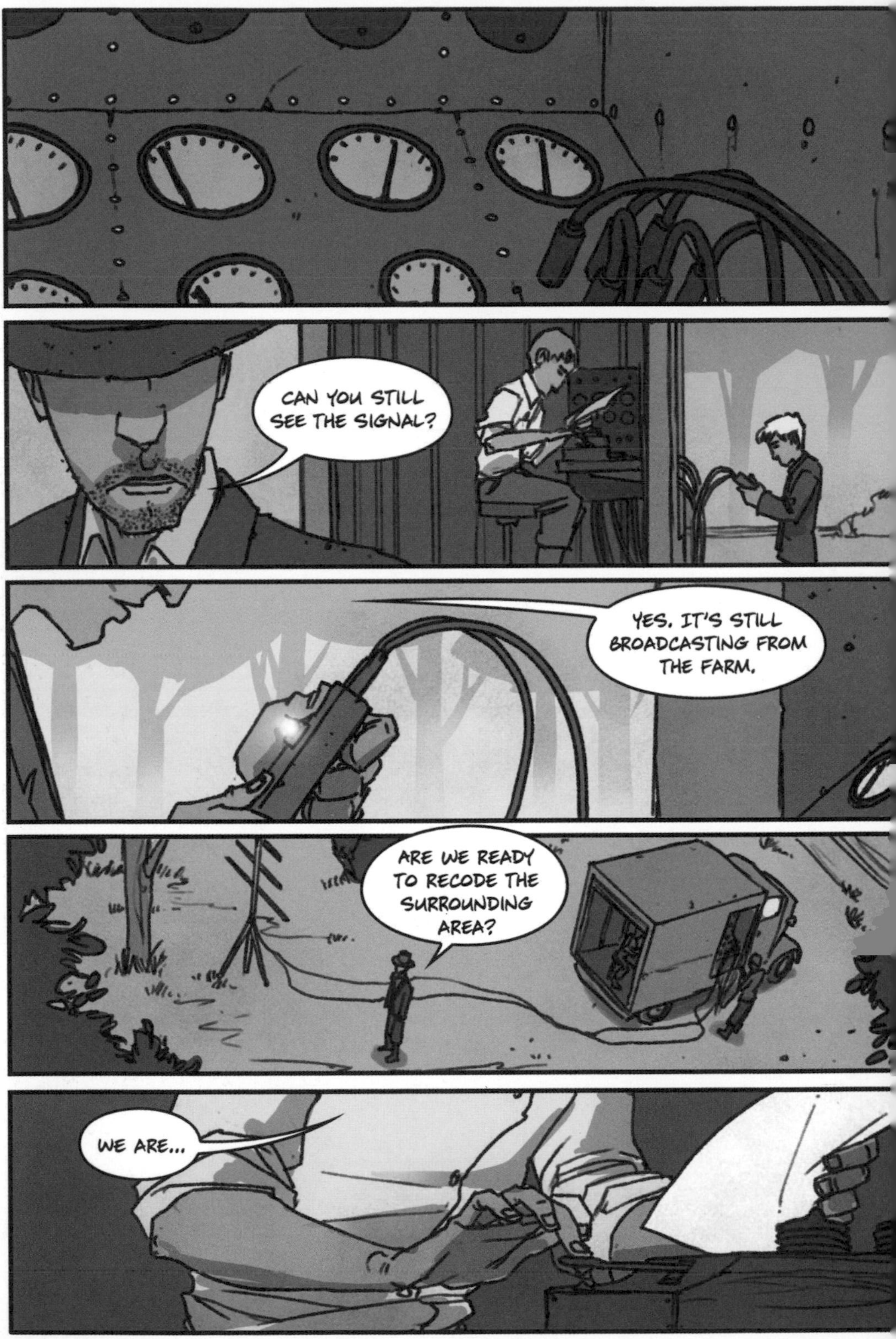
CAN YOU STILL SEE THE SIGNAL?
YES. IT'S STILL BROADCASTING FROM THE FARM.
ARE WE READY TO RECODE THE SURROUNDING AREA?
WE ARE...

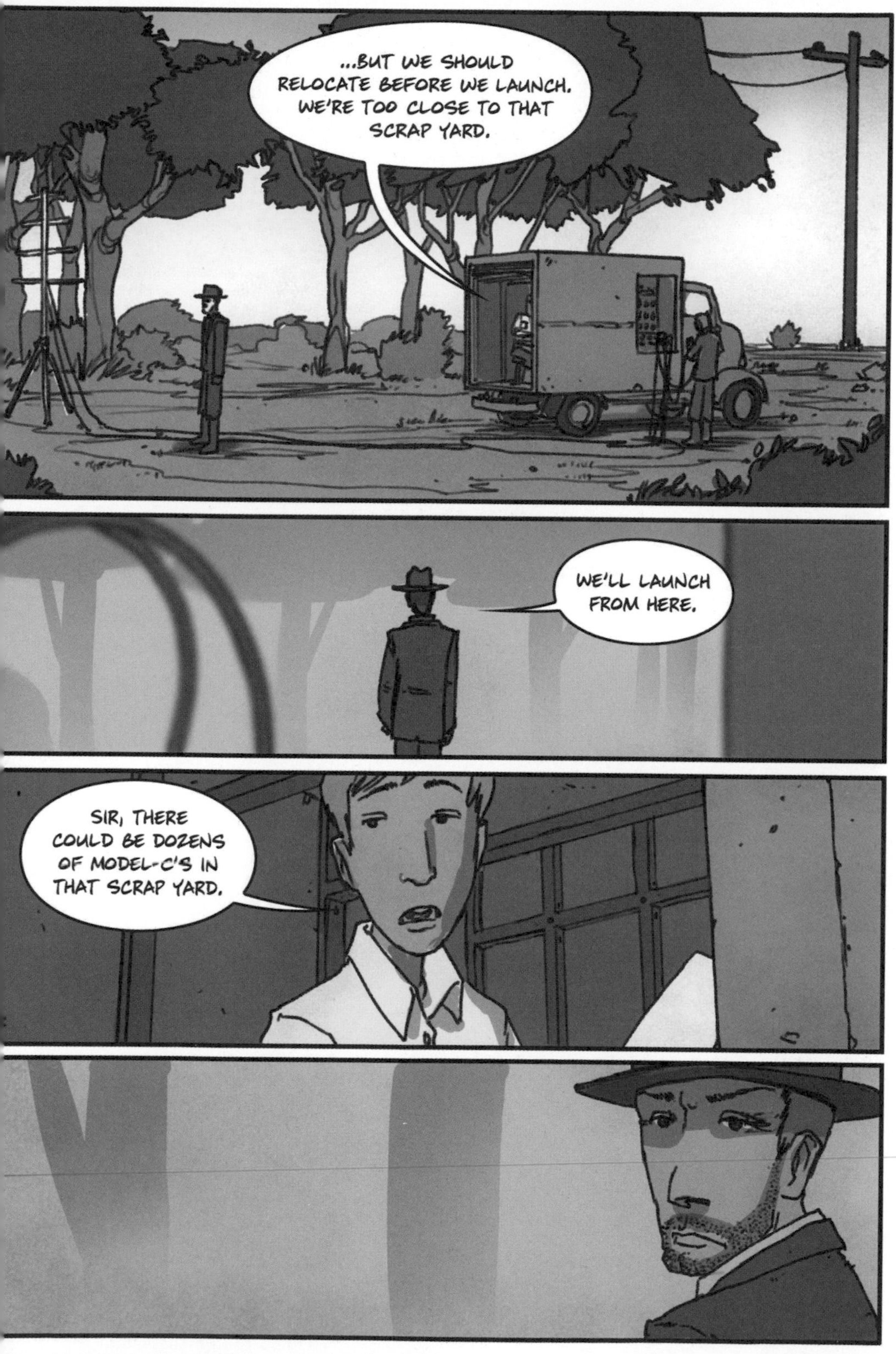
...BUT WE SHOULD RELOCATE BEFORE WE LAUNCH. WE'RE TOO CLOSE TO THAT SCRAP YARD.
WE'LL LAUNCH FROM HERE.
SIR, THERE COULD BE DOZENS OF MODEL-C'S IN THAT SCRAP YARD.

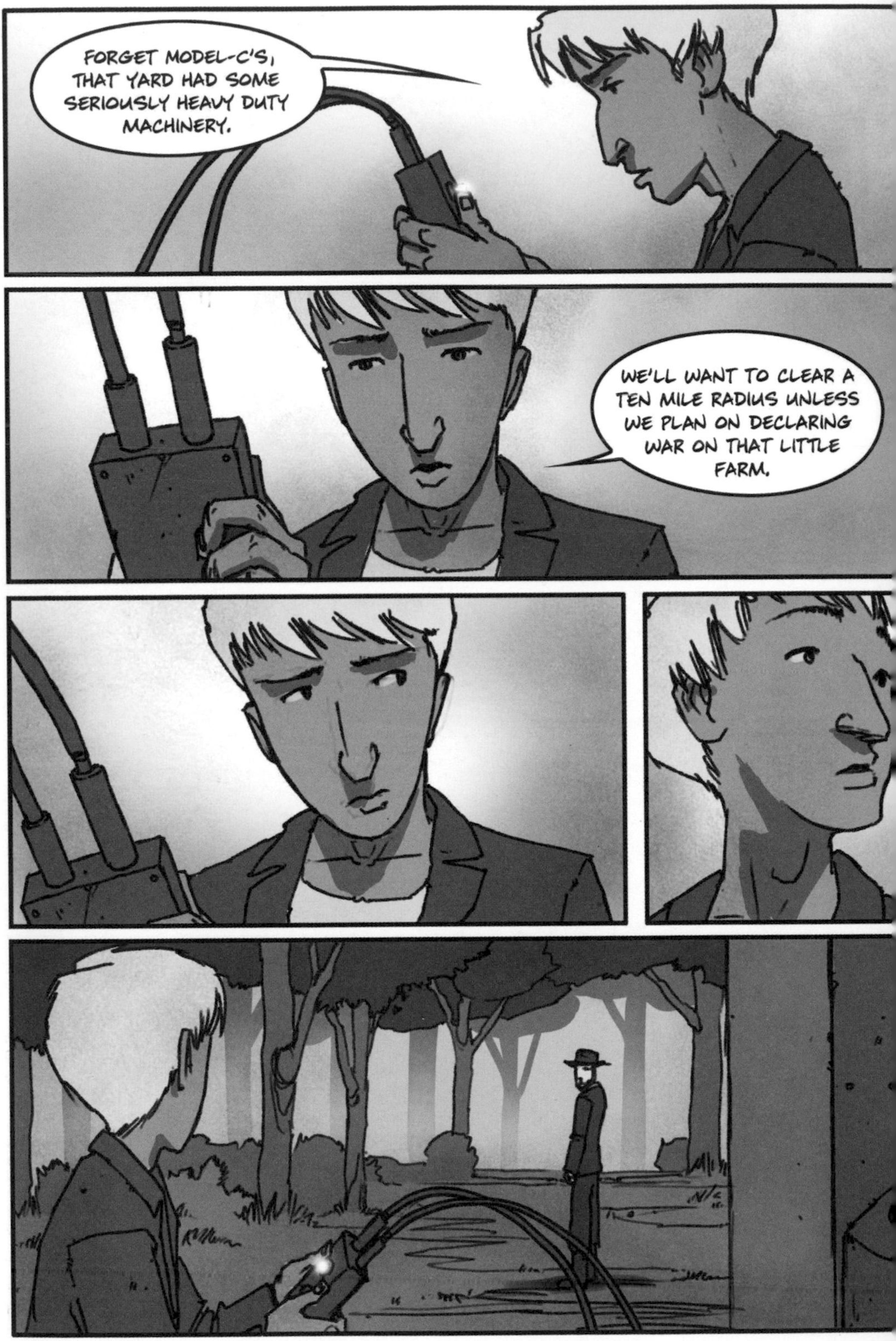
FORGET MODEL-C'S, THAT YARD HAD SOME SERIOUSLY HEAVY DUTY MACHINERY.
WE'LL WANT TO CLEAR A TEN MILE RADIUS UNLESS WE PLAN ON DECLARING WAR ON THAT LITTLE FARM.

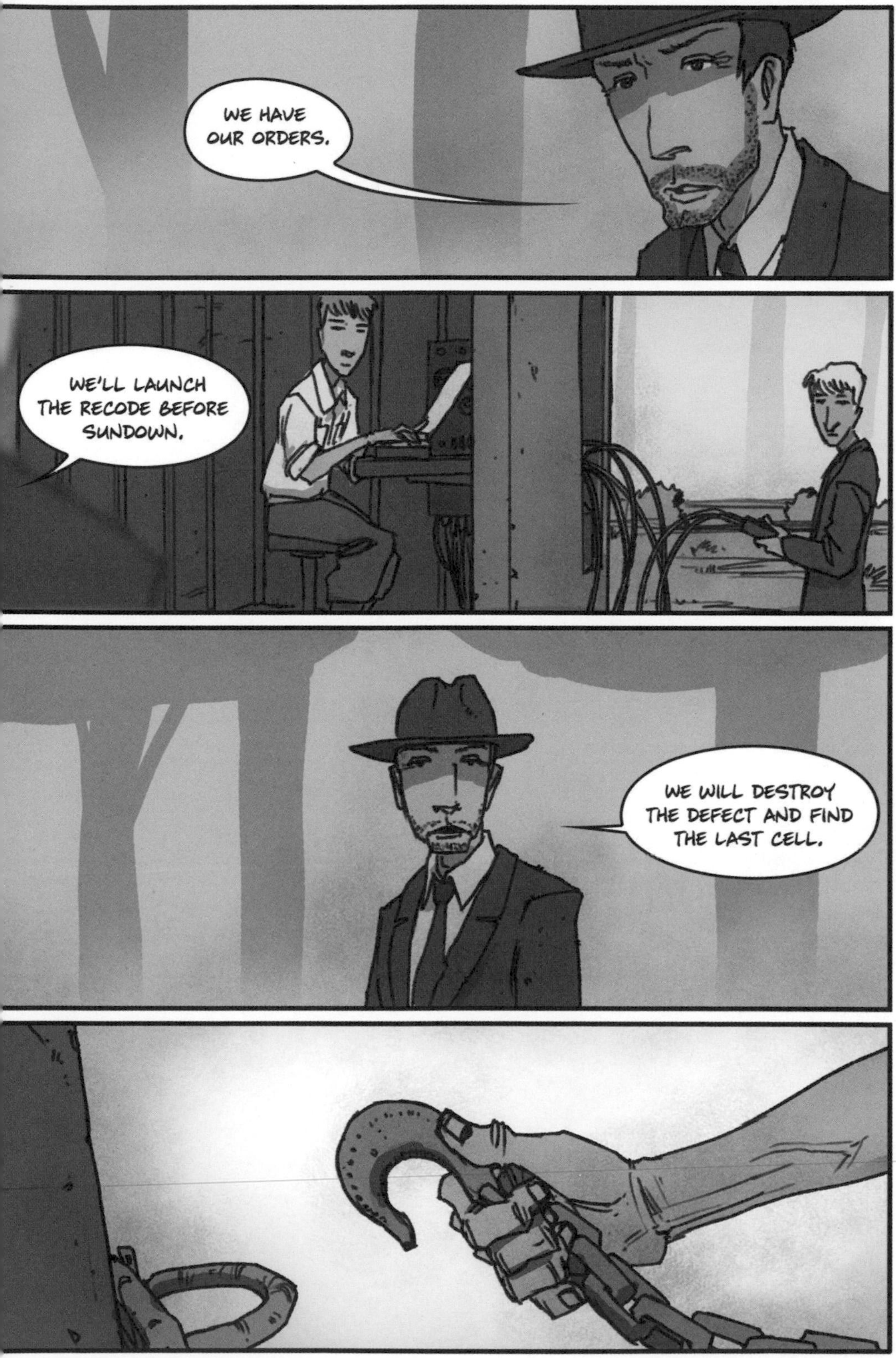
WE HAVE OUR ORDERS.
WE'LL LAUNCH THE RECODE BEFORE SUNDOWN.
WE WILL DESTROY THE DEFECT AND FIND THE LAST CELL.

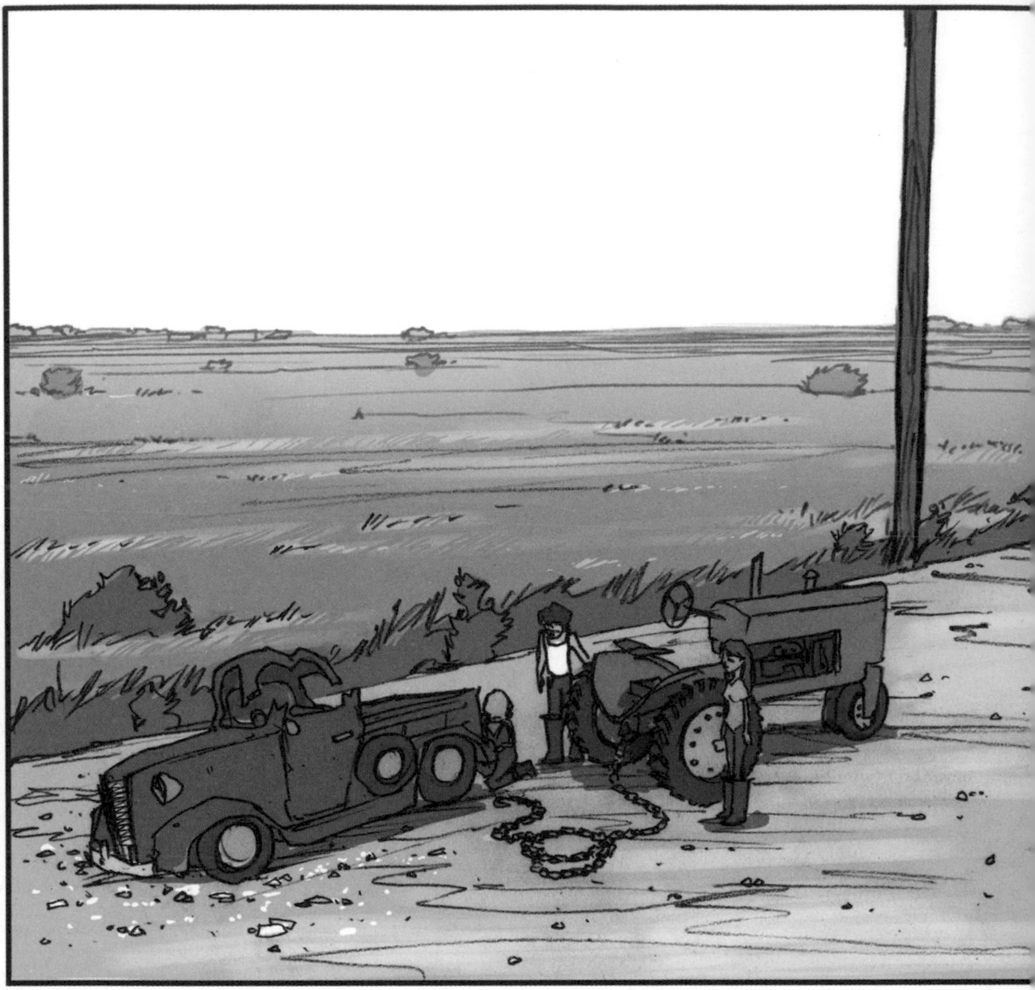

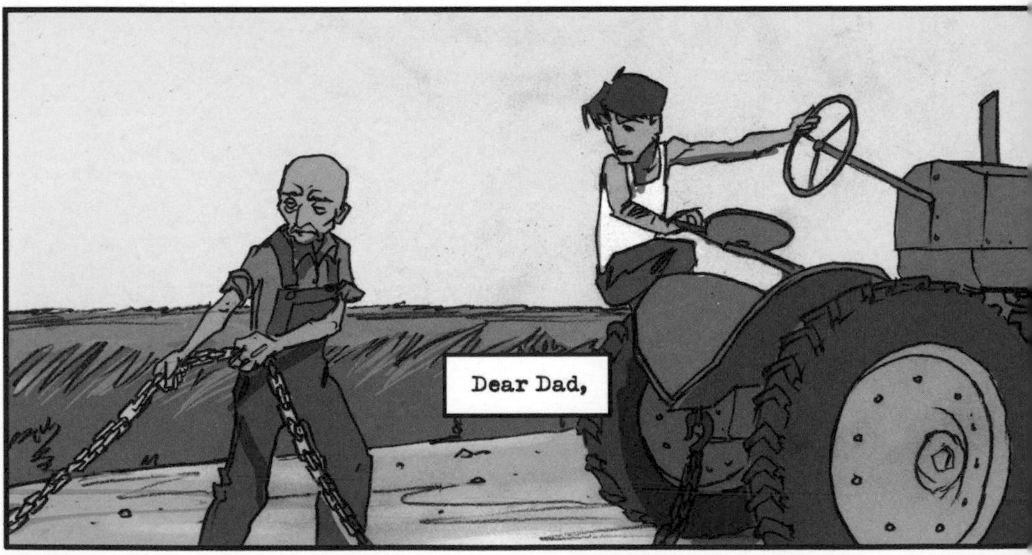
Dear Dad,

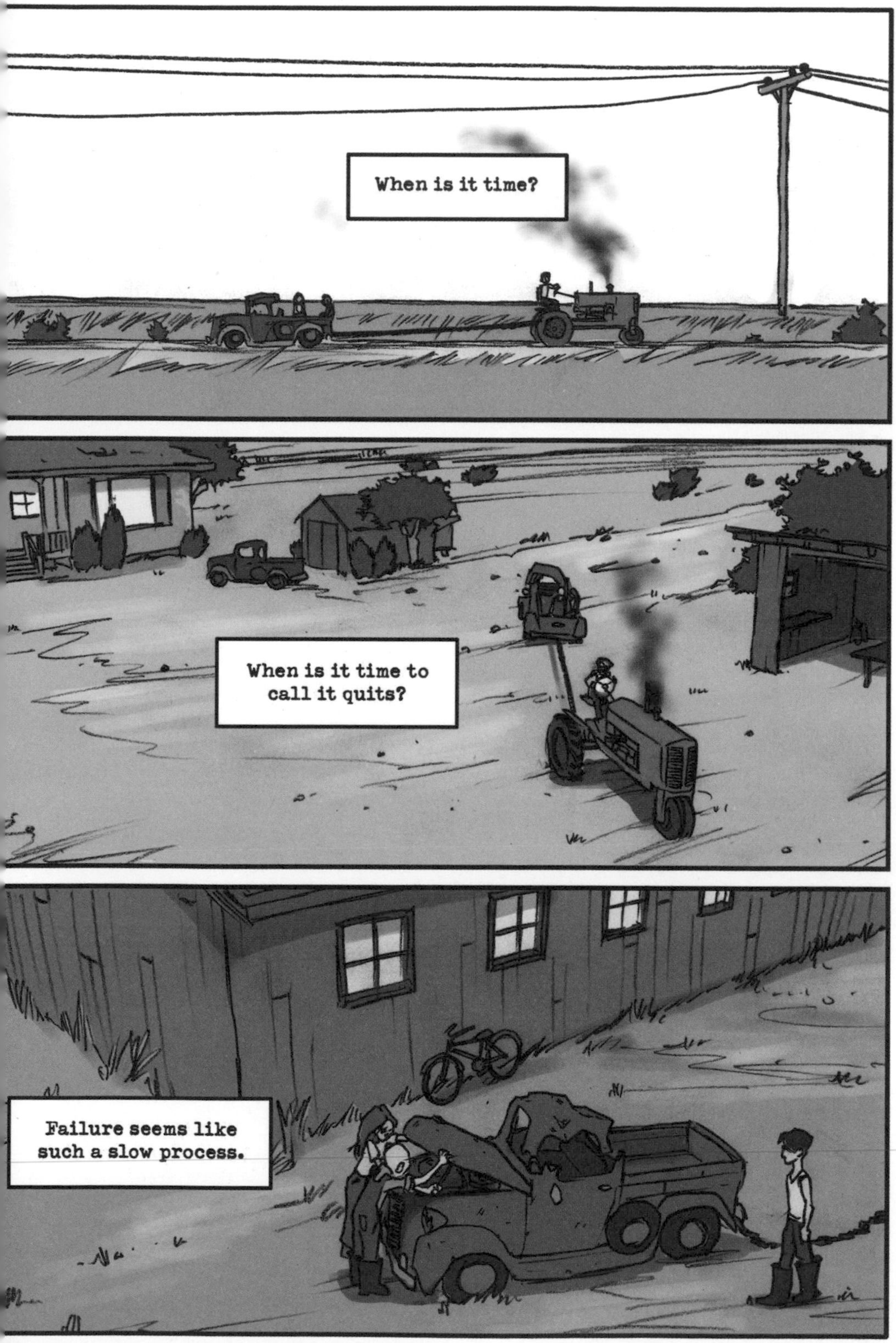
When is it time?
When is it time to call it quits?
Failure seems like such a slow process.

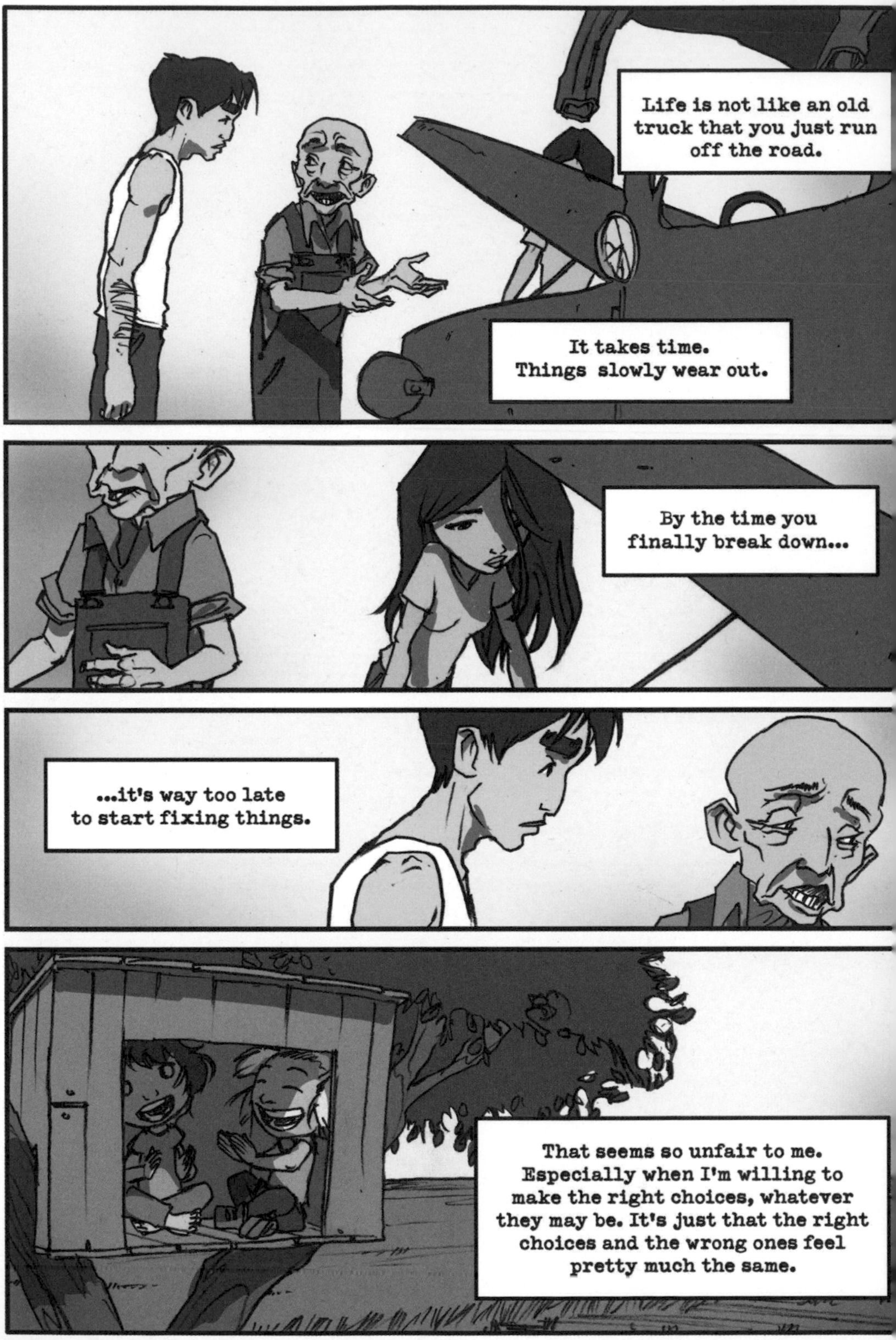
Life is not like an old truck that you just run off the road.
It takes time. Things slowly wear out.
By the time you finally break down...
...it's way too late to start fixing things.
That seems so unfair to me. Especially when I'm willing to make the right choices, whatever they may be. It's just that the right choices and the wrong ones feel pretty much the same.

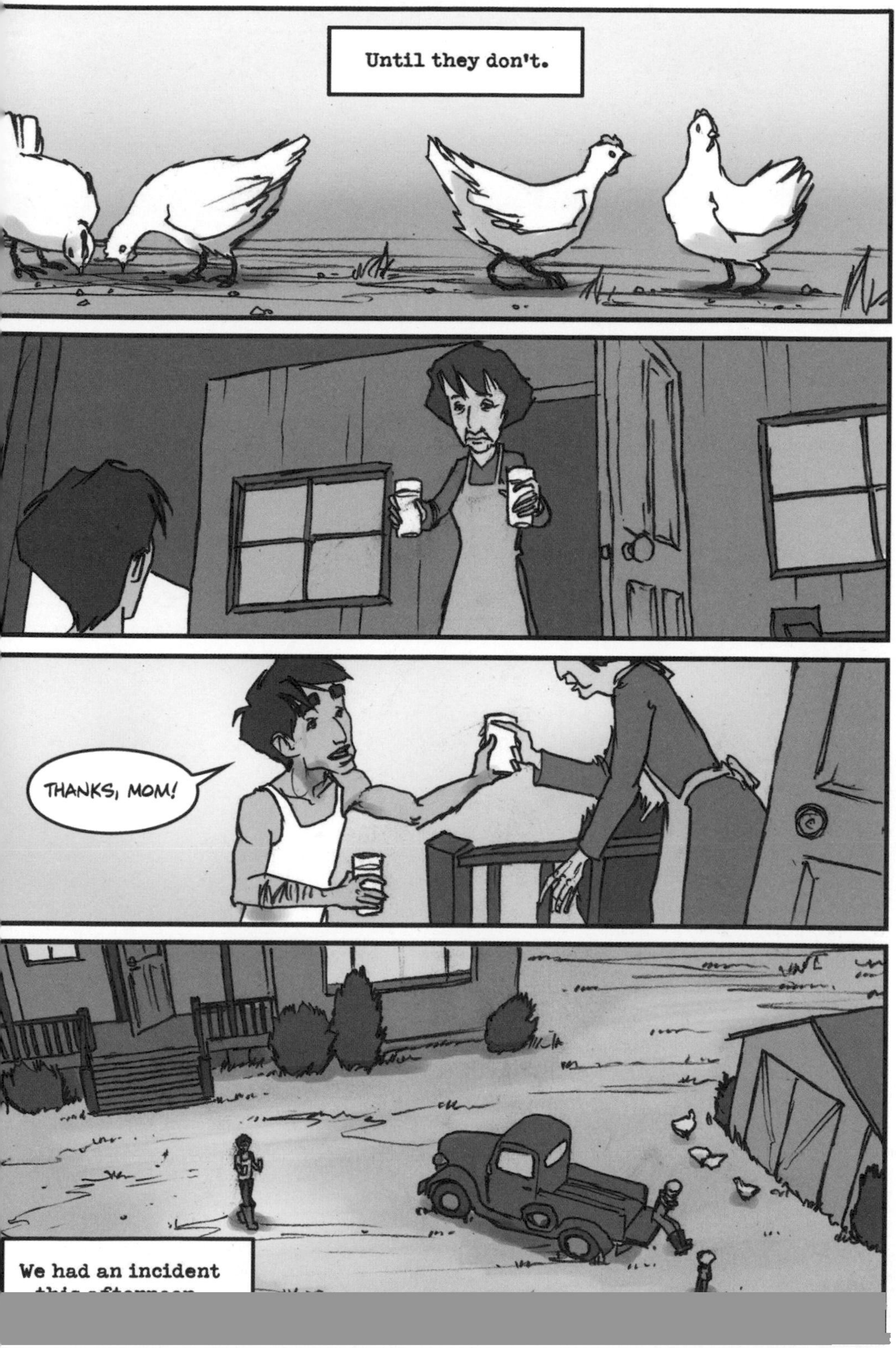
Until they don't.
THANKS, MOM!
We had an incident

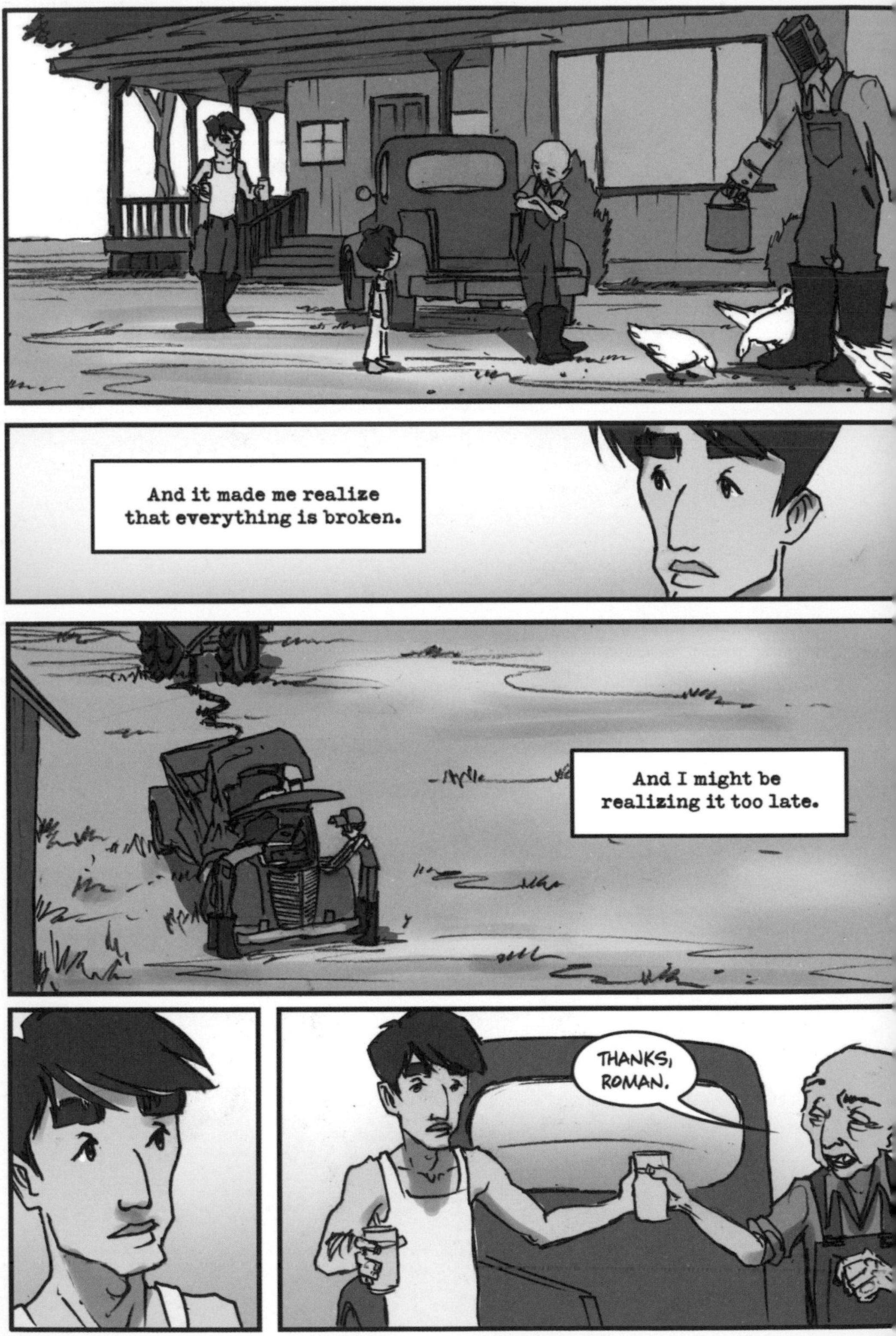
And it made me realize
that everything is broken.
And I might be
realizing it too late.
THANKS, ROMAN.

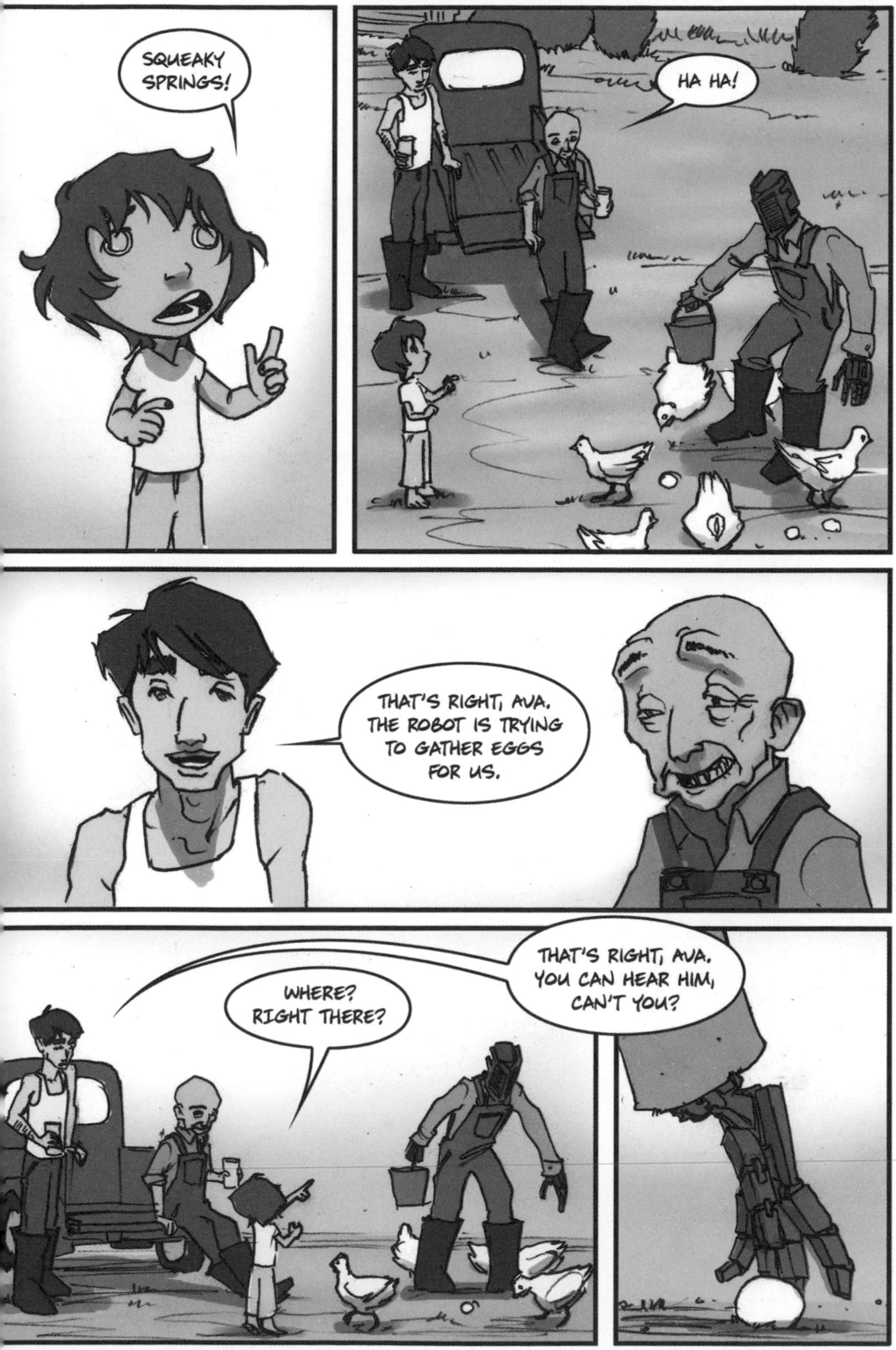
SQUEAKY SPRINGS!
HA HA!
THAT'S RIGHT, AVA. THE ROBOT IS TRYING TO GATHER EGGS FOR US.
THAT'S RIGHT, AVA. YOU CAN HEAR HIM, CAN'T YOU?
WHERE? RIGHT THERE?

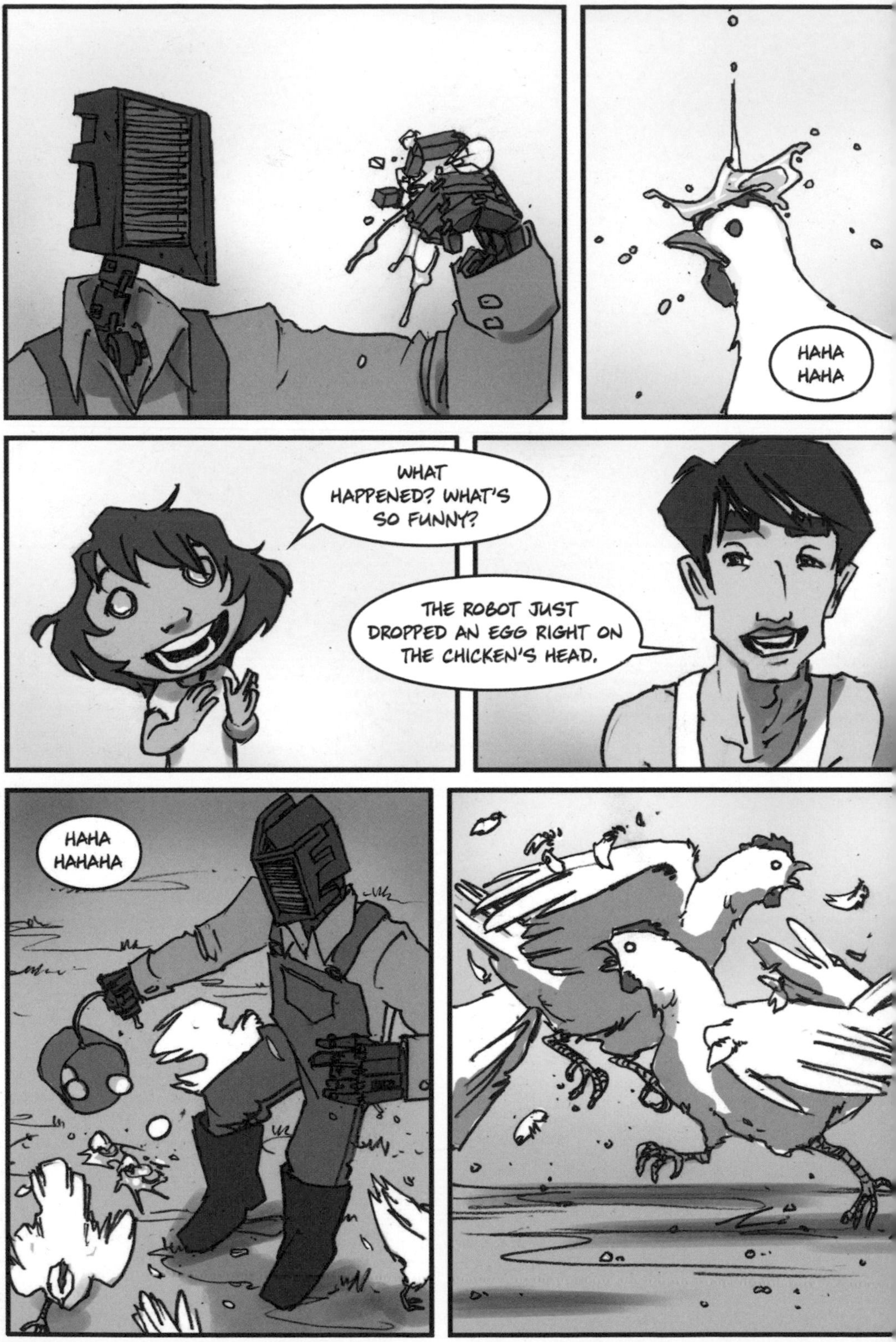
HAHA HAHA
WHAT HAPPENED? WHAT'S SO FUNNY?
THE ROBOT JUST DROPPED AN EGG RIGHT ON THE CHICKEN'S HEAD.
HAHA HAHAHA

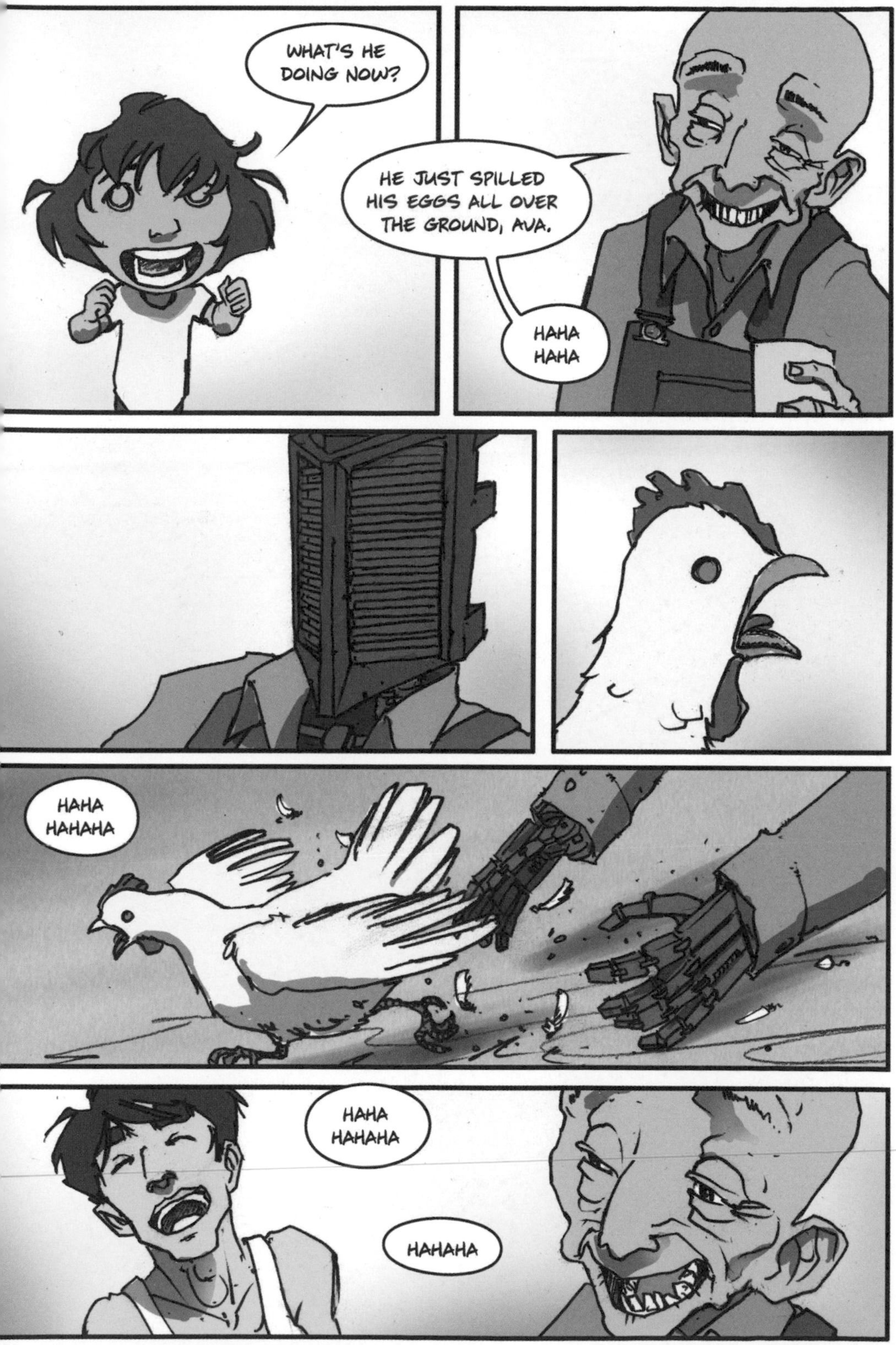
WHAT'S HE DOING NOW?
HE JUST SPILLED HIS EGGS ALL OVER THE GROUND, AVA.
HAHA HAHA
HAHA HAHAHA
HAHA HAHAHA
HAHAHA

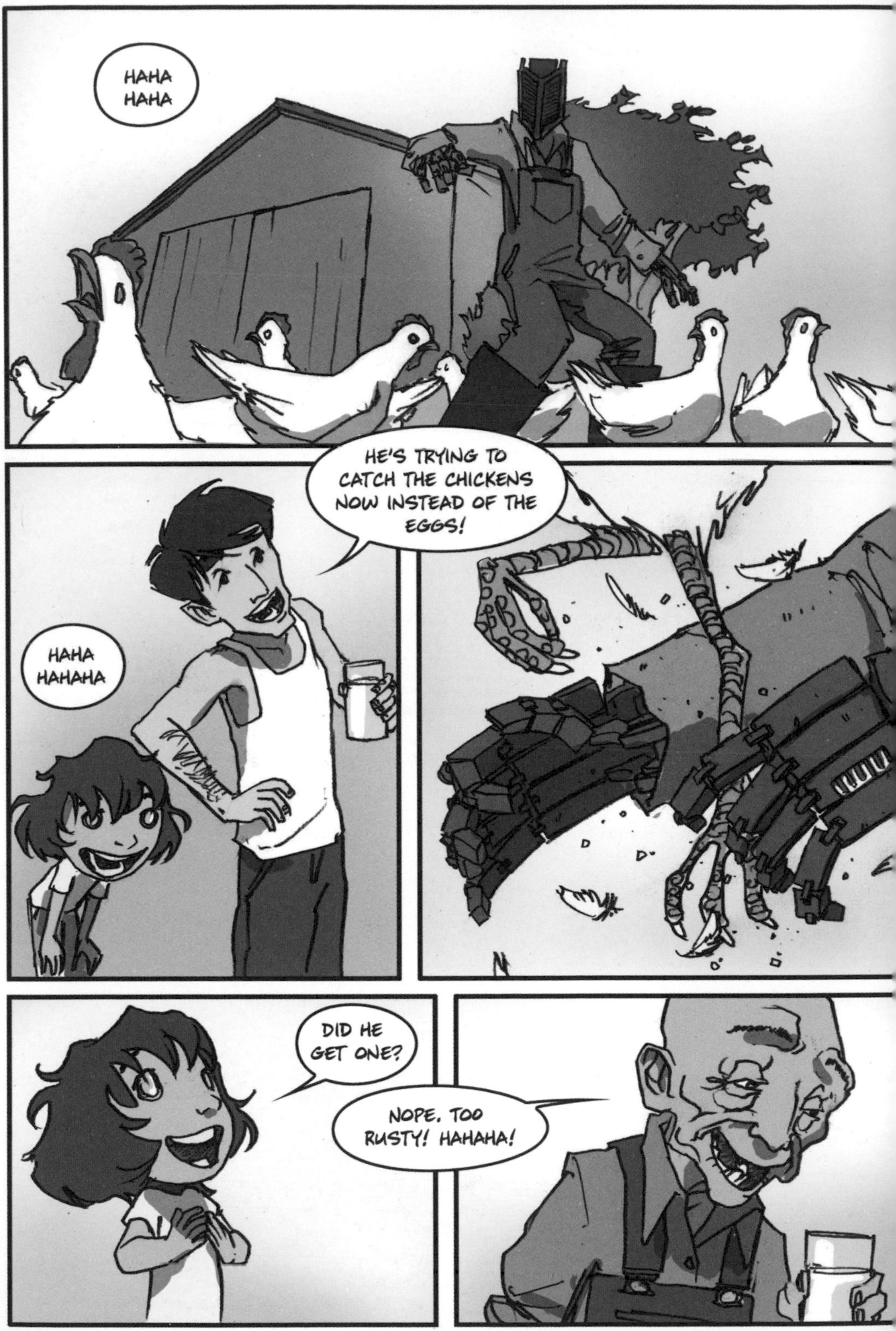
HAHA HAHA
HE'S TRYING TO CATCH THE CHICKENS NOW INSTEAD OF THE EGGS!
HAHA HAHAHA
DID HE GET ONE?
NOPE. TOO RUSTY! HAHAHA!

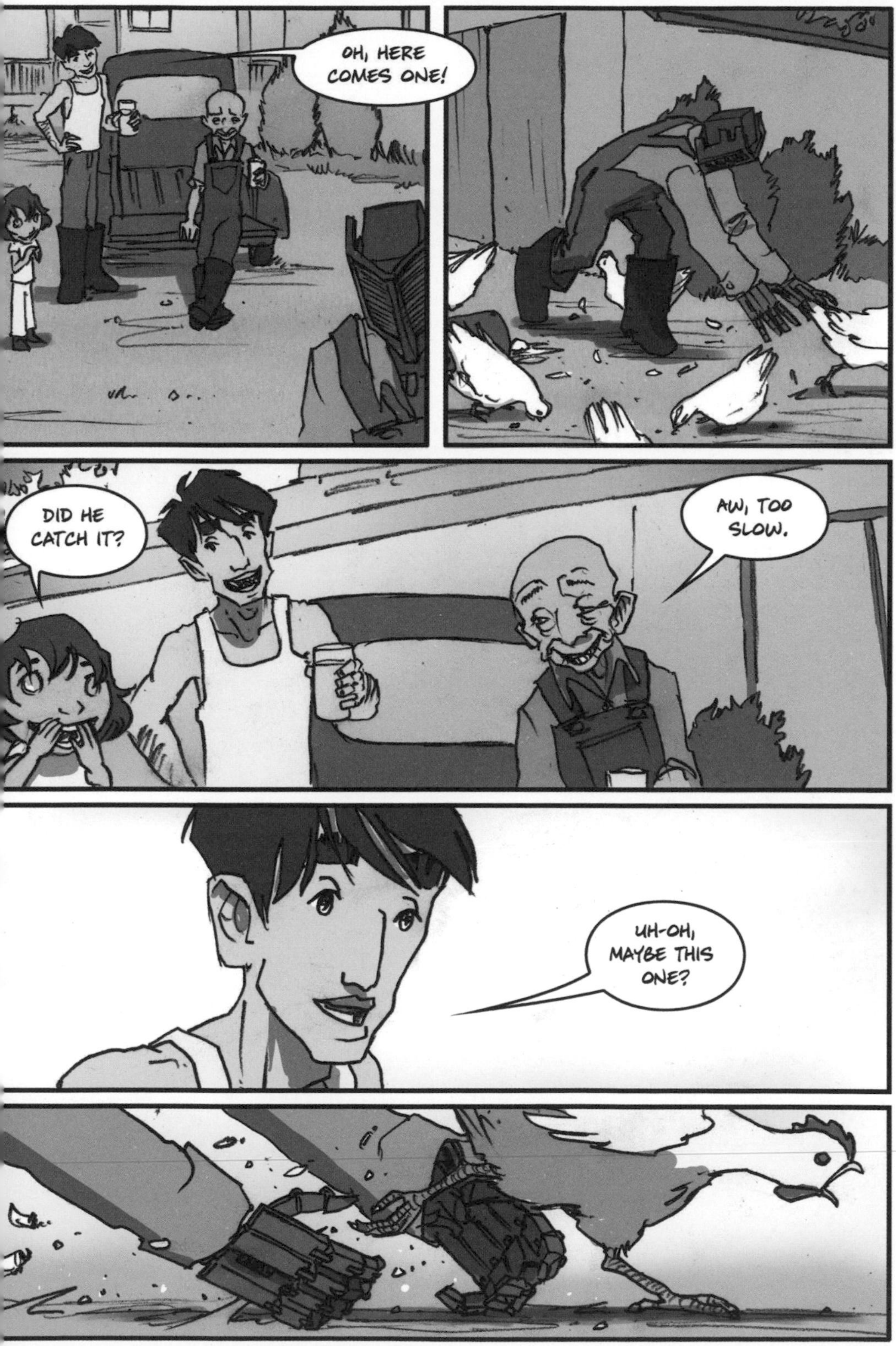
OH, HERE COMES ONE!
DID HE CATCH IT?
AW, TOO SLOW.
UH-OH, MAYBE THIS ONE?

DID HE GET IT?

AW, NOT QUITE!

ALMOST. HA HA!

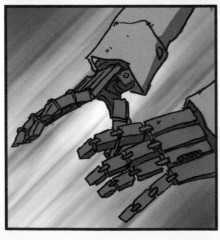

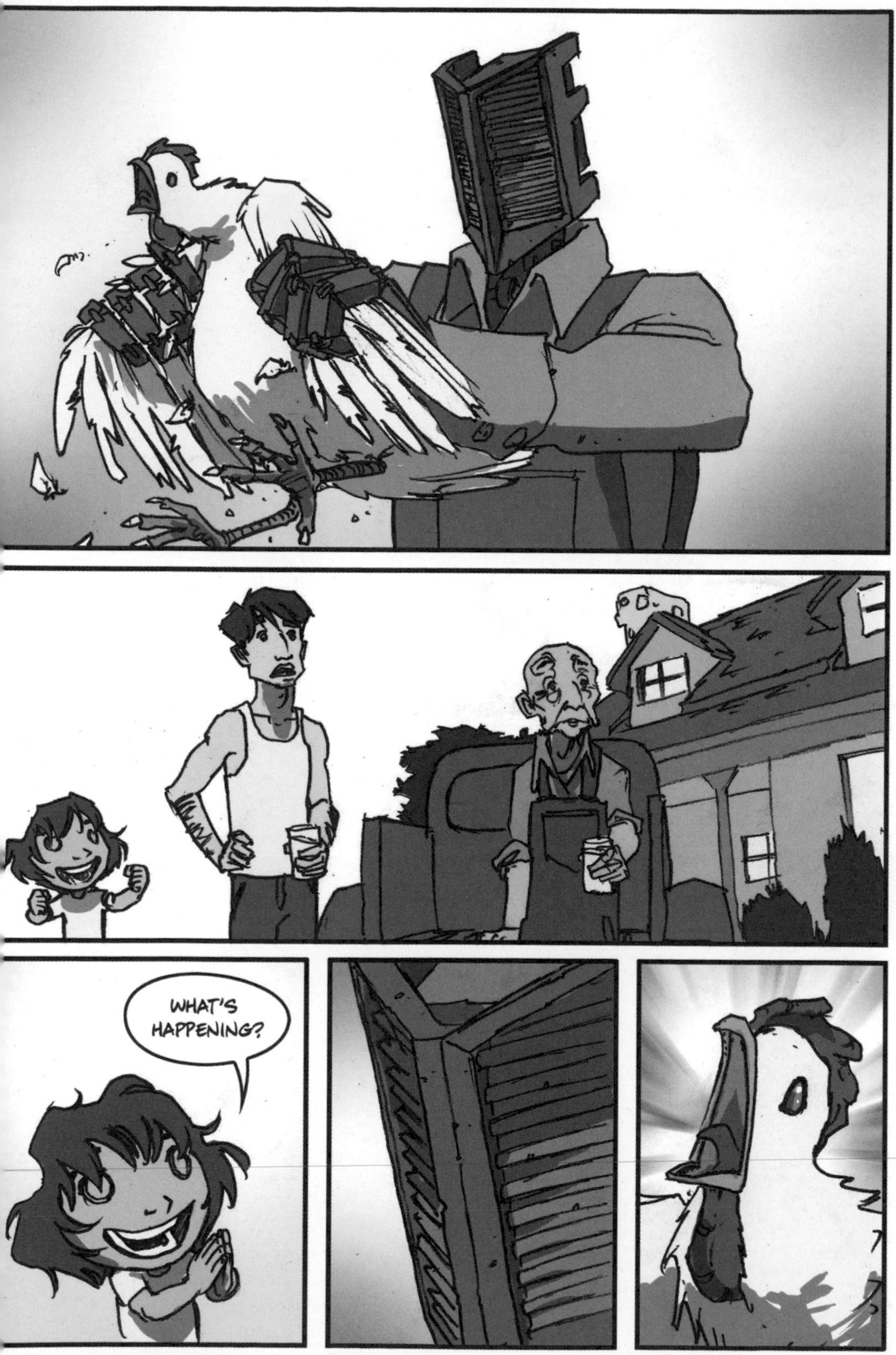
WHAT'S
HAPPENING?

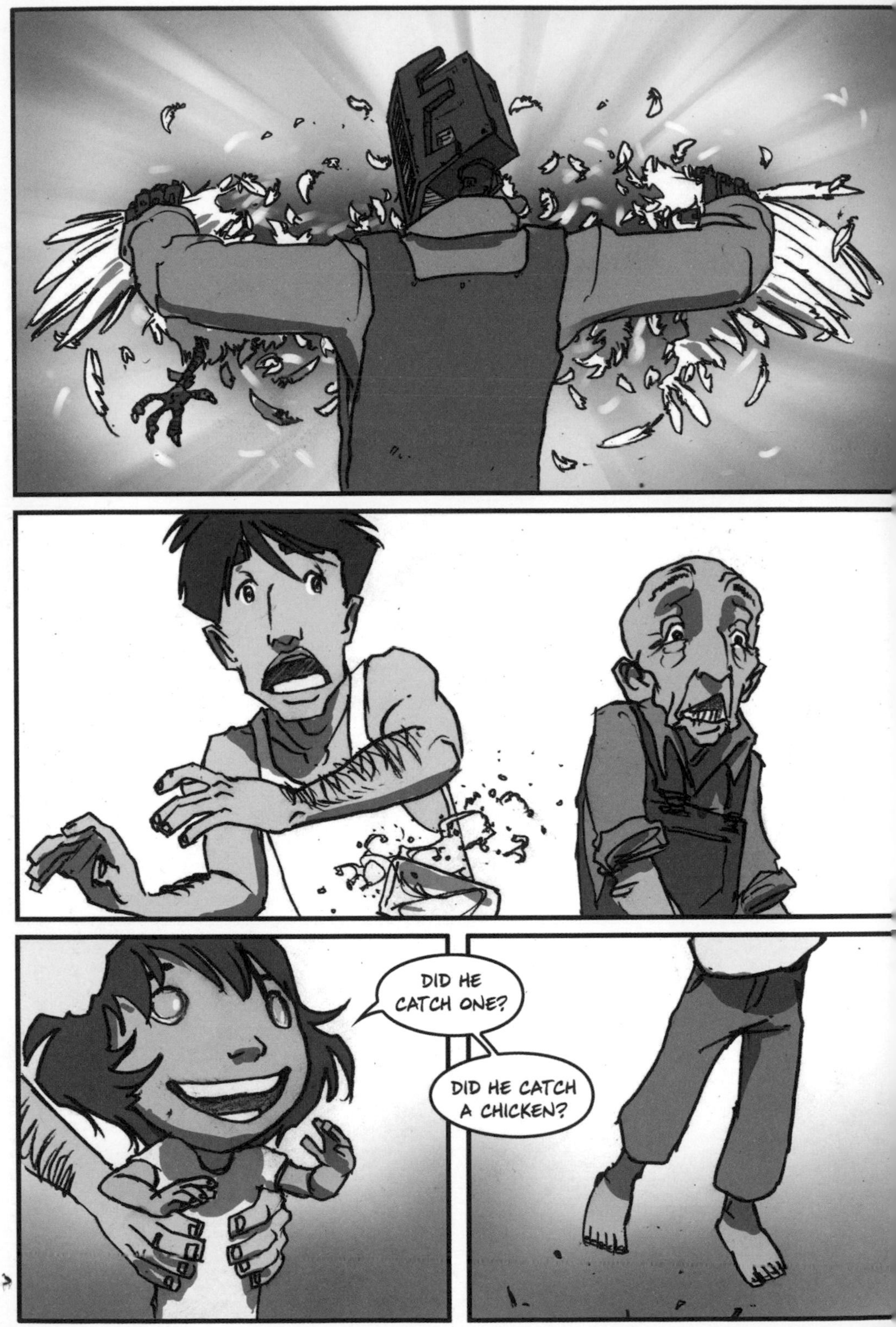
DID HE
CATCH ONE?
DID HE CATCH
A CHICKEN?

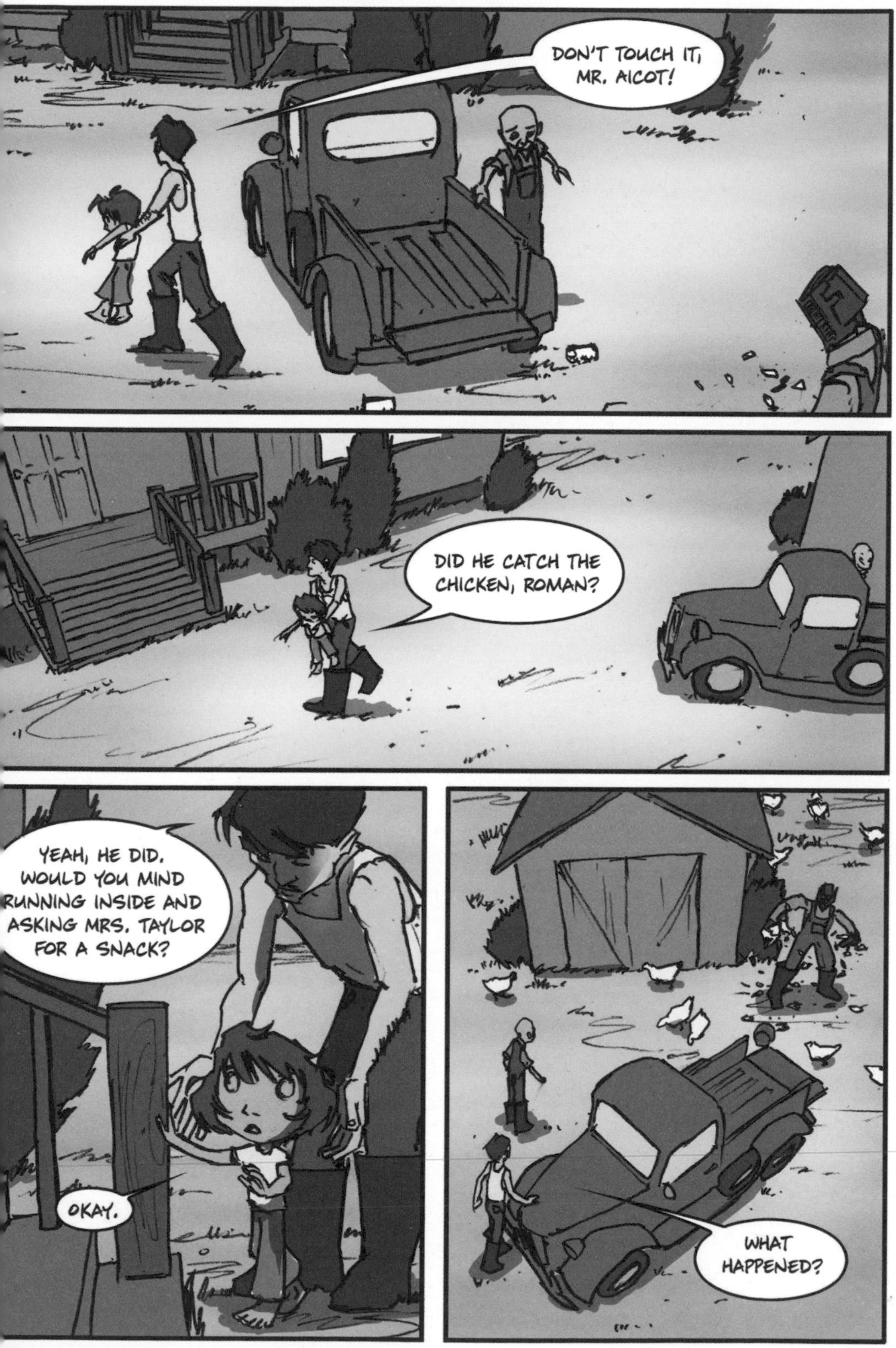
DON'T TOUCH IT, MR. AICOT!
DID HE CATCH THE CHICKEN, ROMAN?
YEAH, HE DID. WOULD YOU MIND RUNNING INSIDE AND ASKING MRS. TAYLOR FOR A SNACK?
OKAY.
WHAT HAPPENED?

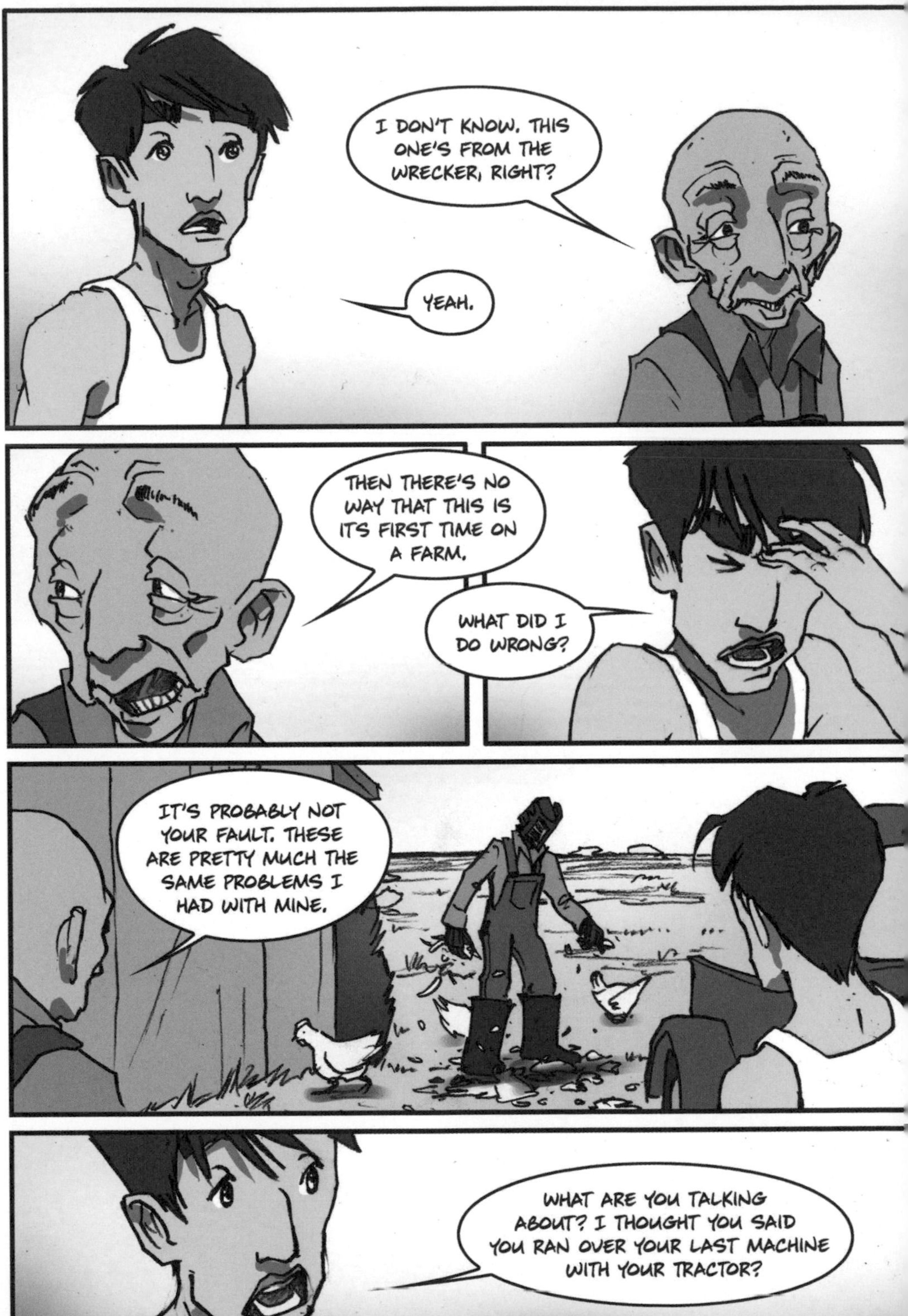
I DON'T KNOW. THIS ONE'S FROM THE WRECKER, RIGHT?
YEAH.
THEN THERE'S NO WAY THAT THIS IS ITS FIRST TIME ON A FARM.
WHAT DID I DO WRONG?
IT'S PROBABLY NOT YOUR FAULT. THESE ARE PRETTY MUCH THE SAME PROBLEMS I HAD WITH MINE.
WHAT ARE YOU TALKING ABOUT? I THOUGHT YOU SAID YOU RAN OVER YOUR LAST MACHINE WITH YOUR TRACTOR?

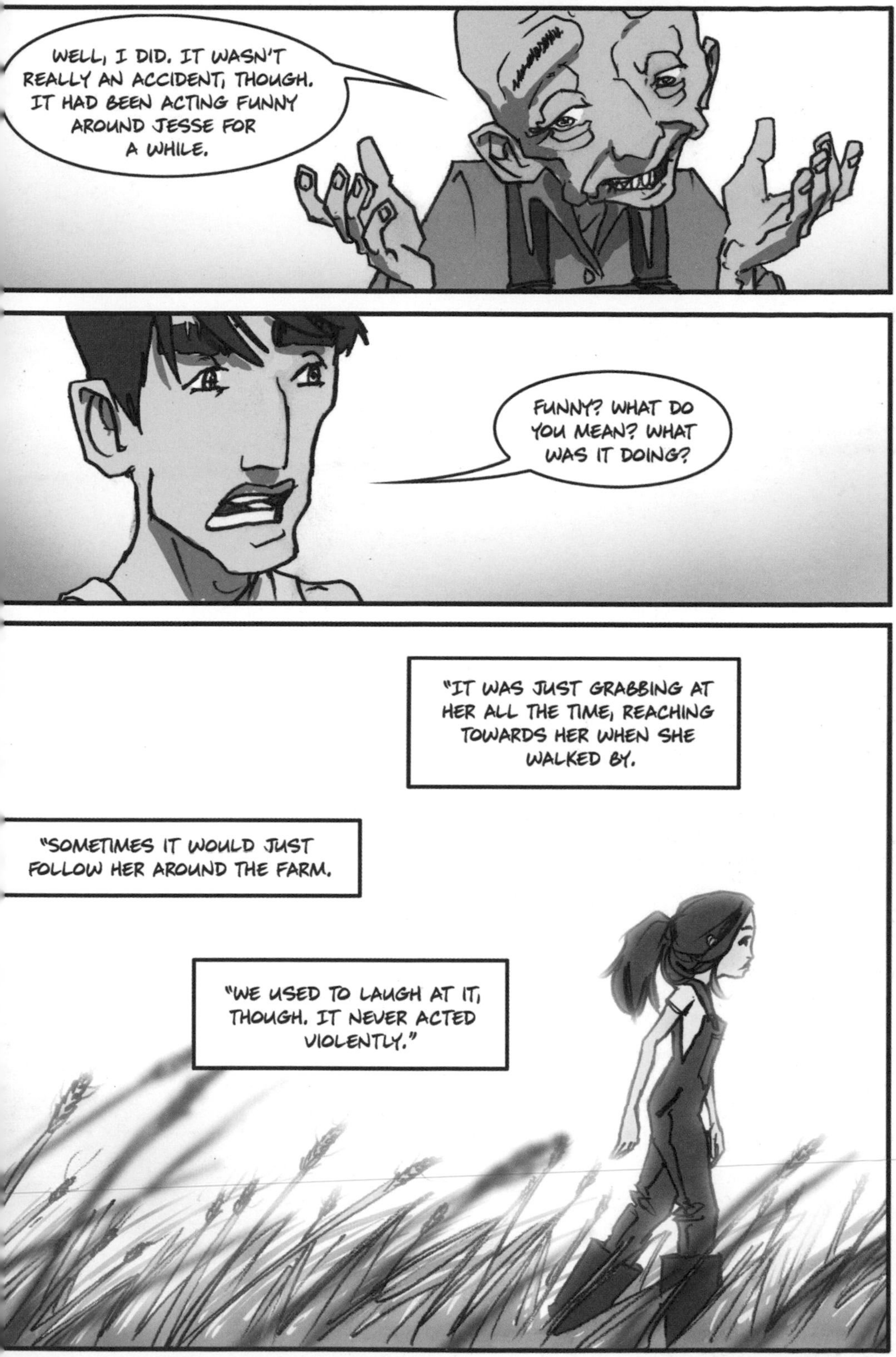
WELL, I DID. IT WASN'T REALLY AN ACCIDENT, THOUGH. IT HAD BEEN ACTING FUNNY AROUND JESSE FOR A WHILE.
FUNNY? WHAT DO YOU MEAN? WHAT WAS IT DOING?
"IT WAS JUST GRABBING AT HER ALL THE TIME, REACHING TOWARDS HER WHEN SHE WALKED BY.
"SOMETIMES IT WOULD JUST FOLLOW HER AROUND THE FARM.
"WE USED TO LAUGH AT IT, THOUGH. IT NEVER ACTED VIOLENTLY."

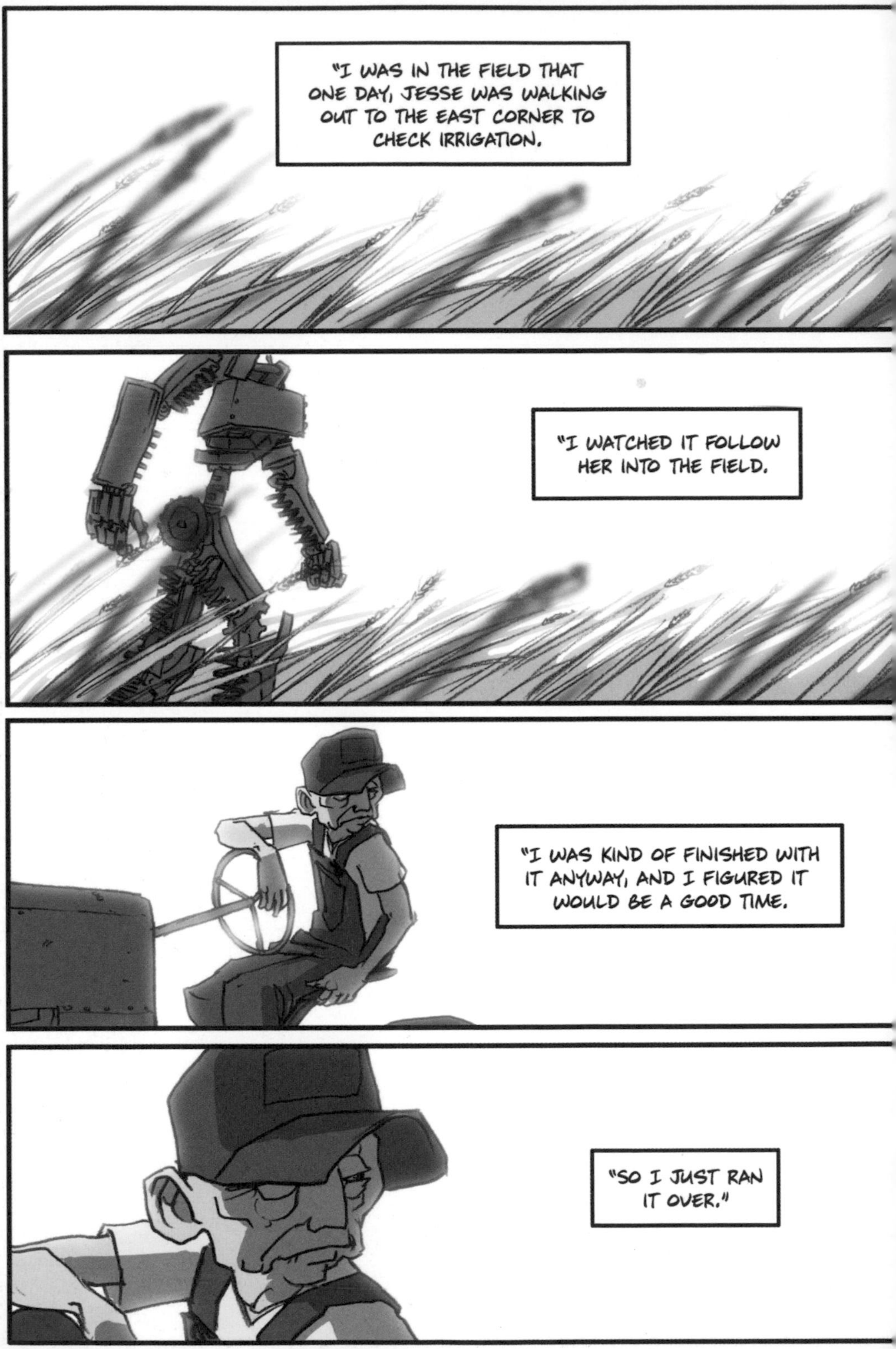
"I WAS IN THE FIELD THAT ONE DAY, JESSE WAS WALKING OUT TO THE EAST CORNER TO CHECK IRRIGATION.
"I WATCHED IT FOLLOW HER INTO THE FIELD.
"I WAS KIND OF FINISHED WITH IT ANYWAY, AND I FIGURED IT WOULD BE A GOOD TIME.
"SO I JUST RAN IT OVER."

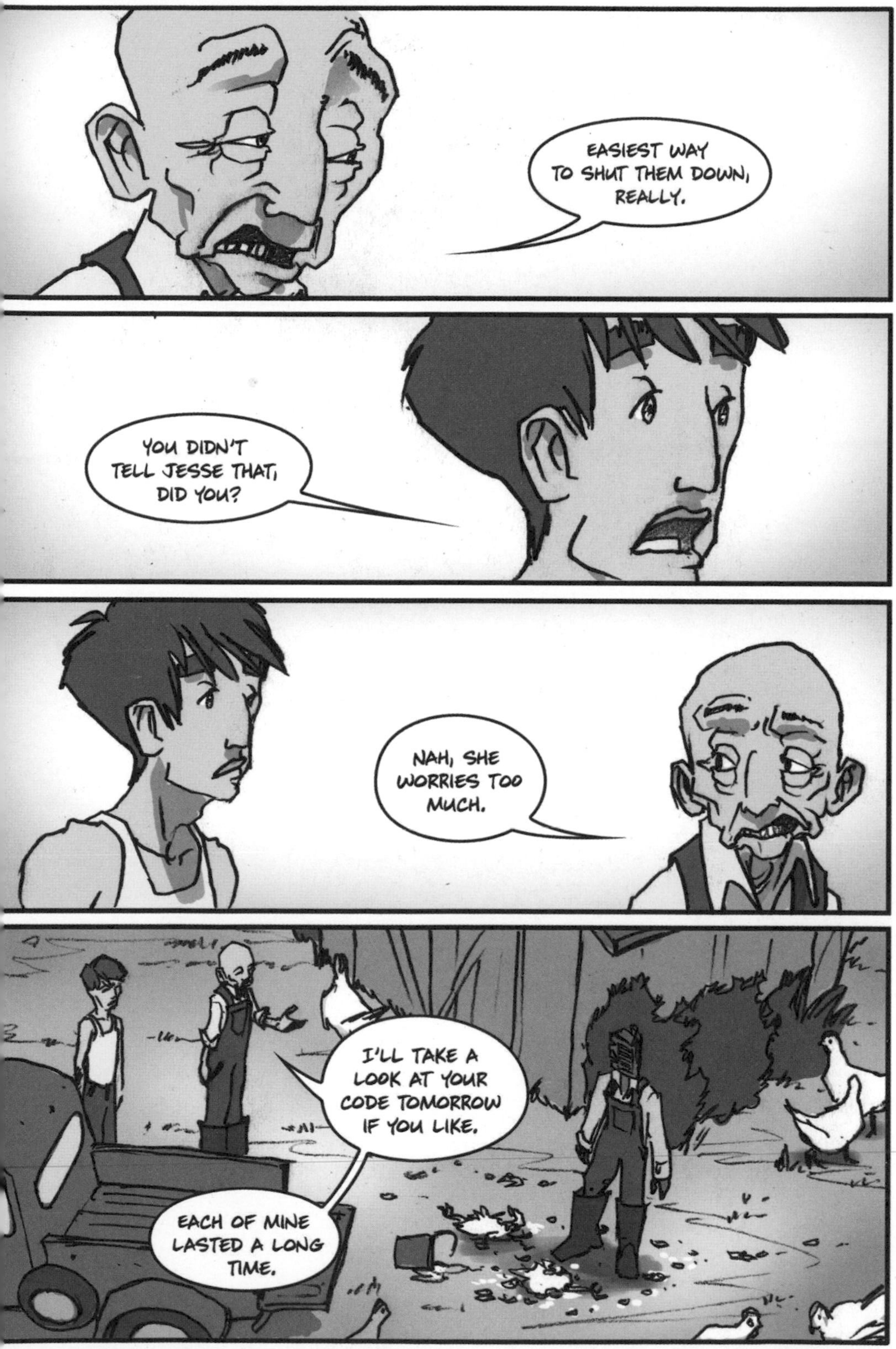
EASIEST WAY TO SHUT THEM DOWN, REALLY.
YOU DIDN'T TELL JESSE THAT, DID YOU?
NAH, SHE WORRIES TOO MUCH.
I'LL TAKE A LOOK AT YOUR CODE TOMORROW IF YOU LIKE.
EACH OF MINE LASTED A LONG TIME.

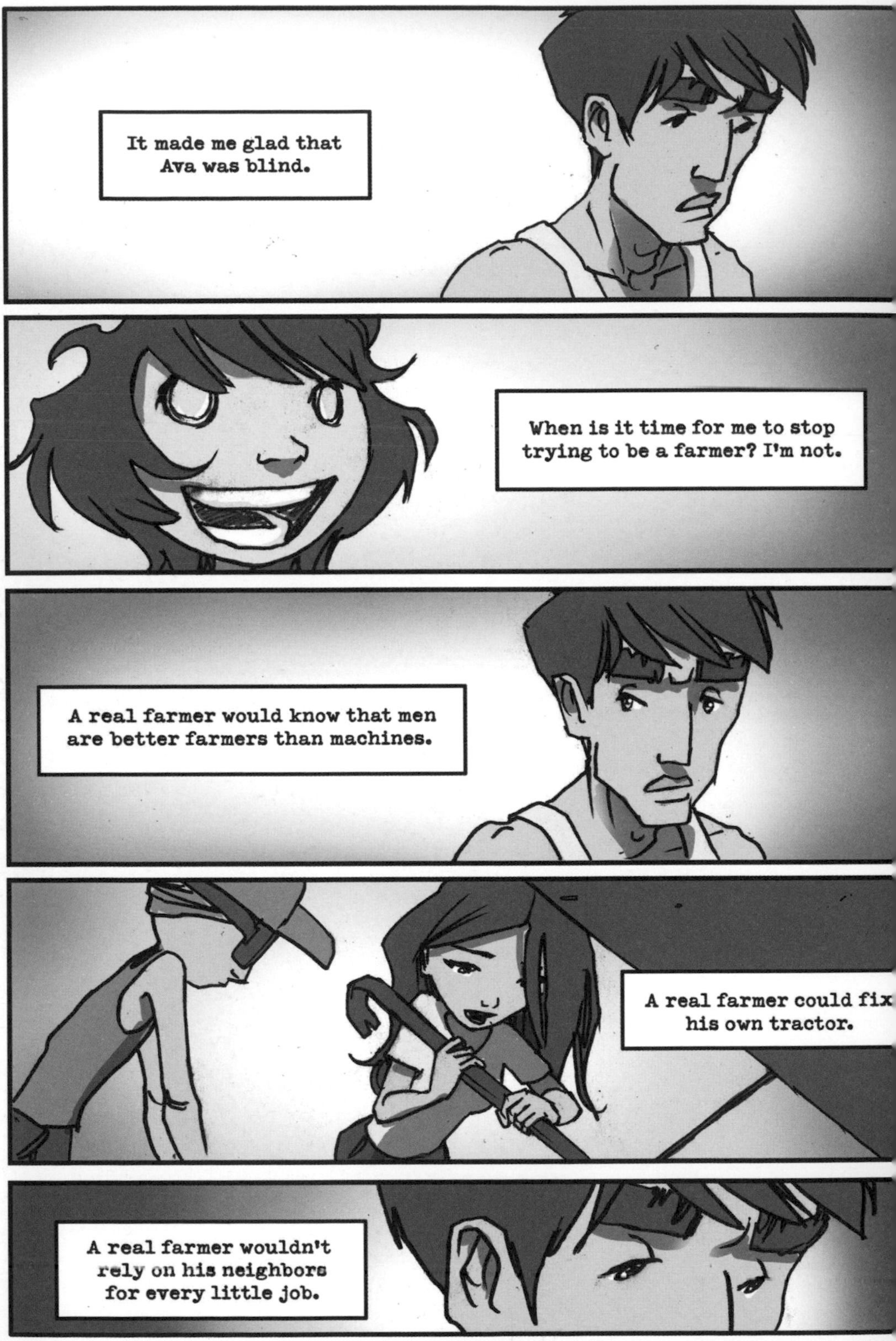
It made me glad that Ava was blind.
When is it time for me to stop trying to be a farmer? I'm not.
A real farmer would know that men are better farmers than machines.
A real farmer could fix his own tractor.
A real farmer wouldn't rely on his neighbors for every little job.

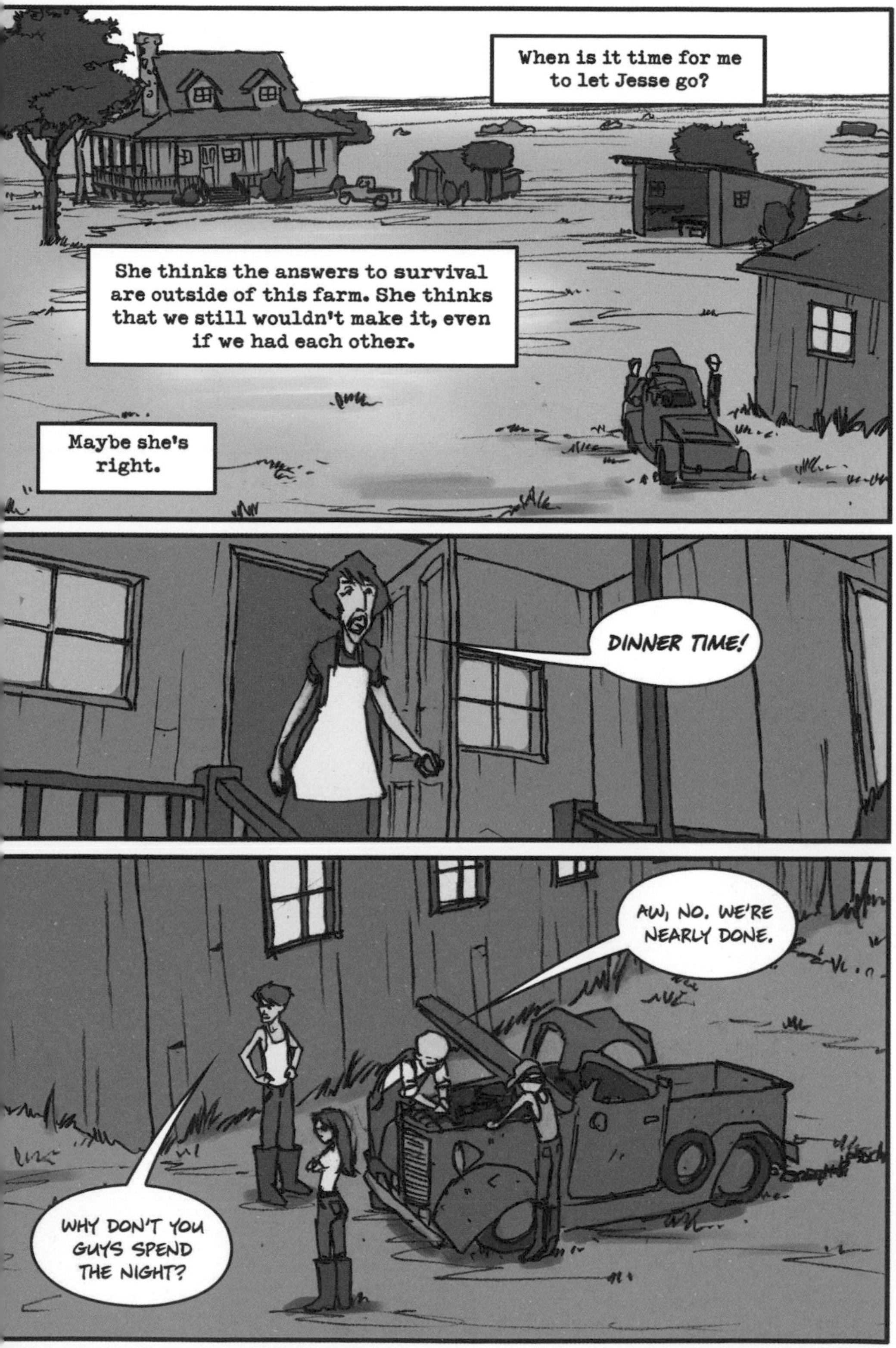
When is it time for me to let Jesse go?
She thinks the answers to survival are outside of this farm. She thinks that we still wouldn't make it, even if we had each other.
Maybe she's right.
DINNER TIME!
AW, NO. WE'RE NEARLY DONE.
WHY DON'T YOU GUYS SPEND THE NIGHT?

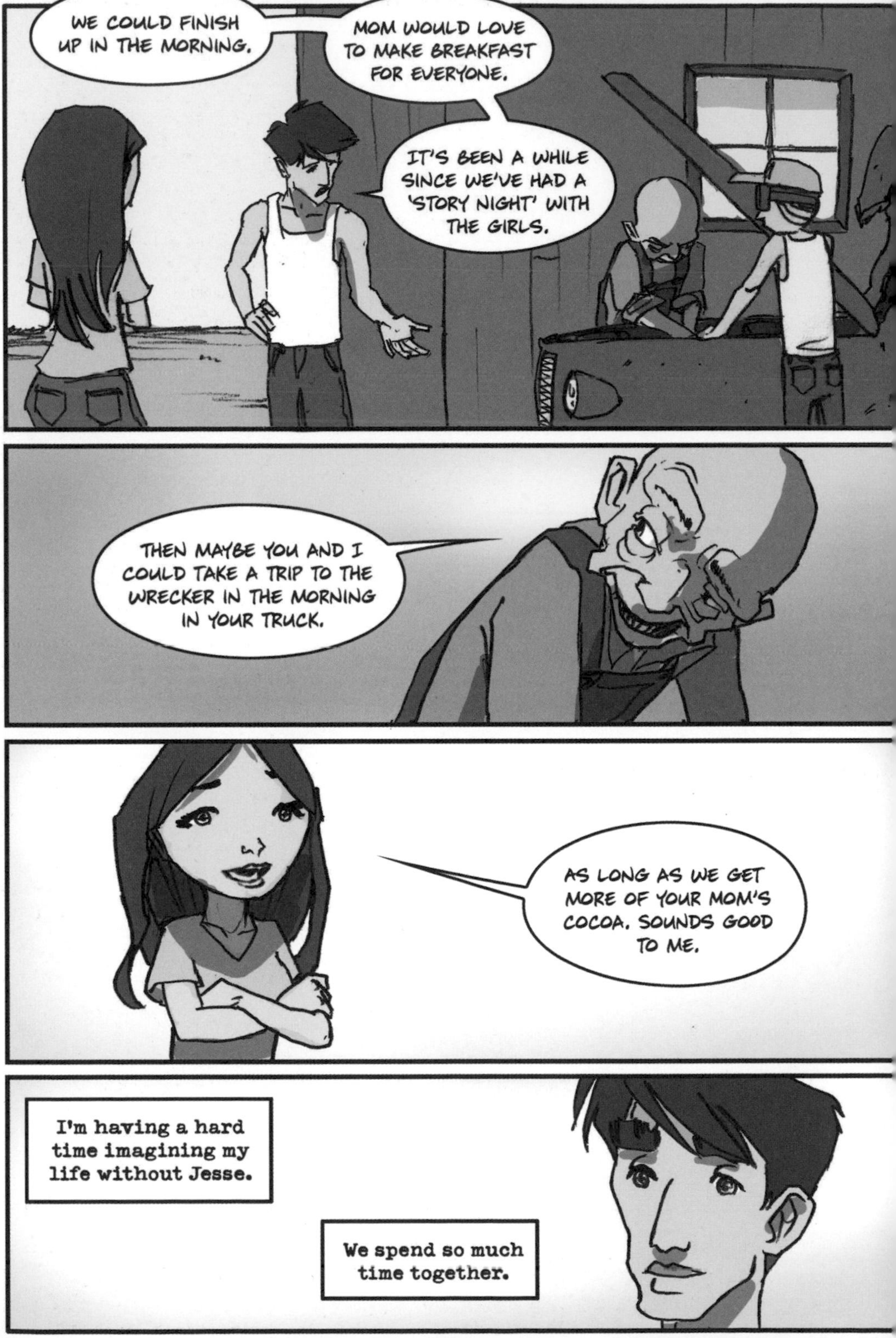
WE COULD FINISH UP IN THE MORNING.
MOM WOULD LOVE TO MAKE BREAKFAST FOR EVERYONE.
IT'S BEEN A WHILE SINCE WE'VE HAD A 'STORY NIGHT' WITH THE GIRLS.
THEN MAYBE YOU AND I COULD TAKE A TRIP TO THE WRECKER IN THE MORNING IN YOUR TRUCK.
AS LONG AS WE GET MORE OF YOUR MOM'S COCOA. SOUNDS GOOD TO ME.
I'm having a hard time imagining my life without Jesse.
We spend so much time together.

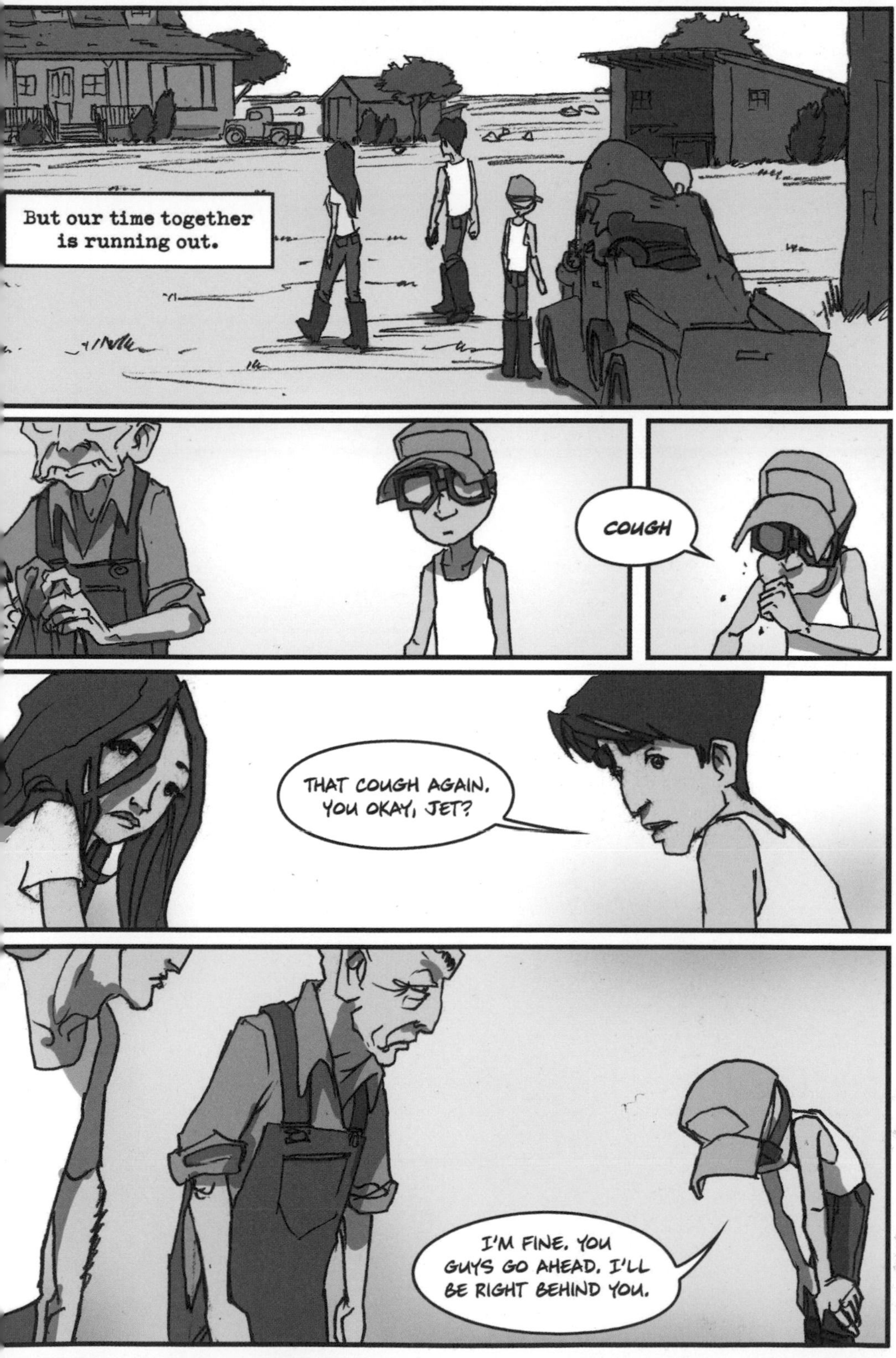
But our time together is running out.
COUGH
THAT COUGH AGAIN. YOU OKAY, JET?
I'M FINE. YOU GUYS GO AHEAD. I'LL BE RIGHT BEHIND YOU.

COUGH COUGH

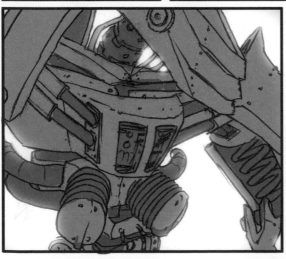

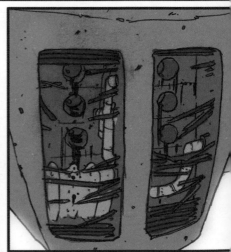

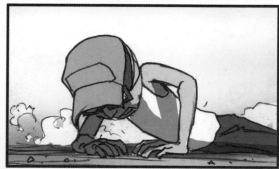

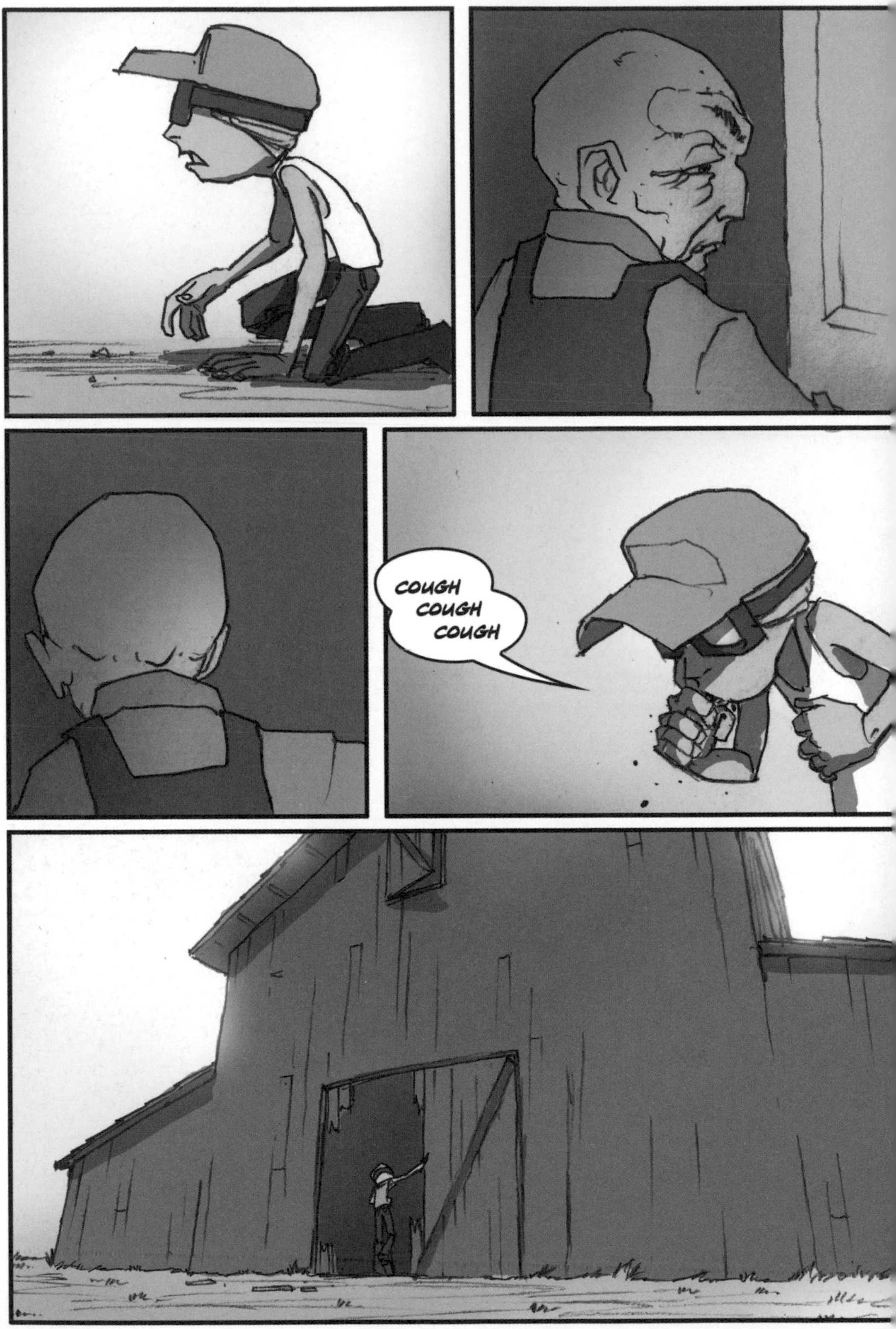
COUGH
COUGH
COUGH

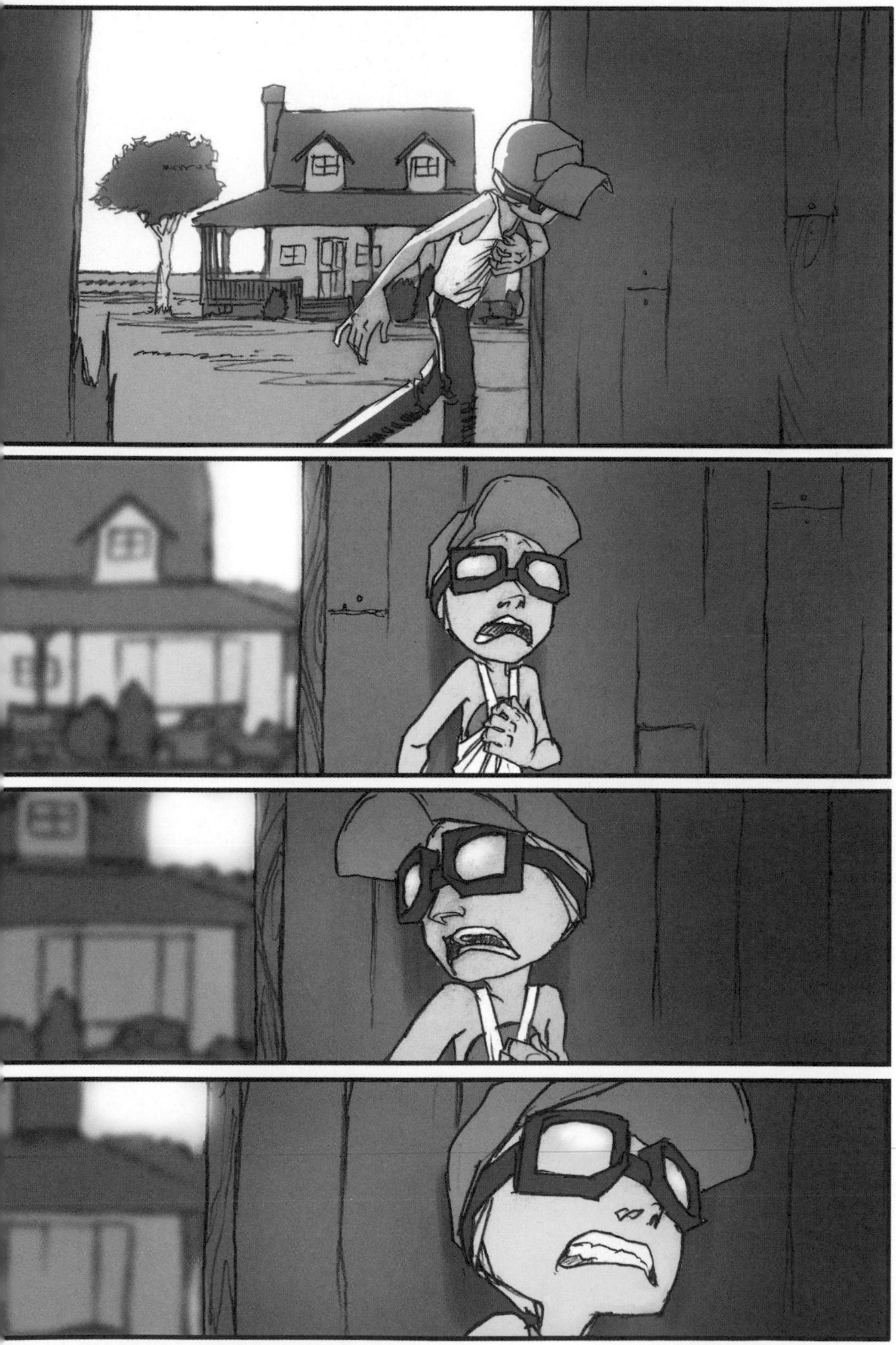

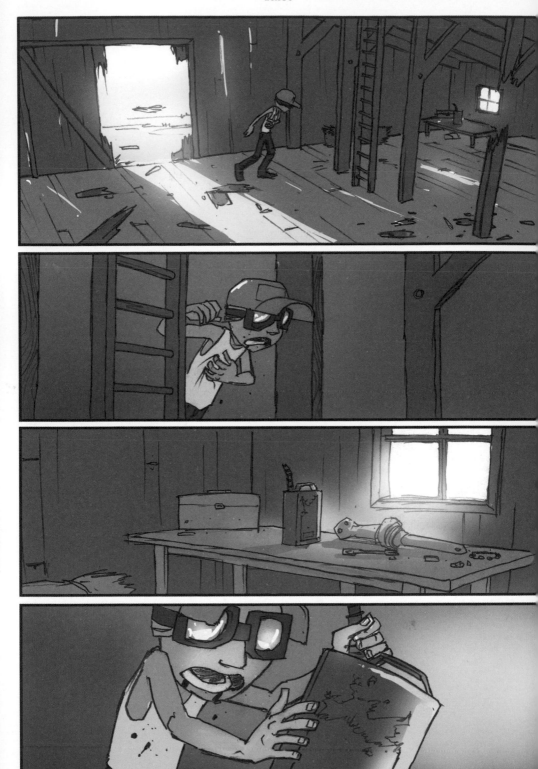

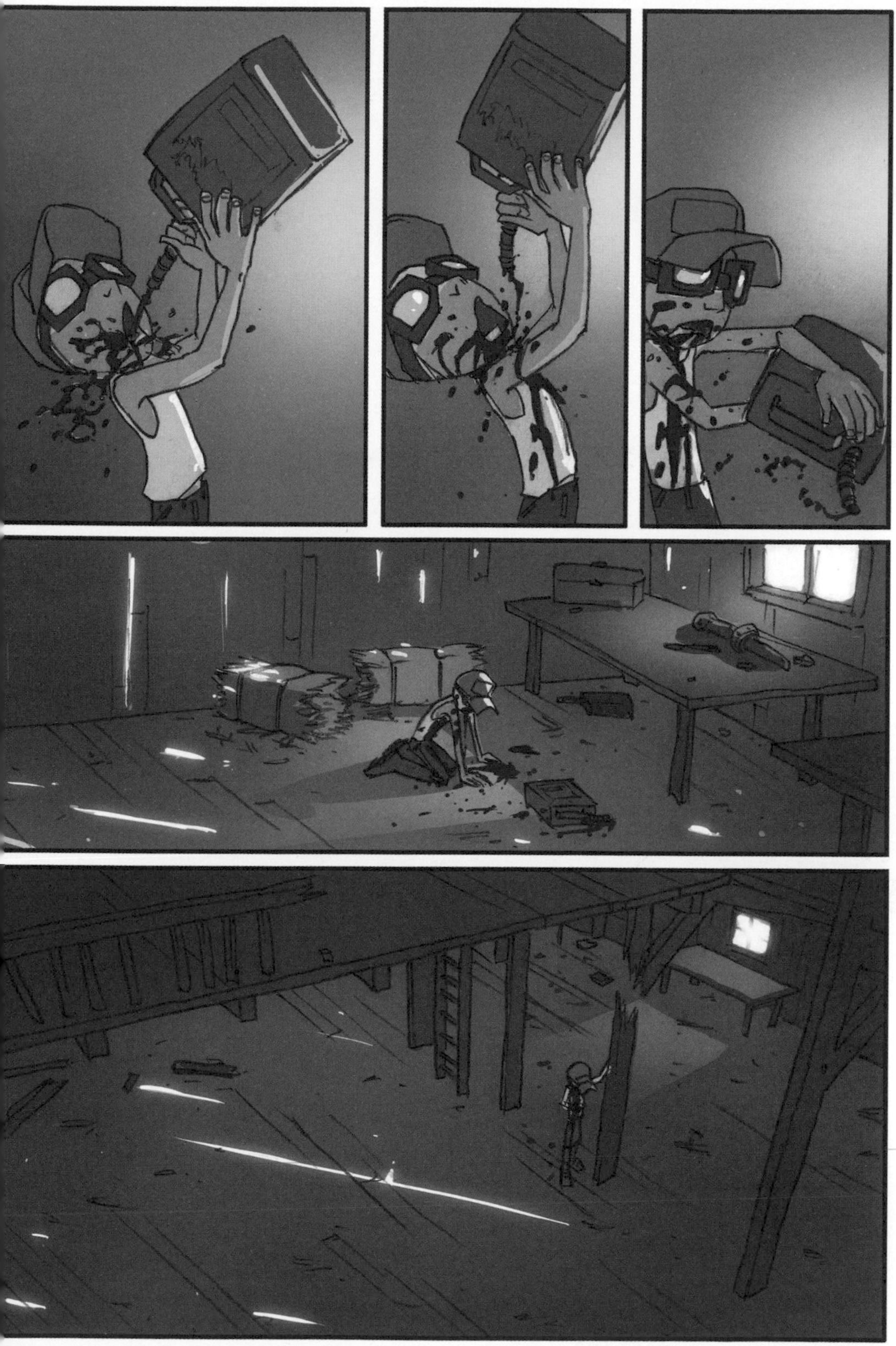

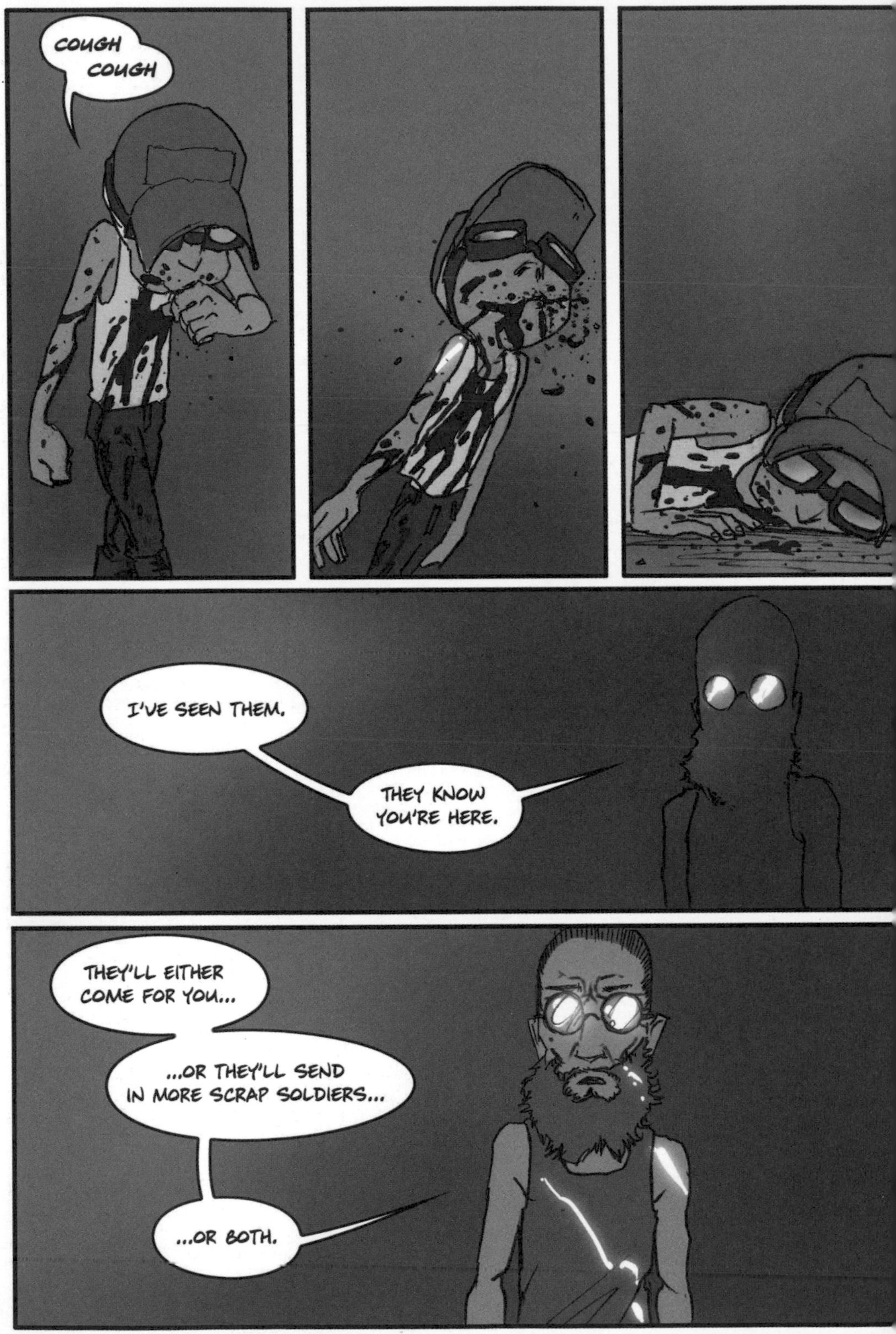
COUGH
COUGH
I'VE SEEN THEM.
THEY KNOW YOU'RE HERE.
THEY'LL EITHER COME FOR YOU...
...OR THEY'LL SEND IN MORE SCRAP SOLDIERS...
...OR BOTH.

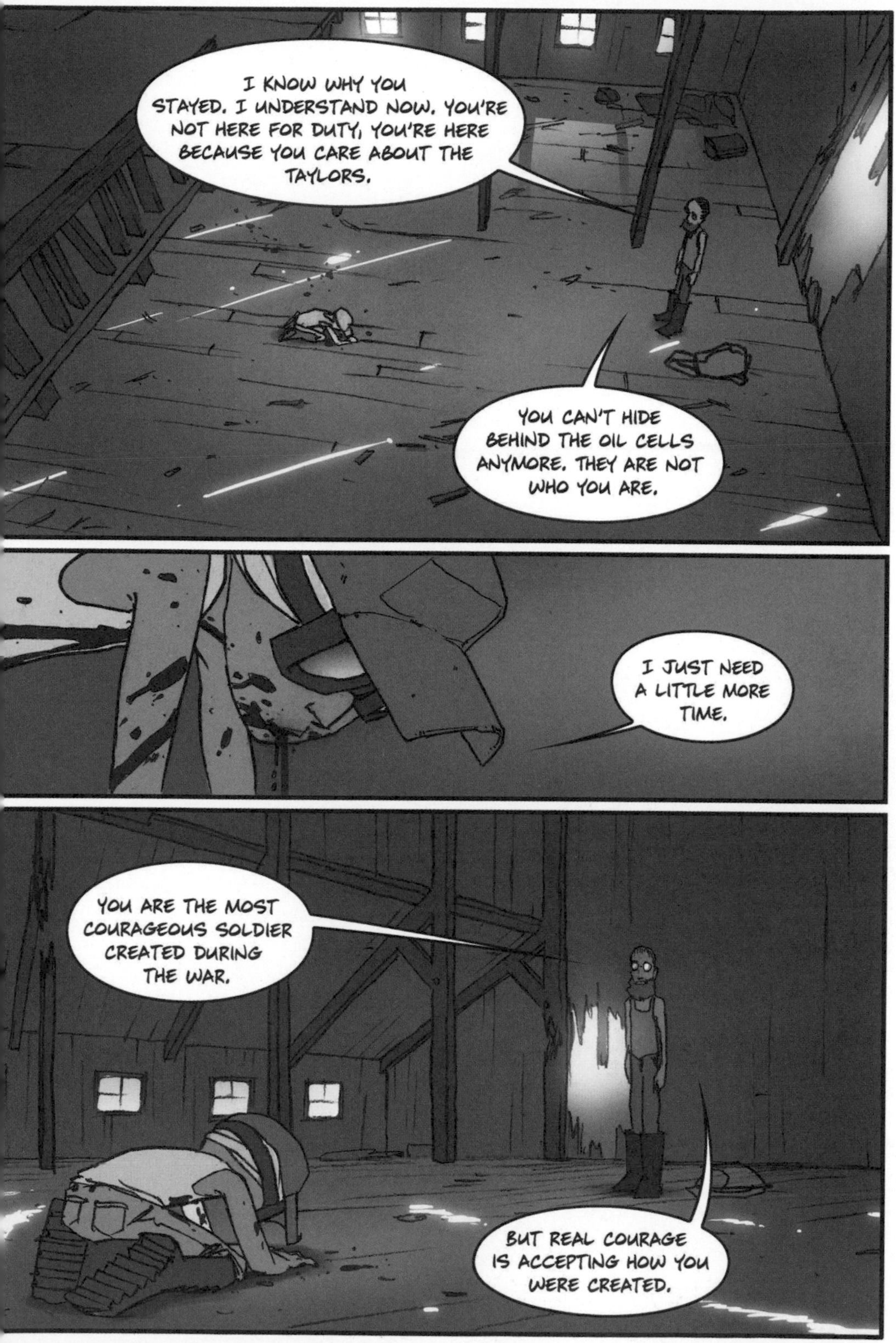
I KNOW WHY YOU STAYED. I UNDERSTAND NOW. YOU'RE NOT HERE FOR DUTY, YOU'RE HERE BECAUSE YOU CARE ABOUT THE TAYLORS.
YOU CAN'T HIDE BEHIND THE OIL CELLS ANYMORE. THEY ARE NOT WHO YOU ARE.
I JUST NEED A LITTLE MORE TIME.
YOU ARE THE MOST COURAGEOUS SOLDIER CREATED DURING THE WAR.
BUT REAL COURAGE IS ACCEPTING HOW YOU WERE CREATED.

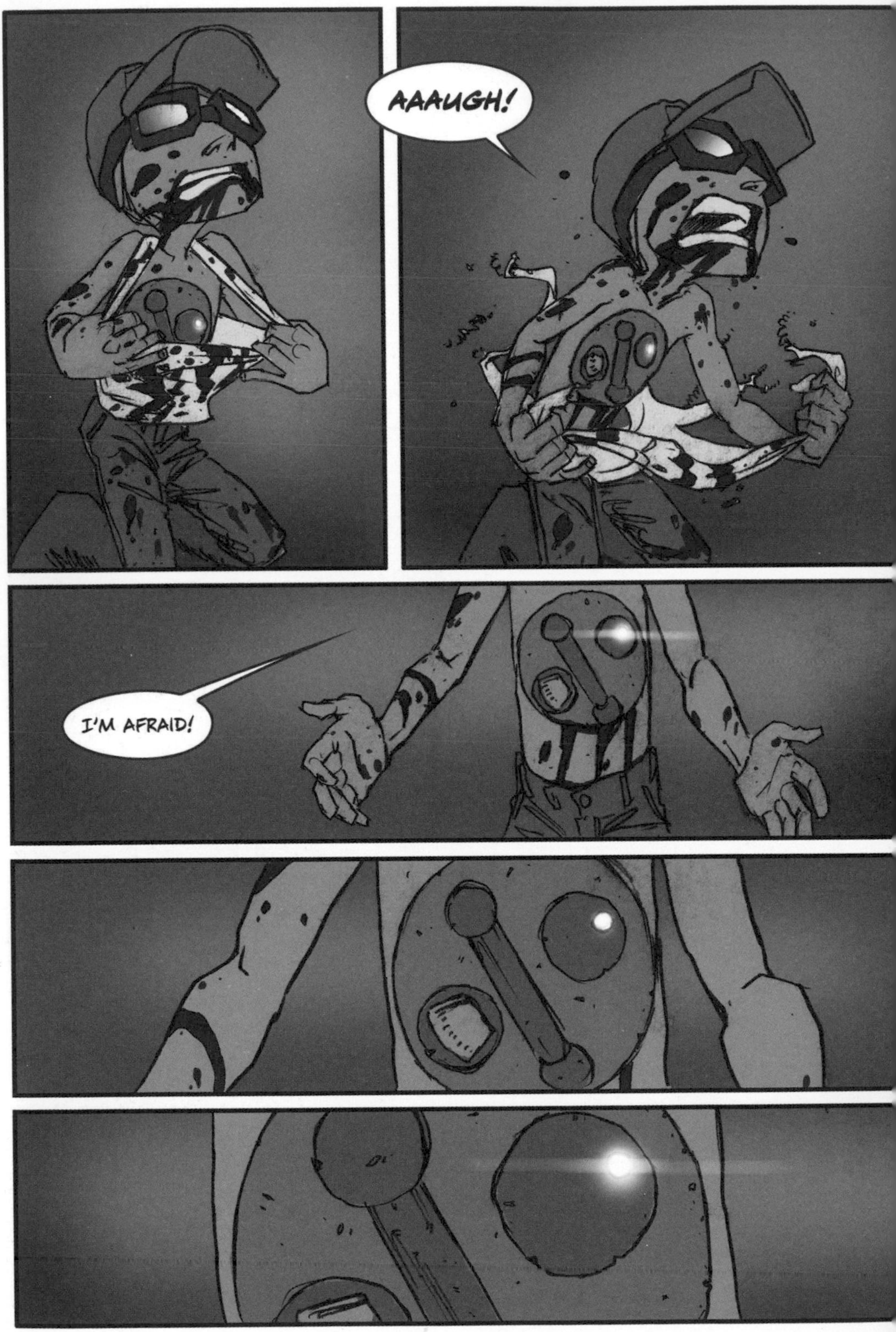
AAAUGH!
I'M AFRAID!

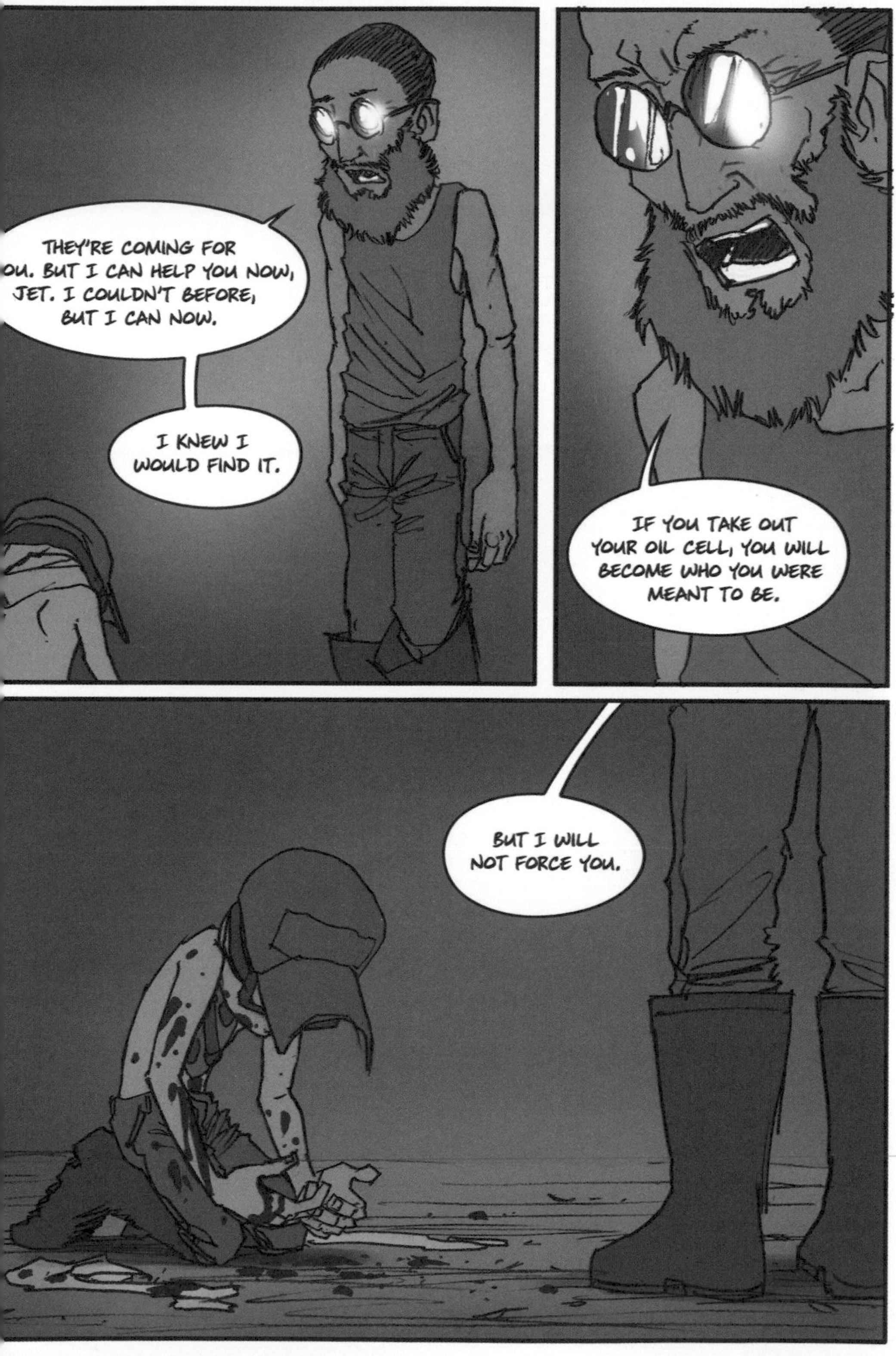
THEY'RE COMING FOR OU. BUT I CAN HELP YOU NOW, JET. I COULDN'T BEFORE, BUT I CAN NOW.
I KNEW I WOULD FIND IT.
IF YOU TAKE OUT YOUR OIL CELL, YOU WILL BECOME WHO YOU WERE MEANT TO BE.
BUT I WILL NOT FORCE YOU.

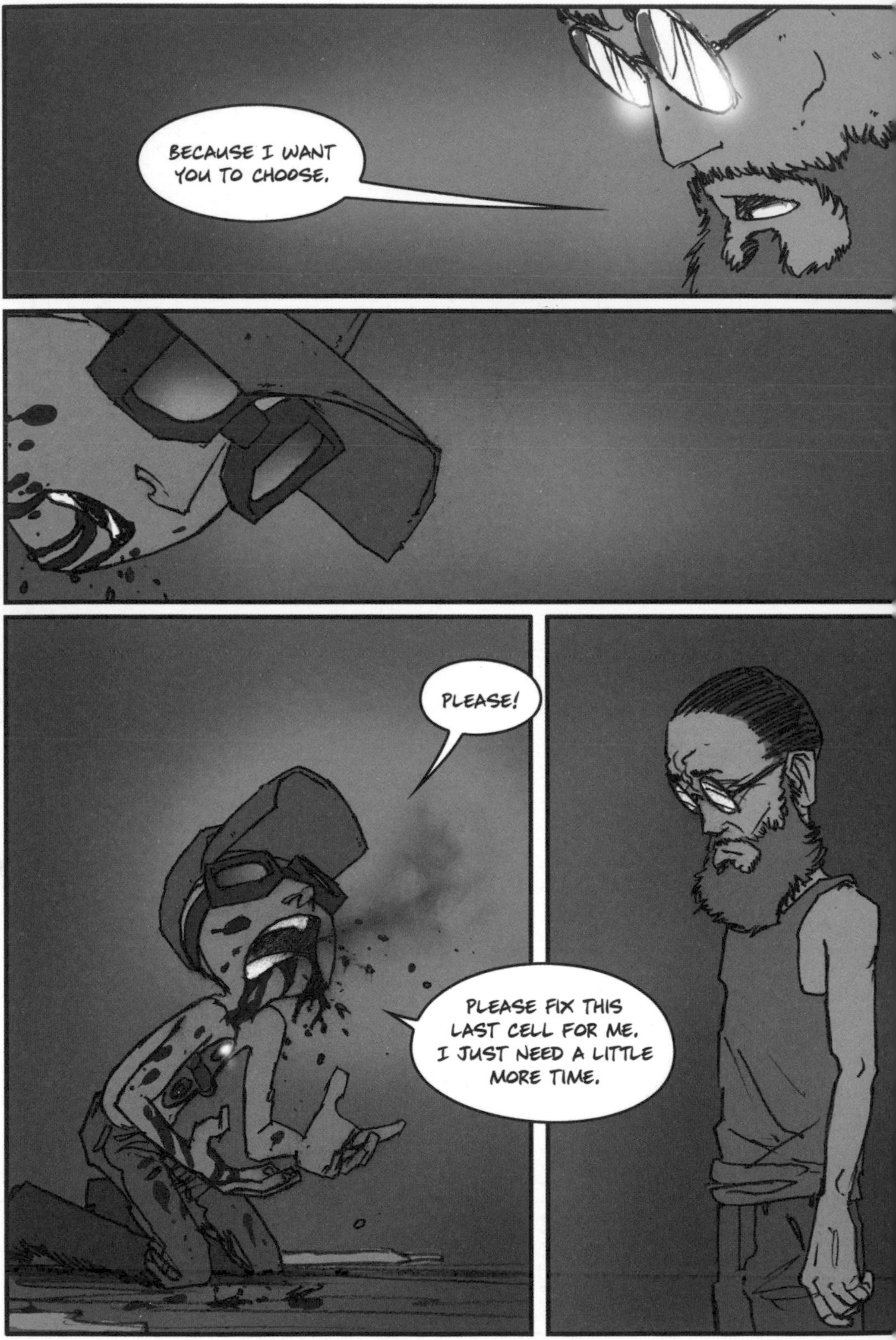
BECAUSE I WANT YOU TO CHOOSE.
PLEASE!
PLEASE FIX THIS LAST CELL FOR ME. I JUST NEED A LITTLE MORE TIME.

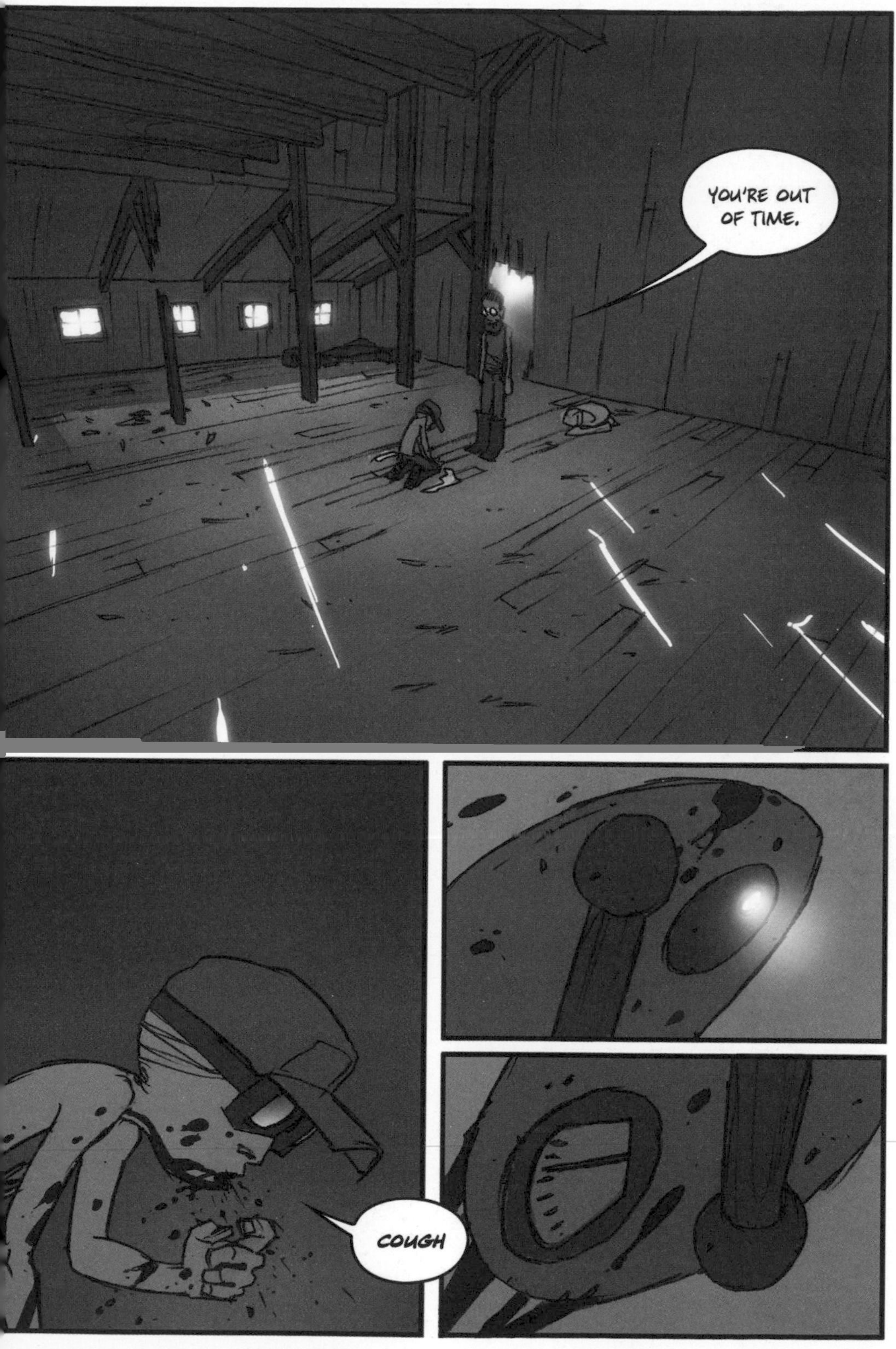
YOU'RE OUT OF TIME.
COUGH

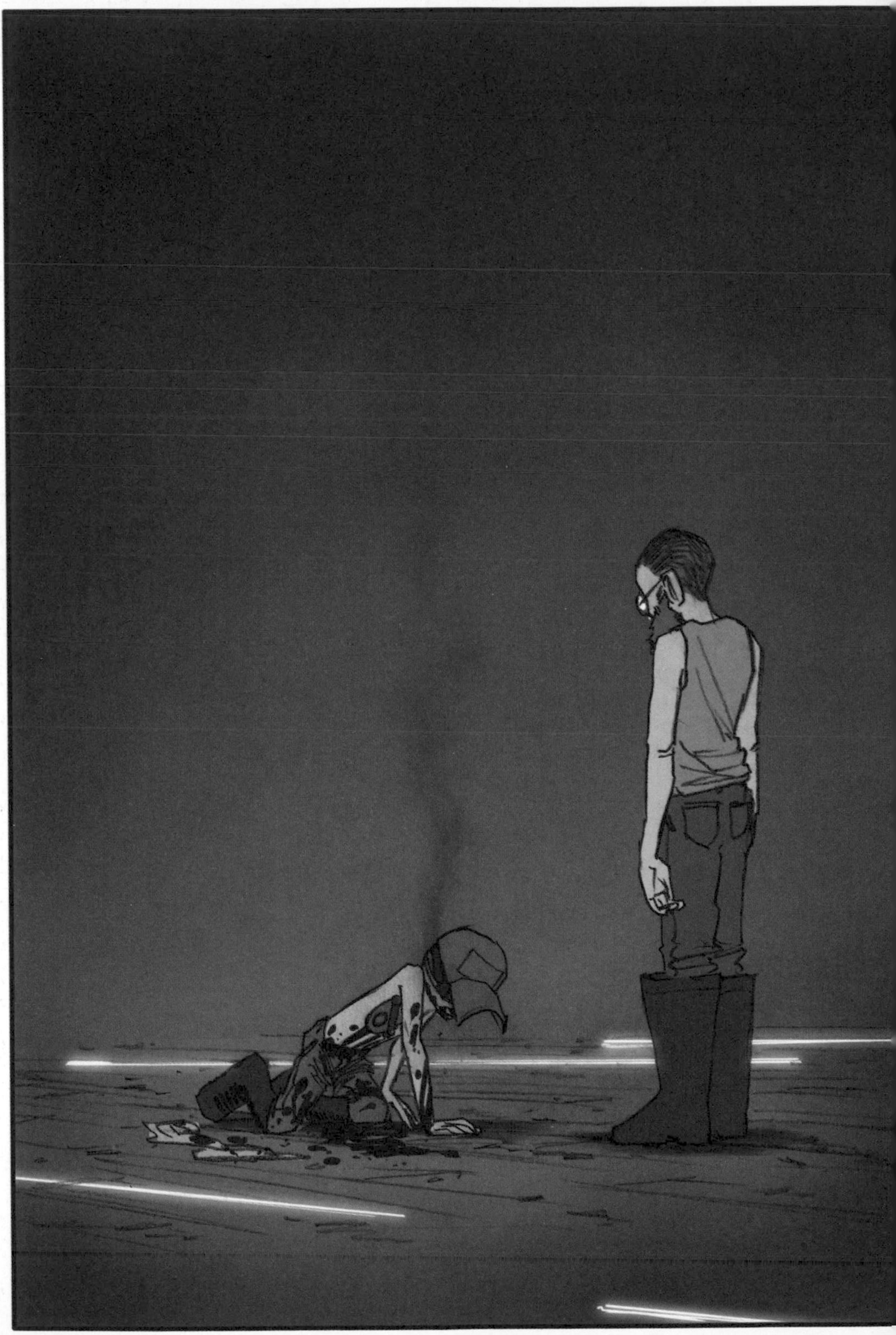

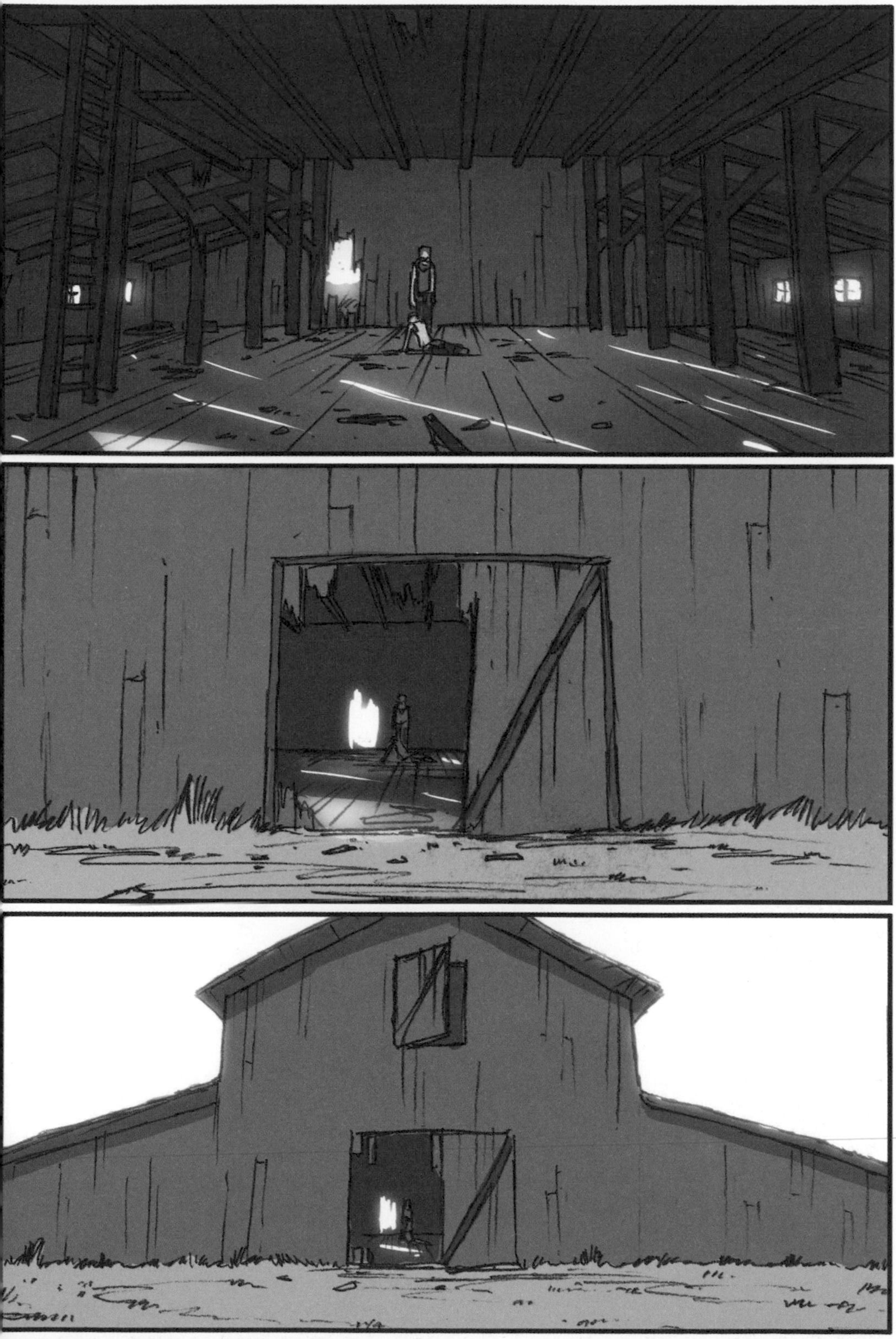

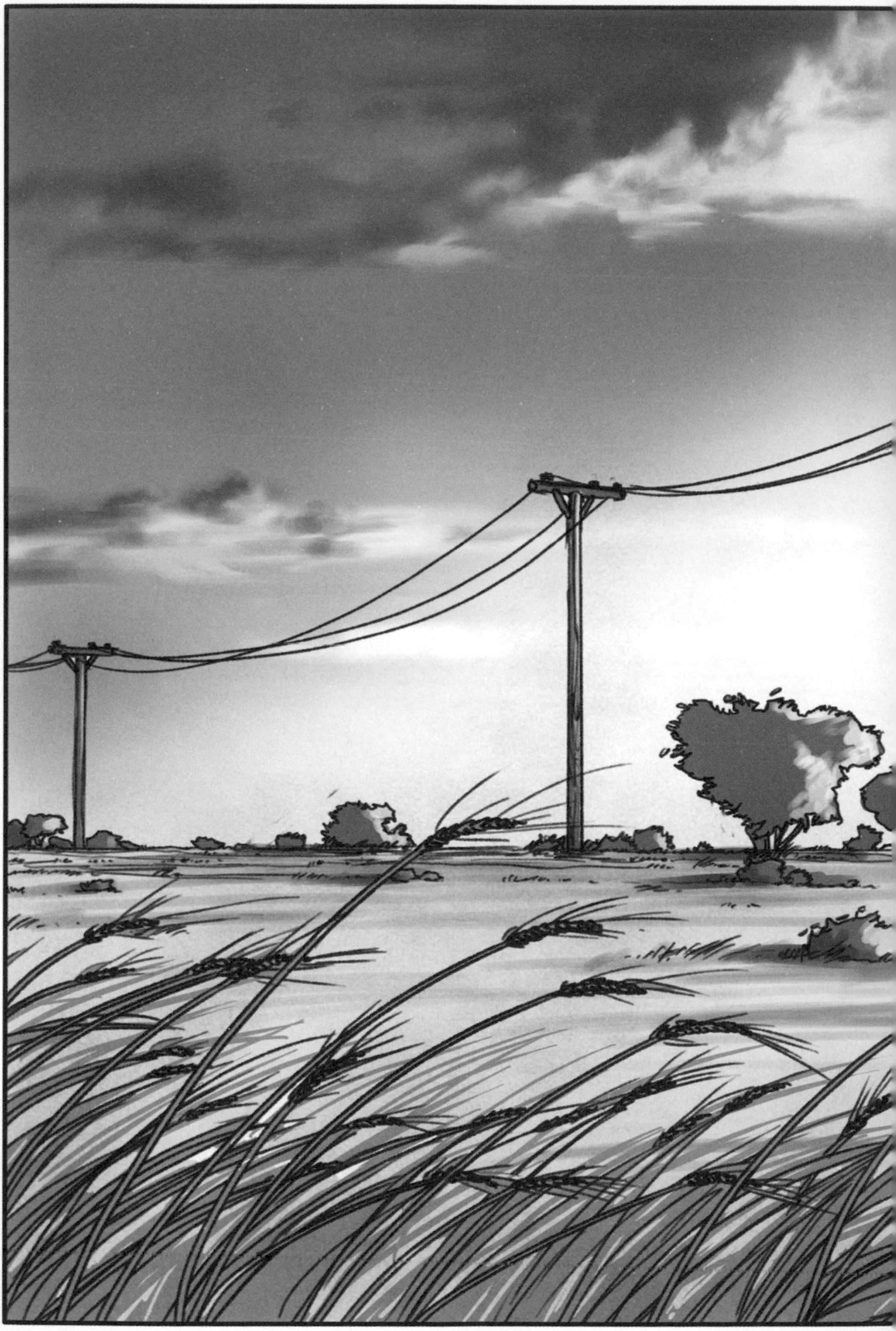

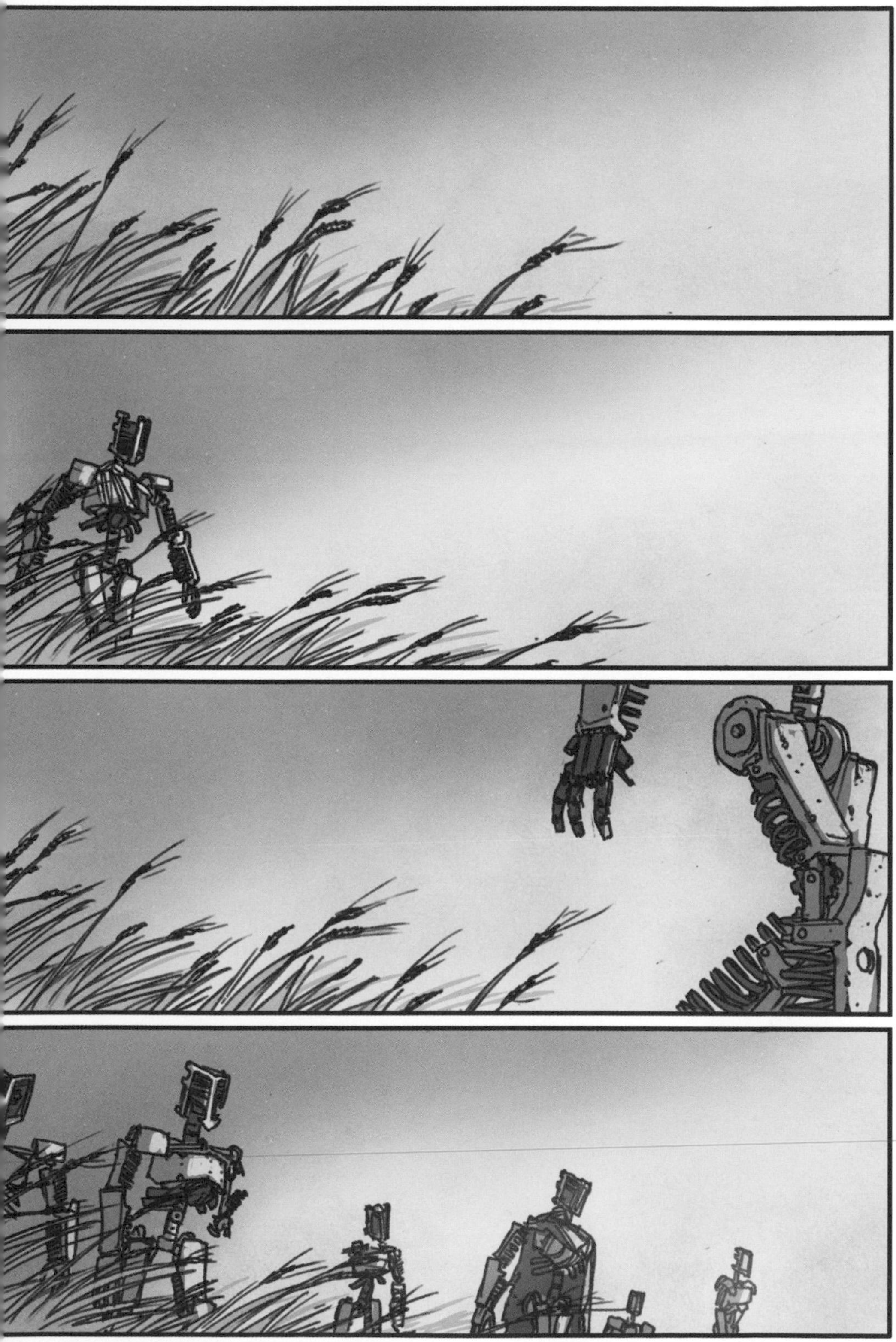

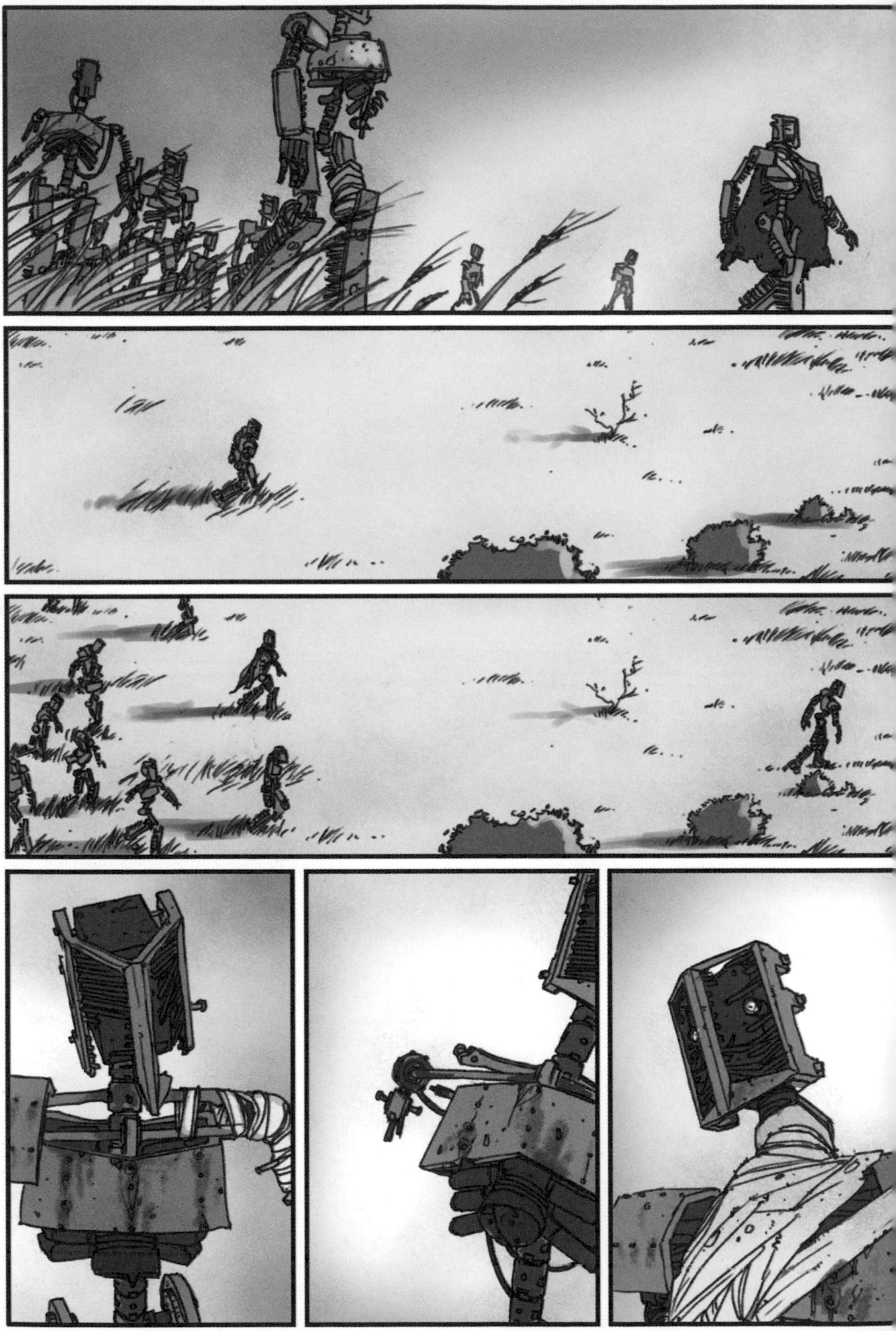

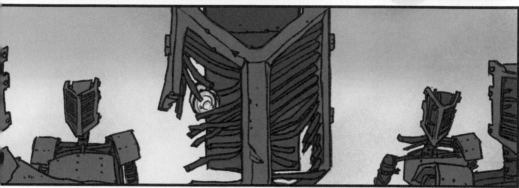

YOUR DAD WAS SURE HE'D DONE SOMETHING WRONG.

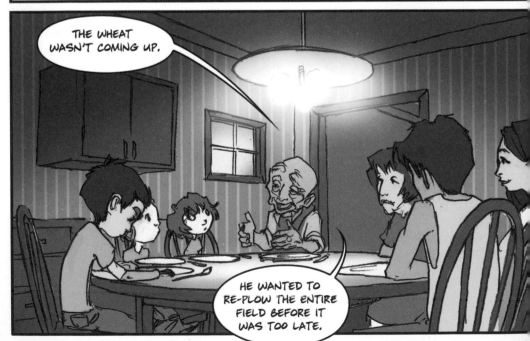

THE WHEAT WASN'T COMING UP.

HE WANTED TO RE-PLOW THE ENTIRE FIELD BEFORE IT WAS TOO LATE.

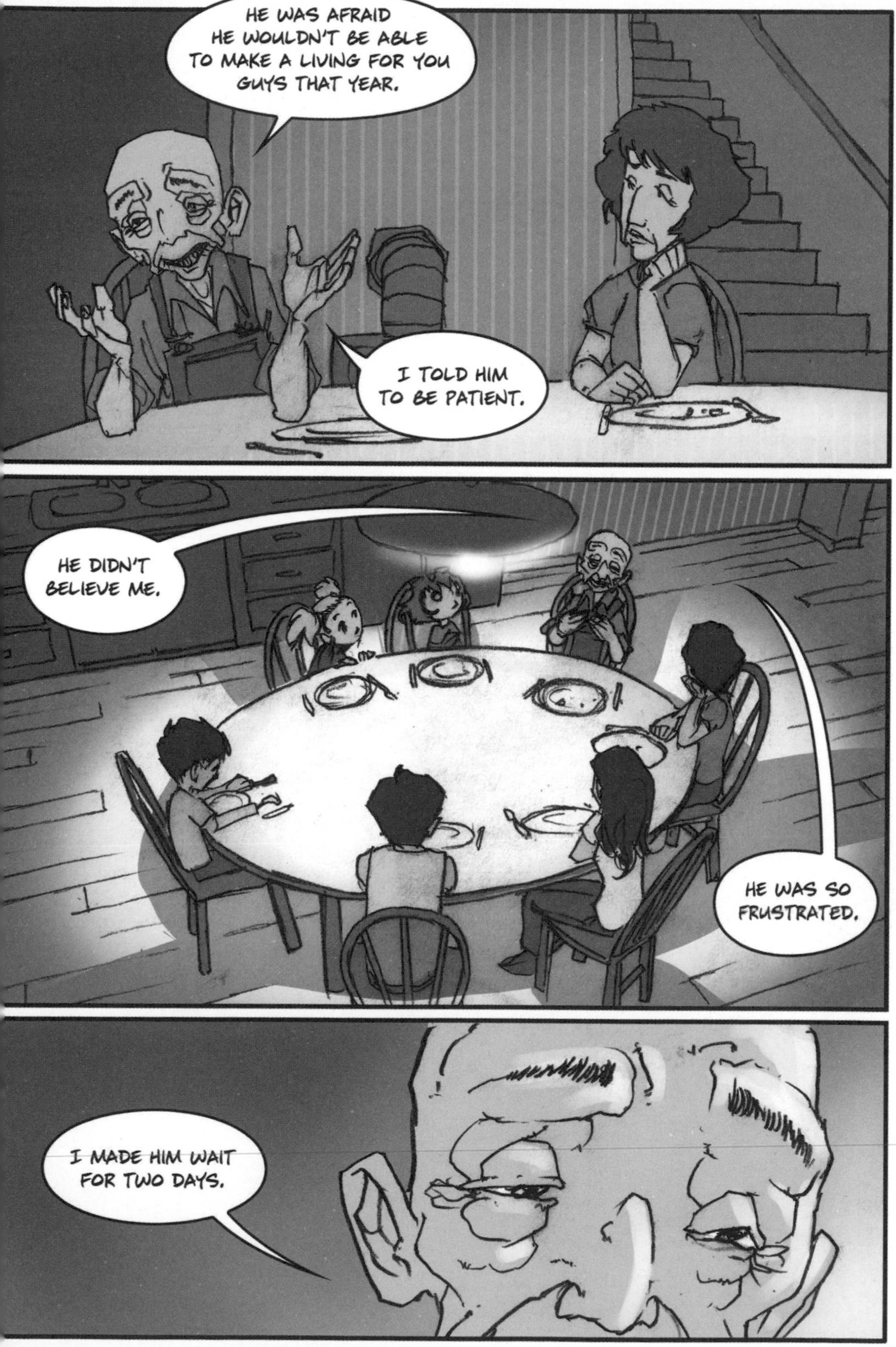
HE WAS AFRAID HE WOULDN'T BE ABLE TO MAKE A LIVING FOR YOU GUYS THAT YEAR.
I TOLD HIM TO BE PATIENT.
HE DIDN'T BELIEVE ME.
HE WAS SO FRUSTRATED.
I MADE HIM WAIT FOR TWO DAYS.

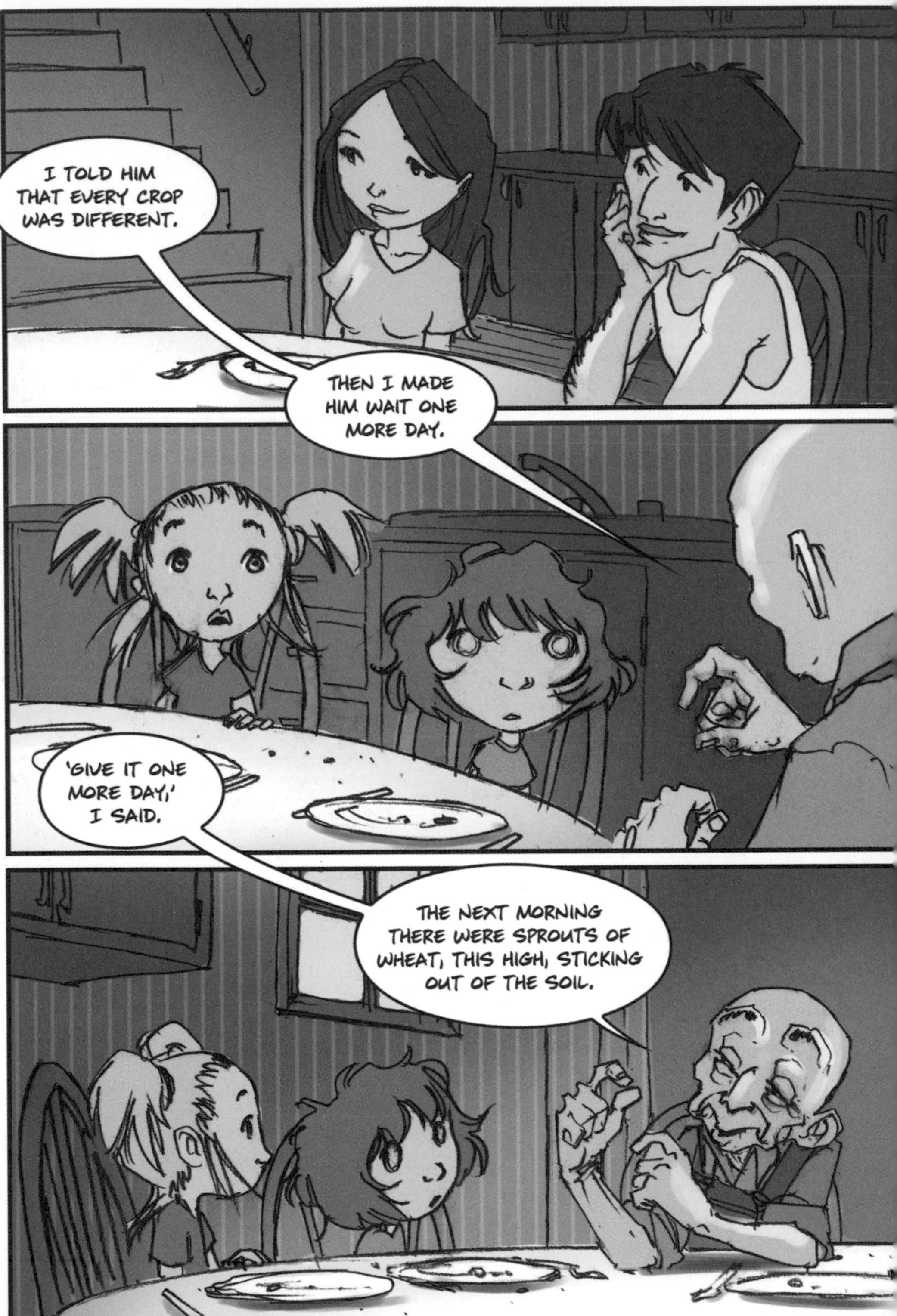
I TOLD HIM THAT EVERY CROP WAS DIFFERENT.
THEN I MADE HIM WAIT ONE MORE DAY.
'GIVE IT ONE MORE DAY,' I SAID.
THE NEXT MORNING THERE WERE SPROUTS OF WHEAT, THIS HIGH, STICKING OUT OF THE SOIL.

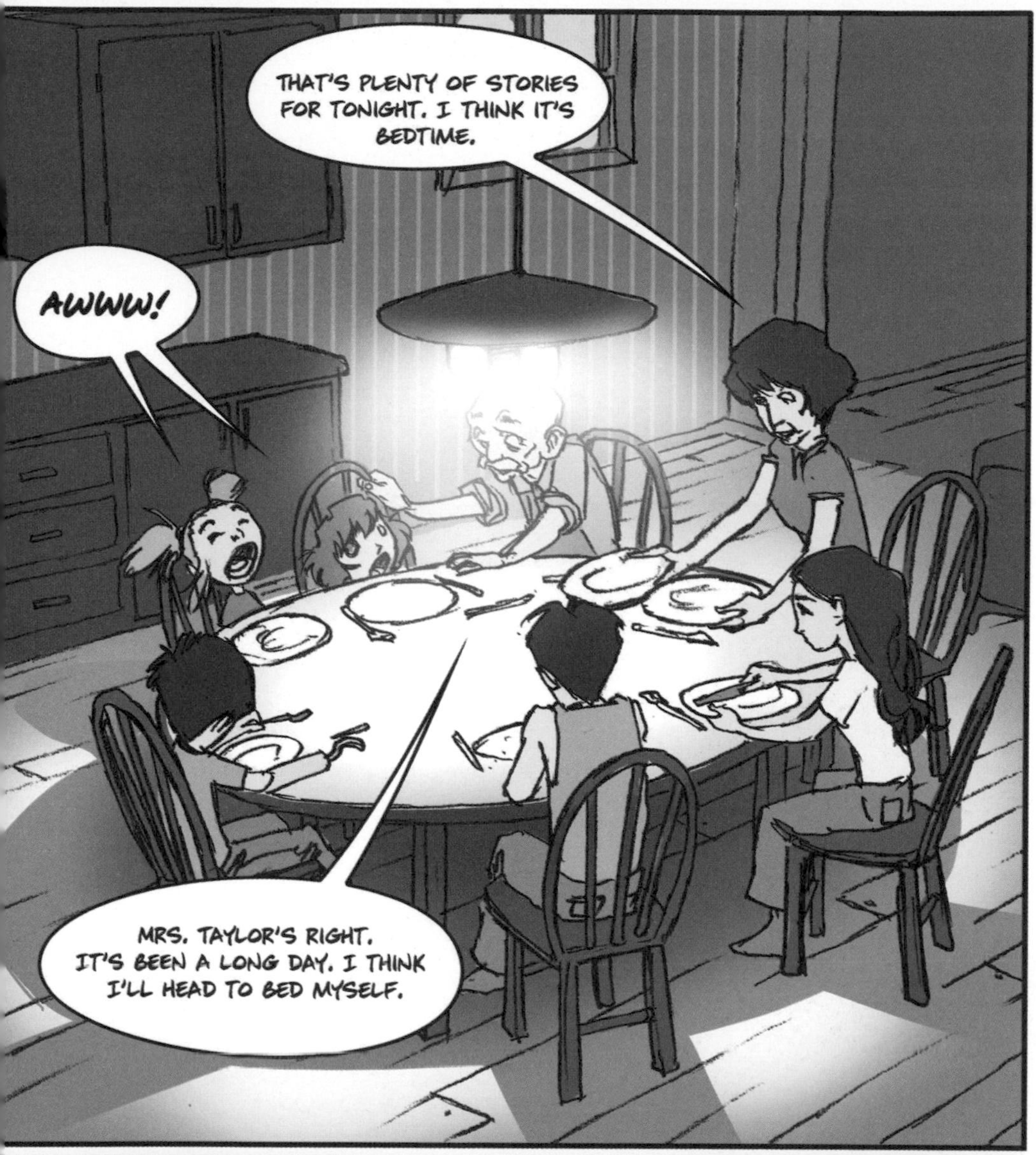
THAT'S PLENTY OF STORIES FOR TONIGHT. I THINK IT'S BEDTIME.
AWWW!
MRS. TAYLOR'S RIGHT. IT'S BEEN A LONG DAY. I THINK I'LL HEAD TO BED MYSELF.

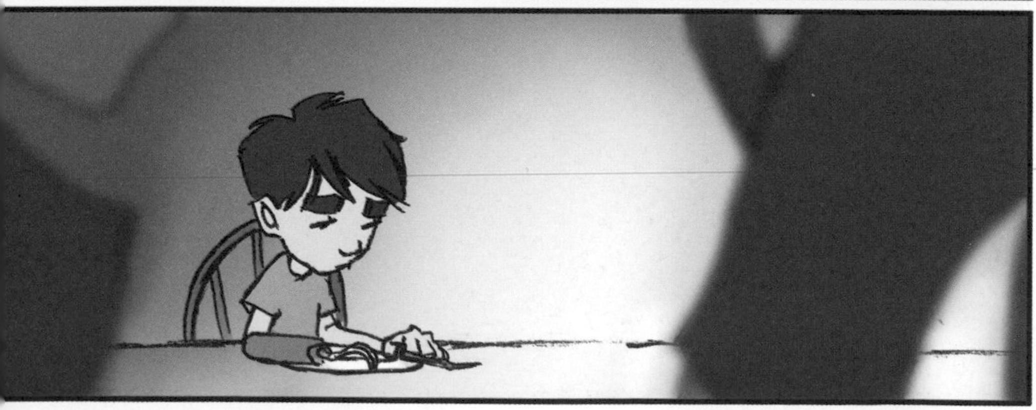

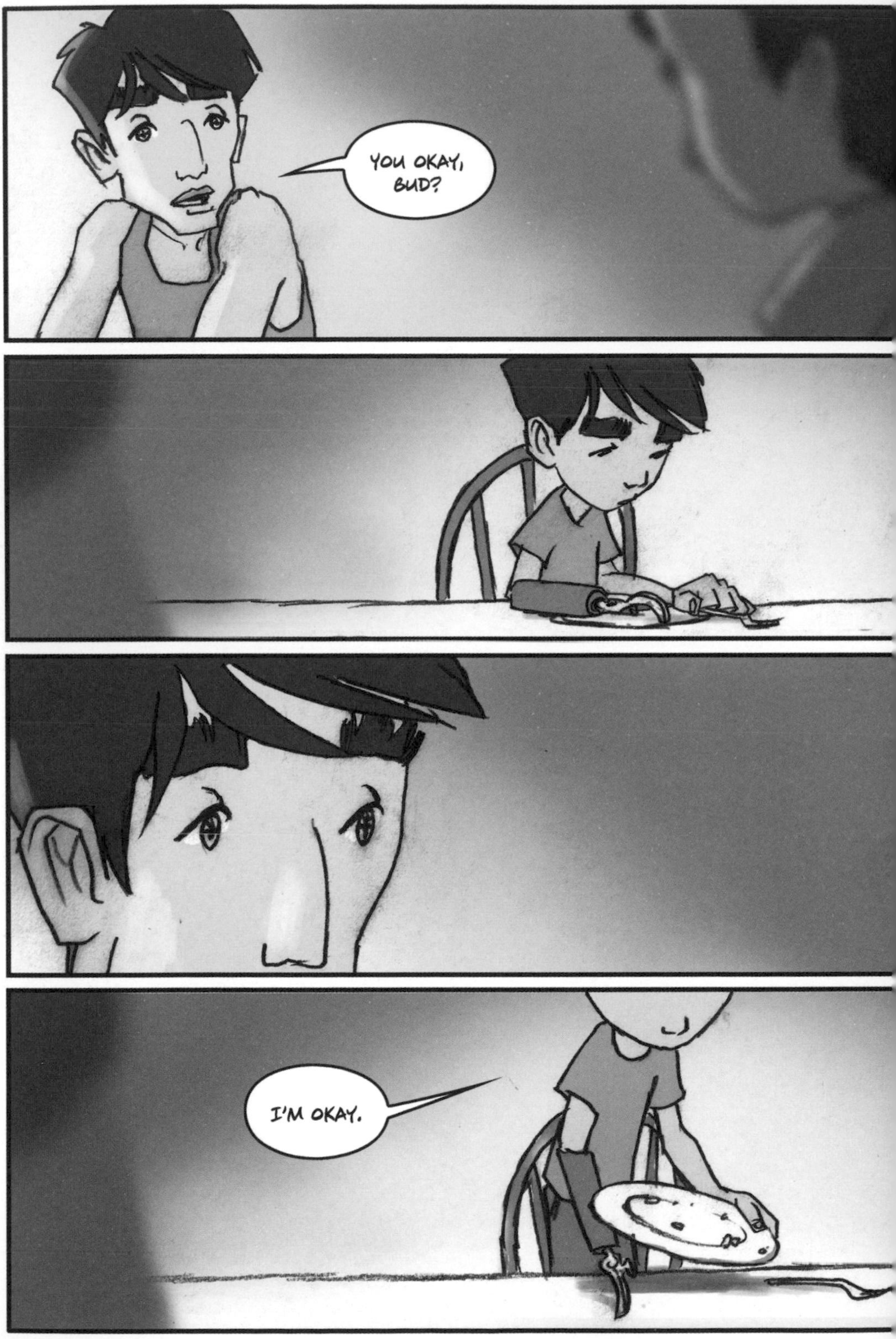
YOU OKAY, BUD?
I'M OKAY.

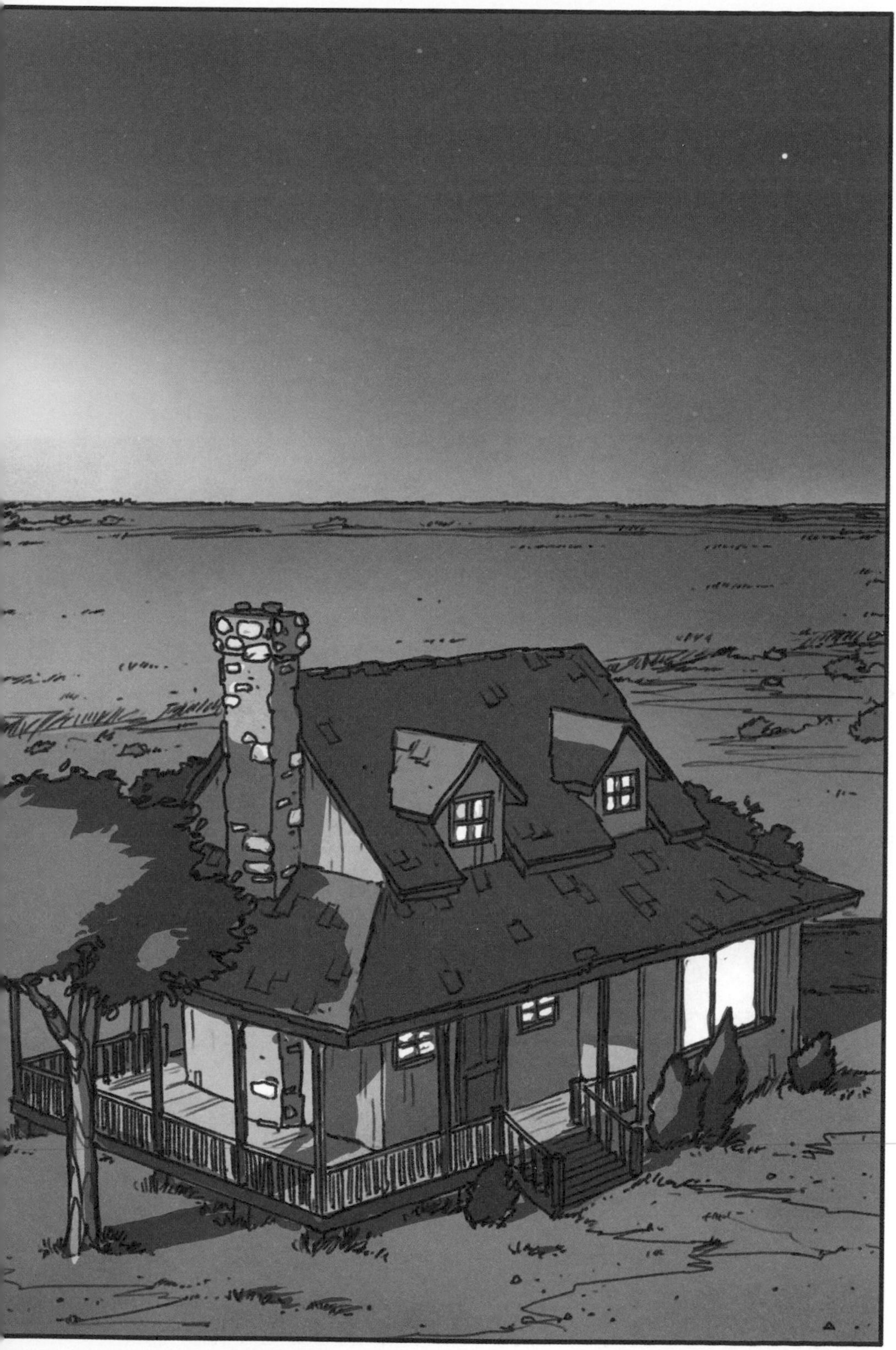

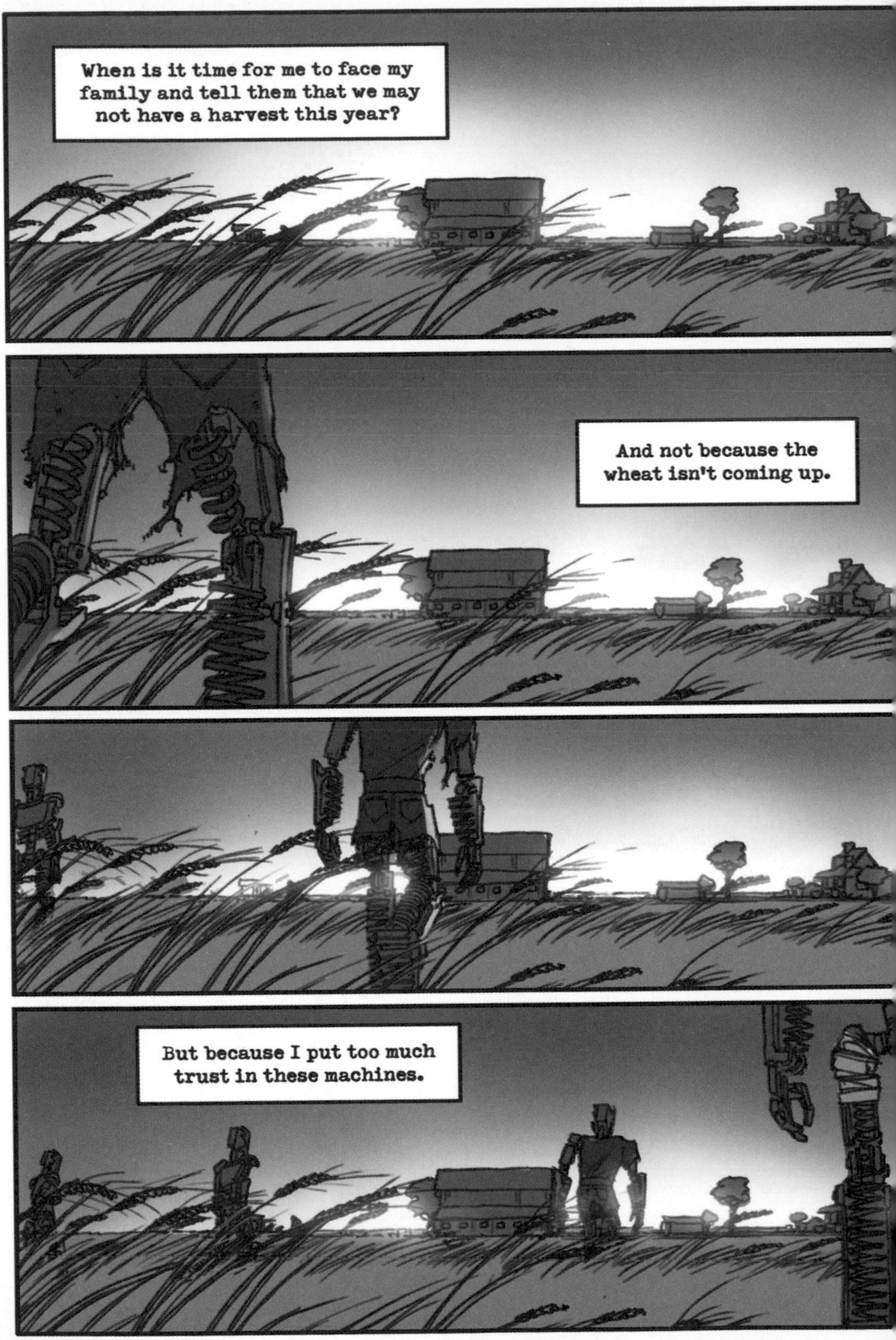
When is it time for me to face my family and tell them that we may not have a harvest this year?
And not because the wheat isn't coming up.
But because I put too much trust in these machines.

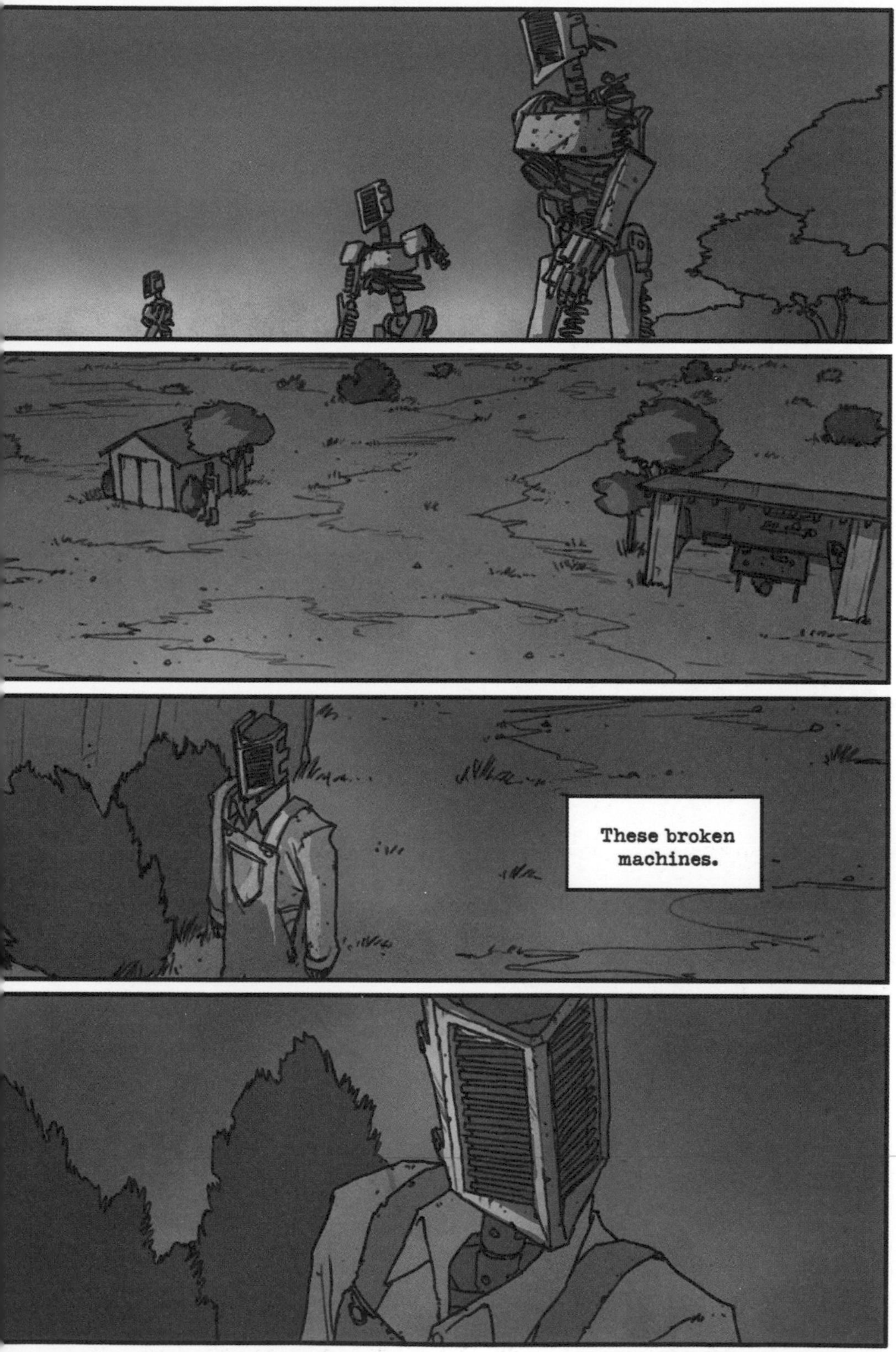
These broken
machines.

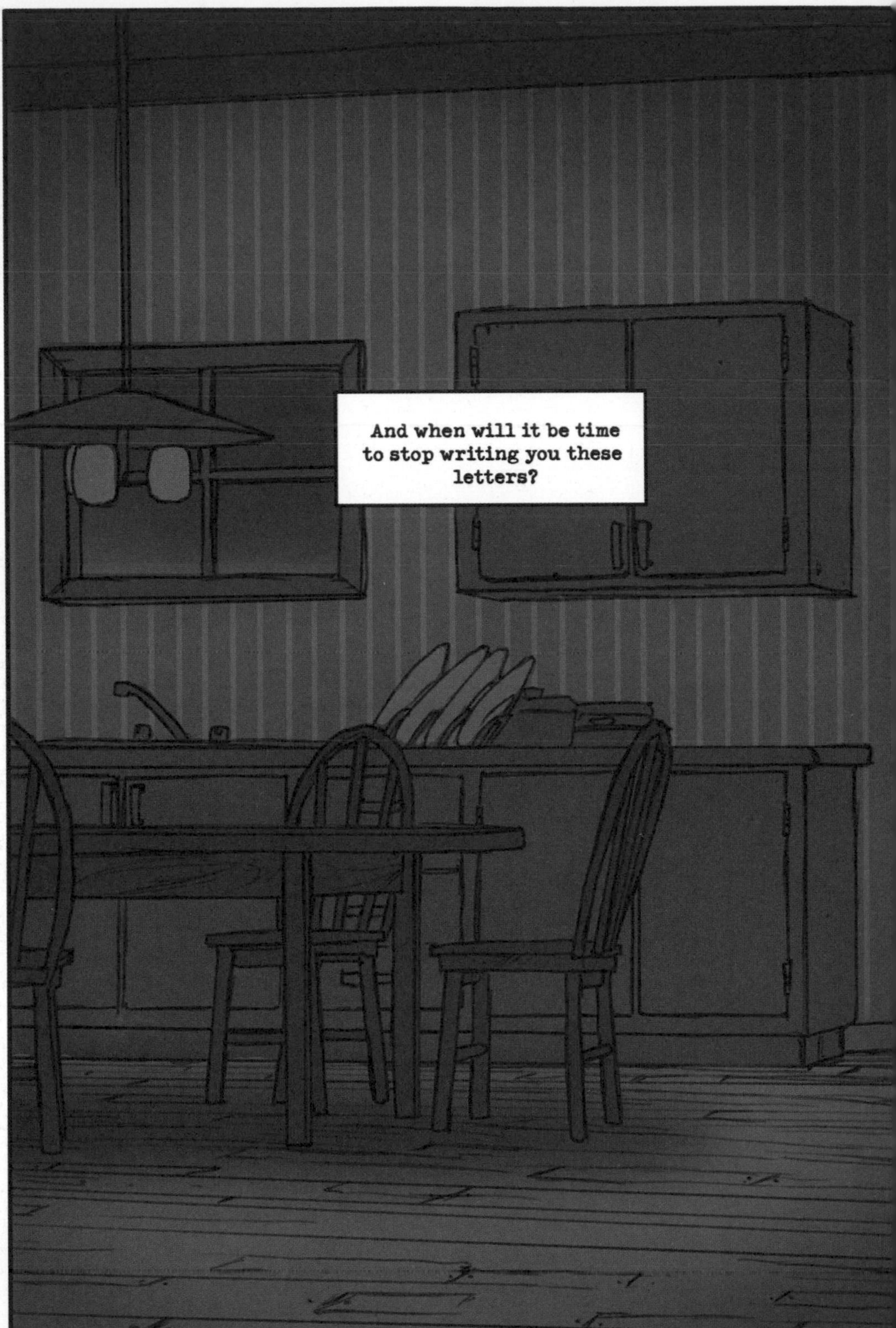
And when will it be time to stop writing you these letters?

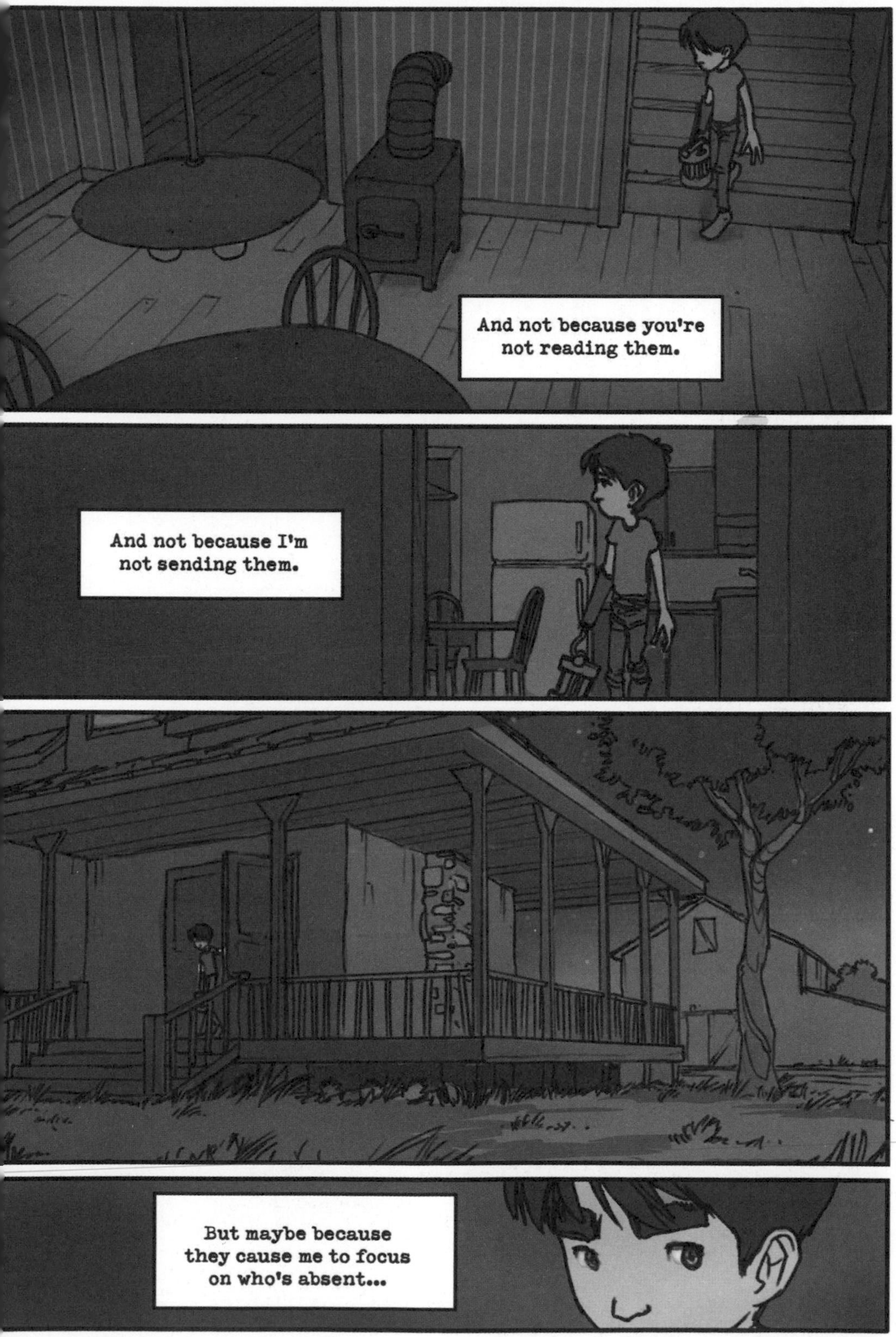
And not because you're not reading them.
And not because I'm not sending them.
But maybe because they cause me to focus on who's absent...

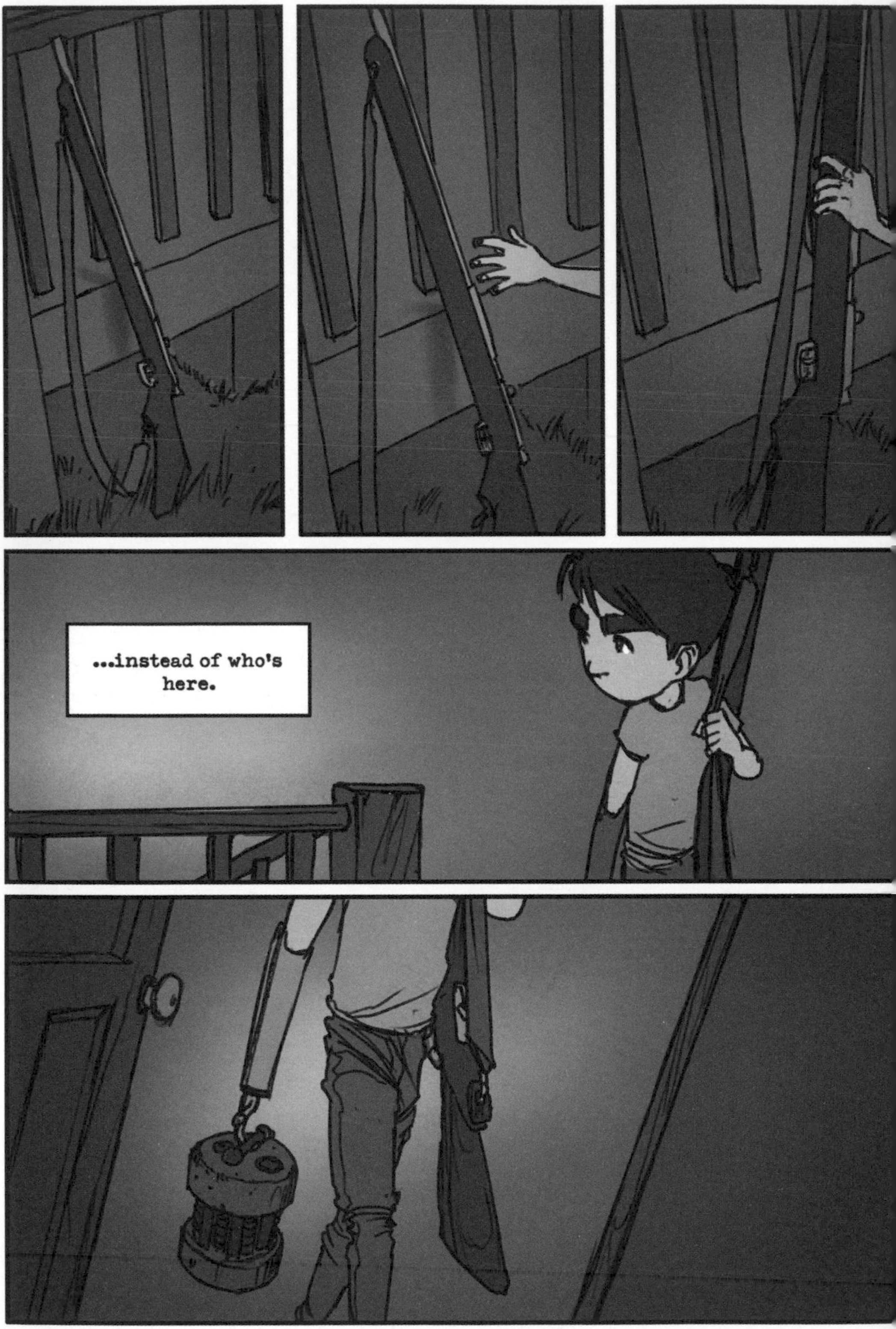
...instead of who's here.

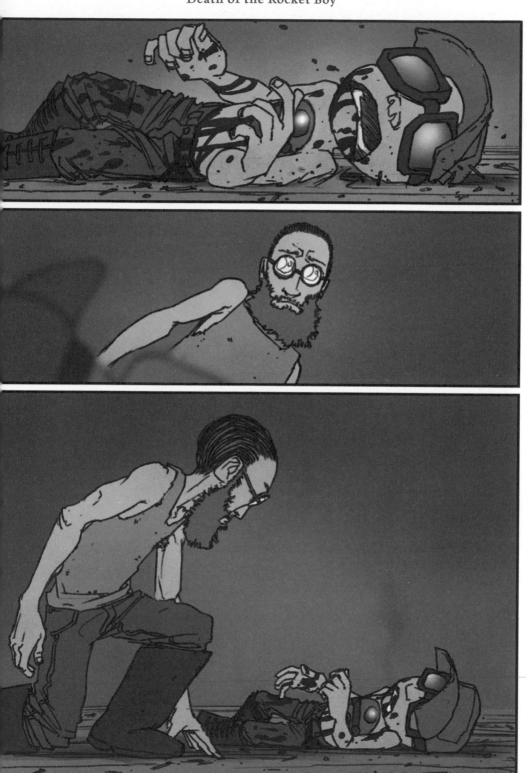

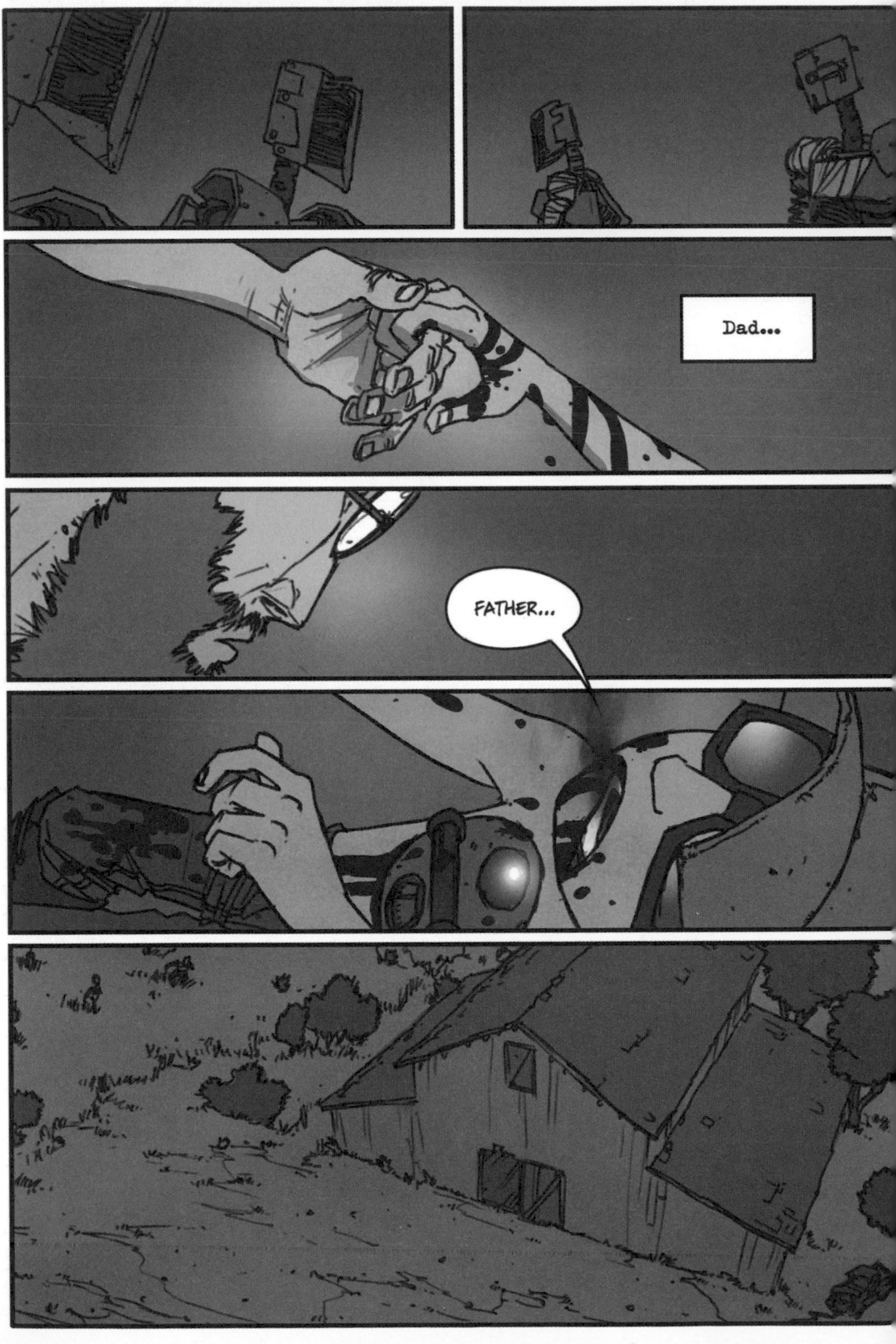
Dad...
FATHER...

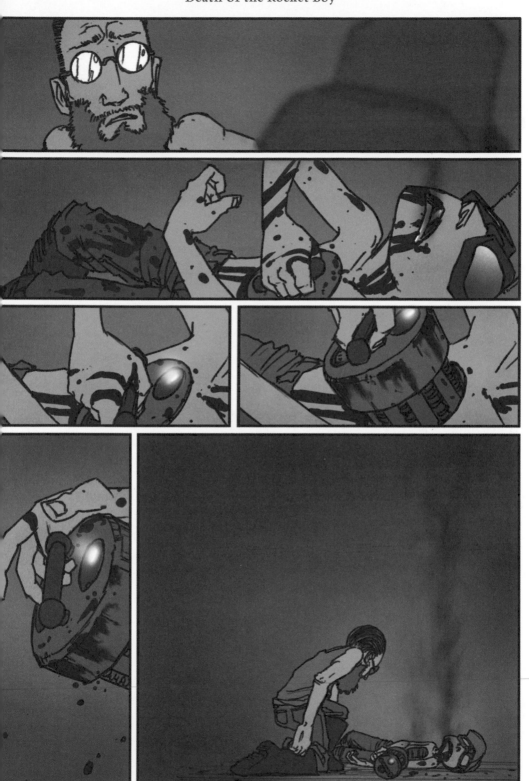

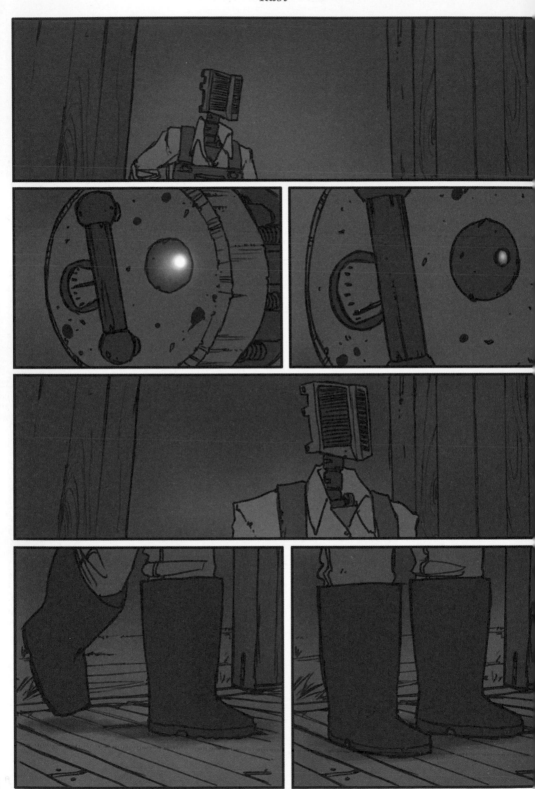

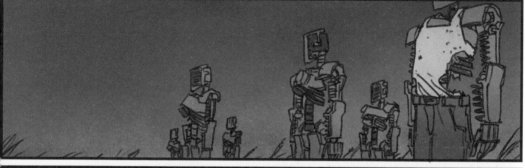

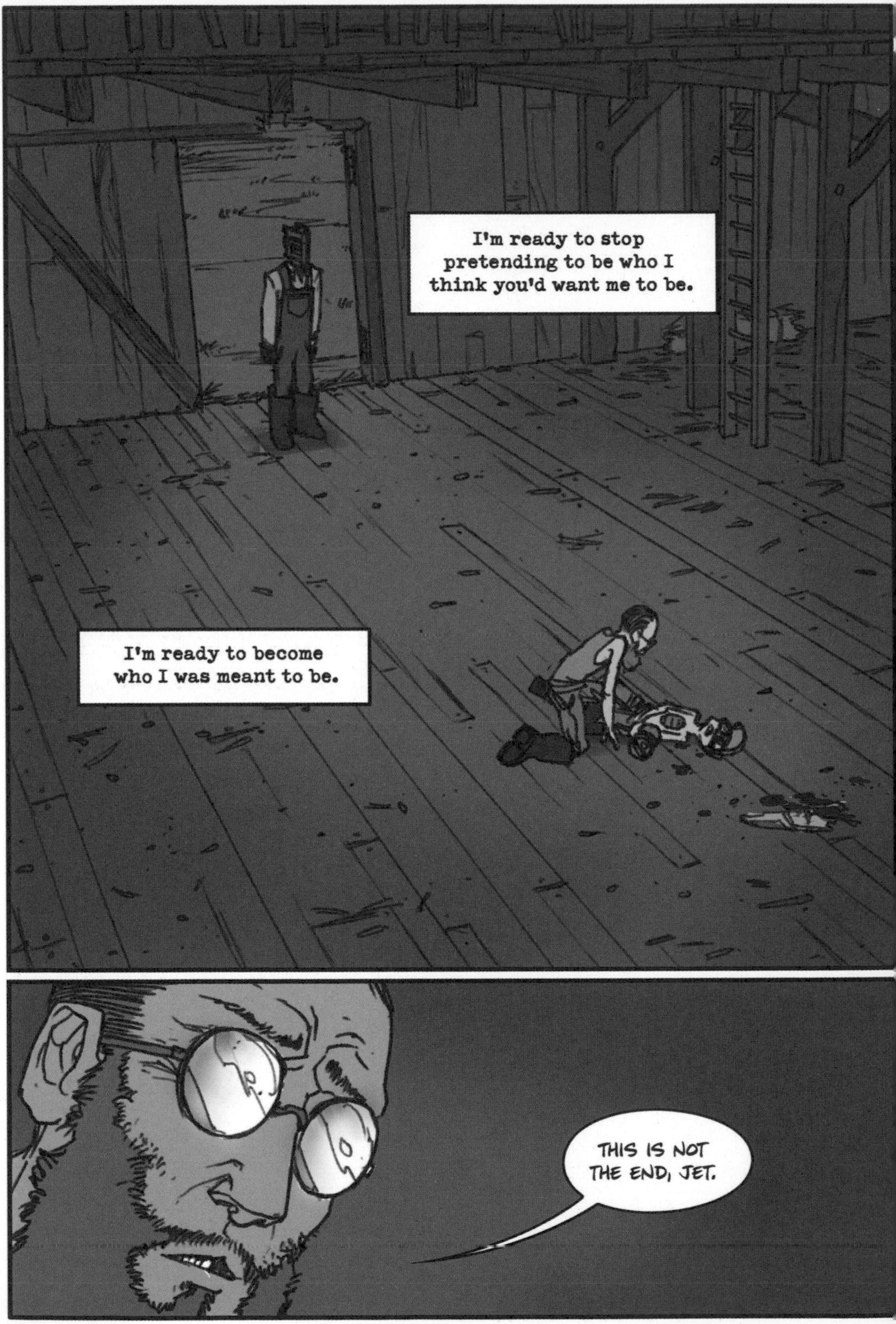
I'm ready to stop pretending to be who I think you'd want me to be.
I'm ready to become who I was meant to be.
THIS IS NOT THE END, JET.

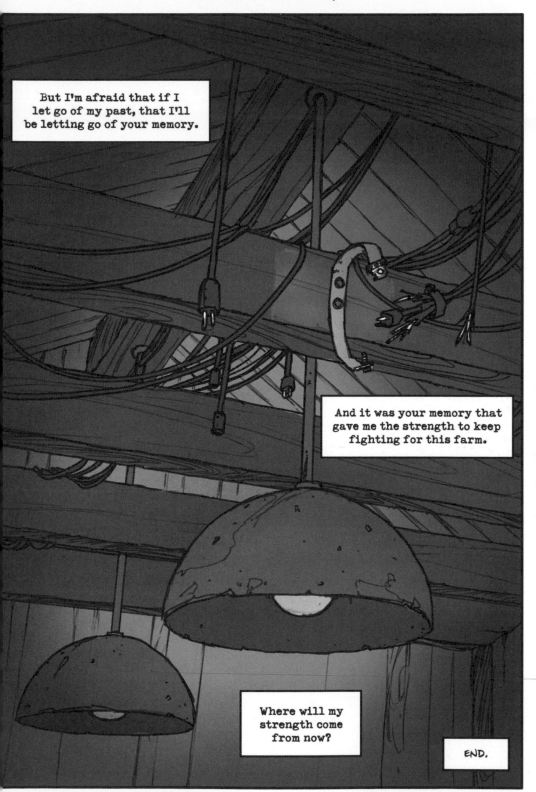

But I'm afraid that if I let go of my past, that I'll be letting go of your memory.

And it was your memory that gave me the strength to keep fighting for this farm.

Where will my strength come from now?

END.

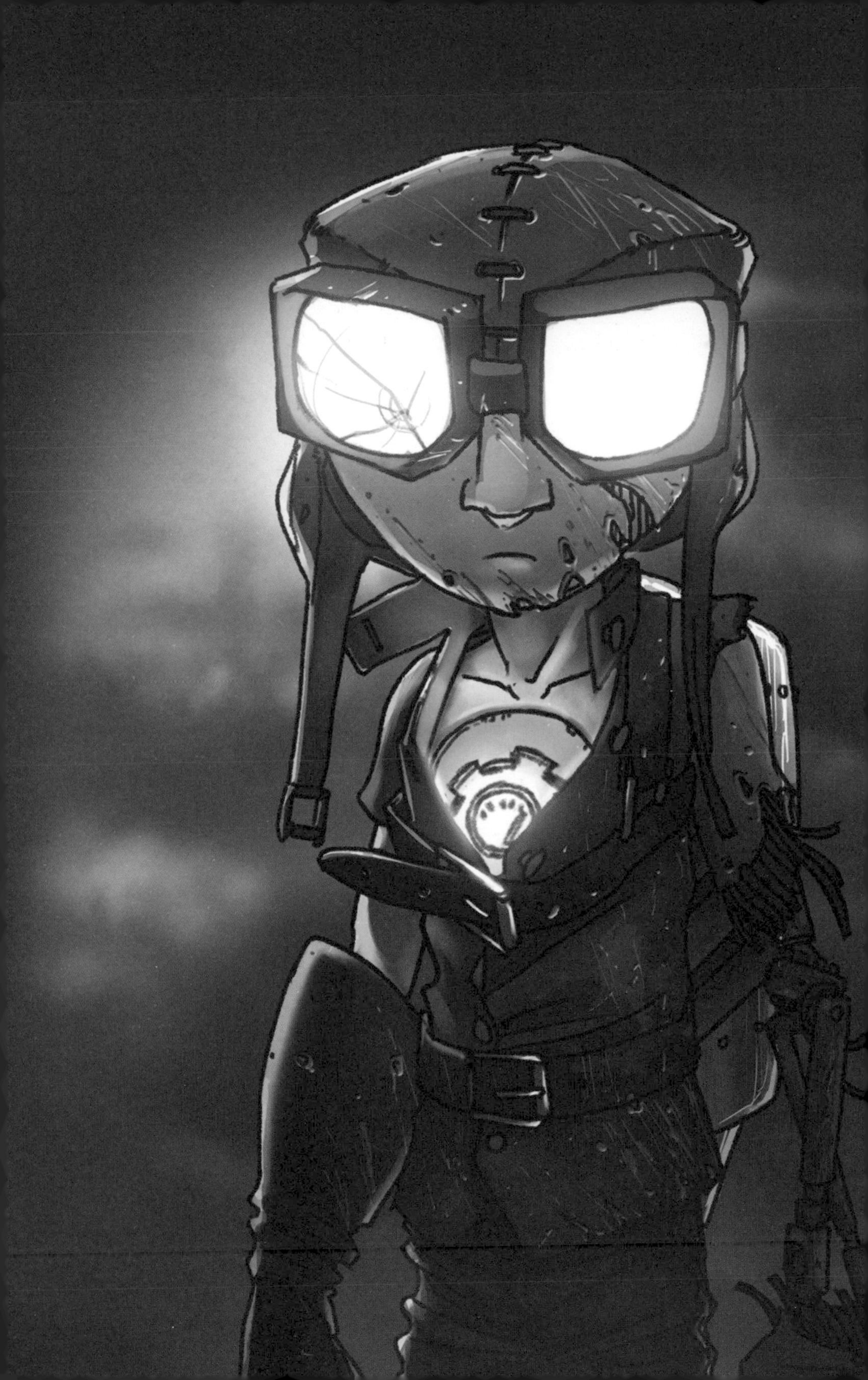

Experience the final adventure of Jet Jones in

RUST™

VOLUME FOUR
SOUL IN THE MACHINE

Coming
Spring 2018

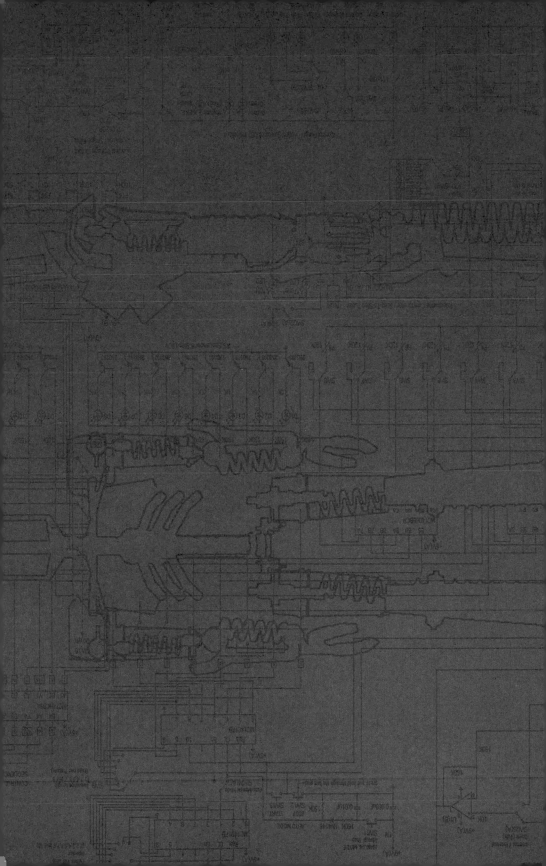

About the Author

Royden Lepp was born and raised on the Canadian prairies. He was kicked out of math class for animating in the corner of a text book, and he failed art class for drawing comics instead of following the class curriculum. He now draws comics and works as an animator in the video game industry. Royden resides in the Seattle area with his wife, Ruth, and son, Edison.

Special Thanks

Special thanks to Aline Brosh McKenna and Simon Kinberg for embracing this story, to Mark Smylie for believing in this book, and to Doug TenNapel, Stephen Christy, and PJ Bickett for all the long talks on the phone.

DISCOVER GROUNDBREAKING TITLES

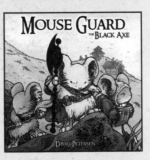

The Realist
Asaf Hanuka
ISBN: 978-1-60886-696-0 | $24.99

The Realist: Plug and Play
Asaf Hanuka
ISBN: 978-1-60886-953-4 | $24.99

Long Walk to Valhalla
Adam Smith, Matt Fox
ISBN: 978-1-60886-692-2 | $24.99

The March of The Crabs
Arthur De Pins
Volume 1: The Crabby Condition
ISBN: 978-1-60886-689-2 | $19.99
Volume 2: The Empire of the Crabs
ISBN: 978-1-68415-014-4 | $19.99

Jim Henson's Tale of Sand
Jim Henson, Jerry Juhl, Ramón K. Pérez
ISBN: 978-1-60886-440-9 | $29.95

Jim Henson's Musical Monsters of Turkey Hollow
Jim Henson, Jerry Juhl, Roger Langridge
ISBN: 978-1-60886-434-8 | $24.99

Jim Henson's The Dark Crystal Creation Myths
Brian Froud, Matthew Dow Smith, Alex Sheikman, Lizzy John
Volume 1
ISBN: 978-1-936393-00-8 | $12.99
Volume 2
ISBN: 978-1-60886-834-6 | $14.99
Volume 3
ISBN: 978-1-60886-435-5 | $24.99

Rust
Royden Lepp
Volume 0: The Boy Soldier
ISBN: 978-1-60886-806-3 | $10.99
Volume 1: Visitor in the Field
ISBN: 978-1-60886-894-0 | $14.99
Volume 2: Secrets of the Cell
ISBN: 978-1-60886-895-7 | $14.99

Mouse Guard
David Peterson
Mouse Guard: Fall 1152
ISBN: 978-1-93238-657-8 | $24.95
Mouse Guard: Winter 1152
ISBN: 978-1-93238-674-5 | $24.95
Mouse Guard: The Black Axe
ISBN: 978-1-93639-326-8 | $24.95

AVAILABLE AT YOUR LOCAL COMICS SHOP AND BOOKSTORE
To find a comics shop in your area, call 1-888-266-4226
WWW.BOOM-STUDIOS.COM